MOTHER'S DAY!

Love Mills & Boon xx

Get swept off your feet in this powerful collection
of glitzy, glamorous stories from your
favourite authors.

It's the perfect Mother's Day indulgence...

HAPPY
MOTHER'S
DAY!

Love Mills & Boon xx

KIM LAWRENCE
MELANIE MILBURNE
CATHERINE GEORGE

All the characters in this book have no existence outside the imagination of the author, and have no relation whatsoever to anyone bearing the same name or names. They are not even distantly inspired by any individual known or unknown to the author, and all the incidents are pure invention.

M&B™ and M&B™ with the Rose Device
are trademarks of the publisher.
Harlequin Mills & Boon Limited, Eton House,
18-24 Paradise Road, Richmond, Surrey TW9 1SR

HAPPY MOTHER'S DAY! LOVE MILLS & BOON
© Harlequin Books S.A. 2010

The publisher acknowledges the copyright holders of the individual works as follows:

Santiago's Love-Child © Kim Lawrence 2005
The Secret Baby Bargain © Melanie Milburne 2006
The Unexpected Pregnancy © Catherine George 2004

ISBN: 978 0 263 88023 6

009-0310

Printed and bound in Spain
by Litografia Rosés S.A., Barcelona

SANTIAGO'S
LOVE-CHILD

KIM LAWRENCE

Kim Lawrence lives on a farm in rural Anglesey. She runs two miles daily and finds this an excellent opportunity to unwind and seek inspiration for her writing! It also helps her keep up with her husband, two active sons, and the various stray animals which have adopted them. Always a fanatical consumer of fiction, she is now equally enthusiastic about writing. She loves a happy ending!

Look out for Kim Lawrence's contribution to the new Balfour Legacy continuity, available from M&B™ in October 2010.

CHAPTER ONE

AFTER trying to sell an idea for ten minutes straight most people would have given up. Dan Taylor wasn't one of them. Some people said that what he lacked in flair he made up for in determination. They were essentially correct.

Santiago Morais, who was considered to have more than his fair share of flair, listened to the younger man explain again why it wasn't just *necessary* for Santiago to make up the numbers this weekend, it was his *duty*.

'No.'

The 'No' wasn't the sort of no that could be confused with maybe, and it wasn't encouraging that the enigmatic expression on Santiago's lean features had given way to mild irritation.

Actually Dan was a little taken aback by Santiago's lack of co-operation. He was showing the sort of stony indifference that Dan had expected five years earlier when he had turned up at the London offices of Morais International. The only thing he'd had going for him then had been a tenuous—*very* tenuous—family link with the Morais family.

He had expected to be thrown out on his ear. Getting to see the man himself had been just as hard as he had expected. When they had come face to face, his resolve had almost deserted him. Santiago was younger than he had expected and much, much tougher.

Faced with a dark, cynical and very chilly stare Dan had instinctively dumped his carefully prepared speech and said instead, 'Look, there's absolutely no reason you should give me a job just because some great-aunt of mine married some distant uncle of your mother's. I'm not qualified—in fact I've never finished anything I started in my life—but if you gave me a chance you wouldn't regret it. I'd give it all I had and then some. I have something to prove.'

'You have something to prove?' The voice, deep and barely accented, made Dan jump.

'I'm not a loser.'

The figure behind the desk got to his feet and became correspondingly more intimidating; this man was seriously tall and was built like an Olympic rower. For a long uncomfortable moment Santiago just looked at Dan in silence, those spookily penetrating eyes not giving a clue to what he was thinking.

'Right, sorry to have bothered you…'

'Eight-thirty Monday.'

Dan's jaw dropped as he swung back. *'What did you say?'*

One of Santiago's dark brows lifted. 'If you want a job, be here Monday morning at eight-thirty.'

Dan sank into the nearest chair. 'You won't regret this,' he vowed.

Dan had come good on his promise. He had quickly proved his worth and, perhaps more surprisingly, a friendship had developed between the two men. A friendship that had survived Dan leaving the company and setting up on his own two years earlier.

Dan adopted an injured expression as he looked across at his Spanish distant cousin, who had put down a file he'd been reading to say something in his native tongue into a Dictaphone. Actually it could have been one of several languages; Santiago was fluent in five.

'I must say I think you're being pretty callous about this.'

'If by callous you mean I will not spend a weekend

amusing a fat, boring and mentally unstable woman—I'm quoting you here—so that you can have your Rebecca to yourself…I am indeed callous.'

'*Rachel*, and the friend isn't mentally unstable exactly. I think she's just having a breakdown or something.'

'You're really tempting me now, but the answer is still no, Daniel.'

'If you'd met Rachel you wouldn't be so heartless.'

'And is your Rachel beautiful?'

'Very, and don't look at me like that. This isn't some casual affair. She's *the one*; I just know she is.' His expression grew indignant when Santiago responded to his emotional admission with a cynical smile that was only slightly less corrosive than neat nitric acid. 'I'd have thought you'd have been more sympathetic considering…' Dan continued falteringly.

Santiago abandoned his attempt to carry on working and pushed his thick sable hair back from his brow. 'Considering what?'

'Aren't you getting married?'

'At some point I imagine it will be necessary.' The exquisite irony of him continuing the precious Morais family name was not lost on him.

'You know what I mean. Aren't you marrying that hot little singer who I keep seeing you photographed with.'

'That hot little singer has an agent with a vivid imagination. Susie is not in love with me.'

Dan's expression grew curious. 'So it's just…'

'None of your business.'

'Fair enough, but I still think you're being totally unreasonable. I'm asking you to spend a weekend in a cute cottage, not donate bone marrow! Look…look,' he said, reaching into his pocket and extracting a photo. 'Isn't she gorgeous? And, as for her being older, I *like* older women...' he added defensively as he shoved the photo under Santiago's nose.

With a sigh Santiago took the creased item from the younger man's fingers and dutifully glanced at the slightly out-of-focus image of a tall blonde who looked to him like many other tall blondes.

'Yes, she is very...' He stopped, the colour seeping steadily from his olive-toned skin as he looked at the person half concealed by Dan's girlfriend.

'Are you feeling all right?' Dan asked, thinking of Santiago's father, who had dropped dead at fifty-five from a massive heart attack several years earlier.

Santiago hadn't inherited his dad's looks, generous girth or taste for copious amounts of brandy—the old man had by all accounts been a bit of a sleaze—but who knew what else he had inherited?

Like maybe a propensity to heart disease and dropping down dead!

Dan had started to try and remember if you bashed someone who stopped breathing on the chest, or gave them mouth to mouth, when Santiago's eyes lifted. He looked bleak, but much to Dan's relief not about to expire any time soon.

'I'm fine, Daniel.' Santiago wasn't about to reveal that he'd recognized the woman in the photograph. 'This woman here, she is the friend who will be there this weekend?' he enquired casually as he indicated the figure in the background.

'Yeah, that's Lily,' Dan admitted without enthusiasm. 'Rachel's had her staying at her place for the past three weeks. They go way back. I never see Rachel alone. Wherever she goes, there's Lily. I don't think she likes men...she *definitely* doesn't like me. Must be the husband dumping her has made her all weird.'

'Her husband left her…?'

Dan nodded. 'Not too sure of the details, but presumably that's what made her fall apart.'

Santiago's eyes lifted. 'Are they divorced?'

'Like I said, I don't know the details. I had a colleague lined up for this weekend to keep her out of our hair, but he got mumps, of all things!'

'That was inconsiderate of him,' Santiago murmured sarcastically, thinking fast and hard—something he was well equipped to do.

'I'm not saying he did it on purpose, but, hell-fire, Santiago, I've been planning this weekend for weeks, ever since I bought the ring.'

'You are going to propose?' He watched as Dan looked self-conscious and thought, *I hope she's not a total bitch.* Being Lily's friend was not the best of recommendations.

'Six years is a very small age gap.'

'Insignificant,' Santiago agreed obediently, amused that it was something as minor as an age difference that bothered his young friend. 'This alters things,' he mused out loud.

'It does?' Dan sounded cautious.

'Being a romantic—'

'Since when?'

'I will come and keep this…*Lily*…company.'

Dan was so grateful that it took Santiago ten minutes to get rid of him.

When Dan finally left, Santiago took the photograph he had slipped surreptitiously into his pocket and laid it on the desk. Hands pressed on the polished rosewood surface, he leaned forward, his eyes trained on the barely distinguishable features of the woman in the background. A quiver of movement tightened the contours of his impossibly symmetrical features. When admirers attributed that symmetry to generations of aristocratic inbreeding, Santiago could barely repress his amusement.

Lily's hair looked dark in the snapshot, but Santiago knew it was a medium brown, not a boring matt brown, but a fascinating intermingling of shades ranging from golden blonde to warm, rich russet.

That heart-shaped little face—thinner than he recalled—those big, kittenish blue eyes, and soft, seductive mouth didn't look as though they belonged to a woman who had the morals of an alley cat.

She had made a fool of him.

But, as Santiago had told himself many times over the last months, he had the consolation of knowing that he had had a lucky escape. *Lucky me!*

He wasn't married to this heartless little cheat—*someone else was.* Another man enjoyed the expertise of those soft lips. Someone else slept with his head cushioned on those soft, warm breasts at night. That man was entitled to touch pearly skin that smelt of roses and vanilla, and wake up with pale, smooth limbs wrapped around him.

Another man was listening to her lies and believing them.

Someone else, but not me.

Oddly enough, thoughts of his lucky escape did not make Santiago feel like breaking into spontaneous song.

Then he remembered Daniel's words and realised that it was possible nobody was enjoying the carnal delights of her voluptuous body. Recalling what a sensual little thing she had been, he doubted this situation would last for long.

He looked at his hands clenched into white-knuckled fists and rotated his head to ease the tension that had crept into his shoulders and neck. He was over the woman; it was the memory of his own criminal gullibility that plagued him, that stopped him fully enjoying what life had to offer. The

obvious way to restore equilibrium was to face his problem.
He needed what the psychologists called closure, and what
he, in the privacy of his own thoughts, called seeing Lily
get what she deserved.

Now, thanks to Dan, he had the chance.

Staring out of the window, seeing none of the panoramic
view over the city, he mulled over what he had learnt and
wondered how it could be used to his advantage.
Apparently Lily was going through a rough patch. The protective instincts that sprang into life at the thought of her
vulnerability didn't survive more than a split second before
good sense reasserted itself.

He smiled grimly. Maybe it was Lily's turn to reap some
of what she had sown...? Or maybe her present *breakdown*
was part of some elaborate scam, which, knowing her as
he did, was entirely possible.

Though he had nothing to prove, it would be good to
confirm what he already knew: *that he was over Lily.*

'You've been crying.'

Lily, who had thought she was alone, jumped at the accusation and gave a surreptitious sniff before lifting her
head. 'No,' she mumbled, pinning a determined smile on
her blotchy face, 'it's this darned hay fever.'

Her friend sighed. 'You don't get hay fever, Lily,' she
retorted, dropping her designer handbag on the floor and
easing one shoe off with a sigh.

Lily watched the second four-inch heel follow suit as
Rachel shrank to a willowy five ten. Her cheeks began to
ache as she continued to smile brightly to compensate for
her blotchy appearance.

She blew her nose defiantly. 'Well, I do now,' she insisted.

Rachel lifted her artfully darkened brows and released a theatrical sigh, but didn't press the point.

'If you say so,' she said, wincing as she rubbed first one aching foot and then the other against her slim calves. 'Now, what shall we do tonight?'

'I fancy an early night, actually.'

'Early night! You've had early nights for the past week.' She looked her friend up and down through narrowed eyes, mentally chucking the top Lily was wearing in the bin—no self-respecting charity shop would want it—and getting her into something, preferably low cut, in a pastel shade maybe...? A nice soft smoky blue would bring out the incredible shade of her eyes.

'It's definitely time you let your hair down, Lily. It'll do us both good,' she contended.

Lily guiltily noted for the first time the lines of fatigue around the older woman's eyes. 'Bad day?'

'Sometimes I wonder why I ever became an accountant,' she admitted.

'The six-figure salary...?'

Rachel grinned. 'I get that because I'm brilliant at what I do. And I won't bother trying to explain to someone who can't even add up *with* a calculator that numbers are sexy. Now, about tonight. Dan has this really sweet mate...single, solvent...admittedly he's no Brad Pitt, but then—'

'Beggars can't be choosers...?'

Rachel adopted an expression of mock gravity. 'Well, I was going to say, *Who is?* But now you mention it women who don't exfoliate regularly, Lily, have to be realistic.' She turned her frowning scrutiny on the younger woman's fair-skinned face. 'Actually, considering your skin-care regime consists of splashing a bit of soap and water on your face, you have the most disgustingly gorgeous skin,' she observed enviously. 'A bit of decent foundation would totally disguise those freckles,' she prophesied, frowning at the bridge of Lily's small, tip-tilted nose. 'Still, some men like freckles. Shall I ring Dan and—'

Lily knew one man who had said he liked her freckles, though she suspected they, like everything else about her, would disgust him now.

'*No!*' Rachel's eyebrows lifted and Lily added more moderately, 'I appreciate what you're trying to do, I really do, but, to be honest, a man is the last thing I need right now.'

It was easy to figure out what she *didn't* need—blind dates featured pretty high on this list. What she *did* need was a much more difficult proposition!

'*Need* and *want* are not always the same thing.'

'This time they are,' Lily insisted quietly.

Rachel looked exasperated and glanced absently at a message on her mobile phone before sliding it back into her bag. 'What are you going to do? Take a vow of celibacy?'

Lily ignored Rachel's question. 'Actually, I was thinking it might be time for me to go home.' Home…but for how much longer?

Lily deliberately pushed the subject of her uncertain future to the back of her mind.

It wasn't easy. Her marital home was on the market, and according to the agents a couple were making interested noises, which, considering their viewing, was nothing short of a miracle.

Lily's thoughts drifted back to the occasion three weeks earlier. Rachel had unexpectedly arrived when she had been halfway through showing the prospective purchasers around. Her friend had taken one look at her, and had calmly informed the startled pair that they would have to come back another day. She had then proceeded to escort them firmly off the property.

Rachel had then packed Lily a bag, arranged a sitter for the cat and asked a neighbour to water the plants. Lily had just sat there and watched her. She supposed her listless inertia had been a symptom of whatever Rachel had seen in her face.

The break had served its purpose, but now, despite the tears this afternoon, Lily was feeling less fragile. She no longer felt so…*disconnected*. She wasn't sure whether to be relieved or not. Being grounded was painful, you had to think about things you'd prefer not to and make decisions… For months now, she realised, she'd just been drifting. She hadn't even begun to look for somewhere to live. All she'd done was sign everything that Gordon's solicitor had sent her.

Yes, it was definitely about time she stood on her own feet.

Rachel didn't agree.

'You can't go home yet. I've got things planned.'

Lily, who didn't like the sound of 'things' frowned suspiciously. She really wished that her friend hadn't taken on the role of social secretary with such zeal. *'Things…?'*

Rachel acted as if she hadn't heard. 'God, but these shoes are murder,' she complained, picking up the culprits, stilettos with black and pink bows.

'Then don't wear them.' It seemed the obvious solution to Lily, who liked clothes but wasn't as much of a slave to fashion as her friend.

'Are you kidding? They make my legs look hot.'

Lily looked at the legs in question and observed honestly, 'Your legs would look hot in wellingtons, Rachel.' She glanced down at her own legs, currently concealed under denim. They were pretty good as legs went, but they weren't in the same class as Rachel's, which stopped traffic on a regular basis.

'Yes, they would, wouldn't they?'

Lily smiled. There was something oddly endearing about her friend's complacent vanity.

'But enough about my legs.' With a little pat of one taut, tanned thigh through her short summer skirt, she turned her attention to Lily, who in turn looked wary, an expression her friend had observed always appeared when the conversation got even faintly personal.

Such tight-lipped reserve was something Rachel found hard to understand. If she had been through hell and back like Lily, she would have *wanted* to get it off her chest, but all her attempts to encourage Lily to let it out had failed miserably.

'Don't you think you'd feel a lot better if you talked about it?'

They both knew what 'it' was: Lily's divorce—the ink was still wet on that—and her miscarriage earlier that year.

CHAPTER TWO

For a split second Lily was tempted to tell Rachel; the urge quickly passed.

Rachel didn't know half the story and the truth was so shocking that she couldn't predict how even her broad-minded friend would react to the unvarnished version.

Besides, the habits of a lifetime were hard to break and 'sharing feelings' had been encouraged during Lily's child-hood about as much as spontaneous hugging!

If she had let her feelings show, her grandmother's im-patient response had been, 'Nobody likes a whiner, Lily.' Lily had learnt not to whine. Her crying had always been done behind closed doors.

'Nothing to talk about.'

'Nobody does the stiff upper lip these days, you know, Lily. All that being reserved does is give you an ulcer.'

'My stomach feels fine.' Lily placed her hand against the curve of her belly and discovered with a sense of surprise that she had lost a lot of the soft, feminine roundness she had always hated.

The softness that Santiago had professed to find sexy and feminine.

She knew from experience that there were times when fighting the flashbacks did no good, that it was easier on those occasions just to go with the flow. Lily, dimly con-scious of Rachel's voice in the background, felt her eyelids grow heavy as she allowed the bitter-sweet memories to wash over her.

She had perfect, total, painful recall of the heat in his

16

incredible eyes as he had tipped her face up to his and smiled a slow, sexy smile as he had drawn her against him, fitting his hard angles into her softer curves and murmuring throatily in her ear.

A woman should be soft and round, not hard and angular.

It was humiliating, but a full twelve months after that first scorching kiss and she still couldn't think about it without getting palpitations.

'Well?'

Rachel's impatient voice acted like a lifeline back to the present. Lily grabbed it and held on. While she was fixated on the past the chances of her rebuilding her life were nil.

She dabbed her tongue to the beads of sweat along her upper lip and gave a strained smile as she rubbed her damp palms against her jeans.

'Sorry, I...' *Am pathetic and living in the past? Can't get it into my thick skull he never loved me? All of the above?*

'You weren't listening. I could tell...' Rachel considered her friend's flushed face. 'You look a bit...?'

'I'm fine.' Smile fixed, Lily pushed the intrusive images away without acknowledging them or *his* presence in her head.

'What you need is a nice glass of wine,' Rachel decided. 'Just don't move,' she said, padding over to the big stain-less-steel fridge in her bare feet. A moment later she returned with a bottle of Chardonnay and two glasses, which she filled.

'A nice night in...yeah, I can live with that,' she conceded, handing Lily her glass. She curled up comfortably on the sofa and reached for the newspaper. 'I wonder what's on the telly tonight?' Turning over the pages, she suddenly stopped and lowered the broadsheet to the table.

'Now there,' she observed with a lascivious smile, 'is something I wouldn't mind finding in my Christmas stocking.'

'I thought you were in love with your delicious Dan.' Lily laughed, looking over her shoulder to see what hunk her friend was drooling over.

'I'm in love, not blind. Now, *there's* a man who doesn't use a shoebox to file his returns. Look at that mouth and those eyes...' she enthused.

'You can tell about his filing system from his mouth?' Lily teased.

'No, that I can tell by the attention the financial pages give him on a regular basis. I wonder if he's that sexy in real life?' She slung a comical look of entreaty over her shoulder. 'And please don't spoil it by saying it's just good lighting. You're such a disgusting cynic.'

Lily went cold as she looked at the half-page photo showing an unsmiling, dark-eyed man. It was a standard moody black and white shot of an incredibly attractive man. Lily knew that the lighting couldn't begin to do justice to just *how* sexy the man was in real life. It didn't reveal the aura of raw sexuality he projected like a force field.

Aware that some sort of response was expected of her, and hyperventilating wasn't it, Lily cleared her throat. 'He does have something,' she admitted, reading the headline above that pronounced MORAIS LEAVES THE OPPOSITION COUNTING THE COST AGAIN.

Me too, she thought.

'*Something!*' Rachel squealed. 'He is off-the-scale gorgeous. That man,' she said, poking the page with her finger, 'not only looks like he could be quite *deliciously bad* in bed—'

Never again will I mock Rachel's instinct, Lily decided. Of course, Rachel's instinct only told part of the story—as well as being deliciously bad he could also be breathtakingly tender and passionately unrestrained. Lily pressed her hands to her stomach as the muscles deep inside tightened.

'He's also a genuine financial genius. His name is Santiago Morais.' Rachel's smooth brow furrowed. 'He's Italian or—'

'Spanish,' Lily inserted in a flat little voice. 'He's Spanish.' *And I am so over him,* she thought, pressing her hand against her sternum to ease the tight feeling in her chest.

'Yeah, you're right. Since when did you start reading the financial pages, Lily?'

'He makes the gossip columns too,' she said, struggling to keep the bitterness from her voice as an image of the pop star Susie Sebastian, her pouting lips aimed like heat-seeking missiles at a willing male mouth, flashed into her mind.

'That figures. You know, I think I'll spend my next holiday in Spain. You never know, I might bump into Mr Gorgeous. He would carry me off to bed and make mad, passionate love to me.'

Lily half closed her eyes, and saw sun-dappled shadows dancing over a lean golden torso as the breeze stirred the leaves of a tree outside the window. 'For five days straight?'

Rachel angled an amused look at Lily's face. 'Hey, get your own fantasy!' she protested.

Lily blushed, which made Rachel chuckle. 'You have hidden murky depths, girl.'

You have no idea, Lily thought.

For a while after she'd come out of hospital Lily had thought she would never feel anything ever again. Now she wasn't so sure that would have been such a bad thing! Oh, when were things *ever* going to get back to normal? So she could get on with being a librarian who lived in a Devon seaside town.

She knew that it wasn't healthy or constructive to go down the 'what if?' road, but she couldn't help wondering what her life would be like now if she hadn't gone down to the pool that morning all those months ago. It had been such a small decision, but the consequences had been life-changing.

An early-morning swim hadn't seemed sinister or significant, just a good way to clear her head after a long, sleepless night alone in the decadent honeymoon suite of a Spanish five-star hotel, which, rumour had it, had been fully booked up for the next decade or so.

It would have been understandable if the thoughts that had kept her awake had concerned her absent husband. Her husband who hadn't been answering her calls. The *same* husband who had texted her the previous morning to say the problem at work that had forced him to leave her at the airport at the start of their holiday had turned into a crisis and, no, he wouldn't be joining her after all.

Gordon wasn't to know that, following his text, determined to make the best of her holiday to this enchanting area, Lily had booked herself onto an excursion to the charming nearby Renaissance town of Baeza. Places like this were part of the reason she had fallen in love with Andalucia.

She hadn't immediately placed the middle-aged man and his wife bearing down on her as the tour guide was in full flow. Then as she'd looked beyond the shorts and garish shirt she'd recognised a colleague of Gordon's and his wife. She'd vaguely recalled meeting them on a few social occasions.

'Matt...Susan.' She called out to the couple.

They did the usual 'small world, fancy meeting you here'

stuff, and then the older man looked around expectantly. 'Gordon not with you?'

'No, he couldn't get away, I'm afraid.'

If he had, there was no way she'd have got to take this excursion; Gordon wouldn't have budged from the five-star luxury of the hotel. If she had suggested that they go and see the real inland Andalucia, with its olive groves and rolling hills, he would have thought she was crazy.

'Not surprised,' the other man confessed. 'He must be up to his eyes in it with his new venture. I couldn't believe it when I heard on the grapevine he was leaving. I admit, I thought Gordon was a permanent fixture like me.'

Miraculously Lily's smile stayed superglued in place. 'So did I, Matt.'

'And he was a sure bet for that promotion.'

Lily nodded in agreement. 'He did mention that.' One of the few things he had mentioned, it seemed.

'But good for him, I say. You need to be a risk-taker sometimes.' He looked across the square. 'Is that your group moving on?'

'Yes, it is. Lovely to see you.'

Blissfully oblivious to the fact that with a few words he had revealed her marriage to be a total joke, Matt shouted cheerily after her, 'Remember me to Gordon and wish him all the luck in the future.'

He's going to need all the luck he can get when I get hold of him. 'I will,' Lily promised with her best sincere smile.

Of course, she had known for some time that their marriage had problems, but she hadn't suspected until now that they might be insurmountable.

My husband is leading a double life! What the hell is he up to?

At the first opportunity Lily slipped away from her tour

group and sought refuge in the town's delightful flower-filled plaza. She sat in a pavement café and ordered coffee, then, changing her mind, asked instead for wine in her clumsy, faltering Spanish. The proprietor brought a bottle.

She sat sipping the rich-bodied red and thinking about what she was going to do next. Didn't a woman in her situation need a plan of action?

She could run up a credit-card bill, one guaranteed to bring tears to Gordon's eyes. It wouldn't be hard. Gordon had a deep, almost spiritual connection with his wallet—in fact, not to put too fine a point on it, he was as mean as hell!

Then again, she mused, she could take the direct approach and get the next plane home, tell him straight if he didn't want her to walk he'd better come clean about what he'd been up to. But was it a good idea to confront him when she wasn't even sure any more if she *wanted* to save their marriage?

She could always cut the sleeves off his favourite designer suits, give the bottles of wine he'd put down as an investment to the church raffle... But, no, that had been done before by other, more imaginative wronged wives. But wasn't she jumping the gun? Maybe her deepest suspicions were off and another woman wasn't involved.

Sure, because Gordon's never cheated before.

Lily toyed with the idea of sleeping with the first attractive man she saw. It would certainly be one way to have her revenge.

She knew the alcohol was partially responsible for her audacious line of thought, but for a while it was good to feel daring and in charge, not a damned victim.

When the bottle was empty she still hadn't decided what course, if any, to take. The helpful proprietor of the café offered to call her a taxi and for once she thought, *Hang the cost,* and let him.

Given the day's revelations and the fact she spent the rest of the afternoon sleeping off the unaccustomed alcohol, Lily never *expected* to sleep that night, and she didn't, but not for the reason she had anticipated. No, all thoughts of her secretive husband and his mysterious new venture were crowded out of her head by the dark, chiselled features of a total stranger! This probably said something about her character. Lily wasn't sure what, but she doubted it was flattering.

The next morning the solitude of the pool and exercise had the desired therapeutic effect, or so she naively believed at the time. After several slow, steady lengths she succeeded in rationalising what had happened in the hotel restaurant the night before. So she had been the victim of instant lust—it happened, she told herself with a mental shrug. Admittedly never before to her.

It was silly to get hung up about it.

It wasn't as if she had done anything awful like cheat— at least only in her mind. And she suspected every woman who ever laid eyes on the tall, dynamic Spaniard with his sinfully sexy smile and incredible voice was guilty of that.

By the time exhaustion forced her to flip over onto her back and get her breath back Lily had reached the comfortable mental position of concluding she had handled the evening pretty well, under the circumstances.

The *circumstances* being she had hardly been capable of stringing two words together in the man's presence, but there was no need to dwell on that! As for that frisson when their eyes had met and the tug, the feeling of *connection*, she had felt, such things did not happen between total strangers except in her feverish imagination.

Sensual fantasies aside, their brief encounter had actually been pretty much a non-event.

Lying on her back in the water, she couldn't help her thoughts drifting back to the moment she had seen him. Lily involuntarily inhaled as the tall figure with a dark, classically featured face crystallised in her head.

He had achingly perfect, chiselled cheekbones, a proud nose, a strong jaw, dark, smouldering eyes and a sternly sexy mouth that just had to have fuelled countless female fantasies.

She had been lending half an ear to the elderly couple who had invited her to share their table at dinner when she had seen him framed in the doorway.

A tall, dark figure, dressed in a pale linen suit and open-necked shirt that revealed a tantalising section of olive-toned skin and undoubtedly had a designer name hand-stitched into the lining.

It hadn't just been her, lots of people had looked, but Lily had carried on looking a lot longer than most others. She hadn't been able to help herself. The stranger had been quite simply *spectacular*!

He'd been deliciously dark in a typically Spanish way, but nothing else about him had been *typical*! For a start he'd been much taller than the average Spanish male; she'd estimated that he had to be six four or five. Even the way he'd moved, with a fluid animal grace that had made her tummy muscles quiver, had been rivetingly different. His features had been classical, but strong. Her fascinated glance had lingered on his sensually moulded mouth.

It had felt like a long time, but it had probably only been a few seconds, before she'd managed to drag her hungry eyes clear, but in the process she'd connected briefly with his eyes. For a split second the rest of the room had faded away, and something that had felt like a mild electric shock had travelled through her body.

Lily had been utterly overwhelmed by emotions that she hadn't recognised or understood. Rachel would no doubt have identified what she'd been suffering from as lust, but Lily knew it hadn't been that simple.

White and shaking with reaction, she'd examined the pattern in the marble floor. Her heart had continued to race while some inner instinct had told her of his approach. By the time he'd reached her side every nerve ending in her body had been taut with anticipation.

She couldn't even think about it now with a clear head, in the cold light of day without her pulses racing. She hadn't been able to breathe; excitement had lodged itself like a tight fist behind her breastbone. Of course, when he'd walked straight past her as though she were invisible and clasped the elderly man beside her on the shoulder she'd felt every kind of fool.

CHAPTER THREE

AFTER exchanging a few polite words with the couple, who were apparently frequent visitors to the hotel, the handsome stranger had walked away. It had only been later in the evening that Lily had found out his identity—his name was Santiago Morais, and he owned the hotel, and, so it appeared, a whole lot else.

He had barely even acknowledged she was there.

Except for a kind of stiff inclination of his head in her general direction, no eye contact—even the most generous of judges would have to conclude that it had been pretty thin material for a night's steamy fantasies. The eyes across a crowded room, soul-mate stuff had been a product of her overactive imagination.

She was shaking her head over her own pathetic self-delusion as she heaved herself out of the pool and sat, knees up to her chin, eyes closed and head tilted back to catch the warmth of the early-morning rays.

When she opened them the cause of her sleepless night, Santiago Morais, was standing there looking down at her.

'Good morning. I trust you slept well?' In contrast to his formal enquiry there was nothing vaguely formal about the restless febrile glitter she saw in his deep-set, heavy-lidded eyes before he slid a pair of designer shades on.

Lily didn't say anything, partly because the sight of him casually peeling off his shirt had paralysed her vocal cords.

She watched, too shocked to guard her expression as he dragged a hand through his dark hair and set off a sequence of distracting muscle-rippling. He really didn't have an ounce of surplus flesh on his athletically lean frame.

'I didn't sleep well at all,' he revealed without waiting for Lily to answer his question.

'Sorry,' she croaked, thinking he didn't look as if he'd had a disturbed night. He was oozing an indecent degree of vitality, or was that testosterone? Things deep in her pelvis tightened and ached as she focused hazily on his criminally sexy mouth. *Bad idea!*

Don't drool, be objective, Lily, she warned herself severely.

'Did you have a good swim?' he asked, unzipping his jeans to reveal a flat stomach with perfect muscle definition and a light dusting of dark hair.

'I was just leaving.'

He had been watching her…? The thought caused a secret shiver to pass through Lily's body. She lifted her arm in a concealing arc over her tingling nipples, and pulled herself up onto her knees just as the worn denim of his jeans slid down his narrow hips.

As she took in his muscular thighs complete with a light dusting of body hair her breath quickened to the point where she was not so much breathing as noisily gasping for air.

If only for the sake of her own traumatised heart, she knew she ought to avert her eyes. Heaven knew, she tried, but she couldn't; her eyes were glued to his body. He was so beautiful. She could remember feeling awkward, clumsy and overweight in comparison to his sleek hardness.

'I meant to lose some weight for this summer,' she explained, feeling the sudden need to apologise for her appearance.

Above his designer shades Santiago's sable brows lifted. Behind the dark lenses it was hard to see what he was thinking, but she could guess—*Crazy woman, where is security when I need it?*

She smiled to show she was actually sane. 'But you know how it is.' *Stupid, of course he doesn't.*

Her attention was irresistibly drawn back to his body. By this point he had stripped down to a pair of black swimming shorts that left enough to the imagination to send her temperature soaring several degrees.

The sensation she experienced when she looked at his streamlined golden body was a lot as she imagined drowning might be. The inability to breathe; the heavy pounding of her heart...only drowning would feel cold and she was hot...*very* hot! She took a deep, shaky breath as she struggled to get her breathing back on track and averted her eyes from the arrow of dark hair that dived below the waistband of his shorts.

'Why would you want to lose any pounds?'

Lily didn't take Santiago's bewilderment seriously. 'You've got very nice manners, but I know I'm fat,' she explained matter-of-factly. 'I can't even blame it on my genes; apparently my mother was slim.' Her grandmother, who like many people equated extra pounds with laziness, had been fond of regretfully observing that Lily had missed out on her mother's good looks.

'*Fat...!*' His incredulity gave way to laughter, deep, warm laughter. Through the smoky lenses of his sunglasses she was aware of his eyes moving in a broad, caressing sweep down the length of her body. When he reached her toes he released a long, appreciative sigh. 'You are not *fat!*' He dismissed the claim with a contemptuous motion of his hand.

Lily was so startled when, without warning, he dropped down onto his heels until his eyes were almost level with hers that it didn't even occur to her to protest when he reached across and took her chin in his hand.

He looked into her round, startled eyes. His slow smile made her stomach flip. In this enlightened age Lily wasn't sure if *predatory* should be turning her on.

'What you are is soft…' His voice was deep and dark and textured like deepest velvet. She trembled violently as his thumb moved in a circular motion over the apple of her smooth cheek and she experienced another debilitating rush of heat. 'And lush.' His glance settled on her slightly parted lips. 'And very, very feminine. An hourglass figure is something that men will always admire.'

Gordon hadn't thought so, and Lily felt qualified to disagree. 'Not all men,' she contended huskily.

He dismissed this unappreciative minority with a contemptuous shrug. 'Why do you constantly run yourself down?' he wondered, letting his hand fall from her face and frowning.

'I don't,' she protested, placing the back of her hand against the place his fingers had touched her skin and feeling ridiculously bereft.

He looked amused. 'It is obviously an ingrained pattern of behaviour.'

'That's me, a hopeless case. Look, it's been very nice talking to you…' Surreal was much nearer the mark. There was no mystery about why she was hopelessly attracted to him, the mystery was why he should even pretend to feel similarly about her. 'But I really must be—' His deep voice cut smoothly across her.

'Not hopeless, *querida*. An appreciative lover, someone who could teach you to enjoy your own body, could cure you.'

Having begun to get to her feet, Lily sank back down as her legs literally folded beneath her. 'Are you offering?' In her head it sounded ironic, the sort of slick comeback that invited laughter. Unfortunately it actually emerged sounding humiliatingly hopeful.

'And if I was would you be interested?'

Lily didn't smile; she was too busy panicking. To take him seriously would obviously be a major mistake and a direct route to total humiliation. 'I suppose that's your idea of a joke,' she snapped.

'I am not laughing,' he pointed out tautly.

Lily, who had noticed this, swallowed. There was a driven intensity in his manner that she didn't understand, but it excited her anyway. As she stared he lifted a hand and again dragged it through his hair. His brown fingers were long and elegant...sensitive, but strong. He had the sort of hands you would like to look at against the bare flesh of your stomach...other places too.

'You did not know your mother?'

She looked at him startled by his sudden change of direction and she stopped thinking about his fingers on her bare skin.

'You said ''apparently'' your mother was slim,' he reminded her.

'Did I?' Lily frowned. Her ability to carry on any sort of conversation was severely hampered by the fact that every time she looked at him she experienced a fresh jolt of mind-mushing sexual longing.

'You did.'

'Will you stop doing that?' She snapped, adjusting her towel.

'What?'

'Checking out my cleavage.' Last night he had blanked her, this morning he was mentally undressing her and not trying to hide it. What was going on?

A laugh was drawn from his throat. 'Don't worry. I can

discuss your family and admire your body at the same time.'

'That's an original slant on multi-tasking,' she replied faintly. Inside her chest her heart was fluttering like a trapped animal. 'But I have no desire to discuss my family with you...'

A white wolfish grin split his dark, lean face. 'Then I will settle for admiring your body.'

Lily gave a frustrated little groan and felt a trickle of sweat pool in the valley between her breasts. *What I need is a cold shower,* she thought, picturing cold arrows of water hitting her overheated flesh.

Think cold water... Unfortunately the mental cooling-down process was hampered by the addition of a slickly wet male body in the imaginary shower with her.

'I don't want you to do that either,' she replied hotly.

'Don't you...?'

Working on the basis that it was better to avoid outright lies whenever possible, Lily didn't respond to this husky question. 'Do you always hassle hotel guests this way?' she demanded huskily.

Slowly he shook his head and the twisted smile he gave her was hard to read. 'No, this is actually a unique experience for me.'

The hell of it was she wanted to believe him. She had always despised women who believed slick chat-up lines and here she was wanting to believe that a man who could have any woman he wanted thought she was unique and irresistible. Delusions didn't get any grander than that!

'Just for the record, my mother gave birth to me, and then dumped me with my grandmother, who brought me up. I haven't seen her...*ever*...and as for my father I don't know who he was, but the odds are she didn't either.' *Now why did I tell him that?*

Lily began to get angrily to her feet. This had to be some sort of game. 'I'm not playing,' she muttered from between clenched teeth.

To her way of thinking there was no way a man who possessed a perfect, hard, streamlined, muscular body like Santiago could possibly find anything to admire in her own over-generous curves.

She gave a startled yelp when halfway to her feet the towel she was clutching was unceremoniously wrenched from her fingers.

'Give that back!' she pleaded huskily.

He shook his head, slung the towel carelessly in the pool and removed his shades. His extravagant lashes lifted from the razor-edged curve of his cheekbones to reveal stunning eyes, so dark as to be almost black and flecked by pinpricks of silver. Lily gasped and shivered uncontrollably; the message glimmering in those mesmerising depths was inescapably sensual.

'You didn't ask me why I didn't sleep last night…?'

Raw and driven, his voice drew a low moan from her throat. Lily pressed a hand to the base of her throat where a pulse was hammering away. 'I find hot milk works a treat.'

This sterling advice caused his mouth to spasm slightly, but didn't alter the hot, hungry expression in his eyes. His voice dropped to a low, sexy rasp as he explained. 'I didn't sleep last night because I was thinking about you, and this morning I come out to cool down and here you are. Do you believe in fate…?'

Lily discovered she believed in everything he said in that sinfully sexy voice of his—which probably made her certifiable. 'I really should be going…' *This is pure physical attraction and not a good thing to act on,* she told herself firmly. 'It takes simply ages to dry my hair; it's so thick—'

His authoritative voice cut slickly through her garbled flow of inanity. 'Your hair is rich and lustrous.' He let the damp strands fall through his fingers.

'You think…?' she echoed weakly.

'I do.'

Lily fought to inject a sliver of sanity into the proceedings and shook her head. 'No, it's mousy.' His incredibly long ebony lashes had golden tips and the fine lines that radiated from around his eyes were incredibly attractive.

'We really are going to have to work on that self-esteem issue.'

'We? There is no we. We can't have this conversation. It isn't…*I don't know you*!' Her voice rose in weak protest as her defences went into meltdown.

'What has that got to do with anything?'

'Everything,' she replied, staring helplessly up into his incredible eyes.

He shook his head. 'It is totally irrelevant. Can you deny this feels amazingly *right*?' he challenged as he took her by the shoulders. 'I can't look at you without wanting to sink into your sweet satiny softness and lose myself.'

'You can't say things like to me!' she gasped while thinking, *You can do just anything to me! Please do it now!*

His earthy laugh made every downy hair on her body stand on end. Either he had meant it, or he was a spectacularly good liar! By that point Lily didn't care which it was; she was burning up from the inside out with need.

His shoulders lifted expressively. 'But I just did.' His smile was a potent mix of tenderness and predatory ferocity.

He didn't make any move to stop her when Lily, unable

to resist temptation any longer, reached up and touched his lean cheek. 'I want to see you, touch you.'

His eyes didn't leave hers for a second as he took her fingers from his face and raised them to his lips.

'And you shall,' he promised. 'If that is what you want?'

Lily shook her head. 'I think…I don't know…'

Santiago turned her hand over and traced a path across her palm with the pad of his thumb before touching the plain wedding band on her finger. His head lifted. 'But you are thinking about your husband?'

CHAPTER FOUR

I'M NOT thinking about him, but I should be.

Sucking in a mortified breath, Lily snatched her hand away. His question hadn't just spoiled the mood, it had killed it stone-dead. And a good thing too, she told herself. Her marriage might be a total sham, but she was still married, and in Lily's mind, despite yesterday's reckless thoughts of revenge, Gordon's repeated infidelities didn't give her a licence to do the same.

If she had stopped to think about it, which she hadn't, she would have assumed that Santiago hadn't cottoned on to the fact she was married.

Easy to see how that could happen. She'd been partnerless when he'd seen her, and, unlike women, most men didn't seem to notice things like a wedding band.

It now seemed that he had known she was married all along, and the fact nothing in his manner suggested he had a problem with it made Lily feel totally disgusted.

Not that she was in any position to condemn him. She hadn't exactly run screaming for the hills, had she?

'You shouldn't feel bad.'

Bad! She deserved to feel wretched. 'I wouldn't expect *you* to understand,' she choked contemptuously. Obviously he wouldn't recognise a moral if someone gave it to him gift-wrapped.

A really stomach-churning possibility occurred to her. Had he zeroed in on her *because* she was married? Lily knew there were some men out there, generally commitment phobics, who targeted married women because they didn't want things to get serious. A married woman had clear advantages for that type of sleaze bag.

'I do understand, and what you are feeling is natural,' he soothed.

The compassion in his manner increased Lily's growing anger.

'Done this sort of thing a lot, have you?' She caught her lower lip between her teeth and turned her head away. Angrily she shrugged off the hand that he put lightly on her arm.

'I have handled this badly,' she heard him observe heavily.

Lily's chin lifted. 'So sorry things didn't turn out the way you planned,' she retorted bitterly.

Santiago studied her face before gravely observing, 'It is natural to feel a degree of guilt, a sense that you are being unfaithful—' Lily goggled incredulously at him; this man had to be the most insensitive '—to your husband's memory. I respect you for the way you feel, I really do. In an age when so many place very little value on their marriage vows, your devotion is admirable.'

There was a short time delay before her brain computed what he had said and arrived at the unlikely conclusion—somehow he had the bizarre idea that she was widowed.

Oh, Lord! It should be fun explaining to someone who thought she was a faithful, devoted, grieving widow that her husband was alive and well, and her devotion was the sort that vanished at the first sniff of temptation.

'But you are alive, *querida*, and you are a passionate beautiful woman, with your life ahead of you.' He took her face between his hands. 'I'm sure your husband would have wanted you to be happy. And though I'm sure you won't believe me, one day,' he prophesied confidently, 'you will love again. And until then...'

'Until then…?'

His hands fell away. 'Until then you have needs… appetites…'

'That's where you come in?' Why was she feeling so let down? He was hardly going to tell her that he wanted anything other than to take her to bed. At least he was honest.

'You're not going to deny the attraction between us exists.'

Lily shook her head and wondered what he'd say if she admitted she had never felt anything that even came close to this before.

'Do not let being hurt once make you afraid to live.'

'I'm not,' she said, and realised that for the first time in a long time—perhaps ever—this was true. She took a deep breath; it was time to put him straight. 'As for Gordon, you've got that all wrong. I'm actually totally furious with him.'

'I believe it is not uncommon to feel angry with a loved one who dies. You blame them for leaving you.'

Eyes closed, Lily gave a frustrated sigh and let her head fall back. *I tried, I really tried, and what do I get? Understanding and amateur psychology!*

'No, my husband isn't—'

A nerve clenched in Santiago's lean cheek as he cut across her. 'We keep those we love in our hearts, but there comes a time when we must let go.'

Lily, who would have preferred to put Gordon in a damp, dark, rat-filled cellar, not her heart, stared up at him, her eyes scrunched up in concentration as she tried to figure out how on earth he could have got the idea she was a widow.

'What made you think that my husband is dead?'

'Everyone knows.'

'People know?' Oh, heavens, that explained some of the

sympathetic looks she'd been getting. They all had her down as a brave, plucky widow on some sort of romantic pilgrimage!

And here was me thinking how lovely and friendly everyone was.

He nodded. 'I know hotels are meant to be anonymous, but a woman alone in the honeymoon suite is a subject of conjecture. The staff knew the booking was made by your husband, so obviously when you turned up without him they speculated.'

'You'd think they'd have something better to do,' she snapped.

'And then you told Javier...'

'I didn't tell *Javier* anything; I don't know any *Javier*.' She stopped. *'Oh, no!'* Her questioning eyes flew to his face. 'Do you mean the boy at Reception...?'

'The "boy" has a three-year-old son, but, yes, he works Reception sometimes. He's actually a trainee manager.'

Lily wasn't really listening to his explanation; she was recalling arriving back from Baeza and going to pick up her room key. The details, due to the after-effects of the wine, were a bit hazy, but she *could* remember the chap behind Reception looking embarrassed when tears sprang to her eyes after he asked when her husband would be joining her.

'He won't be joining me.' The realisation hit her. *He never intended to.* 'He's gone. He's *really* gone for good.'

Lily absently massaged the tight skin around her temples. One problem solved—she now knew the why. She only had now to figure out how to tell him her husband was alive and well and therefore she was not available.

'Have breakfast with me?'

'What?'

'Breakfast. Not here, if that's what's bothering you. I

know a place about half an hour's drive away. You need a four-wheel drive to get there,' he admitted, 'but, believe me, it is worth it. The setting is superb,' he enthused. 'The food is not fancy, but it's made with fresh local produce and beautifully cooked. Luis has a huge wood-burning oven outside and you can eat alfresco.'

He seemed to take her silence as assent, because he said, 'I'll see you outside in, what…twenty minutes…?' He smiled at her and then dived cleanly into the water.

'You're allowed to be upset, you know.'

'What…?' It took several seconds for Lily to drag her wandering thoughts back to the present and away from the man who had ultimately told her to go to hell.

Well, he got his wish.

Though, of course, she was post-hell now. She'd come out the other side, but would things ever get back to normal? She sometimes wondered if this was normal for her now; maybe she would carry this awful empty feeling around with her for ever…?

'I said you're allowed to be upset.'

A frown formed on Rachel's crease-free forehead. 'Are you coming down with something? You look awfully flushed.'

'No, I'm fine,' Lily lied. 'It's just warmed up this afternoon—' she gestured towards the sun shining through the open window '—and this sweater is a bit—'

'Of a disaster,' Rachel completed. 'I don't mean to be brutal, but this bag-lady look doesn't do you any favours, love.'

'This is casual.'

'No,' Rachel denied brutally, 'it is absolutely awful. Perhaps if you made a bit of an effort you might feel a bit better? If I'm down I buy a pair of shoes…'

'Retail therapy isn't the answer to everything.'

'I didn't mean to be terminally shallow,' Rachel, who had flushed, retorted.

'Of course you're not shallow,' Lily soothed, guilty for being snappy.

'I do actually know a new pair of shoes isn't going to fix everything, but it... Dear God, Lily, if you don't have the right to fall apart after what has happened to you, who does? I tell you, if I'd been through what you have, losing the baby and Gordon, the total scumbag running off with that little—'

Lily did not want to talk about Gordon or his girlfriend, or the baby...especially the baby. 'Am I falling apart?'

'Ever so slightly maybe... Don't you hate Gordon?' Rachel turned her curious gaze on her friend. 'If it was me I'd want to—'

'Maybe I could do with a trim,' Lily interrupted, running a hand lightly over her hair.

'And a new pair of shoes?'

Lily grinned. 'Don't push it, Rachel.' Her grin faded and she hesitantly added, 'About Gordon—you know, he's really not the bad guy in this.'

Rachel looked ready to explode. *'Not the bad guy!'*

'And Olivia isn't little.' An image of the athletic red-headed figure of the sports psychologist her ex-husband planned to marry now their divorce was finalised flashed into her head.

'She's six feet in her bare feet and it was hardly a shock when Gordon asked for a divorce.'

Gordon had met her at the airport at the end of her Spanish holiday and Lily, who had been consumed with guilt and more miserable than she had thought possible, had not noticed at first that her husband had been acting oddly. She'd totally forgotten that he had a lot of explaining to do, because so had she.

He had waited until they'd got in the car to admit to her that it hadn't been work that had stopped him joining her, but another woman.

Lily hadn't bothered pretending to be shocked.

'She's called Olivia and she's…well, the thing is, Lily, I want to be with her. I think we should get a divorce.'

'All right.'

Gordon, who had obviously been geared up for a big scene, was gobsmacked by her reaction and slightly suspicious.

'And you don't have a problem with that?'

She shook her head listlessly.

'Don't you want to know…' he flushed '…how long…?'

'If you want to tell me.'

'You do understand what I'm saying, Lily?' He spoke slowly as though he were talking to a child. 'This isn't a fling.'

'Not this time.'

Gordon flushed, and looked defensive. 'Well, if you had been more…' He stopped and made a visible effort to control himself.

She decided to move this along a bit. 'Will there be any fallout…career-wise?'

'I resigned.'

'What about the promotion?' The promotion that was all he'd been able to talk about all year.

A hint of defiance crept into her husband's voice. 'I realised that the civil service was stifling me. I need a change of direction.'

'When did you decide this?'

'I resigned two months ago.'

'Should I ask what you've been doing every morning

when you went off to work...and on those business trips...?'

'Olivia and I are setting up a sports training facility in Cyprus.'

'That's different.' She didn't have to pretend total lack of interest.

'Hell, I didn't mean for it to happen, Lily, but you have to admit we're not...but I don't expect you to understand! The moment I saw her...' he began in a low, impassioned voice.

Lily gazed through the car window not seeing the traffic streaming past. 'Maybe I do understand.'

Gordon didn't say so, but she could see he didn't believe her. For a split second she was tempted to tell him that she had met someone too, and she now knew just how empty their marriage had been. She now knew that love could make a person buy very naughty underwear, and forget every principle she'd been brought up to believe in.

But there was no point. This was Gordon, who had once said comfortingly, 'Of course you're not frigid, you're just not a very *physical* person. Don't worry about it; not everyone is.'

The fact was Gordon thought she was a white-cotton girl. Santiago had made her feel and act like naughty black lace.

Rachel made a scornful sound in her throat. 'Sure it wasn't a shock—you expected your husband to leave you for his bit on the side when you were pregnant.'

Lily pushed her brown hair, which, without its normal monthly trim, had got long and uncontrollable, behind her ears. *Maybe it is time to set the record straight?*

'It's true.' A light flush appeared along the smooth contours of her pale cheeks as she experienced an emotion close to relief as she admitted, 'I really wasn't surprised.

Our marriage had been dead and buried for a long time before Olivia came along.'

Rachel's jaw dropped, but almost immediately she began to shake her head. 'I don't believe it. You two were the couple everyone I know wanted to be.'

Lily looked away. That had been the irony, of course; they had appeared the perfect couple in public. 'It's true,' she said.

'Nobody's *that* good at pretending,' Rachel rebutted. 'I don't how many times I told people that you two proved marriage could work. I mean, you were practically childhood sweethearts.'

Lily ran her tongue over her lips... *When did I last wear lipstick? When did I last wear make-up...?* Rachel was right—it was time she entered the human race again. 'In public, yes.'

There was silence before Rachel sank weakly into the nearest chair. 'So you and Gordon weren't happy? *Seriously...?*'

'I wasn't *unhappy*.'

Rachel folded her long legs underneath her and sighed. 'I don't mind telling you, you've really thrown me, Lily.' Lily lifted her head. 'I never had the slightest hint that things were that bad...or bad at all, for that matter. Why didn't you ever say anything?'

Lily's wide mouth twisted into a bitter smile. 'You make your bed and lie in it—that's what Gran would have said.'

'I'm not your gran, and I know you shouldn't speak ill of the dead but she really was one cold—'

'Leave it, Rachel,' Lily begged.

Rachel acceded with a shrug. 'If you were unhappy, why did you stay, Lily?'

'I thought we might sort things...' Lily stopped and shook her head. 'It's a question I've asked myself a million times. The truth is I don't know why I stayed. Maybe I was lazy, or simply scared of change? Maybe I didn't want to admit I had made a mistake? Perhaps,' she speculated dully, 'a bit of all three.'

'But I never heard you exchange a cross word.' A still-sceptical Rachel gave a mystified frown.

'There were cross words,' Lily admitted, recalling the constant sniping and recriminations. 'But we were past that. The fact is, I think we were both too apathetic to argue by the end.'

'That's so sad.'

Lily, whose own throat closed over with emotion, could only silently echo the sentiment. 'I suppose we were a classic case of two people who grew apart, not together.'

A stunned Rachel exhaled a gusty sigh and shook her head, visibly struggling to come to terms with these calmly voiced revelations.

'I knew straight off that Olivia wasn't like the others.'

It wasn't until the designer bag Rachel had been reaching into to switch off her phone dropped from her nerveless fingers, the contents spilling unheeded over the floor, that Lily realised that she had voiced her thought out loud.

'"The others…!" Gordon had *affairs*?'

Lily met her friend's dazed eyes and admitted awkwardly, 'Two that I know of. There might have been more,' she added in an abstracted voice. *Almost certainly were.*

Rachel released a hoarse laugh. *'I don't believe any of this!'* She shook her head as if to focus her thoughts. 'And you knew…?'

Lily nodded.

'Did you care?'

The flash of her blue eyes lent animation to Lily's pale face. 'Of course I damned well cared!' It had been deeply humiliating, but Gordon had always been filled with remorse afterwards… *They mean nothing to me, Lily.*

Rachel grimaced. '*Sorry.* I still can't believe that you never said a word.' Rachel shook her head in disbelief. 'I'm your best friend.'

Lily's hands lifted in a fluttery, helpless gesture. 'It felt disloyal to talk about it and Gordon begged me not to tell anyone. Can you imagine what Gran would have said if she'd found out, and after she had loaned him the money for that car…?' She stopped and angled a questioning glance at her best friend. 'I suppose this sounds big-time weird to you?'

Rachel didn't deny it. 'And then some!'

'And you think I'm totally pathetic?'

'Well, it's not as if there were children and—' She broke off, a stricken look of horror written on her fair-skinned face. She leapt out of the chair and perched herself on the arm of the chair the other girl occupied. 'Oh, Lily, I'm so, *so* sorry.'

Lily shook her head and smiled reassuringly. 'No, you're right, there weren't.'

'But you couldn't have completely given up the marriage; you tried for a baby?'

Lily fixed her cornflower-blue eyes on her friend's face and shook her head. 'No, we didn't.'

'So it was an accident.' Something that Rachel couldn't identify flickered at the back of Lily's eyes. 'I'm not saying you weren't pleased,' she amended hastily. Nobody who had seen Lily in those early months could have failed to see she was delighted at the prospect of becoming a mother.

'It's the happiest I've ever been,' Lily admitted.

'Well, I don't care what you say, I think he's a total bastard to leave you when you were pregnant.'

'I hadn't slept with Gordon for almost a year before I got pregnant.'

CHAPTER FIVE

THE silence that followed this barely audible announcement stretched until, finally unable to bear it, Lily begged, *'Say something.'*

'You and Gordon…you mean Gordon wasn't the father!'

'Obviously not.' Lily, her eyes closed, passed a hand across her face. She was unable to meet her friend's eyes. 'Nothing you can say could make me feel more wretchedly ashamed than I already do,' she choked.

'What I'm going to say… Oh, Lily, you don't really think I'd pass judgement, do you?'

Lily heard the hurt in her friend's voice and her head came up. 'I wouldn't blame you if you did,' she said miserably. She began to rise, but had not managed to get to her feet before Rachel grabbed her by the shoulders.

'You can't drop a bombshell like that and walk away, Lily,' she protested, still looking totally gobsmacked. 'I want to know everything.'

'There's nothing to know.'

'Nothing! You had an affair. You got pregnant. *You,* of all people. That's *not nothing* in my book. I can't believe that all this time you didn't say a word,' she reproached. 'Who…?' Her eyes widened. 'Are you still seeing him?'

Lily involuntarily inhaled as Santiago's dark, classically featured face appeared in her head.

'Do I know him?'

The words dragged Lily back to the present; she willed herself not to glance towards the open newspaper. 'No, and I'm not still seeing him.'

She didn't add that she was pretty sure he'd cut her dead if he ever did see her, not that that was likely considering the different worlds they lived in.

If things had gone differently she supposed they would have had to meet…? A man had a right to know if he was a father. Very conscious of the leaden weight of misery in her chest, she wondered what his reaction might have been if the baby had survived, and she had told him.

It was possible he might not have wanted to have anything to do with a child conceived by accident, but if he had she supposed they would have had to hammer out some sort of arrangement. Now, though, the speculation was pointless; she'd never know, and neither would he.

'It was a holiday romance, that was all, a fling…' She took a deep breath. 'It meant nothing.' She'd told so many lies and half-truths that another one couldn't matter and if she said it often enough she might even start believing it.

Rachel, her expression serious, studied her friend's pale face, pretty sure the spooky composure she was projecting went only skin-deep. 'When did you meet him?'

'You remember that second honeymoon Gordon and I were meant to have just before he dropped the Olivia bomb on me?'

'The one in that gorgeous hotel in Spain? Didn't Gordon…?'

'Get a call at the airport…yes, that's the one,' Lily confirmed grimly. 'He told me to fly out without him and promised he'd catch a flight the next day. He didn't, and I was pretty mad.'

'Is he Spanish?'

Lily's lips quivered. 'Extremely,' she said drily.

Rachel refilled her glass. 'So, did he work in the hotel?'

'On a…casual basis,' Lily prevaricated.

'Did he *know* that you were pregnant?'

Lily shook her head. 'No, he didn't.' Her voice cracked and she swallowed.

Rachel's eyes suddenly widened to their fullest extent. 'You did know his name, didn't you? It wasn't a one-night stand after too much vino or anything. You shouldn't feel bad. We've all been there done that, and those Spanish waiters can be pretty...well, *pretty*.'

Santiago *a waiter*...! Lily swallowed a bubble of hysterical laughter that lodged in her throat. 'I've not been there done that.'

'No, I don't suppose you have—comes of being a child bride.'

Rachel went to refill Lily's glass, but she shook her head and covered it with her hand. 'No, thanks, and I was hardly a child.'

'In my book nineteen is a child bride. So, you didn't know your waiter's name?'

'I knew his name, and I wasn't drunk.'

Not on alcohol anyhow, no wine had ever affected her the way being around Santiago had. Around him, she'd felt reckless and totally out of control. Now the things she had said to him seemed like a dream. The recollection of how her inhibitions had deserted her when she'd been in his bed brought a dull flush of colour to her cheeks.

'And,' she added, defiance entering her blue eyes, 'if I had the choice, I'd do it again.'

Rachel's eyes widened in comprehension. 'So this one-night stand wasn't so casual?'

'It was for him,' Lily admitted.

A thoughtful expression settled on Rachel's face as she looked at her friend. 'You loved him...?'

Lily sighed. 'Totally,' she admitted, and started to cry.

* * *

'The girls are late,' Dan said, checking his watch for the third time. He turned anxiously to the tall dark figure at his side. 'You know what you have to do?'

'I know.'

'It shouldn't be too hard—just turn on the charm, but not around Rachel,' he warned. 'God,' he said with a laugh. 'I'm really nervous.'

'I'd never have guessed.'

'I've never proposed before, and marriage—well, it's a big step, isn't it?' He took a ring box out of his pocket and stared at it. 'And permanent.'

'Not very often.'

'I don't need cynicism; I need support.'

Santiago looked at the younger man's face. 'No, you need a drink, my friend.'

He found that he needed one too. Not that he shared the prospective bridegroom's nerves, but he was conscious of a certain amount of anticipation.

It had been hard to tell from the snapshot—had Lily changed much…? He'd never forget the moment he first saw her in the village square. His breath quickened at the memory.

Driving through the small town on the motorbike his family had gloomily predicted he would kill himself on one of these days, he had stopped to stretch his legs, recalling the conversation they'd had on the subject before he had left home the previous day.

'You have lovely cars,' his mother protested. 'And you can't attend an important meeting in black leather. Nobody will take you seriously.'

'I will change.'

Grinning, his younger sister, Angel, entered the debate. 'I think he wants to forget he's a paid-up member of the establishment…?'

'No,' his other sister corrected, straight-faced. 'He wants

to feel the wind in his tousled hair? I'm right, aren't I, Santiago?'

'Well, I don't care if he wants to walk on the wild side,' their mother retorted, glaring at her tall son. 'He's driving me into an early grave.'

'I'll be careful, I promise.'

He was smiling at the memory and reaching up to unclip his helmet when he saw her. His smile vanished and a reverent sigh shuddered through his body.

'Madre mia!'

From her pensive, almost other-worldly expression, the girl sitting alone at the café table in the square in Baeza seemed to have no idea whatever that she was attracting an enormous amount of appreciative male attention.

She was wearing an ankle-length floaty dress in white. The dress was modest, but not the body it covered.

Her body, *Dios*…!

Even now, it made his breath grow uneven and his body harden just to think about those lush, gently undulating curves. And if the body from heaven weren't enough, she had been blessed with a rare, flawless complexion, big eyes the colour of the bluest cornflowers and a lush and inviting mouth.

If it had been possible to distil that indefinable aura of seductive promise and innocence that this young woman had in abundance, the queue to purchase it would have been stretched from one end of the continent to the other.

He watched her sip her wine, his heart climbing out of his chest as she leaned forward and in the process revealed the upper slopes of her creamy, smooth breasts.

He didn't have the faintest idea how long he stood there motionless, paralysed with lust like an adolescent, but he didn't move a muscle until she got into a taxi, then without questioning his decision he followed it at a discreet distance.

As the taxi turned onto a road that led to only one place, he knew where she was heading.

The first time he had driven along this road it had led to a ramshackle old *finca* and a collection of equally tatty outbuildings. Now it led to a five-star luxury hotel complex set in almost a thousand acres' nature reserve for the lucky guests to enjoy.

Santiago had been born with a name that opened doors in financial and social circles, but when he had approached potential investors to raise money to develop the place he had never once used that name. Stubborn pride…? *Possibly.* A desire to show his father that he wasn't the hopeless loser he frequently painted him as…? *Almost certainly.*

Somewhere along the way to transforming the place into a viable and very successful business, Santiago had realised he was no longer doing it just to prove a point to his father; he was doing it because it gave him a buzz.

He dismounted on exactly the same spot he had ten years earlier, and as he watched the taxi draw up on the forecourt and a shapely female figure emerge he felt no less determined and focused than he had on that first occasion.

Her destination had fitted in with the whole cosmic fate thing he'd had going on in his head. Now he realised he had been rationalising nothing more mystic than lust. Now he knew that it had been a far more malevolent force that had thrown him into the path of Lily Greer.

'It was that turn there.' Rachel bounced up and down in the passenger seat as they passed the pretty village church—for the fourth time.

'Are you sure?' Lily queried.

Rachel looked hurt. 'Of course I'm sure. Don't you think I know what I'm doing?'

Lily sighed and waited for a tractor to pass before she began to back down the narrow village street. 'I'd feel *surer* if you didn't have that map on the wrong page and we hadn't driven round in ever-decreasing circles for the last hour.'

'Don't blame me. It's these instructions Dan gave me; they're impossible. Of course, if he didn't have his phone switched off I could have rung him. Why are you stopping?' she asked as Lily switched the engine off.

'I'm going to ask someone the way.' Over the churchyard wall she had spotted a fair head. 'Give those directions to me and I'll go ask.'

Five minutes later she returned. Rachel was tapping her red-painted nails on the dashboard of Lily's ancient Beetle. 'You took your time,' she complained as Lily slipped back into the driver's seat.

'Sorry, I got talking.'

'Talking? Who to?'

'The vicar. You were right, it's that lane and then the next right and about a mile down there.'

'I knew I was right.'

Lily's brows lifted. 'Well, I suppose according to the law of averages it had to happen some time,' she conceded drily.

'Very funny. If we'd taken my car at least we'd have got lost in comfort,' Rachel said, easing her spine into a more comfortable position in the cramped seat.

'Ah!' Lily gave a triumphant grin. 'So you finally admit we were lost, then?'

'Don't be such a grump. At least we got to see some of this lovely countryside.' Rachel closed her eyes as Lily negotiated a sharp bend. 'What do we do if someone comes the other way?'

Lily, whose thoughts had been running along similar lines, tried to look confident. 'Well, whatever we do it'll be easier than it would be in that monster you drive.'

Fortunately they didn't meet another car and a few minutes later Lily drew up outside a thatched-roof cottage that was picture-postcard pretty. It even had roses around the door.

'Well, isn't this worth it?'

Lily didn't immediately respond. A small paddock divided the cottage from an area of woodland and she had spotted two figures emerge from the tree-lined perimeter. One of them was Dan.

Rachel began to wave her arms. 'There they are!' she cried, catching sight of the men.

'Please tell me that doesn't mean what I think it does,' Lily begged grimly.

Rachel adopted an attitude of surprise and unlatched the garden gate. 'Why? Didn't I say Dan had a friend staying too?'

'Oh, it must have slipped your mind,' grunted Lily sarcastically as she followed her friend through into the garden with considerably less enthusiasm.

'You'll like him,' Rachel slung over her shoulder.

Lily scowled back; she had no intention of liking anyone. 'You're a manipulative monster.'

'Smile,' said Rachel, 'or you'll scare him.' The two men were closer now, so she dropped her voice slightly as she added wistfully, 'Isn't Dan lovely?'

'You're so transparent!' Lily informed her behind a fixed fake smile.

Rachel carried on waving and Lily wondered rather resentfully why her friend could emerge from the tedious

journey looking as fresh as a spring morning and she felt—
and no doubt looked—as though she'd just been dragged
through the proverbial hedge backwards, forwards and sideways!

'For goodness' sake, Lily, *relax*.'

'Relax!' she exclaimed indignantly. 'You've set me up.'

Her friend didn't deny the accusation.

'What is it about people when they get paired off?' Lily
grumbled. 'I've told you I'm happy being by myself.'

Briefly the laughter died from the tall blonde's face.
'You're afraid, Lily, and after what you've been through I
don't blame you.'

Lily's chin went up. 'I am *not* afraid,' she retorted indignantly. 'I'm cautious.'

'Afraid,' Rachel insisted, kindly, but firmly.

'And I'm not interested.' Lily, who knew she sounded
sulky and childish, did her best to ignore her friend's look
of hurt reproach. Of course she knew that Rachel *meant*
well, and normally she would have accepted her efforts
with a smile, but she simply wasn't up to being a *good
sport* at that moment.

'You're going to have to take a risk some time, you
know.'

That's all you know, thought Lily. She was going all out
to have a boring and predictable life from now on. She had
had enough of impulses to last her several lifetimes.

'So now you want me to jump into bed with a total
stranger.' *Been there done that and look where it got me!*

CHAPTER SIX

'Don't be ridiculous, Lily. The jumping into bed is totally optional,' Rachel returned, straight-faced.

Lily grinned despite herself.

'What does he look like?' Rachel asked curiously, craning her neck to see beyond a hedge that briefly blocked the two men from view.

'I can't see through a bush,' snapped Lily. The frown between her eyebrows deepened as she added. '"What does he look like?" Does that mean you don't know?'

'I've never met him, though Dan's always banging on about his wealthy friend.'

'I thought Dan was well off.'

'He is, but this guy has *serious* money, apparently.'

'And like most seriously loaded men probably a taste for tall, skinny blondes with surgically enhanced boobs.' *Great, just when I thought I couldn't be more humiliated.*

'I suppose *you've* known *hundreds* of seriously loaded men…?'

Only one.

'Let me spell out the facts of life. All men have the same fantasies; the rich ones can indulge them—that's the only difference. And I am no man's fantasy.' *One man had convinced her that she was his once.*

'But you're cynical. I don't know about this guy's fantasies, but relax. Dan says he's a…' her freshly glossed lips tugged into a smile '…I think "top bloke" were his actual words. Dan knows him through family—their cousins married or something like that.'

'I'm not worrying; I'm going home.'

Rachel shot her friend a look of amused impatience. 'I'm not asking you to marry the man; he's just a bit of male company for the weekend.'

Despite her professed lack of interest, Lily's glance did slide towards the tall—*very* tall—figure who was just emerging from behind the beech hedge. She felt a spasm of sympathy. Was he a fellow victim or willing pawn? Had he been as much in the dark as her?

Once out into the open Dan broke into a run. A moment later he reached them. Lily looked the other way while the reunited couple kissed as though they had been parted for a year, not a few days.

'Well, what do you think of it?' asked the proud owner of the cottage when they came up for air. He slipped an arm around Rachel's waist and hugged her to his side.

'It's perfect!' Rachel declared as she snuggled up kitten-like to him.

'Not as perfect as you, darling.'

Oh, please! thought Lily as she averted her gaze for the second time. Rachel suddenly grabbed her shoulder.

'Don't look now,' she whispered.

Naturally, Lily immediately wanted to do just that. 'What is it?'

'Not what, *who*,' Rachel corrected. 'Your date is my dream man—no offence, darling,' she slung hurriedly over her shoulder to an amused-looking Dan. 'How do you feel about swopping…?' Her eyebrows lifted. 'You have Hugh Grant, I get Antonio Banderas.'

'I look nothing whatever like Hugh Grant,' Dan protested.

'I've no idea what you're talking about.' Lily shook her head, laughing.

'You will,' Rachel promised. *'Oh, wow!'* She raised her voice. 'Well, hello there. I'm Rachel.'

Unable to restrain herself any longer, Lily turned around; the half-smile on her lips froze where it was.

Rachel's nonsense now made sense. Nothing much else did! Lily took it all in in the blink of an eye: the mobile, sensual mouth, the strong, hawkish nose, the slanted ebony brows.

During that time she drank in the details her heart stopped; it stopped dead. When it started up again she took several long, gulping gasps to pull some oxygen into her depleted lungs. She could literally feel the blood drain from her face.

'Hello, Rachel,' said Santiago, dressed informally but expensively in faded designer jeans that clung to his long, muscular thighs, a linen shirt that hung open to reveal a black tee shirt underneath. Against the dark cotton his skin had the sheen of dull gold.

'This is Lily.' It seemed to Lily that Rachel's voice came from a long way away.

This isn't happening, thought Lily. She looked up into dark, deep-set glittering eyes. This was a man with eyes that could make a girl forget that she was *nice*, eyes that could make a girl feel like a woman.

'Say hello, Lily.'

She would have taken to her heels right then, regardless of any lingering impression she might have left of lunacy, if a creeping paralysis hadn't nailed her feet to the spot. Despite the glorious hot summer weather and the inappropriately heavy clothing she wore, she felt herself grow icily cold and clammy.

Santiago was not a man who did things by halves; when he loved it was full-on, mind-blowing love...the sort of love that... She sucked in air through her flared nostrils.

Do not go there, Lily. Do not go anywhere near there!
When he hated it was with equal fervour. And he hated
her!

She thought about the expression on his face in Spain
when he had personally delivered a message. *Your husband
rang Reception. He says he is worried because your phone
is switched off, and could you please contact him?*

He really hated her.

Santiago Morais could not be here, but he was! And she
was looking at him. Could there be two men who looked
or moved this way?

She already knew the answer to this desperate question.
'Hello.'

His dark head moved slightly in acknowledgement of her
croaky greeting. Briefly their eyes connected, and there was
absolutely no recognition whatsoever in those dark, enigmatic depths.

His head dipped slightly. 'Hello.'

She *felt* different from the woman he had known a year
ago. She knew she looked different, and, she was willing
to admit, not in a good way, but surely she hadn't changed
that much?

What did you want? she asked herself. A big scene? No,
but an acknowledgement they had met would have been
nice. Well, maybe nice wasn't the right word, she privately
conceded. But it would have been, well, better than *this*.
Was this his way of telling her that as far as he was concerned she or, rather, *they* had never happened?

Colour, hot and uncomfortable, came flooding back into
her face; the first stirring of protest wakened in her tight
chest. Blighting contempt, outright animosity would have
been easier to take than being disregarded.

'Rachel, this is Santiago Morais, my sort-of cousin.' Dan

grinned. 'This man gave me a job when nobody else would.'

'I always was a risk-taker.'

'I thought you were just a good judge of character,' Dan retorted.

The dark, heavy-lidded eyes she still dreamt about skimmed over Lily once more; this time anger slipped past his impassive mask. 'So did I,' he said enigmatically.

Lily caught her quivering lower lip between her teeth. She was denied the comfort of weeping, and for a brief vulnerable moment shimmering hurt was reflected in the swimming blue depths of her eyes.

'Well, I always follow my instincts,' Rachel announced.

'And are your instincts always right?' Santiago asked her.

Rachel looked rueful. 'Unfortunately not,' she admitted.

Santiago smiled at her. Having once been on the receiving end of that smile, Lily understood Rachel's dazed expression. Santiago had a way of smiling that made the recipient feel special.

For a short time Lily had thought she was that special person; now she recognised the smile for what it was: a cynical manipulation.

'Dan has talked non-stop about you, Rachel, and I'm glad to report that none of it was exaggeration—you do look like a summer's day.'

Lily watched the delight spread across her friend's face and felt the most shameful stab of jealousy lance through her.

'Did you say that, darling?'

'I would have if I'd thought about it. I've not the way with words that Santiago has.'

'You don't do so badly, sweetheart.'

'Did you have a good journey?'

Lily's jaw tightened as she felt her control begin to unravel. 'Not particularly.'

The response drew the fleeting brush of Santiago's dark eyes and Rachel's laughing rebuke. 'Lily got cranky because she got us lost,' she teased.

'I didn't get lost.' She spoke automatically, her feverish thoughts occupied elsewhere. Had Santiago known she would be here? That made no sense because, considering how they had parted, it seemed unlikely, bordering remote, that he would actively seek her out.

This had to be some sort of ghastly coincidence.

'The lack of signposts are part of the charm of the place,' Dan claimed. 'And that smell.' He inhaled deeply. 'You get nothing like this in the city,' he said, and then started coughing.

A laughing Rachel patted him on the back. 'The air is like champagne, darling, but I can't wait to see the house.'

Lily supposed a conversation of some sort must have occurred, she might even have participated in it, but the next thing she had any real recollection of was being inside the cottage.

Rachel went around the room exclaiming at the quaintness of it all. She loved it.

'The sound system is concealed in the dresser,' the cottage owner boasted, indicating a dark oak Welsh dresser.

And what's a country cottage without surround sound? Lily thought, leaning heavily on the arm of a leather armchair. The interior of the low-beamed room had been painted white; so, for that matter, had the beams. It was furnished minimally with modern expensive pieces that made no concessions to the age of the building.

'I gutted the place,' she heard Dan unnecessarily announce. 'I wanted light and space, like a loft apartment.'

Dan's interior-design efforts hadn't made the low ceilings higher. In the periphery of Lily's vision she was conscious of Santiago ducking to avoid a low beam as he stepped into the room. She forced herself to breathe more slowly as the feelings of claustrophobia intensified.

Santiago moved with the fluid grace only he was capable of and positioned himself in front of what had once been a fireplace and was now a hole in the wall. 'You already have a loft apartment.'

Dan took his friend's dry comment as a joke and laughed. 'Would you ladies like to see your rooms? Then afterwards I'll give the guided tour of the garden. I've got the barbecue going...well, almost,' Dan added with a grin.

'Great. There's nothing we like more than burnt meat, is there, Lily?'

Not unless that something was being underneath a warm, hard, satin-skinned man who told you you were beautiful, who told you that you drove him crazy and then did the same to you...again and again...

'Love barbecues,' said Lily thickly, her breath coming a little faster as she stared at the wooden floor as though it were the most fascinating thing she'd ever seen. 'Hard wood?' she added brightly as she rubbed her toe along the polished surface.

Dan was happy to supply the information. 'Reclaimed from a local chapel that was being demolished.'

'Yes, but what have you done to the bedroom, darling?' Rachel, who was tired of DIY talk, purred.

Dan grinned. 'Let me show you...?' Rachel laughed huskily. 'We'll be back directly. Santiago will look after you, Lily. Won't you, Santiago?'

Horror swept over Lily at the thought of being 'looked after' by Santiago. Her alarm-filled eyes lifted and connected with Santiago's darkly malicious gaze.

'There's nothing I'd like more,' he agreed smoothly.

'I could really do with the bathroom,' Lily interrupted quickly. She desperately had to get away from him.

Displaying an impressive turn of speed, Lily was already halfway up the steep narrow staircase by the time Dan's 'Second on the right,' reached her. In the bathroom she splashed her face with cold water and tried to recover her composure or, failing that, regain the ability to stop hyperventilating.

She had no idea for how long she stood there with cold water playing over her wrists in the washbasin. But her fingers were icily cold by the time she shook them dry and the voices she had been vaguely conscious of had receded and grown faint.

'Tomorrow,' she promised herself. 'I'll leave, and all this will be a bad memory.' She really wanted to go tonight, but she knew that Rachel would be suspicious if she walked out now and she didn't want to ruin her friend's weekend, even if that friend did set her up with strange men.

Only this man wasn't a stranger!

She closed her eyes and took a deep restorative breath. *Come on, Lily, show a bit of backbone,* she chided herself. One evening; how hard could it be...?

Very hard, as it turned out!

CHAPTER SEVEN

THE start was not auspicious.

Lily walked out of the bathroom and found herself standing, not in the small room with a slanted roof and a single bed she had hurriedly identified as her own in her quick dash through to the bathroom, but a larger room with a double bed. She stood for a moment totally disorientated, before she realised that the bathroom must interconnect with the two guest bedrooms.

Her restless gaze took in the black robe slung across the back of a chair, the damp towel crumpled on the bed suggesting that the owner had stepped out of the shower and dropped it there. The scatter of personal items on the dressing table, the elusive male fragrance that hung lightly in the air, told her who slept in that bed.

Her stomach took a deep and unscheduled dip, and the muscles low in her pelvis contracted violently. A hand pressed to her mouth stopped the involuntary cry escaping her lips, but did nothing to quell the smothering excitement that made her treacherous body literally shake.

Santiago the other side of my bathroom door. Now that should really help me sleep! She tried to laugh and found she couldn't; you couldn't make a joke out of something that had all the making of a tragedy.

Every instinct told her she ought to get out of that room as fast as was humanly possible.

So why am I standing here?

She actually started to walk towards the door. She didn't

get there. Something, possibly an untapped streak of masochism, made her linger.

She never could recall the sequence of events that led to her standing there fingering the heavy watch that lay on the bedside table. The heavy metal was smooth and cold in her palm as she turned it over recalling the occasions when she had seen it against his brown flesh.

'The clasp is faulty.'

The observation came from behind her. Lily almost leapt out of her skin at the sound of the deep, sexily accented voice.

A picture of guilt, her cheeks flaming, she spun around jerkily. Her eyes collided with those of the tall figure who stood, his narrow hip wedged against the door-jamb, his arms folded across his chest.

She experienced a surge of adrenaline that made her feel light-headed as she looked at him. Head cocked at an arrogant angle, his eyes narrowed and that marvellous golden skin stretched taut across the angles of his magnificent cheekbones, he looked dark and dangerous and, she couldn't deny it, quite incredibly gorgeous in a fallen-angel sort of way.

One dark brow quirked expressively and Lily realised that she'd been standing there staring at him...for how long she hadn't the faintest idea.

'Did you get lost again?' His expressive, mobile lips set in a straight line of disdain, his narrowed eyes continued to scan her flustered face without warmth.

'Sorry...I d-didn't mean...I thought this was...I was thinking about someone...thing, *something* else.' *I was thinking about you.* 'I thought I was in my own room, but obviously I wasn't.' Her hands moved in a fluttery gesture as she stopped.

The longer his eyes held hers, the less articulate she became, but he didn't help her out. He just carried on staring her down. Lily felt a surge of resentful anger.

'Anyhow, what are you doing here?'

Her aggressive addition caused his eyebrows to lift in an attitude of exaggerated surprise. 'This is my bedroom.'

The dry reminder made her shift uncomfortably and twist her hands in an anguished knot of white-knuckled fingers.

'I know that now.'

'Now that you have gone through the drawers.'

The suggestion brought her chin up. 'I didn't touch the drawers.' Her eyes held a sparkle of resentment as they rested on his dark, disdainful face. 'I wasn't snooping, if that's what you're implying.'

'How exactly would you define entering someone else's bedroom and rifling through their belongings?'

The feverish spots of colour on her cheeks expanded until her entire face glowed with painful colour. 'I didn't *intentionally*... As I said, I didn't even know it was your room.'

The contention drew a nasty smile from him.

Lily gritted her teeth. 'I was just...it takes me a while to get my bearings.' *Especially when I'm in shock!* And seeing Santiago standing there had to qualify as that.

The fragile grip on her panic slipped as she contemplated the night ahead. *Then don't think ahead!* she cautioned herself sternly. *Better still, don't think at all, and say less.*

'Don't worry, it won't happen again.' The first time they had made love she had said the same thing.

But it had!

Something that flickered in the back of his eyes made her wonder if he remembered too. Recalled how rapidly she had retracted and ended up in his bed, and the memory filled her with a deep sense of shame.

Obviously she was no longer that weak, wanton creature.

You hope!

And with her head held stubbornly high, her eyes focused on anything but him, as she began to edge towards the door she realised that to leave the room would mean getting past Santiago. Maybe even brushing against him!

She came to an abrupt halt, and a shudder she had no control over ran visibly through her frame as she contemplated the inevitable physical contact with warm, hard muscle.

'Excuse me...' He didn't respond to her frigidly polite request to move. 'That's a polite way of saying shift out of my way.' Rudeness had an equally poor result. He just stood there looking at her.

'How have you been, Lily?'

She blinked. 'Do you care?'

'You acted as though you were surprised to see me here.'

'I was...' Her eyes narrowed suspiciously. 'If you're suggesting I angled for an invite because I knew you'd be here, nothing could be farther from the truth. If I'd known you'd be here I never would have come,' she promised him. 'My friend invited me. I came, end of story.'

His upper lip curled.

'Do I get to know what the sneer's for?' she asked. Like everything else, Santiago's look of disdain was perfect.

'So this is a happy coincidence...?'

Lily's spine stiffened. 'I'd prefix that with cruel or painful.'

'So your friend didn't mention my name...?'

'I don't think she knew it.'

She continued to grind her teeth quietly; that sceptical smirk of his was off-the-scale aggravating. 'What the hell else could it be if it wasn't a coincidence?'

'I don't know—'

'Amazing, I thought you knew everything,' she cut in childishly.

'Maybe you thought we might start up where we left off?' he suggested sardonically.

Lily tried to sound calm despite the fact she would have liked to take a swing at him. 'We left off with you screaming abuse at me, as I recall.' Her expression was intended to give the impression she found the recollection amusing. The reality was a long way from the truth.

That traumatic encounter was seared into her psyche. And actually he hadn't shouted. When Santiago got mad the volume dropped, and the deep, soft syllables were more devastating than any bellow.

'But,' she added helpfully, 'if you're worried your animal magnetism might prove too much for my control, you can always lock the door this side. And then you can sleep sound in the knowledge that I won't creep into your bed in the middle of the night.'

The moment the scornful words left her lips she knew she had shot herself in the foot. Santiago might have been suitably put in his place by her scathing wit, but she couldn't look at him to find out.

Some wit! Her imagination had gone into overdrive, or, rather, her memory, because imagination wasn't required when you had actually done it!

With a little jerky motion of her head she began to study the blue-striped curtains at the window—the fabric looked expensive. Fabric patterns were a much safer subject than a naked Santiago.

But it wasn't fabric patterns that flooded her head, but forbidden memories. She had woken and been drawn from the warmth of the bed they had shared by the moonlight that had shone through the open balcony window. The air had been thick with the scent of the sea and the heavy fragrance of thyme and lemon trees planted in the terracotta pots around the wrought-iron railings had hung in the air.

Returning to the bed later, she had stood beside it looking at the face of her lover. The strong angles of his face had been softened by sleep. A deluge of emotion so intense that it had brought a hot flood of unshed tears to her eyes had left her feeling breathless and shaky.

So this is love. I always was slow, she thought. *Who else waits until they're twenty-five to fall in love…?*

'Love hurts' had suddenly had an entirely new meaning.

When she'd pulled back the cover and slipped back into the bed beside him she had been cold. For a breathless moment she could literally *feel* the texture of warm satiny skin against her own, as she'd plastered her cold body against his. The tight, congested feeling in her chest became suffocating. It was all so real: the friction of hair-roughened areas against her bare, sensitised flesh, the heat building up between them as pale limbs entwined deliciously with brown.

Lily was too caught up by the unrelenting stream of images passing through her mind to notice that Santiago's response was a long time coming and with his dark skin a flush was easy to miss.

'I'll keep that in mind.'

She gave a dazed blink and focused on his lean face. 'Yeah, well, just remember I've got a lock my side too, and,' she added defiantly, 'I'll be using it.'

His dark eyes moved over her face. 'Have you looked in the mirror recently?'

Not if I can help it. She had no control over the mortified flush that washed over her fair skin, though she managed not to lift a hand to her hair. 'If I'd known you'd be here I'd have had a makeover,' she retorted flippantly.

'It would take more than a makeover.'

Lily, her eyes shocked, froze when he caught hold of her chin between his thumb and forefinger and tilted her face up to him. Head angled back, eyes half closed, long dark lashes brushing his cheek, he scanned her face, then let his hand fall away before delivering his damning verdict.

'You look appalling.'

The verdict tore a shaky laugh from her throat as she absorbed this ego-bashing body-blow. Lily took a step back. 'You always were a smooth talker,' she said, tucking her hair behind her ears with not-quite-steady hands.

'What the hell have you been doing with yourself?'

Lily found the depth of anger in his snarling demand bewildering. Before she had the opportunity to tell him to mind his own business he added sneeringly, 'I hope he was worth it.'

'I'm a slow learner, but I've come to the conclusion that no man is *worth it*.'

Santiago didn't appear to be listening to her. A distracted expression slid across his face as he extended a brown hand towards her. 'Your skin is still smooth.'

A sibilant little gasp snagged in her throat as his thumb began to travel from the curve of her jaw up her cheek. From somewhere she discovered the strength to pull away. Blindly she barged past him and stumbled towards the door.

She almost made it, but her shoulder caught the sharp corner of a tallboy. A cry of pain was wrenched from her lips as half the items from the polished surface went crashing noisily to the floor. Wiping the wetness from her cheeks with the back of her hand, she dropped down and began to agitatedly gather the things that had fallen on the polished boards.

Above her Santiago swore fluently in his native tongue. 'Be careful; there's broken glass.'

'It's fine,' she sniffed.

Santiago dropped down beside her. 'You're bleeding.'

Lily kept her head down and ignored his husky observation.

'I said stop that,' he snarled, grabbing hold of her wrist. 'You're bleeding over everything.'

'Sorry.' Lily held her injured hand against her chest. 'I'll pay for any damage.'

'To hell with the damage. Let me see…'

The idea of him touching her again made her heart rate kick up another notch. She would sooner put her hand in a flame than invite his touch. 'It'll be fine; it's just a little cut,' she muttered, not looking at him, but very conscious of how dangerously close he was.

'You should clean it. There could be glass in it,' he said, pulling her to her feet and sounding angry. *So nothing new there.*

'Don't fuss,' she gritted, pulling her elbow out of his supportive grasp.

'Let me see.'

Lily ran the tip of her tongue across her dry lips and flickered a wary look at him through her lashes.

'There's no need to make a production of this.'

'Then don't,' he suggested, stony-faced.

'It's a scratch,' she insisted, beginning to clumsily off-load the things she was still holding onto the nearest solid surface, which happened to be his bed.

She grimaced as items from his wallet spilled out untidily over the quilt. Teeth set, she tried to stop them falling on the floor. Her efforts were hampered by the fact she still had one hand pressed against her chest.

'That would suggest otherwise.'

She followed the direction of his finger and saw the red stain spreading across her pale sweater. 'Damn!' she exclaimed, grimacing. 'I'd better change.'

'That would be a good idea. Dan faints at the sight of blood,' Santiago told her drily. 'But *after* I've looked at it.'

'You haven't changed a bit.' As she levelled her angry glare at his face she wondered if maybe Dan wasn't the only one who didn't like the sight of blood. Santiago looked unusually pale. 'You still have to be in control of everything,' she accused, beginning to rub a spot of blood from a snapshot that had fallen from his wallet.

'You never used to mind that I was hands-on.'

The mortified colour flew to Lily's cheeks. 'That's something I prefer not...' Her voice died away as she straightened up, the photo grasped in her fingers. Her eyes, round and shocked, went from it to him.

'You knew I'd be here.'

Santiago took the stained snapshot from her fingers and gave a careless shrug. 'I barely recognised you.'

'But you did,' she snapped accusingly. 'You *knew* I would be here and you still came and then,' she added, her indignation escalating, 'you accused *me* of trying to get back in your bed!'

'You introduced the subject of beds.'

Forgetting her cut hand, she grabbed his hand in both hands and released a long, low, anguished groan. 'We could have avoided this.' Her bewildered eyes locked with his. 'Why did you come, if you knew I was here, Santiago?'

He didn't respond. 'Have you been ill?'

'We're not all as image-conscious as you are.'

Actually Santiago had many faults, but vanity, she admitted, was not one of them. He didn't work on his image; you had to care about what people thought about to do that. Santiago had a 'take me or leave me' attitude that many people took for arrogance. They might well be right, she reflected grimly.

'That's not an answer,' he pointed out impatiently.

'Maybe I don't think I owe you any explanations. It's pretty obvious that you don't think you owe me any.' She shook her head. 'I still can't imagine what you were thinking of coming here?'

'Maybe I wanted to see how many scalps you had added to your belt since me?'

'Oh, my,' she said airily, 'I've lost count. Rachel and Dan will wonder where we are. We should go down.'

'Perhaps they'll think we succumbed to instant lust and have fallen into bed.'

Lily inhaled and shook her head. 'That's enough.'

'Enough of what?'

'Enough of you acting like I'm something that just crawled out from under a stone. Just what is your problem anyway?'

His head reared back, the muscles in his brown throat worked as he looked down at her with incredulous disdain. 'The fact you can ask that question…'

She expelled the air from her lungs in a long, hissing sigh of weary exasperation. 'I was married and I let you think I wasn't.'

'You played the vulnerable, grieving widow,' he condemned.

'And you were only too eager to take advantage of my vulnerability, as I recall.'

'Do you think I don't know that? Do you think I didn't know that at the time…?' He gave a bitter laugh. 'Do you think I didn't despise myself?'

'And now you just despise me…that must be convenient. Oh,' she sighed sadly. 'I shouldn't have deceived you, I'm aware of that, but it was a year ago and it's not like you were left with any permanent emotional scars or anything. It's just your pride. I suppose it's being Spanish, the macho thing.'

Santiago had been moving as she spoke; now he was standing so close they were almost touching. He didn't touch her, but she wanted him to. This, she thought despairingly, was why history kept repeating itself...the human race was incapable of learning by its mistakes, no matter how painful. Or at least she was!

'You sound quite an authority on the subject.'

She was normally sensitive to intonation, but the heavy irony in his voice sailed over Lily's head as she tried to focus her eyes halfway up his chest. Her eyes had other ideas.

'Well, it was only sex...very good sex,' she added fairly. 'But just sex when all said and done...' *You're gibbering,* she thought and closed her mouth. Her eyes stayed stubbornly, some might say suicidally, focused on the severe sexy line of his incredible mouth.

It was a few seconds later that her fuddled brain registered the anger etched on his lean face.

'You're right, the sex was good.' His voice was like warm honey as he leaned towards her. Their eyes connected and the crackling tension went off the scale.

There was no moisture left in Lily's mouth as she swallowed convulsively. The unique scent of his warm male body filled her nostrils and she felt dizzy. She was not aware of the strangled sound of distress that emerged from her aching throat.

Lily closed her eyes and concentrated all her resources on regaining control. A moment later she opened her eyes and managed a shrug.

'Yes, we had a good time, didn't we?'

'The sort of good time that leaves a nasty taste in the mouth.'

The insult made her flinch, but her chin lifted. 'Well, we

both agree on something, then. Now, if you'll excuse me,
I'm going downstairs.'

'Looking like that?'

'Oh!' Lily glanced down at her top and grimaced. 'I'll
get changed... Damn, my things are in the car.'

'Never mind your damned clothes, you need that hand
cleaned up. Come on.' Ignoring her squeal of protest, he
placed both hands on her shoulders and propelled her into
the adjoining bathroom. It was a small room, which got a
lot smaller with him in it. Lily knew that if she dwelt on
the confined space she would start to hyperventilate.

'Right, sit there and let me have a look.'

Perched on the edge of the bath, she glared resentfully
at the top of his dark head as he inspected her cut hand.

'It's deep,' he concluded after a moment, 'but I don't
think it needs stitches.'

She snatched her hand away. 'Damned right it doesn't.'
After the last experience she didn't want to see the inside
of a hospital for a long time.

'You're lucky—there doesn't seem to be any glass frag-
ments in it. It needs cleaning and dressing, though.' He
switched on the cold-water tap. 'Put it under the water and
I'll get something to clean it with.'

'I really don't think—'

'And I really don't care what you think,' he cut in with
blighting scorn. 'So shut up and for once in your life do as
you're told.'

Lily put her hand under the tap, not because he'd said
so, but because she was dripping blood all over the marble
tiled floor. 'Mr Charm,' she muttered darkly as he left the
room.

A couple of minutes later he returned carrying a bottle
of antiseptic, a bandage and several sundry items.

'Where did that come from?'

'The first-aid kit in my car. I told them you'd had an accident. Dan's bringing up your bags.' He dropped down onto his knees at her feet and gestured for her to give him her hand.

Lily did so with reluctance. He was impressively deft and in a matter of moments her wound was cleaned and neatly dressed. After a final inspection he appeared satisfied. His eyes lifted to hers. 'Does that feel comfortable—not too tight?'

She shook her head. 'Thank you.'

'Lily...you asked me why I came knowing—' At the sound of Dan noisily dumping her bags in the adjoining room he broke off. 'You're welcome,' he said, rising to his feet in one fluid motion.

A brief nod and he was gone, leaving Lily to wonder about what he had been going to say.

CHAPTER EIGHT

HAD anyone even noticed when she had excused herself pleading a headache last night? Well, that at least was no lie. Lily pressed her fingers to her temples. This morning the heavy thud from last night had been reduced to the gentle throb of a tension headache. *Me tense…? Now, there's a surprise!*

Her expression sour, she looked at her reflection in the mirror. It was the same image that had looked back at her for weeks, the only difference was this time it shocked her.

I barely recognise myself, she thought, lifting a stubborn hank of hair from her cheek. That at least looked healthy. She let it slide through her fingers, slippery clean and shiny as a conker. Its original cut was a dim and distant memory, but it didn't look too bad.

The same couldn't be said for the rest of her! It wasn't just the fact that she wore no make-up and her clothes had been selected without any concession to style or colour co-ordination. Lily recognised that her body language screamed defeat, the same message was conveyed by the expression in the shadows of her blue eyes.

She was frowning at her frumpy reflection when the sound of laughter drifted up the stairs along with the smell of breakfast. They were having fun; a wave of self-pity washed over her. *Now how daft is that?* she asked herself. *Nobody made you go to bed early. Nobody made you sit in a corner saying nothing all night.* A few inarticulate grunts had been her major contribution to the evening's festivities.

A light of resolution awoke in her wide-spaced eyes and,

purposefully straightening her pathetically hunched shoulders, she stalked to the wardrobe and pulled open the doors.

The contents did not offer much choice. Finally she pulled out a pair of cream linen trousers and a sleeveless, plain, fine-rib black vee-neck sweater that still had the shop label attached. When she pulled them on the trousers were too big for her new slimline self so she substituted them with a butterfly-patterned voile skirt in soft pastel shades.

She chewed her lip for a moment and wondered what to do with her hair, then on impulse she pulled it back in a severe pony-tail high on her head. She secured it with a silk scarf and freed a few long tendrils of soft hair to curl around her face and nape. It had a softening effect and drew attention to the swan-like curve of her slender, pale throat.

'My goodness!' she said aloud to the mirror. 'I've got cheekbones.'

Fascinated by the discovery, she traced the slanting outline, not sharp enough to cut yourself on, but definitely cheekbones. Purposefully, with the occasional glance back at the strange girl in the mirror, she emptied the contents of her bag onto the bed. Sifting through the motley collection of make-up from the bottom of her handbag, all she came up with was a soft apricot gloss, which she applied to her lips then, for good measure, her eyelids and the apples of her cheeks too. The difference the subtle smudges of colour made was amazing.

After breakfast Dan and Rachel announced their intention to walk into the village to buy some milk.

Santiago looked at the spindly high-heeled shoes that the bubbly blonde was wearing and thought about the lane with its numerous potholes. He doubted they would go far. 'Enjoy yourselves,' he said, unfolding the previous day's financial pages.

'We will,' they promised in unison.

He heard the sound of the back door slamming and then seconds later it opening again. 'Forgot my shades,' Dan said in a voice loud enough to reach his girlfriend outside and then, in a lower, confidential tone, he added, 'Listen, Santiago, mate, I'm really sorry about…' With a grimace he jerked his head suggestively upwards. 'My God, was she hard going last night or what?'

'I thought she was a little quiet.' She hadn't laughed once all night. He had liked her laugh. He had made her laugh just to watch her face light up.

'You're being generous,' Dan said, and then wondered at the odd expression that flitted across his friend's face.

'Are you coming or not?' A smiling Rachel popped her blonde head around the door.

Dan smiled. 'Just coming.' He gave a conspiratorial nod towards his friend and made to leave.

'If Lily wakes while we're gone, tell her I won't be long. It's great to see her sleeping late,' she mused. 'I *knew* the country air would do her good,' she confided happily. 'I bet she's glad I persuaded her to come now.'

'Your friend…she has been ill?'

It seemed to Santiago, after considering the alternatives, that illness was the only thing that could explain Lily's altered appearance.

The permanent crease line between his dark brows deepened as he recalled her expression when she had recognised him the previous day. There had been enough shock, pain and desperate hurt in those wide blue eyes to satisfy the most vengeful of ex-lovers.

Wasn't that what he was? Hadn't that been his intention—to see her suffer? Certainly she deserved to. She had done what no other woman ever had; she had made a fool of him. *Though not without my help.*

The truth was it had provided him with no pleasure, no sense of triumph, to see the pinched pain in her face and the shocking dark smudges under her eyes. He supposed it might have if he were the sort of man who got a kick from making a helpless puppy whimper. Damn the woman! Only a sadistic bastard could take revenge, petty or otherwise, on someone who looked as though they had been to hell and back.

So far nothing had gone as planned. He'd had it all worked out, what would happen when he saw her again. He would be able to view her beauty with objectivity, and leave at the end of the weekend wondering what he had ever seen in her. End of story, get on with the rest of his life.

It turned out he had been slightly optimistic about the objectivity part. And he knew *exactly* what he had seen in her.

He had also forgotten to include the unforeseen into his calculations. And he definitely hadn't foreseen feeling a powerful urge to feed her, protect her from cold winds and crush with his bare hands the person responsible for turning a vibrant, glowing woman into a shadow.

'She's had a bad year,' Rachel explained.

Haven't we all? he thought.

'She's a bit…emotionally *delicate* just now.'

And not just emotionally, he thought, recalling the extreme fragility of her wrist bones. They had looked as though a light breeze would snap them, let alone a man holding them—not that he had any intention of holding her or them.

Though it was not immediately obvious because of the bulky outfit she had been wearing, it would seem likely her body had lost its luscious curves. He had woken in the middle of the night on more occasions than he cared to acknowledge with an ache that nothing but holding her soft, fragrant body could assuage.

A man who knew his own weaknesses could guard against them. Last night his guard had come close to slipping. With a frown he pushed aside the intrusive thought.

'Though she looks a million times better than she did a few weeks ago. I don't mind telling you I was really worried…'

A million times better? Madre mia! This information shocked him more than he could say.

Rachel looked as if she might say more, then at the last moment appeared to have second thoughts. With a quick awkward smile over her shoulder, she followed Dan outside.

He smelt Lily before he even heard her soft tread on the flagged passageway. He inhaled the scent of the floral soap she used and the shampoo she washed her hair with.

Lily walked, her feet encased in a pair of silly but pretty sandals, into the kitchen. She stood framed in the doorway blissfully ignorant of the fact the morning sun had made her skirt effectively transparent. When she saw that Santiago was alone she almost turned around.

She took a deep breath and stuck out her chin. 'Good morning.'

His eyes lifted to hers and then dropped as he continued to scan the paper.

Lily entered the room, and when Santiago made no attempt to move his long legs from her path she stepped over them. Clearly her efforts to re-enter the human race were wasted on him. Not that the effort she had made had anything to do with him.

She sat down in a chair opposite him. Arms folded in an

unconsciously protective gesture across her chest, she examined his remote profile.

'Where are Dan and Rachel?'

There was no reply.

'Don't you think this is rather silly?' She sucked in an angry breath and her hands twisted together into a white-knuckled knot as, his dark head turned from her, Santiago continued to scan the page of print.

'I'm talking to you,' she added in an overloud voice that trembled with emotions that threatened to spill over. 'Would a little bit of common courtesy be too much to ask?' she demanded.

The newspaper rustled as he laid it to one side. Very slowly his eyes lifted to hers. 'Frankly, yes.' Though the muscles in his brown throat worked as his eyes meshed with her indignant blue orbs, his expression didn't alter.

'Is that it?' she choked.

'What do you want me to say…?' *You look delicious and I want to take your clothes off.*

The mild question brought a look of confusion to her face. 'I don't want anything from you.'

Santiago appeared to believe that statement about as much as she did. 'Are you annoyed,' he suggested, 'that I have not noticed the trouble you have taken with your appearance this morning?' His dark eyes dropped, moving with slow, insolent deliberation over her slim figure. 'I have.'

Their eyes connected once more and the gleam of predatory heat in Santiago's caused all the muscles in Lily's abdomen to spasm violently. Trying desperately to ignore the flash of suffocating heat that had engulfed her, she lifted her chin in a gesture of empty defiance and swallowed past the dry, tight occlusion in her throat.

'Well, don't think I did it for you.' She shook her head

vigorously and felt her pony-tail bang against her cheek. 'Because I didn't.' *Well, if he wasn't thinking it he sure as hell is now…way to go, Lily!*

'So Dan is the lucky man. Perhaps I should warn your friend.'

Lily tossed her head. *He thinks I'm a conniving tart, why not give the man what he wants?* 'Dan isn't my type, but, naturally,' she added, fabricating an insincere smile out of pure loathing. 'I would steal him from my best friend without a second thought.'

'Then what is your type?'

You are. It made her blood chill to think how close she came to saying it out loud. Her eyes slid from his. 'I have abysmal taste in men,' she confided huskily.

'Is one of these…*men* responsible for your present condition?'

'*Condition…?*' Her voice rose, hoarsely suspicious. Without realising it she pressed her hands to her stomach. 'I'm not pregnant, if that's what you're insinuating.' She might smile about the irony of this conversation later, but at that moment she was fighting back the tears. Anger, she had learnt, was a pretty good way of doing that.

His ebony brows lifted. Hard disdain was etched on his patrician features as he observed, 'I wasn't. You're hardly glowing, are you?'

Determined not to show that his disparaging observation had shattered her confidence, she responded with laughing unconcern. 'Sorry you don't like my new cheekbones, but actually I'm more concerned with the fact I can actually look good in clothes now.' She glanced down and smoothed the skirt defiantly over her hips.

'You always looked good in clothes,' he retorted.

Lily searched his face expecting to find sarcasm. She found none.

'Though you looked a lot better without them.'

The silence that engulfed them seethed with things Lily wouldn't let herself analyse. The sound of her own tortured breathing was loud in her ears. Did the dark bands of colour along the slashing angle of Santiago's high cheekbones mean that he wasn't immune to the possibilities throbbing in the taut atmosphere…?

Did she want to find out?

'You're being so childish,' she stated defensively.

The harassed accusation ignited an astonished flare of anger in his deep-set eyes.

'Sorry,' she drawled. 'I forgot for a moment I was speaking to Santiago Morais. Obviously *you* couldn't be childish. You're brilliant and accomplished and incapable of putting a blessed foot wrong. Doesn't it ever get tiresome being so damned perfect?' He had been perfect in bed. The maverick thought sliced right through her anger and left her feeling uncomfortably defenceless.

'What the hell are you talking about?'

'Forget it. It's nothing you'd understand.' The problem, she reflected wearily, was that Santiago was one of those rare individuals who had never known failure. Had he ever failed at anything he decided to do? Lily studied his lean, autocratic features and doubted it. Failure simply wasn't in his vocabulary.

He folded the newspaper and put it on the table.

'I understand when someone is giving me the runaround.'

'I'm not trying to…' She gave a shrug. 'What's the point?' The spark might still be there between them, but it didn't matter what she said. There was no realistic possibility of them ever rekindling their affair.

Too much had happened.

He angled a disturbingly penetrative glance at her averted profile. 'Was that a question?'

Her eyes lifted and she squared her slumped shoulders. 'Don't worry. I'll make an excuse the first chance I get and leave.'

'You'll lie, you mean. Now why doesn't that surprise me?'

'Look, do you think I like this any better than you?' she demanded, dragging an exasperated hand over her forehead. She wasn't sure how much of this she could take. 'At least you knew what you were walking into. Can't we just make the best of what is an awkward situation?'

Santiago's jaw tightened a notch. *'Make the best of it…'* he repeated slowly. 'How very stoical and British of you.' His nostrils flared as he raked her with an openly contemptuous glance.

'I am British.'

A muscle clenched in his jaw. 'I, however, am not.'

Unnecessary information, she thought as he rose in one fluid motion to his feet.

'I am not stoical; I am Spanish.'

Despite the awfulness of the situation, or maybe because of it, the comment wrenched a laugh from her dry, aching throat. The heritage Santiago so proudly claimed had never been more apparent than at that moment.

'I was just thinking that it shows. You make being Spanish sound like a threat.'

'Do I…?' His shoulders lifted in a shrug, but he didn't deny the husky accusation. 'I am simply stating a fact. It is what I am.' His penetrative eyes continued to scan her face until she wanted to scream or run away…preferably both!

'Did you sleep well?'

At the innocuous enquiry some of the tension slid from

her body. 'Brilliantly,' she said, knowing the smudges of violet under her eyes, the ones she hadn't been able to totally disguise with make-up, gave lie to the claim.

'Then it must have been someone else I heard pacing the floor all night.'

'I don't pace.'

'*Really?* In case you forgot, your room is very near to mine, and one thing about these old houses is that the floorboards creak.'

To hide the mortified colour that sprang to her cheeks Lily bent down and adjusted the strap of her sandal. 'I think we've already established I look like hell,' she grunted resentfully. 'I'm so sorry if I kept you awake.' She extended her bandaged hand. 'My hand was hurting.'

Something flickered behind his mesmeric eyes. 'It wouldn't be the first time you kept me awake,' he admitted throatily. 'Do you want me to look at it, change the bandage...?'

She shook her head, lowering her gaze protectively as the sexy rasp in his voice sent a debilitating shock through her body. Considering the stream of erotic images playing in her head, she managed to keep her voice remarkably expressionless as she added, 'It wasn't just that. Actually my bed is extremely uncomfortable and the pillows have rocks in.'

The extravagant fringe of lashes lifted, revealing the febrile glitter of his spectacular eyes. 'Mine isn't.'

The thud, thud of her treacherous heart made it hard for her to hear her own breathy response. 'Are you offering to swop? How very gentlemanly of you,' she quipped nervously.

'I was thinking more along the lines of...*sharing*?'

Her undiscriminating stomach muscles went into violent,

quivering spasm. 'I'll avoid the obvious been there and done that and simply say that sarcasm is hardly helpful.'

Presumably he *was* being sarcastic…the alternative made her heart beat faster. From under the fringe of her lashes, she scanned his face. It revealed nothing other than his perfect bone structure.

'Helpful to what?'

My blood pressure, she thought, staring at him helplessly.

'And how do you know that wasn't a serious offer? I understand that you're a free agent these days.'

Lily stiffened, her expression growing wary. 'I'm divorced, but how—?'

With a voice like a scalpel he cut across her. 'Although being married never cramped your style, did it?'

She lifted her hands palm-up towards him in an unconscious gesture of submission. 'What am I supposed to say to that?'

Features set, he pressed a finger to the spot on his temple where he could feel a pulse throbbing. 'Being single doesn't suit you,' he rasped.

'Well, I'm enjoying it,' she lied immediately.

His critical dark eyes moved up and down her slim body. 'You look like you haven't had a decent meal in weeks, and don't give me that rubbish about a new image. For starters I think you'll discover the old image had more *pulling* power and, besides, your friend implied that you'd had problems.'

Expression blank, she shrugged.

With a muttered curse in his own tongue he turned and walked across the room. 'I suppose it was a man…?'

She looked at his broad back and gave a bitter little smile he couldn't see. 'I suppose you could say that,' she agreed drily. 'I'm surprised Rachel didn't fill in the details when you were discussing my private business.' The next time she got Rachel alone she was going to warn her not to say a word about the baby to Santiago unless she wanted her designer shoes trashed. 'Was it Rachel who told you about my divorce?'

'Dan. He said your husband dumped you? Not a secret, is it?'

'No, it's not a secret.' She looked at him and gave an exasperated sigh. 'Do you *have* to be so antagonistic?'

'You want to behave like we're old friends? Fine.' His mobile lips sketched a smile. 'Let's catch up…I know about the divorce, and I understand you're having a breakdown because of some man. Anything else of interest been happening?'

I was having your baby and I lost it…does that constitute interesting? Breathing hard, she bit back the retort that hovered unspoken on her tongue. She pressed a hand to her heaving chest until she trusted herself to speak.

'You're a callous bastard,' she announced conversationally. 'And I hate to disappoint you, but I'm not having a breakdown…although after this weekend who knows?' She released a laugh that even to her own ears sounded worryingly wild.

'And there's no need for you to tell me what you've been doing. It's been pretty well documented.' The gossip columns had been full of his latest romance.

'I'm flattered you take an interest.'

'I don't! *Nothing* you do is of any interest to me,' she proclaimed angrily.

One dark brow angled. '*Really?* Me, I have to admit to a certain curiosity. Your husband did leave you. Presumably one infidelity too many?'

She took a deep breath and forced her hands to unclench. '*One* was too many,' she hissed.

'Are you trying to tell me that I was the only one?' His mocking laugh grated against her raw nerve endings. 'I feel so special,' he confided nastily.

'I'm leaving. I must be mad to have stuck it out this long.'

'Leave…?'

Lily, already halfway to the door, stopped and half turned.

'Secure in the knowledge your concerned friend would run after you…'

'You didn't tell her about us, did you?' She sucked in a horrified breath.

'Was I meant to, *querida*?' Eyes narrowed to icy slits, Santiago slowly shook his dark head. 'How little you know me.'

'I wish I didn't know you at all!' she yelled back. After declaring childishly, 'I wish I'd never met you,' she ran from the room.

But did she? Did she *really* wish she had never met him? If she had a magic wand would she wipe out that short period of her life as if it had never been? Even after all the anguish and grief of the last year, would she deprive herself of the intense experience of falling in love?

CHAPTER NINE

'LILY, what do you think you're doing?'

Lily dropped the pile of wood she was carrying and turned around guiltily. 'Now look what you've made me do,' she grumbled, wiping a grubby hand across her face and leaving a dusty smudge along her cheek.

Rachel planted her hands on her slim hips. 'Put that down immediately! I can't leave you alone for a minute.'

'The doctor said light exercise is good for me. Besides, I like it.' The good thing about hard manual labour was, you got too tired to think—at least that was the theory. After the logs Lily planned to mow the lawn.

'I rather think the doctor had a gentle stroll in mind.'

'Then why didn't he say so?'

'I suppose he thought that he was talking to a rational human being,' Rachel retorted tartly before she turned to the tall man standing in the doorway. Her expression was accusing. 'Don't just stand there, pick it up!' She turned back to Lily. 'Anyone would think you *wanted* to hurt yourself?'

Lily didn't hear the exasperated comment. Her eyes were fixed on the tall, silent figure who had not responded yet to Rachel's terse command. How long had he been standing there and what, if anything, had he heard?

Their eyes connected, and it hit her like a sledgehammer—a massive surge of sheer longing. She didn't want to stop looking at his dark, sinfully beautiful, fallen-angel face, but she did.

The sun was hot, the night was dark, those were givens.

So was the fact that she would always be susceptible to Santiago's dark, dramatic looks. She might have to live with this mortifying fact, but she didn't have to put herself in a situation where she had to fight her own blind instincts.

In fact to do so would be criminally insane!

She squared her shoulders. 'Don't fuss, Rachel.' Her tone made Rachel's brows lift. 'Sorry, I didn't mean to snap, but I've had a toothache since last night,' Lily quickly improvised to explain her short temper.

'You have perfect teeth,' Rachel, who had spent a small fortune on cosmetic work to achieve a similar result, protested.

'Apparently not.'

Rachel scanned her face. 'You do look a bit off. How could you be so stupid?' she reproached. She laid a hand on her friend's arm. 'Come and sit down.'

'For heaven's sake, they're not heavy, and I'm not an invalid. It's been six months now.' The moment the words left her lips she knew they were a mistake.

Santiago, who so far had been silent, asked the one question he wasn't meant to. 'Six months since what?'

'Since nothing.'

'Since she lost the baby.'

The two contradictory statements emerged in unison.

Lily found herself looking directly into a dark pair of heavily fringed eyes, even though that was the one place she was trying hard not to look. So hard that beads of sweat had broken out along her upper lip. *Stay calm, Lily. He just looks as though he can read your mind. It's an illusion.*

Isn't it…?

There was a short, static silence before he said in a voice that was not so smooth and assured as normal, 'Baby…?' His eyes dropped to her belly. 'You were pregnant.'

Lily was horrified to feel her eyes fill with weak tears.

Hand across her wet face, she turned; by the time she reached the stairs she was running. She didn't stop until she was in the small attic bedroom.

Rachel winced as the sound of the door slamming above made the cups on the dresser rattle. She felt obliged to offer an explanation for her friend's peculiar behaviour to this tall, urbane Spaniard.

'It's still a bit raw. She doesn't like to talk about it.' Her voice dropped to a soft, confidential whisper as she added, 'She was six months gone when they discovered there was no heartbeat.'

'The child died?' In contrast to the slow way he spoke his brain was making some rapid calculations. A man didn't need a calculator to figure the obvious maths. She had lost the child at six months, six months ago...the child could have been his.

Rachel, oblivious to the fact she was talking to a man who was anything other than mildly curious in the details, elaborated. 'To make things even worse she had to go through labour and deliver him knowing that...'

She sighed and shook her head as she watched Santiago, who had begun to mechanically stack the scattered logs into the basket by the door.

'It makes your heart break just to think about it,' she said half to herself. 'And then as if that wasn't enough something went wrong after the birth and they had to rush her to Theatre.'

There was a full thirty seconds' silence before Santiago straightened up. 'She had surgery?' He casually flicked a piece of cotton off his trousers.

Rachel wondered at his odd tone, but as his head was turned away from her as he examined his trousers for another invisible speck she couldn't read his expression. Though if last night was anything to go by that appeared the norm with Dan's Spanish mate. He was a stud, certainly, and she had seen flashes of humour, but she had been able to honestly soothe Dan the previous evening when she'd told him his distant Spanish cousin was much too intense and brooding for her taste.

'It was touch and go, apparently.'

His head came up and the expression on his rigid features startled Rachel. 'So that is why she has lost so much weight...' He turned to an astounded Rachel, his attitude harshly condemnatory. 'What were her family and friends doing while she wore herself to nothing?'

Driven on the defensive, Rachel responded apologetically to the abrupt demand. 'Well, she hasn't got any family since her gran died last year, and I and others have tried to help, but Lily is very proud...'

Santiago's nostrils flared. 'She is very stubborn.'

Rachel couldn't help but nod in agreement with this bitter observation. 'Tell me about it. I just wish I'd been in the country at the time.'

She might have paused to wonder how he suddenly seemed to know a lot about Lily, if he hadn't closed his eyes and exclaimed, in a low explosive undertone, *'Madre di Dios!'* The words emerged from between clenched teeth. 'She was all alone...?'

Carrying his child had almost killed her, and where had he been while she lay fighting for her life? It could have been any number of glitzy venues, all as instantly forgettable as each other. For a short time he had actually convinced himself that he had enjoyed the whirl of empty activity.

'Are you all right?' Rachel's concerned enquiry received no response. In fact her fellow house-guest gave no sign of having even heard her, as without saying another word he turned stiffly and strode out of the door, down the garden path and out into the lane.

'Now what was *that* about?' Rachel speculated, brushing a stray hair from her face as Santiago vanished from view down the leafy lane.

Spanish men were very unpredictable, she reflected, comparing this man's volatile behaviour with Dan's more predictable conduct. Of course Dan didn't have those eyes or that smile, she conceded, but you couldn't have everything.

She was beginning to suspect that hearing the details of Lily's ordeal had recalled some personal tragedy for Dan's friend. Hoping this wasn't the case, she went to see if Dan could shed some light on the situation.

Dan turned out to be in the car listening to the cricket score. She got in beside him and started recounting the incident; midway through she stopped, an arrested expression on her face.

'He said she'd lost weight. How did he know she'd lost weight?'

Dan looked puzzled, but not for the same reason as his girlfriend. 'Lost weight? She's fat.'

Rachel elbowed him in the ribs. 'She is not fat. It's the clothes she wears, silly. He must know her.'

Dan looked sceptical. 'If he knew her he'd have said so.'

'I suppose so,' Rachel conceded. 'Unless…'

'Unless what?'

'Dan, I think that he's Lily's Spanish waiter!'

Dan decided his beloved had lost her mind.

Unaware of the speculation going on, upstairs in her room Lily lay on the bed, her crooked arm lying across her tightly shut eyes. *I ran away.* She turned over and groaned. If she'd thought about it all day she couldn't have come up with a better way to arouse his suspicions.

Actually, she didn't know why she was so bothered. What did it matter if he found out? She tried to analyse her reluctance to share the truth with him. She'd had the perfect opportunity to explain when he'd brought up the subject of her appearance the day before.

She played out the scene in her head.

I would say—*I was pregnant, there were complications and I lost the baby.*

And he would think about it and ask—*Was it mine?*
Yes.

He would be shocked, of course; what man wouldn't? But as it sank in and he realised that there was no unwanted child to trouble his conscience, wouldn't he be secretly relieved for the narrow escape?

I don't want to see that relief!

She had lost a child that meant everything to her. She didn't expect Santiago to share her grief, but she didn't want to see the father of her child pay lip service when all the time he was thinking what a narrow escape he'd had.

Emotionally drained, she must have dozed because the next thing she knew someone was banging on her door. She lay there for a moment staring at the ceiling, wondering why she had a knot of tension in the pit of her stomach.

Then she remembered.

'Oh, God!' she groaned, pulling a pillow over her head. There was another urgent knock and the door-handle rattled. Lily tossed the pillow on the floor and sat up and rubbed her eyes. 'I'm asleep, Rachel. Go away.' One thing she definitely didn't feel like just now was an interrogation Rachel-style.

The door opened. 'It is not Rachel.'

Not unless Rachel had grown into a lean, muscle-packed,

six-foot-five male who oozed earthy sexuality from every delicious pore. After staring at the tall, dark figure who filled the doorway for a horror-stricken, open-mouthed moment, she recovered from her paralysis.

With as much dignity as the situation allowed she closed her mouth, swung her legs to the floor and tightened the knot of her pony-tail in a determined fashion.

'I can see that.' She eyed the intruder in a wary, unfriendly fashion and willed her racing heart to slow. 'Is dinner ready?' Even mentioning food made her stomach churn nauseously.

The furrow between his brows deepened as he looked at her as though she had lost her mind. 'I've not the faintest idea if dinner is ready.'

'Pity, I'm feeling quite peckish,' claimed Lily brightly. 'Then why...?' He didn't respond to her prompt, just carried on looking at her with a bone-stripping intensity that negated all her attempts to keep things light and normal.

Normal! Santiago Morais in your bedroom, normal? You should be so lucky, mocked the ironic voice in her head.

'What can I do for you, Santiago?' There had been a time when she would have meant that quite literally; she would have done anything for him.

'You can tell me if you were carrying my child.'

Lily gave up trying to be composed as with a sharp gasp she leapt to her feet and reached out as if to physically haul him into the room. 'For goodness' sake!' she cried. 'Lower your voice, and shut that door!'

Santiago did neither. 'I am waiting.'

She released a long, frustrated sigh through her clenched teeth. 'Closing the door was a suggestion, not an order, if that makes it easier for your macho pride. Now, please...please close the door before someone hears you,' she begged.

Santiago did as she requested, which was a mixed blessing as being inside the small room in his presence was almost unbearable. Even in the midst of her blind panic she felt dangerous swirls of excitement as their eyes touched. *Eyes to lose yourself in…*

'Now will you give me an answer?'

'Are they downstairs?' she asked in a hushed undertone.

He gave one of his maddening shrugs. The action made her belatedly aware that handfuls of his pale blue shirt were clamped between her clenched fingers.

'Sorry,' she mumbled, ineffectually patting the creased fabric. The fact she carried on patting just a bit too long might have had something to do with the hard, muscular contours of his perfectly developed upper arms.

All right, there was no *might* about it. Touching Santiago had always been addictive. In fact she hadn't been able to keep her hands off him, and he had always been more than willing to indulge her obsession, but not so now. He was looking down at her with an expression of impatient disdain etched on his hard features.

She mumbled a mortified, 'Sorry,' for the second time. 'I was afraid they might have heard you,' she explained, tucking her hands safely behind her back. Her thoughts, the ones that involved her hands gliding over satiny golden and perfectly formed hard muscles, were less easily disposed of.

'Your friends knowing we have been lovers bothers you?'

Lovers. He sounded so indifferent when he said it, as though he were discussing the weather, but hearing their relationship described this way in his deep accented voice sent an illicit shiver through her hopelessly receptive body.

'Too right it bothers me,' she grunted, lifting a hand to her tangled hair as she watched him lean against the wall.

Unless his fitness levels had decreased dramatically the shallow flight of stairs that led to her room could not account for the rapid rise and fall of his chest.

'The truth bothers you.'

'I don't like to advertise my mistakes,' she stressed in response to his sarcastic interjection. 'And you were the one who acted as though we had never met when I arrived.' She heard the note of dissatisfaction in her voice and almost groaned out loud.

Santiago's lips formed an ironic smile as he recalled the moment he saw her standing there. Every time he thought about those seconds before his self-control and pride had kicked in, the moment when fierce delight had permeated every cell of his body, he experienced a wave of self-disgust.

'I was just following your lead.'

This outrageously false claim drew a snort of derision from her dry throat. 'Well, that would be a first.'

He gave a dangerous grin that didn't reach the hardness in his eyes. 'Meaning what, exactly?'

Quiet mad. Santiago did quiet mad well, but then Santiago did *everything* well! The thought inevitably took her in the direction of the bedroom. She closed that mental door and in a burst of reckless frustration she told him exactly what she meant.

'Meaning that you never follow *anyone's* lead, certainly not mine. You are autocratic, overbearing and it never even occurs to you that people won't do exactly what you want them to. You see something you want and take it regardless of the consequences. I can see how this dark, brooding Spanish-lover thing has worked for you over the years, but a word to the wise…if you want a long-term relationship, you'd better start giving a little more and taking a little less!' she finished on a breathless, bitter quiver.

Even though she felt good at that moment, she was pretty sure she'd regret her cathartic diatribe—if she could remember exactly what she'd said, that was. It was already a bit of a worrying blur.

His eyes were hot as if lit from within as he responded in a husky voice that vibrated through Lily all the way to her toes.

'I was under the impression that I took nothing you were not anxious to give to me.'

And I gave and gave… Lily veered her thoughts firmly in the opposite direction. Her chin was up, but she couldn't prevent the flush that ran up under her fair skin as their eyes met.

Her recent emotional outburst took its inevitable toll as, without warning, her knees folded under her. Fortunately the bed was there to break her fall…

'I wasn't looking for a husband,' she said bitterly. 'Just a bit of fun.'

'I was light relief?' The muscle in his lean cheek throbbed like a time bomb and she couldn't tear her fascinated eyes from it.

'What else?'

If Santiago had been angry before, he was furious now. Her heart climbed into her throat as she watched him struggle to contain his feelings of outrage.

'You already had a husband, didn't you, Lily? Though I wonder at your choice of…playmate. I'm amazed you were prepared to sleep with such an arrogant, selfish, abusing bastard.' Through his long dark lashes she could see the furious glitter of his jet eyes and they had a strangely mesmeric effect upon her.

'I didn't know you when I slept with you, and you're not selfish in bed.'

She heard his splintered gasp and froze suddenly because

instead of hostility the room seethed with an equally volatile, but infinitely more dangerous, emotion—the sexual charge hung heavy in the air between them.

'Neither are you,' he admitted thickly.

Through the open window she could hear bird song. The carefree sound provided a sharp contrast to the tense atmosphere in the room.

'Like I said before, it was a mistake. One I'm not terribly proud of.'

Something dark and dangerous flared in his eyes as his brooding features hardened. She watched as his clenched hands unbunched. Very slowly he exhaled silently and folded his arms across his chest. 'And did that "mistake" include getting pregnant?'

CHAPTER TEN

STRICKEN to silence, Lily just looked at Santiago.

'It is not a difficult question so why is it so hard for you to answer?'

Good question.

And one Lily had never anticipated having to answer. She hadn't thought she would ever see Santiago again. To lie was the simplest and most expedient solution. Yes, it was almost definitely the way to go, and she opened her mouth to do just that, but strangely the required words wouldn't come.

She walked across the room and straightened an already straight insipid print on the wall and twitched a curtain.

As the silence lengthened a spasm of impatience twisted Santiago's mobile mouth. Her dark curling lashes gave her very little protection when his interrogative gaze locked onto her flustered face. *'Well…?'* he rapped, obviously holding on to his temper with difficulty.

Her lips formed a mutinous line. 'Well what?'

She heard the audible snap as his white teeth came together in a frustrated grimace. 'I know how much you like playing games, Lily,' he said, levering himself off the wall and rotating his broad shoulders in a way that made her visualise the knots of tension in his tight muscles that he was trying to relieve.

She could recall smoothing away the tension, letting her fingers glide over his smooth, oiled skin.

His expression was set and bleak as he added softly, 'But, believe me, now is not the time.'

Neither was it the time to get distracted by a sexual fantasy, but she was doing it anyhow. She bit back the bubble of hysterical laughter that rose to her lips. 'I don't play games. And I'd like you to leave my room.' The latter was said with no real belief he would do so.

He didn't.

'And *I* want to know if you were carrying my child.'

Lily dragged her eyes clear of the frenetic nerve spasming beside his wide, sensual mouth—never a good idea to look at his mouth—and she stuck out her chin. Despite the body language inside she felt about as defiant as a limp lettuce leaf. She took a deep sustaining breath and angled an enquiring look up at his dark lean face.

'Why do you want to know?'

Santiago's jaw clenched; he looked at her in furious disbelief. '*Why?* Are you *serious*?'

The colour began to creep into her pale cheeks. 'It seems a reasonable question to me.'

'You know nothing about reason!' he contended loudly.

'Will you lower your voice?' Lily yelled back even louder.

'You know nothing about the truth! You...' With a visible effort he controlled himself and gritted, 'I warn you, Lily...'

'Warn me?' she parroted, breathing as hard as he was now. There had been times when she had needed him, when she had wanted him and he hadn't been there. No, he turned up now, just when she was about to put her life back together again...*typical*! She looked at his hands clenched white-knuckled at his sides. Clever hands that had moved with infinite variety over her tingling flesh... *Don't go there, Lily!*

The instruction came too late. A visceral shudder was

already passing through her body as heat ignited deep in her belly.

'What the hell right do you have to warn me about anything?' she demanded, shrilly desperate as she tried to ignore what was happening. 'We only slept together.' She dug deep and managed a more than passable 'so what?' shrug.

The effort produced a rash of cold sweat over her body. But maybe, she reasoned, if she annoyed him enough he might get sidetracked and forget his original objective. 'It's history, and not a very important piece of history at that.'

Strangely objective, she watched his nostrils flare and the strong, beautifully sculpted lines of his incredible face tighten until the golden skin pulled taut and glistening with a fine sheen of moisture across the angles of his jutting cheekbones. He looked the epitome of Southern Mediterranean fury as he loosed a flood of low, hoarse words in his native tongue.

He was awesome!

He really was the most incredible-looking man. *Excitement…?* It was with horror that Lily identified the illicit thrill that tingled along her raw nerve endings.

Even in the midst of his fury Santiago's hot eyes strayed to Lily's slim, ringless fingers that plucked fretfully at the neckline of her tight-fitting sweater. The deep vee gave a tantalising hint of the creamy swell of her soft breasts, whose fullness was emphasised by the extreme slenderness of the rest of her body. His already rock-hard body reacted violently to the feminine image.

'What's the point?' She smiled and recklessly ignored the hoarse growl of incredulity that issued from his throat. 'Think about it,' she advised. 'I mean, what difference does it make? There isn't a baby…*not now.*'

Santiago flinched at the bleak little addition, but his ex-

pression didn't soften. 'Was the child mine, Lily? I'm asking for a yes or no. How hard is that?'

Extremely hard, she knew that, it was the why she
couldn't figure. Why couldn't she just say, Yes, I was having your baby, end of story?

'You know we used…we were c-careful.' Or at least *he*
had been. It shamed Lily to be forced to admit that the
desperate urgency Santiago had aroused within her had
been matched by a negligence to consider the consequences
that in retrospect horrified her.

He pointed out the obvious. 'Careful doesn't always
work,' he said bluntly. 'The only sure form of contraception
is celibacy.'

The comment made Lily wonder about all the women
who had fallen for his fatal charm since they had parted.
'Not really your style, is it?'

His upper lip curled. 'And it's yours…?'

Lily flushed and desperation drove her to retort defensively, 'It was purely physical.'

His dark eyes signalled contempt as they swept across
her flushed face. 'And here was I thinking it was a meeting
of souls. Imagine my devastation.' His sarcastic drawl taut-
ened as he added, 'I am asking you for the last time, were
you carrying my child?'

'I don't respond well to ultimatums, Santiago.'

Her delaying tactics were beginning to have visible effect
on his anger. 'And I don't respond well to being lied to,
Lily.'

'I haven't lied to you.'

One dark brow arched sardonically at her protest. A tide
of hot colour rose up to Lily's hairline. Her shoulders
slumped, she gave a tiny nod of assent. 'I think the baby
was yours.'

'Think…?'

Lily barely heard him, the feelings were rushing back, and for a moment she could feel the tiny body in her arms. The pain and loss, the feelings of total hopelessness, threatened to overwhelm her. She barely registered Santiago's hands on her shoulders forcing her to sit down. He then dropped down on his haunches so that his dark face was level with hers.

'Take some deep breaths,' he ordered.

The concern underlying the rough instruction made her look at him. Their faces were close, close enough for her to see the individual lines radiating from his deep-set eyes and the tiny silver pinpricks of light deep in the darkness of the irises. She inhaled a quivering breath that drew in the warm male scent of his body, evoking forbidden memories.

The memories caused the empty, aching feeling in the pit of her belly to intensify. She felt his fingers tighten against her collar-bone just before his hands fell away completely.

'Don't be nice to me,' she begged huskily. That, she reflected, shouldn't be too hard for him. Not that he hadn't had cause to be mean to her. She had let him think she'd been single when she'd still been married; that constituted just cause in most people's book.

She had *tried* to explain she hadn't set out to deceive him, that it had just happened, but he hadn't wanted to listen to her explanations. Then in her turn she had got angry.

'Come off it, Santiago. Are you trying to tell me that you've never lied to a woman to get her into bed...?' She deliberately goaded him with a light, scornful laugh when he confronted her with her deceit.

For a split second she thought he was going to throttle her. Then he too laughed, a harsh laugh that sent a chill down her spine. 'You didn't have to lie to get me into your bed, *querida*.' His contempt seemed aimed as much at himself as her.

Lily couldn't let this sort of blatant hypocrisy pass without comment. 'I thought you didn't sleep with married women.'

'*I don't!*' he gritted back. The explosive silence that followed his words lengthened until a full minute had passed before he added, 'For you I would have made an exception.'

'Because I'm irresistible?' she fired back with withering sarcasm.

Something hot that made her stomach flip moved behind those dark, impenetrable eyes. '*Yes.*'

She sucked in her breath and felt the heat travel through her body. '*Santiago…?*' Her husky voice was infused with entreaty that it later shamed her to recall as she reached out to him, emotionally and physically.

In hindsight she recognised that moment as one of those crossroads in life, the ones that you didn't know you stood at until later. If he had reached out and taken her hand, as she was sure he almost had, things might have turned out differently.

But he hadn't.

'I'll do my best not to be too nice,' he promised. Her expression vague and distracted, her big blue eyes meshed with his as the past collided with the present. With a soft cry she turned her head.

'No!' He caught her chin in his fingers. 'Don't turn away, Lily,' he said, angling her face back to his.

Lily felt as if her heart would break. 'I think your best will be more than sufficient,' she croaked back.

His lips formed a twisted smile. 'So now I am a brutal monster, am I?'

She shook her head. 'No,' she admitted huskily, 'but you have a very cruel tongue when you're angry.' And when he had discovered she had lied to him, when he had discovered that she had still been married, he had been *very* angry.

'*Madre mia*, but it's true.'

The angry admission surprised her.

'You have this strange ability to bring out the extremes in my personality. Be it anger...' his eyes dropped to the soft outline of her mouth '...or passion...' She gasped and drew back fractionally as his thumb brushed her lower lip.

A deep sigh vibrated through her body as her eyes half closed and her body swayed towards him as though drawn by an invisible thread.

Neither of them spoke while she stayed with her head resting against his chest. When she eventually raised her head she took a step away from him and absently swept the wispy strands of hair from her face with her forearm.

She took a deep, resolute sigh. 'Right, what do you want to know?' she asked, connecting with his sombre eyes.

'When did you...when did...?'

She had no problem understanding what he was trying to ask. 'I was in the sixth month,' she cut in quietly.

'Sixth month.' She watched the muscles in his brown throat move as he swallowed convulsively.

'Babies sometimes live when they are born at that stage? Is that not so?'

She nodded. 'But my baby was already dead,' she told him huskily, while in her head she relived that awful moment when the young woman doing the scan had given her a bright professional smile and excused herself. *I just need to go and get the doctor,* she had said.

The professional smile had not fooled Lily; she had known that something was wrong. The doctor, with his kind, tired eyes, had held her hand when he'd told her.

'You're sure…you're absolutely sure?'

'Yes, though naturally we will double-check. Can I contact your husband…partner…?'

She had shook her head. 'No, he isn't…he's not around any longer.'

'Is there someone you'd like me to contact?'

'No, I'll be fine, thank you.'

'*Our* baby.'

Still trapped in a nightmare of recollections Lily lifted her eyes to Santiago's face. She shook her head. 'Sorry…?'

'Our baby. The child you were carrying was *our* child, and apparently it did not occur to you to tell me?' His low voice was flat and devoid of expression; not so the blazing eyes that were fixed on her face.

'I suppose I had other things on my mind.' Lily, whose face moments earlier had been snow-white, was now suffused with angry colour. 'There was no conspiracy to keep you in the dark.'

'From where I'm sitting that's hard to believe.'

'Well, believe it or not, it's true. I was waiting for the right time.' Even to Lily this sounded lame.

'How hard was it to pick up the phone and tell me?'

'And you'd have believed me, I suppose?' she charged. 'Right, that was *very* likely.' Despite her defiant attitude, she was actually shaken by the depth of his reaction. 'I had to think about what I'd do if you wanted to go down the DNA court-case route.'

His darkly defined brows twitched into an interrogative line above his aquiline nose as he gave a baffled frown. '*Court case…?*'

'Isn't that how it works when a celebrity dad denies paternity?'

His lips twisted in distaste. 'I am not a celebrity.'

'You do things and people write about them. You have more money than any one person could spend in a lifetime. In fact,' she accused, 'I bet you don't even know how much money you have.'

He didn't deign to respond to this angry claim, but said in a taut, controlled voice, 'I do not court publicity, and I protect my private life.'

'You didn't protect it much when you took Susie Sebastian *almost* wearing *that* dress to the music awards…' she began darkly.

'Shall we leave aside for one moment the definition of celebrity? We are talking about you keeping me in the dark about my child.'

Lily wouldn't leave it alone. 'Newspapers don't pay you for stories about people unless they're celebrities.'

His brows lifted. 'Should I expect to see a kiss-and-tell story in the tabloids in the near future?'

Her lips formed a mirthless smile. 'Very funny.' *Maybe he's serious.* Her eyes flew to his face, and what she saw in them soothed her suspicions. At least he didn't think she was capable of that. 'My finances are not stretched that thin yet.' Actually, they probably were. She pushed the worrying state of her bank balance to one side for a moment and added provocatively, 'But who knows in the future…?'

'Why would you assume that I would have denied paternity?'

She tilted her head to look into his dark, hostile eyes and shrugged. 'Well, you must admit the idea of you embracing fatherhood under those circumstances is worth the odd laugh.'

'Do you see me laughing?'

CHAPTER ELEVEN

LILY accepted the invitation and studied Santiago's dark, lean face. She felt the first flicker of uncertainty.

'Your actions were based on the assumption that I wouldn't have wanted to take a full and active role in my child's life. I think that's a pretty big assumption to make, don't you…?'

'So what…are you saying you'd have proposed?'

'That would have been difficult, as you were already married, wouldn't it, Lily?' Lily was too startled to resist when without warning he took her left hand in his. She watched as he looked at her index finger and then, turning her hand over, looked at the palm.

She found it impossible to look away as he stroked the soft skin. The hand that wasn't captured curled into a tight fist as she tensed. She winced as the action caused the bandage to dig into her skin.

'You've taken off your rings.'

'I gave them to a charity shop.' She pulled her hand away. 'Gordon was furious. And,' she reflected absently, 'he was probably right. It was a grand gesture I can't afford.'

'If I had been there to make you take care of yourself our baby might have lived.' He exhaled a long, shuddering sigh and, head in his hands, sank down onto the bed beside her.

Lily froze and missed totally the strong element of self-condemnation in his voice. She heard only the accusation, the levelling of blame. Santiago had hit a raw nerve.

Despite the doctor's repeated assertions that what had happened would have happened no matter what she had done, Lily hadn't totally shaken off the guilt that had afflicted her after the miscarriage.

'You're saying it was my fault…?' Her voice cracked as she added with a harsh laugh, 'I suppose you think I'd have made a terrible mother.'

'At least you'd have had the opportunity to try.' He met her blank look of incomprehension with a twisted smile. 'I was never going to have the opportunity to even meet my son, let alone be his father. Years in the future I could have passed my own son in the street and not known him!' His accusing eyes swung back to her. 'You would have denied me my son.'

Her face suddenly crumpled. 'We were both denied our son.' Biting back the sobs that refused to be subdued, she pressed her hands to her face and turned her back on him.

For a moment Santiago watched the grief-stricken figure before he reached across and pulled her roughly into his arms.

'I'm sorry. It must have been a terrible experience for you, but it's just I've learnt I had a child and lost him all in an hour.'

Lily lifted her tear-stained face from his chest. 'I'd say time makes it better, but I'm not sure it would be true.'

Santiago took her pony-tail in his hand and wrapped the gleaming strands around his fingers. 'You've had a hell of a time, haven't you? I don't want you to take this the wrong way, but I need to know something.'

'Then you'd better ask.'

'Were you going to pass the baby off as your husband's?'

Lily stiffened. Shaking with anger, she lifted her shimmering eyes to his. 'You are the most hateful man I know!'

Her voice ached with feeling as she leapt from the bed and backed away.

'I don't know why you look so outraged…'

The man was just unbelievable! 'You just accused me of passing off another man's child as my husband's. How do you expect me to look?'

'You didn't answer the question.'

'And I'm not going to.'

'You would hardly be the first woman to do so and under the circumstances it was a perfectly legitimate question.'

'What circumstances?'

'As you have pointed out, I know to my cost that lying is second nature to you…and even if you hadn't slept with him during the relevant period you could have been vague about the dates.'

Not when the relevant period had been nearly a year. 'For your information, when Gordon left me I didn't even know I was pregnant.'

'And when you did your first thought was to tell the father.'

His ironic tone made her delicate jaw tighten. 'It's really easy for you to act all hurt and offended now…now there isn't a baby.' She blinked as her eyes filled with the sting of hot tears.

'Actually things worked out pretty well for you, didn't they?' she accused in a voice that shook with emotion. 'Now there is no baby.'

'You think this makes me happy!' he yelled furiously.

'And, anyhow, I couldn't have passed the baby off as Gordon's. We hadn't even…' She stopped and flushed to the roots of her hair. 'Well, anyway,' she ended lamely, 'I didn't.'

'You hadn't even what?' His eyebrows lifted. 'Had sex…?'

Lily struggled to maintain a semblance of calm, though inside she was shaking with anger. 'I have no intention of discussing my private life with you.'

He directed a speculative look at her pale face. 'Is that why you slept with me? You wanted a child? And your husband wasn't willing, or able?'

'You really think that I'm that manipulative?'

His eyes slid from hers as he slowly shook his head as the anger left his body. 'No.' The sweep of his long lashes lifted from his cheekbones. 'You do realise when it must have happened, don't you? It must have been the first time.'

Her eyes slid from his. 'Probably,' she admitted, trying not to think about warm air caressing her naked skin.

It hadn't even crossed her mind that she would ever be uninhibited enough to make love out of doors. Not that the place had been exactly public. The mountain restaurant had been just as remote as Santiago had suggested. Lily hadn't seen a single other car on the journey there and when Santiago had drawn the car onto a grassy verge on the way back they still hadn't encountered another living soul.

'Why are we stopping?'

'Not for the reason you think.'

'How do you know what I think?' she countered crossly.

'It's written all over your beautiful face. Come on,' he urged, sliding out of the driving seat. 'I want you to see something.'

He took her by the hand and led her through a copse of tall cedar trees. As they cleared the trees she gasped.

'It's incredible, isn't it?' he said, gazing out at the view stretched out before them. 'You can see for miles.'

'Yes, incredible.'

Santiago turned his head and caught her looking at him, not the view. She saw the surprise in his eyes, followed by the heat. Lily could have pretended he was wrong, that she wasn't looking at him and thinking he was more gorgeous than any view, but she didn't. She just carried on looking at him.

'Are we trespassing?'

'No, I own it,' he said huskily.

'You bought it?' She looked at his mouth and wanted very badly to kiss him.

'It's a special place and you are a special person, Lily.'

Lily could remember the emotional thickness in her throat making her unable to speak when he took her face between his hands. 'Maybe we should go back,' he said, releasing her almost immediately.

She shook her head and, lower lip caught between her teeth, looked up at him through her eyelashes. 'Couldn't we stay just a little longer?' She watched his eyes darken and felt quite dizzy with power.

His eyes slid down her body, his stillness had an explosive quality. 'That's not a good idea,' he said huskily.

Her chin lifted. 'I don't want to be good.'

She heard him inhale sharply and, smiling, pushed her hands under his shirt. She laid them flat against his warm, tight belly and felt the sharp contraction of his muscles. His skin was warm and satiny textured; low in her pelvis things tightened and shifted. She closed her eyes and, head thrown back a little, sighed with unconcealed pleasure as she began to stroke him, light, teasing movements that drew a faint groan from his throat.

'You have absolutely no idea how much I wanted to touch you,' she revealed, watching him breathe in and out fast. To want someone this much was scary and wildly exciting at the same time. 'All the while we were talking I wanted to touch you.' She saw the beads of sweat break out across his upper lip.

'I'm getting the idea,' he said, sounding slightly breathless.

Lily thought about her bare skin touching his and, shivering, she slid her fingers lower down his belly. With a muttered imprecation he pulled back and caught both her wrists to prevent her fingertip exploration getting any more intimate.

He doesn't want me!

Before the humiliation could totally crush her, Lily connected with his eyes and felt a surge of relief. Those were not the eyes of a man who was about to reject her. They were the eyes of a man who was clinging to the shreds of his self-control. *One push,* she thought, watching his jaw clench.

'You don't know what you're doing,' he accused.

She smiled and leaned forward until her lips were about a centimetre away from his mouth. 'I know exactly what I'm doing,' she said against his lips.

He sucked in a deep breath, then with a soft curse grabbed her face between his hands. The driven ferocity in his kiss made her dissolve. With a soft cry of relief she kissed him back with everything she had.

He carried on kissing her until her knees gave way instead of supporting her. Santiago slid down to the floor with her, pulling her body on top of him.

For a second she didn't move, just lay there wondering what was going to happen next. Then he said, '*Kiss me. I want you to kiss me.*'

It was a good sign, she decided as she pressed her mouth to his, that they seemed to both want the same things. Santiago did several things she hadn't even known she had wanted until he did them!

A shudder ran through Lily's body as, suddenly drawn

back to the present, she banished the steamy images of their two naked bodies intimately entwined from her head.

She swallowed and looked at Santiago. His skin was covered in a light sheen of sweat, and the feverish brilliance in his painfully expressive eyes told her that she hadn't been the only one revisiting that memory.

Sharing memories was almost like foreplay. The shocking idea sent a thrill of heat through her body.

Santiago let his glance move from hers to the bed, then slowly back to her flushed face.

She knew she should make it clear that this wasn't going to happen. She didn't; neither of them spoke. Words weren't needed.

Lily was conscious only of his dark, mesmeric eyes, and the need that burned inside her as they kissed, not gently, but with a raw, bruising urgency. Then when they broke apart he took her hand and led her to the bed.

Lily let him pull her down beside him and they lay side by side, not touching, just breathing hard.

Lily tried to understand how this could be so mind-blowingly erotic when he was not even touching her. When he did she sucked in a deep, shocked breath and felt everything inside tighten.

'The thing I remember is how, whenever I touched you, you were always hot.' The hand that was on her hip slid a little lower as he added thickly, 'And ready for me.'

Lily licked her lips, so aroused she could barely breathe. When his hand moved under her skirt she stuck her fist in her mouth to stop herself yelling out. He touched the lacy edge of her knickers and she could no longer stop herself moaning.

'That's right, let go,' he rasped, watching her face as he parted her legs and slid his fingers into the soft, warm heat between.

'Oh, my God!' she moaned, pushing against his hand and squirming. 'I want…'

'You want me.'

'I want you,' she sobbed as he lifted her skirt around her hips. *'Right now,'* she added from between clenched teeth.

She reached for him, fumbling with the clasp of his belt. He took her shaking hands and pinioned them above her head with one hand, while with the other he completed the job she hadn't been able to. He left her for a moment, but only to rip off his shirt and kick aside his jeans.

Lily held onto the bars of the headboard, her body arching as he slid into her. He felt so incredible that she wanted to cry. She closed her eyes and felt his breath come heavy and hot against her neck as he began to move. She moved with him, gasping, feeling the familiar pressure slowly building inside her to a dark rhythm she could feel roaring in her blood.

Then without warning the wave she was riding broke and pleasure, wave after wave of nerve-tingling pleasure, exploded through her body.

CHAPTER TWELVE

IT WAS the sort of thing you wondered about. What would you do if you put your foot on the brake and nothing happened?

Lily had never actually expected to find out.

The situation was complicated by the bend she was fast approaching and the double-decker bus coming in the opposite direction.

Was this the moment her life was meant to flash before her eyes? Lily's didn't; she was too busy trying to save her skin. She succeeded. A nifty bit of steering, some frantic use of the gears and a lot of luck landed her on the grass verge with the front end of her car wedged in a hedge.

The car door, partially against a branch, was difficult to open, but after a short, determined tussle she emerged scratched by the brambles but otherwise unharmed.

The bus driver was inclined to want to yell at her, she couldn't blame him, but when she explained that her brakes had failed he calmed down and even said a few nice things about her driving skills.

The horse and rider she had driven at a snail's pace past a few hundred yards back reached them and she began the explanations all over again.

'I thought I was going to hit her for sure,' the bus driver confessed, wiping his forehead with his sleeve. 'Have you ever seen a car after it's hit a double-decker head-on?' he asked. Nobody had. 'There's not much to see.'

Everyone laughed, except Lily, who was starting to experience what she assumed was a delayed reaction to the shock. She clenched her teeth and tried to stop them jarring against each other.

'What's the procedure? Do I call the police or a recovery service?' Lily asked, trying to stay focused and practical.

'My God, you were lucky!' one of the passengers who had left the bus remarked for the third time.

Lily, who was starting to realise just how lucky, nodded and felt sick. The adrenaline rush that had got her through the ordeal this far was definitely bottoming out and her knees were literally shaking. She was looking around for somewhere to sit down when a big, gleaming, low-slung car drew to a halt a couple of yards away.

The occupant took in the scene of near averted disaster and was heard to swear at length. Although it was hard to be positive on this point because he was talking a foreign language. The group of people around Lily fell silent when he vaulted athletically from the vehicle and stalked towards them, looking like a dark avenging angel in designer sunglasses.

Oh, no, he'd followed her!

Lily dabbed her dry lips nervously with the tip of her tongue as the tall figure approached. Pale but resolute, she waited to be the target of his blistering anger, as she usually was.

Santiago was angry. Possibly, he recognised, *more* angry than he had ever felt in his entire life, but then why should that surprise him? he reflected bitterly. This woman was capable of extracting the most extreme emotional response from him.

On this occasion he actually embraced the anger that seethed through his veins because it was infinitely preferable to what had gone before. He never wanted to feel the way he had when he had broached the hill and seen Lily's car slewed across the road and embedded in the hedge. He never wanted to relive those seconds when he had thought the worst, but he suspected he was doomed to in his nightmares for some time to come.

'Hello, Santiago.' She had never been so glad to see anyone in her life, which was totally irrational considering she had been driving away from the cottage to avoid seeing him when her brake had failed.

'Hello,' he echoed. The simple greeting made his eyes flash. *'Hello…?'* he repeated, dragging a hand through his dark hair as he scanned her face.

There was no visible damage to Lily other than torn clothes and a few scratches. The nightmare images of mangled bodies were still there, but they were receding as he realised she seemed to have escaped the impact apparently unscathed.

His big hands settled on her shoulders and in a husky voice he enquired, 'Are you hurt?'

Lily assumed that he was running his hands down her body to check her out for injury. Unfortunately her response to the light clinical examination was anything but clinical.

'What are you doing here?'

'What do you think I'm doing here? I woke up and you were gone.'

'Don't shout!' Lily begged, painfully aware of their interested audience. 'Didn't Rachel tell you I remembered an appointment I just had to keep?'

'Do not insult my intelligence; I am not your gullible friend. And, just for the record, after Rachel walked in and found me asleep and stark naked in your bed I doubt she's falling for the appointment story either.'

'She didn't!' Lily gasped in horror.

'She did and…' Santiago stopped and scanned her paper-white face. 'Sit down before you fall down.'

'I'm fine,' she croaked. Actually her ribs where the seat belt had cut in were beginning to ache. Later, she recognized, they would be painful.

Her claim seemed to inflame him further. 'And would you tell me if you weren't?' The band of dark colour etched along the ridge of his sharp cheekbones deepened as he drew in a deep, unsteady breath.

Deeply conscious of the thumbs that were now resting on the crest of her hip-bones—his fingers were curved possessively across her bottom—she tried to resist the almost overwhelming impulse to simply sink against him.

'You're acting as if I drove into the hedge just to irritate you.'

'It wouldn't surprise me if you had,' he contended grimly. 'How could you be so criminally careless?' he wanted to know, lifting a hand from her bottom, but only to roughly stroke the hair back from her cheek.

She tried to sound matter-of-fact as she explained what had happened. 'The brakes failed.' Her breathing quickened as she experienced the moment of panic a second time.

The colour seeped from his olive-toned skin as he sucked in a deep shuddering breath. If Lily hadn't closed her eyes in a futile attempt to blot out the images in her head she would have seen the strain that was evident in the taut lines of his lean face.

'Yes, I put my foot down and nothing happened, and there was a bus coming…so…'

His hand fell from her face. *'Failed…?'* His oddly flat voice cut across her.

'Yes, they failed. I'm trying to explain.'

'Explain! What is there to explain?' The muscles in his throat worked as he swallowed. *'Madre mia*, what is wrong with you? You drive around dangerous roads in a car that is clearly fit only for the scrap heap. Heaven knows how you escaped serious injury.'

'Just because it didn't cost a fortune, and doesn't go at a hundred miles an hour, doesn't mean it's not roadworthy. For your information it passed its MOT last month.'

'Whoever passed it should be flogged.'

This brutal conclusion made Lily blink. 'It was just an accident.'

Her weak protest triggered another long stream of Spanish curses. 'It was an accident. It wasn't my fault. No, it's never *your* fault, is it? Nothing is your fault. You blithely go through life wrecking lives left, right and centre and it's *never* your fault.'

Lily lifted a hand to her brow in a fluttery motion. The unsteady gesture made her look intensely vulnerable, which irrationally made Santiago more livid than ever.

The red dots dancing before her eyes had begun to thicken to a mist. Through it she could see his face as a dark blur. 'Whose life have I wrecked?'

'Yours…mine…' she heard him say thickly just before she slithered gracefully to the ground.

Lily was only out for a couple of minutes. When she came to she found she was lying on the grass verge with something warm and heavy draped over her. Someone was holding her wrist between their fingers.

'Her pulse is strong.'

The fingers left her wrist.

The warm and heavy thing smelt of Santiago. His jacket? She half opened her eyes and discovered she was right. The two men continued to talk above her.

'Like I said, she just fainted, mate. I wouldn't worry.'

'Yes, I am fine,' said Lily.

'I told you so,' said the bus driver as Santiago squatted down beside her prone figure.

'How do you feel?' he asked, scanning her face.

'I'm fine,' she repeated and tried to sit up. Santiago's hand on her chest pinned her gently but firmly to the ground.

'You will not move until the ambulance arrives.'

She decided not to fight him on this, mostly because when she did move her head swam unpleasantly. 'Fine, have it your way.'

He sketched a grim smile. 'I intend to.'

So nothing new there. 'So you expect me to lie here…?'

'Yes.'

She eased herself up on one elbow and this time met with no resistance. 'How about if I move six inches to the left…?'

Santiago settled back onto his heels. 'Why?'

'I'm lying on a dirty great rock; it's sticking in my back. I'll be black and blue tomorrow.'

'You'll be alive tomorrow,' Santiago retorted grimly as she shuffled away from the offending item.

He lifted his head and frowned into the distance. 'Where is that damned ambulance…?'

When he turned back to her, still frowning, Lily noticed for the first time the signs of extreme tension in his face. The most noticeable clue was the greyish tinge of his normally vibrant skin tone.

'I don't need an ambulance. Do I look like I need an ambulance?' she asked, pushing aside his jacket. 'Talk about an overreaction,' she grumbled tetchily. 'And I thought you were the sort of man who would be useful in a crisis.'

'I have no interest in what *you* think you need. Or what you think of me.' This demonstration of his high-handed attitude brought an angry frown to her face. 'And I don't think you have the faintest idea what is good for you,' he continued patronisingly.

'You could be right, but I do know what is bad for me.' She glared pointedly at his face.

He rolled his eyes. 'And yet here we are together again.'

'That's not any of my doing,' she retorted. 'You shouldn't have followed me.'

'What did you expect me to do? You left before I woke up.'

She swallowed. 'I thought you'd be relieved. Goodbyes are always awkward.'

'I had no intention of saying goodbye.'

To her intense frustration the sound of an ambulance siren meant she didn't get to hear what he had intended to say.

When the ambulance reached the local hospital Santiago was already standing outside the casualty department. How someone who could beat an ambulance to the hospital had the cheek to criticise her driving beat her; clearly he was allowed to risk his life.

A couple of hours later a doctor armed with X-ray results and her medical notes gave her a clean bill of health. 'I'm afraid you're going to be pretty stiff and sore for a few days, but nothing's broken. You can get dressed. I'll go and tell your partner he can take you home.' She twitched the curtains to one side. 'He's been pacing up and down the waiting room like a caged panther.'

Lily gritted her teeth. 'I don't have a partner.'

The other woman grinned and pushed her glasses up the bridge of her nose. 'I'll let you explain that to him, shall I? He doesn't seem like a listening sort of man to me.'

That doctor was a very astute judge of character, Lily

soon decided as Santiago proceeded to pick up the plastic bag her clothes had been dumped in and marched Lily to the carpark and his waiting car.

'You can rest up at my place,' Santiago instructed as he helped Lily into the passenger seat.

'But I'm not going home with you!' Lily protested.

He slung her a look of total scorn as he turned the ignition. 'Do you imagine even for one second that I'm going to let you stay in Rachel's flat alone?' he asked incredulously. 'You may have conned the medical staff into believing that you're fit enough to go home, but I—'

'I didn't con anyone about anything!' She directed a frustrated grimace at the back of his neck and added, even though she knew there was little chance of him paying any heed to her protestation, 'I *am* well enough.'

'I know you like the sound of your own voice, and I admit it has pleasing qualities when you are not yelling abuse, but we will not discuss the matter farther,' he pronounced calmly.

Lily, who was starting to feel sleepy now the car was moving, couldn't decide if there had been a compliment in there somewhere... 'I'd be much happier on my own, and I'm sure you'd be much happier with me out of your hair,' she continued to argue feebly.

'This is not a matter of what makes me happy. You were driving erratically because I upset you, so I must accept at least part of the responsibility.'

'I keep telling you—the brakes failed.'

'It is late, we are both tired and are liable to say things we might later regret. Tonight you will stay at my house. Tomorrow...'

'Tomorrow you'll have worked off your guilt?'

Briefly his eyes met hers in the rear-view mirror. 'It will take longer.'

CHAPTER THIRTEEN

LILY hadn't expected to, but she'd slept the moment her head had touched the pillow. She had been too exhausted the previous night to take any interest in her surroundings, but this morning she was curious to see where Santiago lived when he was in London.

The place was massive, three storeys and, according to the housekeeper who had presented her with a selection of outfits when she'd brought her morning tea, had a swimming pool and gym in the basement.

'Mr Morais will be in the breakfast room when you're ready. Is there anything special you'd like for breakfast?'

'Thanks, but I'm not hungry.'

'He said you'd say that. Couldn't we tempt you…?'

Santiago could tempt me any day.

'I'll get into trouble if you don't eat.'

The other woman didn't act like someone who thought she was about to lose her job, but for a quiet life Lily relented. 'Scrambled egg and juice would be good.'

The housekeeper beamed approval. 'Excellent.'

It was about half an hour later that Lily, dressed in a silk shirt and classic black trousers, discovered by a process of elimination the breakfast room. She took a deep breath before stepping inside.

Santiago, his long fingers curved around a coffee-cup, turned his head as she walked in. His dark eyes moved up and down the length of her body, but he vouched no opinion on her appearance. 'Did you sleep?'

Lily, who had thought when she'd pirouetted in front of the mirror that she looked rather good, felt quite peeved.

'Yes, thank you.'

As if by magic her breakfast appeared. Lily smiled her thanks and sat down. One eye on the silent man at the end of the table, she broke a warm roll and spread it with butter.

'Would your housekeeper really be in trouble if I didn't have breakfast?'

'I'd sack her without a reference.'

Their eyes met and she grinned. 'You really are a piece of work. I didn't really think you would, you know.'

'You weren't *quite* sure, though, were you, Lily? And you are eating, so it had the desired effect.'

'I'm not anorexic or anything, you know,' she said, putting a forkful of fluffy golden egg into her mouth.

'I realise that.'

'I just forget to eat sometimes. You have a beautiful home.'

'Thank you.'

'Are you here often?'

'Not often enough to call it a home.'

She looked at him curiously. 'What makes a house a home?'

'I prefer to put my faith in people, not brick and mortar.'

'Home is where the heart is?' she suggested.

'Something like that. The clothes—they fit, I see, and, no, they do not belong to an ex-girlfriend. They are my sister's.'

'How did you know I thought…?' she began, and then, meeting his eyes, she blushed and subsided into silence. If he really could read her that well she was in big trouble.

It was a silence he made no attempt to break until she was drinking her second cup of coffee. Then he said in a casual voice, 'You have an appointment with a gynaecologist this morning.'

Lily stiffened. *'What did you say?'*

'If it suits you I think we should leave at ten-thirty to allow for the traffic.'

He was incredible! Did he really think all he had to do was snap his fingers and she would fall in line?

'The only place I am going is home, and you're not coming with me. I'm expected at work tomorrow.' She frowned.

'Under the circumstances it makes sense to get yourself checked out.'

This brought a fresh sparkle of anger to Lily's eyes. 'Frankly I don't give a damn what you think, and even if I did there would be no way I'd be able to see a gynaecologist today.'

'Why not?'

She rolled her eyes. 'Hospital waiting lists?' She supposed his ignorance of the working of the NHS was understandable.

'We are not going to the hospital. Mr Clement has consulting rooms in Harley Street,' he revealed casually. 'His secretary was most helpful.'

'I don't doubt she was,' Lily said bitterly. 'You seem to be under some misguided impression that you have a right to order my life. Let me spell it out for you—I can't afford a private consultation.'

He gave a careless shrug and pulled a folder from the briefcase that was propped up against his chair. 'You don't have to.'

Lily was out of her seat and beside him before he could open it. Breathing hard, she leaned across him until their faces were level. Her voice dropped to a dramatic quiver as she announced, 'I'd prefer to die than accept your charity.'

'You almost did die, because of me.'

'That's ridiculous!' she exclaimed.

'Carrying my child almost killed you.'

She saw it all there in his bleak eyes: self-recrimination; the terrible burden of guilt he was carrying. Everything he was doing, she realized, was about expiating that guilt.

Lily would have drawn back, for his long brown fingers curled over her forearm. The ache inside her chest intensified. She didn't want his guilt. She wanted his love, but that wasn't an offer.

'I was not there then—'

'It wouldn't have made any difference if you had been.'

His shoulders lifted fractionally. 'Maybe...? We will never know, but I am here now, and intend to make amends.'

'And you expect me to be grateful?' She saw a baffled expression filter into his deep-set eyes, but didn't pause long enough to let him respond to her hostile enquiry. 'You're feeling guilty. Well...tough. I didn't ask you to. In fact, I didn't ask for *anything* from you.'

She began to tick off a list on her fingers of the things she *didn't* want from him. 'I don't want your money. I don't want your concern. I don't want you interfering in my life and conspiring with my friends—' She broke off, wincing as the fingers around her arm spasmed.

His grip immediately loosened, and he pulled his hand away. His eyes touched her and then dropped before she could analyse the puzzling expression she had glimpsed in the dark obsidian depths. *'Sorry.'*

She watched through her lashes as he got up and walked over to the window.

'Sorry enough to let me walk through that door and leave me alone for ever?'

Until she had thrown the challenge at him Lily had been convinced this was exactly what she wanted. She would have signed a declaration to that effect.

Now the possibility was out there, perversely she wasn't so sure. It was awfully final. *Final is what I need,* she told herself, irritated by her sudden doubts.

He turned. 'You don't want to be left alone.'

The confident contention was so close to her own thoughts that Lily flushed and responded spikily. 'Sure, I love to have a control freak taking over my life,' she drawled. 'I am quite capable of taking care of myself.'

The muscles around his mouth tightened. 'You have a remarkably casual attitude to your own health,' he condemned harshly.

'Would you prefer I was a hypochondriac?'

'I would prefer you faced facts,' he countered impatiently. 'You've been extremely ill...'

Did he honestly think she needed reminding of the fact?

'You have just endured a slow recovery,' he continued. 'Can you honestly tell me that you're not concerned that yesterday's accident has not in some way compromised that recovery?'

She slung him an exasperated glare. 'Not until you suggested it.' Now of course the uncertainties were going to nag at her.

'Don't let your dislike of me and your stubborn pride prevent you from doing the right and proper thing.'

'You wouldn't know right and proper if you fell over it!'

Her indignant accusation made him laugh.

'Let's work together on this, shall we?'

The casually charismatic smile and the melting-chocolate, coaxing tone alerted her to Santiago's abrupt change of tactics.

'Don't bother with the smoothy charm stuff. I'm immune.' If only, Lily reflected bitterly, this were true. Where Santiago's smiles were concerned she was wide open and vulnerable.

He threw out his hands in a frustrated gesture. 'Fine. I won't waste my time talking to you as though you were a rational human being because clearly you are not. I try and be pleasant and you become abusive.'

'That wasn't pleasant; that was calculating and manipulative,' she contended stubbornly.

'You are the most impossible woman!' The only woman he had ever wanted to wake up next to for the rest of his life. 'Well, calculate this—if you refuse to go willingly to get checked over, I will—'

'*What?*' she cut in scornfully. 'Drag me there kicking and screaming?' An image formed in her head of her slung over his shoulder caveman fashion. Her sensual reaction to the image added an extra layer of venom to her voice as she added, '*I don't think so.*'

Eyes narrowed, nostrils flared, he folded his arms across his chest and looked, Lily had to admit, like a man perfectly capable of slinging a woman over his shoulder and marching through London.

'I don't know why you're making such a big thing of this. You're not going to wear me down, if that's what you think. I've been checked over,' she reminded him. 'Are you suggesting that the staff in Casualty didn't know what they were doing?'

'I'm not saying that,' retorted Santiago impatiently. 'They were obviously dedicated people,' he admitted, thinking of the nurse who, but for his intervention, would have been struck by a drunk.

When the young woman had thanked him he had made a discovery that had appalled him: being physically attacked and verbally abused by drunken patients was considered the norm, not the exception. He had been inclined to encourage his youngest sister's laudable ambition to train as a nurse; now he wasn't so sure that this was such a good idea.

'I am not casting aspersions on their professional ability, but they were tired and overworked. People who are tired make mistakes and miss things.' His eyes burnt with an almost frightening intensity as they swept across her face. She saw the muscles in his brown throat work as he swallowed. 'Have you any idea how damned...breakable you look?'

Lily lifted a self-conscious hand to her neck, and watched his eyes get that dark bleak look that made her heart feel as though it were being squeezed in a vice. 'I did that to you,' Santiago added bitterly.

'Santiago, you haven't done anything to me.'

'I wasn't there when you needed me, but this time I am.'

'What makes you think I need you?'

'Driving around a corner and seeing your car in a ditch.'

Unable to respond to this, she dropped her gaze. Sometimes you had to accept defeat gracefully. 'I'll go and see the damned doctor!' she gritted.

As they approached the Harley Street offices Santiago's phone rang. He fished it out of his pocket and scanned the screen.

His eyes lifted to hers. 'I have to take this.'

'Fine. I don't even know what you're doing here.'

'I'll follow you in.'

'I wish you wouldn't.'

Her childish retort brought a grim smile to his lips. 'It won't take long.'

'Don't hurry on my account.'

Inside, the doctor's rooms were considerably more plush than the NHS outpatients' clinic she had last visited. There was only one other person in the tastefully furnished room she was directed into. The man's face was hidden behind the pages of a broadsheet. She took a seat at the opposite end of the room.

'Can I get you a coffee, tea?' the attentive receptionist asked.

'No, thank you.'

'Mr Clement won't keep you long,' she promised, excusing herself with a smile.

Lily reached for a glossy magazine from the table and began to flip through it.

'Excuse me?'

With a smile she moved her knee and bag to allow the stranger access to the magazines. 'Sorry…' The smile froze on her lips. She gave a gasp of astonishment. 'G-Gordon…?'

'Lily…heavens, this is a surprise…' Her ex-husband cleared his throat.

'Isn't it?' Lily agreed. She wondered if she looked as uncomfortable as he did; she probably did.

'What are you doing here?'

Good question, she thought. *What am I doing here…?* 'This being a gynaecologist's office, shouldn't I be asking you that…?'

'Right, well, if it's private…'

'It is.'

Gordon looked momentarily taken aback, then glanced towards the closed consulting-room door. 'I'm here with Olivia.'

'I thought you might be.'

'She's pregnant.'

Given the meeting was taking place in the waiting room of an obstetrician Lily had been half expecting this, so the impact of hearing that the husband who had said he didn't want children, not *ever*, was about to become a father was not as great as it might have been!

It would seem that Gordon had simply not wanted children with me.

'Congratulations.'

Gordon frowned warily, as though her calm reaction had surprised him.

'We're both very happy about it.'

Did she hear a touch of defensiveness in his voice? Lily realised that she didn't care enough to analyse it. Gordon had stopped having the power to hurt her a long time ago.

'I'm sure you are.' *We never did have a lot to talk about,* she reflected as the uneasy silence stretched. 'You look well. Your new life must suit you.' Gordon's fair, freckled skin had acquired a ruddy hue, he hadn't tanned, but his freckles had joined up.

'It's great,' he enthused. 'I feel like a new man.'

Well, the old one needed some work, she thought and smiled neutrally.

'And you're looking…' The mechanical response faded as his eyes drifted over her. 'Good gracious, Lily, you look *marvelous*,' he said, sounding almost comically amazed. '*Thin.*'

The contrast between her ex-husband's and Santiago's reaction to her new shape brought a wry smile to Lily's lips. It must have been hell for Gordon to be married to a curvy wife, she reflected, feeling surprisingly unemotional about this discovery. Still, he had what he had always wanted now: a skinny wife. She felt sure that Olivia would receive a lot of encouragement after the baby was born to get back her trim figure.

'A bit too thin?'

Gordon looked shocked at the suggestion. 'No, it suits you. I suppose it's after… I was sorry to hear about your miscarriage.'

Lily's expression froze, but Gordon, never being the most perceptive of men, failed to notice the distress suggested by her rigid posture and added with an upbeat smile, 'Still, I expect it was all for the best, as I'm sure you've realised.'

'The best…?'

'Well, I'm assuming you didn't intend to get pregnant, but accidents happen,' he conceded magnanimously. 'I should know,' he added under his breath. 'I said to Olivia at the time, good on Lily for going through with it. Given the circumstances a lot of people would have got rid of it.'

It…? Lily gritted her teeth. She wasn't sure now she shouldn't have followed her initial knee-jerk reaction and clobbered him!

'Circumstances…?'

'Well, I'm assuming that the father didn't want to know…?' When a stony-faced Lily didn't volunteer any information, Gordon shrugged. 'I have to tell you, when I heard I was shocked. A tacky casual affair just didn't seem like the Lily I knew,' he observed with, as far as she could tell, absolutely no irony. 'I suppose you were on the rebound,' he mused, as though this partly excused her lapse.

'It happened before we split up.'

Gordon's eyes widened. 'You were unfaithful to me?' he gasped, visibly shaken by her confession. 'My God, Lily, how could you?'

Lily was perfectly prepared to take responsibility for her behaviour and own up to her faults, but she wasn't going to take a lecture on morality from her serial adulterer ex-spouse. 'We don't choose to fall in love, but then I don't have to tell you that, do I?'

Their eyes met and he flushed. 'I suppose you think I'm a hypocrite.'

Satisfied she had made her point, Lily let her silence speak for itself.

'I wasn't a perfect husband, I admit that, but whether you like it or not it's different for men. And we both know a child needs a stable home environment and two parents. I know you couldn't have afforded to stay at home or decent childcare... By the way, I've heard the agents have a buyer prepared to pay the asking price on the house...'

'Talk to my solicitor,' she said automatically. 'The child would have had me.'

The sentence felt like a knife sliding between his ribs to the figure framed in the doorway. Upon realizing that the man Lily was chatting to had to be her ex-husband, he'd deliberately not entered the room.

'I'm sure you'd have done your best,' Santiago heard the ex concede pompously.

Dear God, what had she ever seen in him? Santiago wondered. There was no escaping it, the man was, not to put too fine a point on it, a pathetic loser.

He knew that love was not an exact science, but what he had seen and heard had convinced him that this sad individual had nothing to recommend him but a moderately pretty face.

Presumably a face that Lily had liked...maybe still did...?

It was a face that Santiago was discovering he could not look at without longing to rearrange the bland features on it. His hands curled into fists as he fought the impulse to do just that.

'The day would have come the kid would have wanted to know who his dad was, and what would you have told him? No, in the long run it was for the best.'

Lily felt light-headed with anger. That anyone could suggest losing the baby she had wanted so much was 'for the best'—well, she just couldn't let it pass. The irony was this was Gordon's idea of empathy. *How did I ever contemplate spending the rest of my life with this pompous prat?*

She got to her feet and realised that she was shaking. She pressed her interlocked fingers against her chest and took a deep sustaining breath.

Santiago, who had started to move forward into the room, stopped as Lily began to speak.

'I would have told my baby he was much wanted and loved…' Her tremulous voice firmed and got louder as she added, 'I would have told my baby his dad was more of a man than you ever could be!' She stopped and brushed the tears that had spilled onto her cheeks angrily away with the back of her hand.

Gordon, who didn't like tears, looked away. 'Well, really, I don't think personal attacks are called for,' he responded huffily. 'And if this man was so damned great, where is he now?'

'He is right here.'

CHAPTER FOURTEEN

WITH a startled gasp Lily spun around and collided with a hard breadth of male chest. Her wide blue eyes flew upwards.

'Who says that eavesdroppers hear no good of themselves?'

'S-Santiago.' Before she could get any less articulate he fitted his mouth to hers.

Oh, but it always had been a very good fit, she thought in the split second before an invisible button clicked and her mind switched off. Another one clicked and her hormones switched on.

Oh, boy, did they switch on!

When his head lifted she was breathing as though she'd just run a marathon.

If Gordon hadn't grasped the significance of Santiago's opening gambit, after that kiss she could hardly pass Santiago off as a casual acquaintance. Though she had to concede that the offending kiss might not have been quite so lingering if she hadn't opened her mouth without any coercion.

Her struggle to regain at least a semblance of composure—not easy when she was feverishly shaking from head to toe—suffered a set-back when she allowed herself to think about the stabbing, sensual incursion of his tongue and how her insides had dissolved lustfully. Her eyes went automatically to his mouth and they dissolved all over again.

Show some control, woman! Lily told herself as her

breathing went haywire once more. *This is a public place.* She was peripherally aware of Gordon, standing there with his mouth half open as he gazed at her in the arms of the tall, incredibly good-looking Spaniard.

She made a concerted effort to untangle her thoughts as she forced herself to breath slowly. Clearing her throat, she removed her hands from Santiago's shirt front.

'How long have you been standing there…?' she hissed hoarsely at the man who had her face cradled between his large hands. If Gordon hadn't been watching she would have pulled away.

It didn't even cross her mind that Santiago's comment had been unintentional. He had *meant* for Gordon to know that he had been the father, that they had been lovers.

Why the hell would he do that…?

Still puzzling the motivation behind his behaviour she frowned up into Santiago's lean face. His dark eyes crinkled at the corners as his features relaxed into a lazy, languid smile that made her tummy flip and her knees tremble.

'Long enough to know that I'm finally meeting your ex-husband.' Letting his hands drop from Lily's face, he lifted his dark head and subjected the shorter man to a critical stare before stretching out his hand formally.

If Gordon had picked up on the violent dislike that Santiago was barely repressing, he might have been even slower to take the proffered hand. What he did pick up on, and it made him feel deeply resentful, was Lily's lover's dark, handsome looks, his expensive clothes and his confident, take-control manner.

Gordon, who retained a quaint Victorian assumption that Britain was the centre of the universe, reminded himself that this guy wasn't English. He gave a charitable smile as he complacently observed, 'You're foreign.'

Santiago, who no longer saw any reason to disguise the

fact he didn't like the other man, deliberately allowed his accent to thicken as he replied, 'You're correct. I am not English—I'm…'

A faint, despairing, 'Dear God,' escaped Lily's lips as she heard him outrageously introduce himself.

'Santiago Morais, the Spaniard who stole your wife.'

It seemed to Lily that his wolfish smile challenged Gordon more eloquently than the words.

Suddenly Gordon looked like a man who wished he were somewhere else, and for her part Lily didn't blame him.

Santiago could look daunting when he tried, and he appeared to be trying. What with the arrogant angle of his head, the contemptuous half-smile that pulled lightly at one corner of his fascinating mouth and, most of all, his eyes. He had very expressive eyes and it seemed to Lily that the molten anger gleaming in them at the moment was far in excess of anything Gordon's patronising comment justified.

She could have told him that Gordon didn't mean anything by it, he was just a bit of twit really. The sort of man who thought all women who weren't attracted to him were lesbians and that anything bad that happened to him was someone else's fault. When they had been married that someone had almost always been her!

Contrast was a strange thing, she reflected. Until Santiago had walked into the room Gordon had appeared an above-averagely attractive man. It wasn't that he wasn't attractive; it was that Santiago was *more* attractive.

So I'm not the most objective observer, but… Lily's generous lips curved into a slow, covetous smile as her glance slid over the contours of his lean, powerful body…*he really is gorgeous.*

It wasn't just that Santiago was taller by several inches. Or that he had not an ounce of surplus flesh on his hard, muscled frame and was considerably broader across the shoulders. It wasn't even his startlingly handsome face, charismatic smile or glorious, vibrant colouring. No, it was his effortless air of command, his aura of immutable confidence, the raw male sexuality he projected that drew all eyes, and held them.

Her fingers closed urgently around Santiago's upper arm to draw his attention. It did. His head turned and some of the hostility faded from his face as their eyes connected.

'*Querida...?*'

'You didn't steal me, I gave myself willingly.' *Now why did you think that was a helpful comment?*

Santiago's dark eyes flamed as they moved over her face. 'Yes, you did give,' he agreed. 'And very beautifully.' His voice dropped to a low, intimate drawl that sent a shiver along her raw nerve endings. 'Did I ever say thank you?'

Lily didn't say anything. She had to dig deep into the reserves of her self-control just to keep standing.

'If not...' he ran his thumb caressingly down her smooth cheek '...I'm saying it now. Thank you.'

Gordon, who was standing there watching this intimate interchange, found his voice.

'I had no idea you were with anyone, Lily...'

The hint of reproach in his voice brought a sparkle of annoyance to Lily's eyes as she turned her head. 'That makes us quits. I wasn't meant to know you were with anyone while we were married, which probably makes me very weak for turning the other cheek.'

Gordon flushed at her dry tone, and beside her Santiago looked thoughtful.

This was the first hint he had had of Lily's husband's infidelity.

'And, anyway, I'm not *with* anyone.'

'There is no need to be embarrassed,' Santiago interjected. 'We are both civilised men of the world?' One dark brow elevated, he angled a questioning look at Gordon. 'Is that not so?'

Gordon nodded uneasily. 'Of course.'

'There will be no violence.'

'Don't be too sure of that,' Lily hissed under her breath.

Gordon looked at the athletically built figure of the man who was looming behind Lily and swallowed hard. 'Good grief, no, it's all water under the bridge as far as I'm concerned. And anyway I'm having a baby...that is, my wife...my *present* wife is having a baby.'

His wife appeared at that moment and Lily looked curiously at the woman Gordon had left her for. She had only seen the other woman from a distance before now. She hadn't wanted to—that much hadn't changed, but she had to admit to being curious.

What woman wouldn't want to see what her husband thought was an improvement?

A very tall, slim redhead, she was dressed in a tailored white trouser suit that was cut to minimise the soft swell of her belly. She was deeply tanned and her hair was cut in a short, flattering, feathery style that minimised a prominent square jaw.

For quite a while after she had lost the baby Lily had been unable to look at a pregnant woman or a mother with a baby without feeling a terrible toxic mixture of anger, pain and gnawing loss. Now what she felt had more in common with sadness.

That *had* to be an improvement, didn't it?

'Olivia, look who I met. Lily.'

The other woman came forward showing no signs of the discomfort Lily was sure she would have felt in similar circumstances.

Her manner was confident and composed as she said, 'Hello.'

Lily nodded. She felt quite sorry for the other woman being put in this situation. 'Sorry about this.'

The other woman looked blank. *'Sorry...?'*

'The dumped wife meets mistress thing. It is a bit awkward.'

The redhead looked amused. 'Don't worry your head. I don't feel awkward. Nobody expects a marriage to last for ever these days, do they? And I know yours was over long before me. We're all grown-ups, aren't we? People are far too sentimental about marriage, I think. Treat it like any other contract, that's what I say.' Her smile invited agreement.

Lily, who doubted the other woman would feel quite so 'grown up' if the roles had been reversed, didn't smile back. When Santiago's arm snaked around her waist she allowed herself to be drawn into his side. This was a stressful situation, and she reasoned that she needed all the support she could get—it also felt very good.

'So you think a marriage should be dissolved like a partnership that doesn't work out?' Santiago injected interest into his voice as he gave the woman just enough rope to hang herself.

Lily recognised that the approval in the other woman's eyes wasn't just related to his question. It would be hell to be married to a man who aroused lustful admiration in every woman with a pulse, she thought.

Wow, you really had a lucky escape, the intrusive voice in her head mocked.

'Exactly. I mean love is only for ever in trashy romances.'

She'd never thought she would, but Lily actually started to feel quite sorry for Gordon. 'I like trashy romances,' she felt impelled to protest.

Olivia gave her a look that suggested she wasn't surprised. Lily wondered if Santiago liked tall, athletic red-heads and then inwardly mocked herself. *All* men liked tall, athletic redheads, she thought gloomily. Men were idiots!

'And the accumulated assets of the union divided?' Santiago persisted.

Lily was amazed that no one else had picked up on the ironic edge in his voice, and she realised that, far from being smitten by Olivia, Santiago had taken a dislike to her. She couldn't help but be a little bit pleased by the discovery.

'Right down the middle,' she agreed readily. 'California has it exactly right.'

'A child is hard to split.' Santiago wondered why guys went for women who looked like boys, especially ones who had eyes like calculators. Women were meant to be... A great wave of profound realisation washed over him. Women were meant to be like Lily.

'Would you stay with a woman just because of a child?'

Beside him Santiago was aware of the tension in Lily's body stepping up a notch. He looked at the glossy top of her head just below his shoulder and gently increased the pressure around her waist.

'Call me old-fashioned, but I'm working on the assumption that I will be in love with the mother of my child.' He drew Lily even closer.

'The doctor is ready to see you.' The smartly dressed receptionist's brisk words broke the tension, and Lily grate-fully extracted herself from Santiago's embrace to follow the woman down the corridor to the consulting room.

CHAPTER FIFTEEN

'THIS is charming,' Lily admitted as the girl who had taken their order disappeared with a rustle of starched apron.

'I thought you'd like it. My mother always has me bring her and my sisters here for afternoon tea when they visit London.'

'You have sisters…?'

'Two. Carmella is twenty-four. She graduated top of her class from law school.' The pride in his voice was obvious. 'She was married last year.'

'And the other?'

His voice softened. 'Angelica is eighteen.' He frowned. 'She wants to be a nurse. She has her heart set on training in London.'

'And you don't want her to?' Lily speculated, planting her elbows on the table.

'I want her to be happy, but Angel is very quiet and reserved,' he explained. 'The hospital last night…' He appealed to her. 'Tell me, would you want your baby sister to be exposed to that? I admit it was quite an eye-opener to me.'

It was obvious that Santiago took his responsibilities as head of the household very seriously. 'Perhaps you underestimate her?' Lily suggested quietly.

'Perhaps I do.' Their eyes met, and when Lily analysed the happiness that suddenly suffused her she realised it was directly attributable to the smile in his eyes.

Oh, hell, am I in trouble!

'And there's nothing you can actually do to stop her if that's what she wants to do, is there?'

'You think not?' He sounded amused.

'Well, short of locking her in her room, and that's hardly a long-term solution, is it?'

'If I forbid her she will accede to my wishes.'

Lily stared at him. They obviously occupied two very different worlds.

He arched a brow. 'You find that surprising?'

'I find that medieval—' Lily began, and stopped as the waitress delivered their tea and cakes. The cakes distracted her momentarily from her indignation on behalf of this unknown girl.

'Cream?' asked Santiago.

'Milk.' For some reason she felt the need to support his unknown sister's cause. 'You're only her brother, not her keeper. Why should you have the right to decide what's right?'

'She is young.'

'And female.'

His sculpted lips quivered faintly at her acid insert. 'And being female she might very well change her mind before it becomes a problem.'

Her chin went up at this provocative response. 'Because females are capricious and frivolous?'

A grin spread across his face, making him look, much to Lily's weary dismay, even more devastatingly attractive. He was a doubly dangerous proposition because he wasn't just a pretty face; Santiago had an intellect to match his startling good looks.

'You don't really expect me to answer that, do you?' he asked, sounding amused.

'You don't need to. I already know what you think,' she returned tartly. 'You're a total, unreconstructed male chauvinist.' She levelled her rebellious gaze at him and was shocked by the expression she caught on his face.

'If you knew what I was thinking you wouldn't be...' he began from between clenched teeth.

As Lily watched him breathing hard it was obvious that he had exerted considerable will-power to curtail his sudden and totally uncharacteristic emotional outburst. When he picked up the thread again, or rather *didn't*, the incendiary heat had gone from his eyes and his tone was flat and even.

'Let us just agree to disagree. Angel knows that I have her best interests at heart.'

'That's what all the despots say,' Lily contended, unwilling to be pacified. 'Benevolent or otherwise. I'm just glad I never had a brother like you,' she added crossly.

'I am also glad I am not your brother,' he concurred silkily. Connecting with his eyes, she hastily averted her gaze from the dangerous warmth shimmering in his unblinking regard.

'But if you had had a brother like me perhaps he would have stopped you making a disastrous marriage when you were not much older than Angel,' he observed.

Far from encountering opposition from her grandmother, who had been convinced that marriage was the only true career for a woman, Lily had been positively encouraged to marry.

'If you hang around playing hard to get,' the old lady had cautioned, 'you'll lose him. After all he could have any girl he wanted.'

'You really don't know much about teenage girls, do you?'

His expression hardened. 'I know about men who prey on teenage girls.'

'Gordon didn't ''prey'' on me.'

'And still you defend him!' Santiago exploded.

Lily stared at him while he swore with fluency and venom.

'Women are stupid!' he said when he had stopped swearing.

Lily knew Santiago didn't mean women, he meant her. As she had pretty much come to the same conclusion herself, though not for the same reasons, she didn't defend herself. Instead she steered the subject in a safer direction.

'Don't you know that teenagers thrive on opposition? Do you have to be so hands-on?' *Cool, skilful hands moving over her damp flesh.* Lily blinked hard to banish the hot, steamy images in her head and willed her expression not to change as she added crankily, 'Couldn't you just sit back, say nothing, and be supportive of your sister's decision?'

He looked at her as though she had lost her mind. 'You think I should be *nice* while she ruins her life?'

'I'll take that as a no, shall I? Perhaps you should try reverse psychology?' she suggested helpfully.

'Rather than say what I honestly think?' The fight not to do so was trying Santiago's patience to its limit.

'Saying what you think isn't always a good idea.'

Santiago's expression didn't change.

Lily looked at the strong, sexily sculpted outline of his lips thinking, *If I told you what I was thinking right now, you'd run a mile. Or maybe you wouldn't run?*

Colour heightened, Lily lowered her eyes. She wasn't sure which possibility scared her most!

Santiago, his expression cloaked, watched as she fiddled with the flowers arranged in a porcelain vase on the table.

'Were you a teenage rebel, Lily?'

Her eyes lifted. She was relieved to see Santiago looked less likely to spontaneously combust at any moment.

'Rebel! Me? No, I wasn't,' she admitted, unaware of the wistful note in her voice.

'Angel isn't a rebel either,' Santiago asserted confidently. He reached across the table and pushed a plate bearing a vast creamy confection towards Lily. 'Eat. It's chocolate.'

Lily took a forkful. 'Some women prefer chocolate to sex. I can see why.' Her eyes lifted from her plate. 'What about you?'

Santiago's long, tapering brown fingers pushed his own plate to one side. 'I prefer sex, and I do not have a sweet tooth.'

Lily had no more control over the colour that flooded into her face than she did the soft, fractured sigh that left her lips.

'So you're just going to sit there and watch me?' she accused, uncomfortably aware of deep-set, disturbing eyes following every move she made, every flicker of expression on her face.

'That was certainly my plan,' he agreed, tilting his chair back as he stretched his long legs out in front of him. 'I enjoy watching you.'

This silky admission did not help Lily relax; it just caused her to miss her mouth.

'You're frowning. Are you still worrying about my sister?' he asked, looking at her soft mouth and feeling hungry. 'As I said, Angel might change her mind so my intervention might not be necessary.'

Lily dabbed her mouth with a napkin and prayed the fine tremor in her fingers wasn't too obvious. 'And then again she might not.'

'True.'

'So what will you do?'

'On past experience I'd say the wrong thing.'

His unexpected frankness made her laugh before she

reapplied herself to the chocolate cake and tried to blank out everything else.

Santiago watched her lay down her fork and looked pleased. 'You enjoyed that. I told you so.'

Lily pushed aside her plate. 'It was very good chocolate cake.'

'I was surprised when you agreed to come here without a fight.'

'I like to keep people guessing.' It made her sound interesting and enigmatic, which she wasn't, but hopefully he wouldn't realise this.

His eyes followed her hand as she added a second spoonful of sugar to her coffee. 'Why did you come?'

Lily stirred her coffee, watching the swirl of the liquid in her cup. 'You asked me,' she reminded him, feeling tense and twitchy because she kept getting increasingly powerful impulses to touch him.

'That is generally enough to make you do the opposite. This unusual compliance,' he confided, 'makes me nervous.'

She slanted a glare at his handsome olive-skinned face. He didn't look nervous; he looked spectacularly gorgeous. She felt an irrational desire to cry and lowered her lashes in a protective screen.

'Well, this is a sort of goodbye, isn't it?' She needed to look to the future, her new life. Santiago was part of the past, and anyway goodbyes were better made on a neutral ground. And there was a limit to how much of a fool she could make of herself in a public place. *I hope.*

Lily smiled, conscious she should be projecting the more upbeat, positive aura of someone who was looking forward to a brand-new start.

His head tilted to one side, though his eyes didn't leave her face. *'It is?'*

Her eyes lifted. 'Please don't act as if you're stupid, Santiago. I know you're not.'

'Why, thank you.'

Lily ignored his sarcastic interjection. 'We both know that the only reason you're hanging around is because you feel guilty. There's no need. You just have an overdeveloped sense of responsibility.' Her eyes slid up from his highly polished handmade shoes to the open neck of his designer shirt. 'Nobody would ever know it to look at you,' she admitted.

'So when you look at me, what do you think?'

That you could make me forget where I end and you begin and I want you to do it again. The sharp inhalation as she gasped for breath made her nostrils flare and her chest lift. 'Sure you want to know?' she taunted weakly.

He smiled and planted his elbows on the table-top. 'I think I can take it,' he said, his eyes trained on her cleavage.

I'm not sure I can.

Lily's smile became even more fixed as she continued to studiously avoid his eyes. 'You look…' she swallowed and exhaled a shaky breath '…not vain and shallow, exactly…'

'I'm relieved,' he came back as dry as dust.

'More dangerous and brooding.'

'*Brooding…?*' he repeated, looking so astounded that any other time she might have laughed.

'Some men spend all their lives trying to look *that* dangerous, brooding, and never get anywhere near.'

'Are you calling me a poseur, Lily?'

'It would be easier if you were.' That was the thing Santiago didn't try at all, she acknowledged despairingly.

'Will you talk sense?' he demanded, running an impatient hand along his firm jawline.

Lily's focus briefly slipped as she indulged her wilful

imagination and visualised doing the same thing. Her fingers flexed as she imagined feeling the rasp of stubble under her fingertips.

'Fine,' she said hoarsely. Blinking, she laid her palms flat on the table-top and fixed him with an earnest gaze. 'Does this make sense to you? I crashed my car...'

She saw anger stir in his eyes. 'Though it wasn't your fault,' he inserted in his flat, cold voice, the one she now recognised he used when he wanted to break things, generally her neck, and yell.

'Does it matter *whose* fault it was?' she asked him in exasperation. 'Anyhow, no matter how you look at it, it wasn't *your* fault, but even if it had been, as you see—' she held her arms out from her sides '—I'm fine.' She pinned a smile on her face to underline the fact.

His dark brows twitched into a straight line and his expression became uncomfortably intense as he studied her face. 'I suppose it wasn't my fault you got pregnant either?'

She gritted her teeth and closed her eyes. 'Not this again. I thought we'd agreed to draw a line under that like rational human beings.'

'You are not rational, and I agreed to nothing.'

Aware that Santiago's raised voice had attracted several curious glances, Lily lowered her own voice to compensate. 'Well, if we didn't, we should have,' she retorted. 'I know you're on some major guilt trip.'

'Naturally, I regret that I was responsible for what you have suffered. What sort of man would I be if I did not feel some guilt?'

She clutched her head between her hands as she let her head flop forward; her hair fell in glossy, concealing bangs around her face.

'If I had had a termination I wouldn't have needed to ask your permission.'

The fine muscles around Santiago's mouth quivered as his jaw tightened. Some of the colour seeped from his olive-toned skin.

'You didn't.'

She had never heard that particular note in his voice before and Lily knew that she never wanted to again. The victim of a sudden and inappropriate wave of tenderness, she was momentarily unable to respond.

'No, I didn't.' Lily had to bite her tongue to stop herself assuring him that this was a course she had never even considered. 'But that was *my* decision. And it was *my* decision to go ahead with the pregnancy. Anything that happened after that was down to me.' She sketched a brief sad smile. 'And fate.'

Her blue eyes met his as she searched in vain for some flicker in those dark, enigmatic depths to show he recognised the point she was desperately trying to get across.

There was nothing.

She gritted her teeth with sheer frustration. 'I take responsibility for my own actions, Santiago. And I am capable of taking care of myself. I realise that you feel you have to go through some sort of penance, but I don't want to be it.'

'*Penance!* That's ridiculous.'

'I don't think so. Why else would you be here with me?' Sniffing, she reached behind her for the bag she had slung over the back of the chair.

Seconds before Lily, Santiago was on his feet looking very tall and *very* angry as he stood the other side of the table glaring at her. A waitress heading in their direction caught the tail-end of his glare and changed direction.

'Maybe I just like looking at you?'

A look of stricken hurt in her eyes, Lily turned her head while she regained control. The irony was he had said *ex-*

actly what she longed to hear. The problem was the comment had been delivered in such a tone of ferocious dislike that even she didn't make the mistake of imagining that he meant it.

From somewhere she dredged a mocking smile. 'Sure, that's *really* likely,' she agreed huskily. 'Considering you've not lost a single opportunity to tell me how dreadful I look. If you want to feel better about yourself, go give something to charity, because I don't need anything from you. I don't need chocolate cake and I don't need you!'

Santiago opened his mouth to assure her the feeling was totally mutual and saw a solitary tear sliding slowly down her pale cheek. He swore softly under his breath, pulled some notes from his wallet and, without even looking, slammed them down on the table.

'Come on. Let's get out of here before someone throws us out,' he said without looking at her.

Robbed of her chance to make a dignified solitary exit, Lily was left with no choice but to follow in his wake.

CHAPTER SIXTEEN

LILY tried to leave Santiago at his car. 'I need to go home.'

Santiago stared at her impatiently. 'We are going home.'

'My home.'

'Get in, Lily, we need to talk.'

'We have talked, Santiago. I'm all talked out.' She shook her head sadly from side to side. 'The truth is, talking isn't going to change anything. Let me spell it out for you: I don't need rescuing. You feel guilty. You're one of the good guys. I understand that. It might make you feel better to act as my protector, but quite frankly being around you only reminds me of things I'd prefer to forget.'

His head reared back as though she had struck him. Shock registered in his face, then slowly his lean features settled into a blank mask.

'You look at me and think of losing the baby.' He met her eyes and gave a bleak smile that made Lily's tender heart ache. 'I must admit I had not thought of that.'

Neither did I until ten seconds ago, she thought, and felt wretched. She stuffed her hands into her pockets to stop herself reaching out to him. *This is the right thing to do,* she told herself. *In the long run it will be less painful. Guilt is no basis for any sort of relationship, and even though he hasn't got around to it yet I'm pretty sure that's what he's going to suggest.*

And if he did she wasn't sure she would have the strength to say no.

'Get in,' he said tersely. 'And I will drive you home.'

Just like that. If he really cared he would have put up some sort of fight. 'To Devon?'

'Certainly to Devon.' He frowned, then added, 'Where is Devon? And I thought you lived with Rachel now?'

She shook her head. 'God, this is stupid. I can catch the train.'

'I have driven across several continents. I think I can find my way to Devon.' Lily watched him run his hand along his jaw; she had never heard him sound so tired before. 'Get in, Lily.'

It was the worrying note of exhaustion in his voice that made her stop arguing. 'Thank you.'

They travelled in silence, the rain, grey, depressing sheets of it, began to fall before they had even left the city. By the time they got on the motorway the visibility was abysmal and the traffic heavy. Then, twenty miles on, the traffic came to a complete standstill.

'Accident…?' she suggested tentatively, after they had moved ten feet in half an hour.

'It would seem likely.'

Lily pushed her hair back from her brow and wound down the window, which let in fumes and rain. 'How can you be so calm?' So far he had not even drummed his fingers on the dashboard, and she felt like tearing her hair out. Listening to him rant and swear would be preferable to the nerve-shredding silence.

'There is no point stressing over things that are outside your control. Would you like to listen to the radio or some music?'

'You're not human.'

He turned his head. 'I'll take that as a no, shall I?'

Lily took a map from the glove compartment just as the traffic started creeping forward at a snail's pace. 'I thought so,' she said, after she had located the right page. 'There's an exit in about a quarter of a mile.' She traced a route along minor roads with her fingers. 'It's less direct, but it should be faster than this.'

'Building a new motorway would be faster than this,' he said, indicating to manoeuvre into the inside lane.

About half an hour later, after several miles of incident-free driving on a minor road, they hit the first diversion sign. Santiago slowed as a policeman approached and wound down the window as he came to a stop.

'Flash floods. The road ahead is closed, sir. If you follow the diversion signs it'll get you back on the motorway.'

'I don't believe this,' Lily groaned under her breath. She turned to Santiago. 'What are you going to do?'

He scanned her pale face and made a rapid mental calculation. 'We're going back.'

'What?'

'You're clearly exhausted, and I'm not getting any younger while I drive around the west country. It will be quicker to go back to London than go on, unless you prefer to stop overnight in a hotel here? The choice is yours, but first—' he pulled into the forecourt of a roadside pub '—I need to ask you something.'

Lily looked across at him. Santiago didn't quite meet her eyes. Her brow furrowed into a quizzical frown.

'You don't usually find it difficult to say what's on your mind, Santiago.'

'This is a difficult thing to ask,' he continued. 'I need to know if the complications of the birth and surgery affected your fertility. Will you be able to have more children?'

The question was so totally unexpected that the breath snagged in her throat. Almost immediately her lashes lowered in a protective screen over her eyes. When her head came up her expression was as devoid of emotion as her voice.

'I rather think that's my business, don't you?'

'I am only…'

She lifted her hand to silence him. 'The *only* person it might concern would be the person I intended spending the rest of my life with.' The muscles along her delicate jaw quivered. 'And that's not you, is it? I expect *your* wife when you eventually take one, poor woman, will need to supply a medical certificate to certify she is good breeding stock. You and your precious family pride,' she sneered. 'I suppose it's understandable if you have an aristocratic bloodline that stretches back to the year dot.'

A look of frustration settled on his dark saturnine features as he studied her expression. *'Lily…?'* His long brown fingers touched her wrist and she flinched and pulled her hand away as though burnt.

'If I say I can't have children, what are you going to do, Santiago?' Inside her tight chest her heart was hammering; for some reason she was so angry she felt light-headed.

'How are you going to fix it?' She saw him flinch and told herself she didn't care. 'Offer me money? How much is it worth, do you think? Isn't that what men like you usually do—throw money at a problem until it goes away? Well, I don't want your guilt money. And, just for the record, I have no intention of remarrying.' *Like he actually cares, Lily.*

'That would, I think, be a pity,' he said quietly.

'But if I did, it wouldn't be to a man who thought of me as a baby machine.' Lily didn't know why it was, but around Santiago she seemed to regress to childish retorts.

Rather than the annoyance she had anticipated there was curiosity and something else she couldn't put a name to in his face as he asked, 'You really think that is what I want in a wife?'

'I can't say I've given any thought to what you might

want in a wife,' she declared, and then almost immediately contradicted herself by adding, 'Oh, I'm sure she'd have to be talented, beautiful. And probably blonde.' She tossed her head.

Santiago's eyes followed her hair as it bounced and settled back around her shoulders. 'No,' he said, smiling in a way that made her stomach muscles quiver. 'My preference is for brunettes.'

'Am I meant to be flattered?' Lily knew what she definitely meant *not* to be, and that was turned on. Turned on to the extent that she was only a whisper away from salivating.

Very conscious of his dark, smouldering gaze lingering on her lips, she attempted a scornful laugh, but all that emerged was a hoarse whimper.

Pathetic, Lily, she told herself.

'And for the record, my preference is for men who don't make personal comments.'

'I don't have an aristocratic bloodline,' he said, still looking at her mouth.

'Sure, you're a regular man of the people.'

'And I cannot trace my family back to… "the year dot".'

'Your family tree isn't actually something I stay awake at nights wondering about.' No, just his voice, and hands, his eyes and the way he had of turning his head to one side when he was about to ask a question…

'I have.'

'You have what?'

'I have stayed awake nights wondering about my family tree. You see, I actually have no idea who my biological parents were.'

Lily's jaw literally dropped. She blinked at him, not quite sure of what she'd heard. 'Your "biological" parents…?'

The frown between her brows deepened. 'What are you saying? *Biological…?*'

'I'm saying that I was adopted.'

'*You* were adopted?' She shook her head. 'No, that can't be right?'

His sensual, dark, delectably velvety eyes shimmered with emotions she couldn't even begin to decipher as they connected with her own.

'It was not something my parents advertised,' he admitted drily. The upward curve of his lips was self-derisive as he added, 'Not even to me.'

She looked at him in horror as the significance of his words sunk in. 'They didn't tell you…?'

'I was going through my father's papers after his death when I came across the paperwork.'

'Oh.' Lily just couldn't begin to imagine how devastating that must have been.

He scanned her horrified face, a half-smile on his lips. 'Be careful, Lily, your empathy is showing.'

'Empathy! I should think so! You found out you were adopted by accident.' She unfastened her seat belt and thought angrily about his parents. 'It must have been a…' She stopped, unable to come up with anything that wasn't totally trite.

'I was shocked,' he admitted.

She flashed him an incredulous look. '*Shocked…*' she repeated. *Oh, well,* she thought, *I suppose that is one way to describe having your life shaken to its foundations. A discovery like that would make your average person question a lot of things they had taken for granted before…things like who they were!*

She slid a searching look at Santiago; he didn't look like a man who had an identity crisis. He looked like a man who was totally at ease with who he was.

'Have you tried...tried to find your birth mother?' She caught him looking at her strangely and added awkwardly, 'I only ask because I've heard that a lot of people feel the need to discover their birth parents.'

'That would be difficult as I was adopted in Argentina.'

'Argentina!'

'My mother has family there. My parents tried for children for some years. Adoption was something of a last resort and they were very discreet. They went to stay with relatives in Argentina. My father came home and later my mother returned with me. Even when I found the adoption documents she initially denied it. Finally she broke down and admitted it.'

Lily listened with growing astonishment to his calm recitation. 'You know, you're so good at hiding your feelings that some people probably think you don't have any.'

His eyes flickered her way. 'But not you?'

'You forget I've seen you lose your temper—on more than one occasion,' she added drily. 'I just don't understand why it was a secret. They must have realised you would find out eventually.'

He shrugged. 'Maybe they didn't think that far ahead.'

She just couldn't believe he was as relaxed as he appeared. 'Weren't you angry?'

'Actually it explained a lot of things.'

'Such as?'

'My relationship with my father.'

'Which wasn't good,' she speculated.

'Which wasn't good,' he agreed calmly. 'My father told me from an early age that I was a disappointment to him. He continually tried to undermine me. I suppose my early life was defined by my attempts to prove him wrong. It was a long time before I realised that that wasn't possible.'

Lily literally bounced in her seat as her feelings of indignation threatened to overcome her. 'Well, he was wrong,' she cried, brushing an angry tear from her cheek. 'And if he was here I'd tell him so.'

His eyes moved across her face. 'I believe you would; you're quite a tigress.'

'And I just think it was stupid not to tell you from the start. If I ever adopted a child I wouldn't make a secret of it.'

'You didn't know my father.' He gave an ironic smile. 'But then neither did I. You have to understand that, to him, not being able to produce an heir was a source of intense shame. I was a reminder of his failure.' He twisted around in his seat and angled a questioning look at her face. 'And is it likely that you would one day adopt a child, Lily?'

Lily's shoulders tensed, then relaxed. Why not put him out of his misery? 'If I did it wouldn't be because I couldn't have one of my own.'

It was only when he relaxed that Lily appreciated just how much her reply had meant to him.

'You are sure?'

'It was one of the things that the doctors made a point of telling me,' she recalled, unaware of the bleak expression that had settled on her face as her thoughts drifted back to that black period. 'They seemed to think it would be a comfort to me.' Her smile was bitter. 'But I didn't want another baby. I wanted *my* baby.'

Her eyes lifted and the expression in his dark eyes made her stiffen. The one thing she didn't want was his pity.

'So you can put your hair shirt back in mothballs,' she snapped.

He looked at her for a moment in silence. 'Why are you angry with me?'

Damn him and his spooky perception! 'I'm not angry with you,' she snapped crankily.

'Then what are you?'

'I'm...I'm *mad* with you because you're only around because you feel guilty.' *I want you to be around because you want to be with me. I want you to feel as if your life is empty without me in it!* Her eyes were filled with a helpless longing as they moved across his lean face.

I want you to feel the way I do.

Blinking back tears, she turned her head away, mumbling, 'Well, like I've already said, I'm not some pathetic charity case.'

'I'm around because your mouth is sweet and hot and I'm hoping at some point to get to taste you again. How the hell can you think I'm just around because I feel guilty after what happened between us at Dan's cottage?' he demanded.

Sniffing, Lily slowly turned her head. *'Seriously...?'*

He looked into her wary eyes. 'Does it look like I'm not serious? Look, I'm willing to walk away if looking at me brings back a pain I can't even begin to imagine. But why do you think I took you to bed? Out of some weird sense of duty?'

'I suppose I might have read the situation wrongly?'

He heaved an enormous sigh and looked relieved. 'Well, thank God for that. My motivation is far less noble.'

'It is?'

He nodded and the hungry gleam in his eyes, the one that made her feel breathless, got more pronounced. 'I can't look at you without imagining you naked. I can't think about you without wanting to be inside you.' There was a dangerous gleam in his eyes as he added firmly, 'Not noble.'

This was good, she told herself. Love would be better.

She gave a ghost of a grin—but she could settle for lust. It was miles better than the alternative, which was never kissing Santiago again. No, she would definitely settle.

'Not noble, but…exciting.'

He looked into her face and swallowed. 'I think we should continue where we left off.'

'But what about what happened between us in Spain?'

With a frustrated sigh, he pushed his dark head into the upholstered seat. 'Fine, let's get this out of the way. I now know that your husband was a total bastard who cheated on you.'

Her eyes flickered in surprise. 'In a nutshell, yes, but—'

'A nutshell works for me,' he promised. He closed his eyes and covered the lower part of his face with his hands. 'Have you any idea what the scent of your skin is doing to me?'

Lily would have loved to have him describe this in detail, but she really needed to clear the air. 'It wasn't all Gordon's fault.'

Santiago's hands fell away. 'You're defending him?'

'I'm trying to be fair. He had flings, because he said, and please don't laugh, he said I didn't understand him.'

'The man is a complete fool!' Santiago observed contemptuously.

'Yes, I know that *now*, but at the time I didn't. I think habit was the only thing holding us together by the end. There had been signs, lots of them,' she recalled. 'But I just didn't want to admit that I'd failed. If I'd been stronger I'd have ended it a lot earlier,' she admitted. 'So I am partially responsible.'

'The Spanish holiday…' She shot him a sideways look and saw he was listening intently. 'It was meant to be a fresh start, a second honeymoon. Only he got called away at the airport. He said he'd follow on, but he didn't.' She shook her head. 'I didn't set out to lie to anyone,' she told him earnestly. 'I was going to tell you the truth about being married, but then it was too late and…'

He leaned across and laid a finger to her lips. 'I can see now how it happened.'

A twinkle appeared in her eyes. 'You're just saying that so that you can kiss me,' she teased.

He trailed a languid finger down her cheek. 'I can see that you will be hard to fool.'

He began to edge towards her and Lily pulled back. 'About the kissing…'

'You have a problem with the way I kiss?'

'Not the kissing, only the stopping,' she admitted. Then, correctly anticipating that Santiago was about to pull her into his arms, and knowing that she wouldn't be able to think, let alone talk, rationally when she got there, she added quickly, 'I was thinking, if we're going to be…an item…?'

He placed a hand on her thigh. 'That is one way of putting it,' he agreed, smiling as he felt a shiver run through her body.

'Then maybe we should do things properly this time?'

He stilled. '"Properly"…?' he echoed. 'Last time felt *faulty* to you…?'

She flushed and felt her nipples harden. 'The sex is not a problem.'

One dark brow elevated. 'Do you think you could work on the enthusiasm for the sake of my ego?'

'Your ego could withstand an earthquake,' she contended with a quick nervous laugh. 'I'm just trying not to think of sex with you, because when I do my mind turns to mush. And I want to say this.'

'"Mush"?'

She nodded. 'There's no need to look so smug,' she choked.

He adopted a grave expression. 'Fine, I am listening.'

'I just thought we could go on dates…the theatre…things like that.'

Or we could just go to bed. 'Anything you like. What food do you like—Chinese, French, Thai…?'

'I'm serious, Santiago.'

Eyes narrowed, he studied her face. 'Is this some sort of test? You want to know if I just want you for your body. Do you want me to love you for your mind?'

She didn't try to laugh, because she knew she wouldn't be able to pull it off. 'I *know* you only want me for my body.'

About to speak, Santiago closed his mouth when she added quickly, 'Which is fine. I want you for your body too. Only I thought it might be nice to talk, and things, sometimes, otherwise…' she flushed and her eyes dropped '…I'd feel like your mistress. I'm not really mistress material.'

She looked at him, frowning as she remained unable to interpret his dark stare.

'Fine, you want to date, we will date.' He went to turn the ignition, then changed his mind and turned back to her. 'I thought we had been talking. And just how many people do you think I have discussed the circumstances of my birth with? I'll tell you, shall I? Nobody.'

Before she had chance to consider this startling piece of information, he added, 'It is getting late. We should start back.'

Lily glanced over at the pub, which was now illuminated by a garish set of multicoloured lights. 'We could stay there. It doesn't look busy. Probably the weather.'

Santiago looked at the building with an expression of fastidious distaste. 'Or the peeling paintwork?'

'Don't be such a snob,' she chided. 'I'm sure it's lovely inside.'

'Your optimism is admirable.'

She gave a reluctant smile. 'All right, it does look a bit tatty, but do you really want to drive all the way back?'

'No,' he admitted. 'That is not my first call.' A thoughtful expression slid into his eyes as he looked at the building. 'This dating, Lily—how far do you want to take it?'

'How do you mean?'

'I mean do you want single rooms?'

'You mean…' A look of horror spread across her face. 'God, no,' she gasped. 'I didn't mean that at all.'

He smiled. 'In that case I think we should by all means spend the night in this delightful establishment.'

CHAPTER SEVENTEEN

LILY spent most of the week packing and looking for somewhere to rent that was reasonably close to work. There was no possibility of buying in a town where the property prices had been artificially inflated by the influx of people buying second homes close to the sea. And the rental market did not offer too much choice—not on her limited budget anyway.

But by the end of the week she had signed a lease on a tiny bedsit. It was cramped, but if you stood on a chair and looked through the skylight in the bathroom you could just see the sea. When the agent had assured her with no trace of irony that a sea view was a real selling point she had tried not to laugh.

She was really trying to be upbeat and put a positive slant on the whole downsizing thing, but it was difficult. The future was still a question mark, but one good thing was the library had offered her a full-time post. The extra money would make life a lot easier.

She looked around at the packing cases in the living room, and thought, *Shouldn't I feel something? This was my home for most of my adult life.* Maybe Santiago had been right, she reflected. Maybe it did take more than bricks and mortar to make a home.

Santiago... She sighed as his lean face materialised in her mind. In theory she should not have had time to miss him; in reality she had thought about something he had said, or did, or just the sound of his voice, just about every minute of the day. Twice he had rung her during that week, and on each occasion the conversation had been strained and awkward. And after she had put the phone down she had cried her eyes out.

She could acknowledge that it was a pathetic way for a grown woman to behave, but she couldn't stop missing him so much it hurt. As she locked the door for the last time and headed for the station it was the thought of seeing him again that gave her step a new sense of urgency as she carried her case to the London-bound train.

'Why are we doing this?' she asked as the taxi drew up outside the restaurant.

She had arrived in London dizzy with anticipation. The rather reserved reception she had received had left her feeling distinctly deflated. Then, instead of whisking her off to bed, Santiago had said he was taking her out to dinner and then a show—*a show, for God's sake*!

Maybe he had gone off her already?

Santiago, who was saying something to the cab driver, turned his head. 'Doing what?'

'What are we doing here?'

'You prefer another restaurant? This place comes highly recommended and tables here are like gold-dust since they got the second Michelin star, but if you prefer some place else, fine.'

'I *mean* why are we here at all? It's pretty obvious you don't want to be.'

'I don't know what you mean.'

'Not looking at me I can take, limited conversation I can take, but it would be nice to get more than a grunt in response to a question. Since it's quite obvious you'd prefer to be somewhere else I wonder what we're doing here at all.'

Something flashed in his eyes. 'It is true I would prefer to be some place else.'

Lily's throat tightened. She would have died rather than show him how much his admission hurt. Through a miasma of misery she heard him add angrily, 'But you wanted this.'

'I wanted what?' *I wanted to be ignored and insulted…?*

'You wanted to take things slowly…'

'Yes…' she said, not seeing where he was going with this.

'A date, you said,' he reminded her through clenched teeth. 'This is a date.'

Lily stared at him. 'You think that I want this?'

There was a thunderstruck silence. 'Are you saying you don't?'

She shook her head. 'You said that there was somewhere else you would prefer to be,' she said. 'Where's that?'

If she was wrong, if he said with someone who didn't bore him silly, she was going to feel pretty stupid. No, actually, she was going to feel much worse than that.

'I would prefer to be naked in bed with you.'

A choking sound was heard from the front seat, but neither of the occupants of the back seat noticed.

'Me too,' said Lily.

'Well, why didn't you say so sooner?' Santiago tapped on the glass partition. 'Change of plan.' He leaned back in the seat and loosened his tie. His dark eyes moved over Lily and her stomach flipped. 'Come here…'

Lily scooted across the intervening inches and placed her hands behind his dark head. 'Will this do?'

'Dios…!' he breathed brokenly as she pressed her soft breasts against his chest.

'Santiago…you remember what I said about not being mistress material?'

He looked at her mouth, soft pink and inviting, and nodded. 'I do…it doesn't matter,' he promised.

'No, it doesn't,' she agreed, 'because I've changed my mind.'

'You want to be my mistress?'

'I'll be anything you want me to be. I don't care so long as I'm with you.' Tears sprang to her eyes. 'The last few days without you have been hell,' she confessed.

A huge silent sigh shuddered through his body as he took her face between his hands. 'We will discuss your official title later,' he promised, rubbing his thumb along the trembling outline of her lips. 'Because right now if I don't kiss you I will go mad.'

'Oh, me too!'

Ten minutes later Santiago opened the door of the Georgian town house and they almost fell into the hallway. Still kissing the woman in his arms, he began to fight his way out of his jacket. Once it was gone he slid his hands into her hair, twisting his fingers into the shiny mesh and tilting her head back to expose the length of her pale neck.

Their lips parted as they both gasped for air. Santiago looked from her half-closed blue eyes to her deliciously pouting lips and groaned.

'You are driving me crazy. Do you know that?'

'*I am?*' Lily said

His smouldering eyes zoned in on her parted pink lips. 'I'm on my way to being certifiable.'

She lifted a hand to his cheek and ran her finger down the hard, strong curve of his jaw, feeling the rough growth of beard that gave him a wildly attractive, piratical air.

Head thrown back, she looked up at him through her lashes. 'Is there anything I can do to help?'

Santiago swallowed and his tense grin grew even more wolfish and hungry. 'What did you have in mind?'

'I'm open to suggestions.' At that moment Lily couldn't

think of any request he might make that she would deny him. Anticipation made her senses swim.

'*Querida!*' he breathed, wiping the beads of sweat from his forehead with the back of his hand. The primal hunger coursing through his veins made it hard to think of anything but having her softness underneath him, then she nibbled his neck and his eyes flickered open. Looking into her sweetly flushed face, he grabbed both her hands in one of his and held them lightly behind her back.

'This is crazy,' she said as he bit the side of her mouth.

'Do you like crazy?'

'Oh, yes…'

Lily's feet barely touched the ground until her back made contact with the wall. Breathing hard, she stood there with her hands now pinioned against either side of her face and her passion-glazed eyes lifted to the dark, lean face of the man whose body, every rock-hard, sinfully delicious inch of it, was plastered up against hers.

His mouth brushed softly against hers and she closed her eyes and shivered.

'Have you the *faintest* idea how much I want you?' he demanded thickly.

His words jolted through her body like a mild-electric shock. Her lips quivered faintly as her eyelids half lifted. Through the sweep of her lashes she tried to focus, but his face was so close his features were just a dark blur.

She swallowed. 'Quite a lot?' she suggested.

'*Quite a lot…*' he repeated slowly.

She started to nod, and stopped as his tongue began to trace the outline of her full, quivering lower lip. 'I'm never going to let you out of my sight for this long again.'

Neither heard the drawing-room door swing open, or registered the light that spilt out into the hallway from that room.

CHAPTER EIGHTEEN

'GOOD evening, Santiago.'

Against her, Lily felt Santiago's warm body stiffen and lift from her own. The quarter-inch of air between them made her feel suddenly icily cold and irrationally bereft.

Eyes closed tight, he exhaled a ragged breath. Swearing softly and fluently under his breath did little to relieve the frustration that coursed through his veins. Families, he decided, were totally overrated, especially when they turned up uninvited at crucial moments in a man's life.

As his head lifted Lily's eyes meshed with his for a moment. She was too mortified at finding herself in this cringingly embarrassing position to be capable of reading the message in his eyes. Maybe Santiago recognised this because just before he turned away from her he said in a rough velvet voice meant for her ears alone, 'Don't move, *querida*.'

If Lily hadn't been literally paralysed with embarrassment she would have had no problem ignoring this husky instruction, sexy endearment or no sexy endearment, and getting the hell out of there! As it was it took her thirty seconds before she lowered her hands from the wall; running at that point was not a serious option.

'What are you doing here, Mother?' he asked, sounding composed but seriously irritated.

Lily, who wanted quite badly for the floor to open up and swallow her, was deeply envious of his composure. Other than the dark lines of colour scoring the high angles of his cheekbones and the ruffled condition of his normally sleek sable hair, he looked relaxed.

Santiago's mother! Lily was briefly diverted from her own misery as she looked across at the older, dark-haired woman. The slim figure standing there didn't look much like the mental image of scary matriarch Lily had nursed. For a start, she didn't look nearly old enough.

Patricia arched a delicate eyebrow, but her serene smile didn't waver at her son's accusing tone. 'When you weren't at the airport to pick me up we got a taxi,' she explained calmly.

Santiago dragged a hand through his dark hair and frowned. His thoughts, not totally committed to this conversation, kept straying back to moments before when Lily had melted into his arms, all sweet softness and heat. He thought about the way she had shuddered from head to toe, the fine muscles just under the surface of her silky skin contracting as he had laid his fingers on the bare skin of her thigh. It took all the will-power at his disposal to prevent himself grabbing her again and burying his face between her breasts.

He inhaled and cleared his throat.

'*Airport…?*' he snapped abruptly.

'It slipped your mind, no doubt?' A smile quivered on Patricia Morais's lips as her dark eyes moved from her son's face to that of the young woman at her son's side. 'Are you not going to introduce me to your friend, or is this not a good time?'

The older woman's dark almond-shaped eyes flickered towards Lily, who was standing there with her lace-edged pink camisole and a lot of flesh on show. Moments before her skin had been flushed with passion; now it was mortification that produced the heat that made Lily's cheeks burn. Her fingers shook as she dragged her shirt together and tried to fasten the buttons.

The only discernible expression on Santiago's mother's face was mild curiosity, but of course it wasn't hard for Lily to imagine what the elegant older woman was thinking. Probably wondering where her playboy son had picked up this one.

Comparing me to the others...? I wonder how I score?

Lily suddenly felt as wretchedly cheap as she was sure the other woman thought her.

Santiago gritted his teeth and tucked his own shirt back into his trousers. 'No, it damn well isn't a good time.'

'I thought it might not be.' As his mother spoke a young woman with big dreamy dark eyes and a serious expression appeared at her shoulder.

Lily saw that the girl's heart-shaped face was attractively framed by a barely tamed mass of dark curls. She had a natural pout and her golden Mediterranean skin glowed with youth and vibrance.

She was quite breathtakingly beautiful.

'Is Santiago here *finally*?' There was no trace of accent in her loud voice.

Lily's spirits took a predictable nosedive. A beautiful girl asking for...no, *demanding* Santiago. Why should this surprise me? she asked herself sardonically.

The brunette's voice dropped to a more acceptable level as she unplugged the earphones from her ears and asked cheerfully, 'What's his excuse for leaving us stranded? This ought to be good,' she anticipated.

She saw Lily and stopped. Her big eyes widened as they turned in enquiry first to her, then Santiago and the older woman.

'Angel! Dear God, you as well?' Santiago demanded in

a less-than-welcoming tone that drew an amused grin from the dark-haired beauty.

'Hello, big brother. I'm glad to see you too,' she quipped drily. 'I would be here, wouldn't I?'

He shook his head as his normal acute mental capability failed him. 'Would you?' he responded with caution.

'I'm here for my interview on Friday, for the nursing degree.' The way she studied her brother's face, with her head tilted a little to one side, reminded Lily of Santiago. 'You'd forgotten,' she concluded.

'I had not forgotten,' Santiago contended. 'It had simply temporarily slipped my mind.'

The last remnants of gravity vanished from Angel's face as she gave an impish grin. 'Which is an entirely different thing.' She laughed a little at her brother's expression and stepped forward, her hand outstretched to Lily. 'I'm Angel, Santiago's sister.' She cast a sideways glance at her brother. 'What have you done with him?'

'Not now, Angel. I'll talk to you later.' He took a step forward, interposing his big body between Lily and his family.

Lily's vision misted; the action seemed painfully symbolic to her. When he said, 'Not now' what he really meant was, *Not ever!* It was obvious that the last thing Santiago wanted to do was introduce her to his family. She blinked and swallowed past the emotional constriction in her throat.

Get used to it, Lily. There's going to be a lot of this. The reality of what she was doing suddenly hit her like a truck-load of bricks.

She told herself it wasn't reasonable to feel hurt, but then when did loving someone have anything to do with reason? It wasn't as if Santiago had lied at any point to her. She had entered into this knowing that he didn't love her—knowing that he wasn't able to return her feelings.

The bottom line was she had been willing to take what she could get and she didn't regret her decision, but she was starting to appreciate how hard that was going to be.

As she turned she didn't have the faintest idea where she was going—she just knew she had to escape this situation before she did something really daft like cry.

'If you'll excuse me,' she mumbled, sure that he would. She was wrong.

'No, I will not excuse you,' Santiago announced, in a tone that made the female members of his family stare in amazement at him.

'I thought you were embarrassed by my presence.'

His glittering midnight eyes swept across her pale-as-paper face; the tears standing out in her eyes made him frown. 'Then you thought wrong, and not for the first time. For the record, you're not going anywhere. You're staying right here with me.'

Lily's chin went up in response to his autocratic pronouncement. Emotional basket case or not, she wasn't going to let him get away with talking to her like that. She might have no pride where he was concerned, but she wasn't a doormat.

'Are you telling me, or asking me?'

His mobile lips quivered and some of the severity died from his face as the lines around his eyes deepened. 'Would it make any difference?'

Their eyes meshed. His were dark and warm and so tender that for a moment she couldn't get her breath.

Lily thought about what they'd be doing now if his mother hadn't walked in and her hand went to her neck where her skin prickled hot and sticky.

'You're incredibly bossy,' she charged gruffly.

'It is part of my charm,' he claimed.

Lily looked into his face and thought, *I love you so much*

it hurts. 'Your problem is you've started believing your own press releases,' she taunted, trying to sound amused and just not getting there at all.

'Do I have press releases?'

Lily wasn't sure whether he was serious. 'Don't you know?'

'Well, if I do, in future you shall have control over all press releases. That should keep my ego from spiralling out of control,' he added with an ironic twist of his lips.

'That would be nepotism.'

He shrugged. 'I don't have a problem with that.'

'The people who work for you might if you invented a job for your mistress.' She didn't have the faintest intention of working for him, but she felt this was something that needed saying.

'What did you say?'

Lily immediately realised why he looked so furious. He didn't want her advertising their relationship in front of his mother and sister, which was pretty unfair considering he had initiated the conversation in the first place.

'She's your mistress?'

With a curse Santiago rounded angrily on the round-eyed teenager. 'No, she is not!'

'Keep your hair on. I was only asking.'

'If I'm not your mistress, what am I?'

Before Santiago could respond to this challenge Patricia Morais, who had been watching the interchange, released a soft cry. 'Goodness, I know who you are.'

Glad someone does, Lily thought, unable to tear her eyes from Santiago's face.

'You're the girl Santiago told me he was going to marry. A year ago...*August.* It was my birthday,' she recalled. 'So I remember the date exactly. You rang, Santiago. It was after midnight and you said you couldn't come to my birthday celebrations because you'd met the girl you were going to marry.' She released a reminiscent laugh. 'At first I thought you'd been drinking.'

Santiago didn't confirm or deny his mother's words; he didn't even turn his head. His dark, implacable gaze remained trained unblinkingly on Lily's shocked face.

'*Marry…?*' Lily, her smooth brow furrowed, shook her head.

'It is her, isn't it?'

'You told your mother you were going to marry me a year ago?' Lily's head swung slowly from side to side as she tried to make sense of this information. 'No, that can't be right.'

She saw something move behind Santiago's dark eyes before his lashes came down in a concealing screen. '*Why?*' The single word fell heavily into the charged atmosphere.

Lily looked at Santiago, who was nursing his dark head between his hands. 'Because in August we'd only just met.'

His head lifted; the pain in his eyes shocked Lily. 'And how long does it take to fall in love?'

Somewhere in the distance Lily heard Angel squeal. 'That's *so* romantic!'

Santiago tore his eyes briefly from Lily's face to beg of his mother, 'Will you get that girl out of here?'

'I'm not a girl!' his sister protested indignantly. 'Does this mean I'm finally going to get to be a bridesmaid?'

After the sound of the door slamming, there was silence for a full sixty seconds.

Lily, whose heart was trying to climb out of her chest, trained her eyes on the floor. 'You're not in love with me,' Lily said in a manner that invited contradiction.

A nerve clenched in Santiago's lean cheek. 'Are you asking me or telling me?' he rasped huskily.

She turned her head away from him and caught a glimpse

of herself in a mirror. The light in the brightly lit hall was pretty unforgiving and she looked quite desperately pale. Her eyes, which seemed to fill half of her face, held a feverish glitter.

'I don't know what I'm doing. I don't know what I'm saying,' she confessed weakly. Just when she had come to the conclusion she knew nothing at all, she remembered something she did know. It actually seemed like the only constant in her turbulent life just now. For once she wasn't thinking of the consequences as she blurted out, 'I love you, though; I know that much.' A wave of fatigue swept over her so intense she sought the lower step of the elegant, sweeping staircase and sat down without even looking at him.

Her eyes were trained on her shoes as she heard his soft tread on the marble floor. The brief contact as his thigh lightly touched hers sent a hot tingle through her body. His hands felt heavy as they came to rest on her shoulders.

'You love me...' In profile it was hard to read his expression, but she could feel the explosive tension coiled in his lean body.

Lily's eyes lifted.

'When I first saw you...'

Lily nodded encouragingly. 'In the restaurant that night,' she prompted.

'No, earlier in the day in Baeza.'

'Baeza!'

'You were sitting outside a café drinking wine.'

'You saw me there?'

He nodded. 'You were wearing this long floaty dress in white. Your hair was tied back here.' He touched the nape of her neck. 'You looked like a sad, sinfully sexy angel,' he recalled, pushing his fingers deep into the slippery thickness of her shining hair and pressing a long, lingering kiss to her soft pink lips. He stayed there with his nose brushing the side of her, his breath warm on her cheek. Lily didn't move; she didn't want this magical moment to end. Part of her was a little afraid that she might wake up and discover this had all been a dream.

His expression suggested that the memory was painful for him. 'I was totally blown away, Lily.'

'You were…?' Lily wanted to believe him more than she had ever wanted anything in her life. She was almost there, but that last leap in the dark scared her. 'You know, you don't have to say what you think I want to hear. I'll love you anyway.'

'And I will spend the rest of my life trying to be worthy of that love.'

A dry sob escaped her aching throat as she let her head fall forward onto his shoulder. 'I can't believe this is happening.'

Santiago placed a finger under her chin and forced her face up to his. Holding her eyes, he moved until his mouth was positioned over hers and then slowly…very slowly…he moved forward until their lips were sealed. Lily gave a little shudder, moaned into his mouth and pressed herself against him.

'Do you believe it's happening now?'

Lily let her fingers remain where they were tangled in his hair. 'Something is happening,' she whispered. 'I'm just not sure what.'

'I thought I was dreaming when I saw you,' he told her huskily. 'I had never seen anything so beautiful in my life.' He gave a shuddering sigh. 'I think I fell in love with you at that moment.' He reached out and touched a finger to the tear running down her cheek.

'But if I made such an impression why did you ignore me later that night in the restaurant?'

'Ignoring you was not my intention when I followed you back…'

A look of blank astonishment swept across her face. 'You followed me back in the taxi…?' Her nervous tension found release in a shaky laugh. 'You're not serious…?'

'I was very serious,' he promised her. 'You don't think I was about to lose the woman of my dreams, do you? Of course I followed you back, but between watching you walk into the hotel and seeing you in the bar I had learnt that you were newly widowed. My plan was to be sensitive, and take things slowly…respect your need to grieve…' His smile was loaded with self-mockery as he turned his head and met her amazed eyes.

'We both know that things didn't exactly go to plan. My self-control has never failed me in the past, but it was not robust enough to withstand the sight of you wet in that black swimsuit. I told myself that another man might see you in that swimsuit, a man not so sensitive, and then where would my patience get me? When love is involved it is possible to rationalise any decision.'

'You don't have to tell me that. Did you…was what your mother said true? Did you really ring her and say…?'

'That I had met the woman I was going to marry?' He nodded. 'Yes, I did.'

'That doesn't sound like something you would do.'

'It wasn't something I would do. You know, when I was young I used to swear that I would never marry. I never wanted to put a woman through what I saw my mother suffer.'

The pain in his eyes made her want to hug him. Her eyes widened as she realised with a sense of shock that she could. She touched the side of his face lightly with her hand

and when he looked down she kissed him on the mouth. It lacked the passion they had shared earlier, but the tenderness as his lips returned the pressure brought a lump to her throat.

When they drew a little apart she left her hand on his cheek. 'Your parents' marriage wasn't good?'

'He had a series of affairs, and he wasn't discreet. He seemed to take pleasure from rubbing my mother's nose in it. It was my fear that I had inherited a genetic propensity to hurt women. Then I learned I hadn't inherited anything at all from him—after the first shock it was actually quite a relief.' His self-recriminatory gaze lifted to hers. 'He made me loathe people who cheat on their partners, which is probably what made me go over the top when I found out you were married.' His eyes closed. 'God, when I think what a judgemental idiot I must have sounded...' His head dropped into his hands and he groaned.

Lily stroked his dark head. She couldn't bear the note of bitter self-recrimination in his voice. 'It wasn't your fault!' she exclaimed. 'I knew I shouldn't have, but when it comes to you I just can't be trusted.'

His head lifted. 'No...'

'It's true. I have no will-power around you and my sense of morality gets dangerously skewed.' Which might be handy, considering the role she was taking on. 'You know, I'm going to enjoy being your mistress.' She gave a little grimace. 'Sorry about blurting it out in front of your family that way. I'll be more discreet in future,' she promised earnestly.

'*Mistress!*' he echoed, looking at her as though she'd gone mad. 'What are you talking about? I don't want you to be my mistress. I never wanted you to be my mistress. I want you to be my wife.'

The look of frozen astonishment on her face slowly gave way to one of rapturous joy. 'You want to marry me?'

He framed her face with his hands. 'Of course I want to marry you.' He laughed. 'I love you, *querida*, I always will, and I can't imagine my life without you.'

'But don't you think that if I've cheated once I'd do it again?'

'No, never. I'd trust you with my life.'

The sentiment and the raw sincerity in his voice made Lily's eyes fill.

'Do you remember where we were before we were rudely interrupted?'

She sniffed and wiped the tears from her cheeks, responding to the wicked gleam in his eye with a smile of her own. 'Roughly,' she admitted.

'I was always told that a man should finish what he starts. It is character-building.'

With a sigh Lily looped her arms around his neck and dragged his dark head down to hers. 'What about a woman finishing?'

A broad grin slit his dark face. 'Oh, a gentleman always lets the lady finish first.' He watched the hot colour spread across her face as she got his meaning. 'Does that blush stop or does it go all over?'

Lily lifted her chin. 'There's one way you could find out.'

It was an invitation that Santiago was not about to refuse. With his bride-to-be in his arms, he took the stairs two at a time.

EPILOGUE

'COME on, Lily, the photographer's waiting.'

'Coming,' Lily shouted to Angel, who was already running out onto the terrace where the rest of the guests were gathered.

Lily's eyes were drawn towards the gilt-framed photo on the baby grand. She hoped the photographer would be as successful in capturing the spirit of the day as he had been a year ago when that had been taken.

She picked it up and looked at the glowing bride gazing up at her handsome husband. She must have been one of the few brides who had been congratulated on putting on ten pounds for her wedding day. The only person who hadn't been delighted had been the poor dress designer, who had been horrified at the final fitting when she hadn't been able to get the zip of the glorious silk gown up. Santiago, she recalled, had been particularly pleased she had regained her curvaceous figure.

It had been the happiest day of her life. So happy she hadn't believed Santiago when he had promised had better days to look forward to.

He had been right and this was one of them, a very special one: the christening of their son, Raul.

'They're waiting for you, Lily.'

Lily lifted her head and smiled at Santiago, who stood there with their baby son in his arms.

She replaced the photo and tiptoed towards him. 'He looks like an angel,' she said, peeking at the dark-haired bundle.

'Yes,' agreed the proud father. 'But wait until they point a camera at him. He will start howling his lungs out,' he predicted. 'Just as he did during the service.' The church had echoed to ear-splitting shrieks.

'You're probably right.' She glanced back towards the photo. 'Does it seem like a year to you since we got married? Such a lot has happened. You know, I'm so happy it scares me sometimes,' she confided, lifting a hand lovingly to his face.

Santiago's eyes travelled from the child in his arms to the face of the woman he loved and he smiled. 'Don't be scared, *querida*. I will always be there for you.'

Lily, her heart full to bursting, blinked away a happy tear. He had been there for her during her pregnancy, soothing away her fears that fate would again rob them of the child they so desperately wanted. 'And I'll always be there for you, my love, and we'll both always be there for this little one,' she said, touching the dark head of their much-wanted baby. 'You know, I once thought I was unlucky. Now I know that I'm the luckiest woman alive!'

THE SECRET
BABY BARGAIN

MELANIE MILBURNE

Melanie Milburne says: "One of the greatest joys of being a writer is the process of falling in love with the characters and then watching as they fall in love with each other. I am an absolutely hopeless romantic. I fell in love with my husband on our second date, and we even had a secret engagement, so you see it must have been destined for me to be a Mills & Boon® author! The other great joy of being a romance writer is hearing from readers. You can hear all about the other things I do when I'm not writing, and even drop me a line, at: www.melaniemilburne.com.au."

Don't miss *The Mélendez Forgotten Marriage*, the exciting new novel by Melanie Milburne available from Mills & Boon® Modern™ romance in July 2010

To Mal and Val Innes. Mal, I owe you so much for changing my life. You not only taught me to swim, you taught me how to overcome some of life's biggest hurdles. And Val, it's true what they say about the wonderful woman behind the successful man, except you are not behind him but right beside him.
Love you both.

CHAPTER ONE

ASHLEIGH knew something was wrong as soon as she entered her parents' house on Friday evening after work.

'Mum?' She dropped her bag to the floor, her gaze sweeping the hall for her three-, nearly four-year-old son before turning back to her mother's agitated expression. 'What's going on? Where's Lachlan?'

Gwen Forrester twisted her hands together, her usually cheerful features visibly contorted with strain. 'Darling…' She gave a quick nervous swallow. 'Lachlan is fine… Your father took him fishing a couple of hours ago.'

Ashleigh's frown deepened. 'Then what on earth is the matter? You look as if you've just seen a ghost.'

'I don't quite know how to tell you this…' Gwen took her daughter's hands in hers and gave them a gentle squeeze.

Ashleigh felt her heart begin to thud with alarm. The last time she'd seen her mother this upset had been when she'd returned from London to deliver her bombshell news.

Her heart gave another sickening thump and her breathing came to a stumbling halt. Surely this wasn't about Jake Marriott? Not after all this time… It had been years…four and a half years…

'Mum, come on, you're really freaking me out. Whatever's the matter with you?'

'Ashleigh…he's back.'

Ashleigh felt the cold stream of icy dread begin to flow through her veins, her limbs suddenly freezing and her stomach folding over in panic.

'He called in a short while ago,' Gwen said, her soft blue eyes communicating her concern.

'What?' Ashleigh finally found her voice. *'Here? In person?'*

'Don't worry.' Gwen gave her daughter's hands another reassuring squeeze. 'Lachlan had already left with your father. He didn't see him.'

'But what about the photos?' Ashleigh's stomach gave another savage twist when she thought of the virtual gallery of photographs her parents had set up in the lounge room, each and every one of them documenting their young grandson's life to date. Then, as another thought hit her like a sledgehammer, she gasped, 'Oh, my God, what about his toys?'

'He didn't see anything. I didn't let Jake past the hallway and I'd already done a clean-up after your father left with Lachlan.'

'Thank God…' She slipped out of her mother's hold and sank to the telephone table chair, putting her head in her hands in an attempt to collect her spinning thoughts.

Jake was back!

Four and a half lonely heartbreaking years and he was back in Australia.

Here.

In Sydney.

She lifted her head from her hands and faced her mother once more. 'What did he want?'

'He wants to see you,' Gwen said. 'He wouldn't take no for an answer.'

So that much hadn't changed, she thought cynically. Jake Marriott was a man well used to getting his way and was often unashamedly ruthless in going about it.

'I can't see him.' She sprang to her feet in agitation and began to pace the hall. 'I just can't.'

'Darling…' Her mother's tone held a touch of gentle but unmistakable reproach. 'You really should have told him about Lachlan by now. He has a right to know he fathered a child.'

'He has no right!' Ashleigh turned on her mother in sudden anger. 'He never wanted a child. He made that clear from the word go. No marriage—no kids. That was the deal.'

'All the same, he still should have been informed.'

Ashleigh drew in a scalding breath as the pain of the past assaulted her afresh. 'You don't get it, do you, Mum? Even after all these years you still want to make him out to be the good guy.' She gave her mother an embittered glance and continued, 'Well, for your information, if I had told Jake I was pregnant he would've steamrollered me into having a termination. I just know he would've insisted on it.'

'That choice would have been yours, surely?' Gwen offered, her expression still clouded with motherly concern. 'He could hardly have forced you into it.'

'I was barely twenty years old!' Ashleigh said, perilously close to tears. 'I was living overseas with a man nine years older than me, for whom I would have done anything. If he had told me to jump off the Tower of London I probably would have done it.' She let out a ragged breath. 'I loved him so much…'

Gwen sighed as she took her daughter in her arms, one of her hands stroking the silky ash-blonde head as she had done for almost all of Ashleigh's twenty-four years.

'Oh, Mum…' Ashleigh choked on a sob as she lifted her head. 'What am I going to do?'

Gwen put her from her gently but firmly, her inbuilt pragmatism yet again coming to the fore. 'You will see him because, if nothing else, you owe him that. He mentioned his father has recently passed away. I suppose that's why he's returned to Sydney, to put his father's affairs in order.'

Ashleigh's brow creased in a puzzled little frown as she followed her mother into the kitchen. When she'd asked Jake about his family in the past he'd told her that both his parents were dead. During the time they'd been together he had rarely spoken of his childhood and had deliberately shied away from the topic whenever she'd probed him. She'd put it down to the grief he must have felt at losing both his parents so young.

Why had he lied to her?

'Did he say where he was staying?' she asked as she dragged out one of the breakfast bar stools in the kitchen and sat down.

Gwen busied herself with filling the kettle as she answered. 'At a hotel at the moment, but I got the impression he was moving somewhere here on the North Shore.'

She stared at her mother in shock. 'That close?'

'I'm afraid so,' Gwen said. 'You're going to have a hard time keeping Lachlan's existence a secret if he ends up living in a neighbouring suburb.'

Ashleigh didn't answer but her expression communicated her worry.

'You really have no choice but to see him and get it over with,' Gwen said as she handed her a cup. 'Anyway, for all you know he might have changed.'

Ashleigh bit back a snort of cynicism. 'I don't think people like Jake Marriott ever change. It's not in their nature.'

'You know you can be pretty stubborn yourself at times, Ashleigh,' her mother chided. 'I know you've needed to be strong to be a single mother, but sometimes I think you chop off your nose to spite your face. You should have been well and truly married by now. I don't know why poor Howard puts up with it, really I don't.'

Ashleigh rolled her eyes, gearing herself up for one of her mother's lectures on why she should push the wedding forward a few months. Howard Caule had made it more than clear that he wanted to bring up Lachlan as his own, but every time he'd tried to set a closer date for their wedding she'd baulked. She still wasn't entirely sure why.

'You do love him, don't you, Ashleigh?'

'Who?' She looked at her mother blankly.

'Howard,' Gwen said, her expression shadowed with a little frown. 'Who else?'

Ashleigh wasn't sure how to answer.

She cared for Howard, very deeply, in fact. He'd been a wonderful friend to her—standing by her while she got back on her feet, offering her a part-time position as a buyer for his small chain of antique stores. But as for love... Well, she didn't really trust such volatile feelings any more. It was much safer for her to care for people in an affectionate, friendly but slightly distant manner.

'Howard understands I'm not quite ready for marriage,' she said. 'Anyway, he knows I want to wait until Lachlan settles into his first year at school before I disrupt his life with any further changes to his routine.'

'Are you sleeping with him?'

'Mum!' Ashleigh's face flamed with heated colour.

Gwen folded her arms across her chest. 'You've known Howard for over three years. How long did you know Jake before you went to bed with him?'

Ashleigh refused to answer; instead she sent her mother a glowering look.

'Three days, wasn't it?' Gwen asked, ignoring her daughter's fiery glare.

'I've learnt my lesson since then,' Ashleigh bit out.

'Darling, I'm not lecturing you on what's right and wrong.' She gave a deep and expressive sigh. 'I just think you might be better able to handle seeing Jake again if things were a little more permanent in your relationship with Howard. I don't want to see you hurt all over again.'

'I won't allow Jake to hurt me again,' Ashleigh said with much more confidence than she had any hope of feeling. 'I will see him but that's all. I can't possibly tell him about Lachlan.'

'But surely Lachlan has the right to meet his father at some point? If Jake stays in Sydney for any length of time you will have no choice but to tell him of his son's existence. Imagine what he would think if he were to find out some other way.'

'I hate to disillusion you, Mum, but this is one thing Jake will never budge on. He would be absolutely furious to find out he had a son. I just know it. It was one of the things we argued about the most.' She bit her lip as the memory of their bitter parting scored her brutally, before she continued. 'He would be so angry…so terribly angry…'

Gwen reached into her pocket and handed Ashleigh a card. 'He left this card so you can contact him. He's staying at a hotel in the city. He apparently wants some work done on his father's house before he moves in. I think it would be wise to see him on neutral territory.'

Ashleigh looked down at the card in her hand, her stomach clenching painfully as she saw his name printed there in silver writing.

Jake Marriott CEO Marriott Architecture.

She lifted her gaze back to her mother, resignation heavy in her tone. 'Will you and Dad be all right with minding Lachlan if I go now?'

Gwen gave her a soft smile. 'That's my girl. Go and get it over with, then you can get on with your life knowing you did the right thing in the end.'

Ashleigh stood outside the plush city hotel half an hour later and wondered if she was even in her right mind, let alone doing the right thing. She hadn't rung the mobile number printed on Jake's business card to inform him of her intention to see him. She told herself it was because she didn't want him to have the advantage of preparing himself for her arrival, but deep down she knew it had more to do with her own cowardice.

In the end she had to wait for him, because the reception desk attendant refused to give Jake's room number without authorisation from him first.

She decided against sitting on one of the comfortable-looking leather sofas in the piano lounge area and took a stool at the bar instead, perching on the edge of it with a glass of soda water in her hand, which she knew she'd never be able to swallow past the lump of dread blocking her throat.

As if she could sense his arrival, she found her gaze tracking towards the bank of lifts, his tall unmistakable figure stepping out of the far right one, every scrap of air going out of her lungs as he came into full view.

She knew she was staring at him but just couldn't help it. In four and a half years he had not changed other than to look even more devastatingly handsome.

His imposing height gave him a proud, almost aristocratic bearing and his long lean limbs displayed the physical evidence of his continued passion for endurance sports. His clothes hung on his frame with lazy grace; he had never been the designer type but whatever he wore managed to look top of the range regardless. His wavy black hair was neither long nor short but brushed back in a careless manner which could have indicated the recent use of a hairbrush; however she thought it was more likely to have been the rake of his long tanned fingers that had achieved that just-out-of-bed look.

She was surprised at how painful it was to look at him again.

She'd known every nuance of his face, her fingers had traced over every hard contour of his body, her gentle touch lingering over the inch-long scar above his right eyebrow, her lips kissing him in every intimate place, and yet as he strode towards her she felt as if she had never known him at all.

He had simply not allowed her to.

'Hello, Ashleigh.'

Ashleigh had trouble disguising her reaction to his deep voice, the smooth velvet tones with just a hint of an English accent woven through it. How she had longed to hear it over the years!

'Hello.' She met his dark eyes briefly, hoping he wouldn't see the guilt reflected in hers at the thought of what she had kept hidden from him for all this time.

'You're looking well,' Jake said, his gaze running over her in a sweeping but all-encompassing glance. 'Have you put on weight?'

Ashleigh pursed her lips for a moment before responding with a touch of tartness. 'I see your idea of what constitutes a compliment is still rather twisted.'

One eyebrow rose and his mouth lifted in a small mocking smile. 'I see you're still as touchy as ever.' His eyes dipped to her breasts for a moment before returning slowly to hers. 'I think it suits you. You were always so bone-thin.'

'It must have been the stress of living with you,' she shot back before she could stop herself, reaching for her drink with an unsteady hand.

A tight little silence fell in the space between them.

Ashleigh felt like kicking herself for betraying her bitterness so unguardedly. She stared at a floating ice cube in her glass, wishing she was able to see Jake without it doing permanent damage to her emotional well-being.

'You're probably right,' Jake said, a tiny frown settling between his brows and, as he took the stool beside her, lifted his hand to get the barman's attention.

Ashleigh swivelled on her stool to stare at him. Was that regret she could hear in his tone?

She waited until he'd given the barman his order and his drink had arrived before speaking again.

'My mother told me why you're here.'

His gaze met hers but he didn't answer. Something indefinable flickered in the depths of his coal-black eyes before he turned back to his drink and took a deep draught.

Ashleigh watched the up and down movement of his throat as he swallowed. He was sitting so close she could touch him but it felt as if there was an invisible wall around him.

'Why did you tell me when we met that both your parents were dead?' she asked when she could stand the silence no longer.

'It seemed the easiest thing to say at the time.'

'Yes, well, lying was always something that came very naturally to you,' she bit out resentfully.

He turned to look at her, his darker-than-night eyes holding hers. 'It might surprise you to hear this, but I didn't like lying to you, Ashleigh. I just thought it was less complicated than explaining everything.'

Ashleigh stared at him as he took another sip of his drink, her heart feeling too tight, as if the space allocated for it had suddenly been drastically reduced. What did he mean—'explain everything'?

She let another silence pass before she asked, 'When did you arrive?'

'A couple of weeks ago. I thought I'd wait until after the funeral to see if he left me anything in his will.' He drained his glass and set it back down with a nerve-jangling crack on the bar in front of him.

There was a trace of something in his voice that suggested he hadn't been all that certain of his father's intentions regarding his estate. Ashleigh was surprised at how tempted she was to reach out and touch him, to offer him some sort of comfort for what he was going through. She had to hold on to her glass with both hands to stop herself from doing so, knowing he wouldn't welcome it in the bitter context of their past relationship.

'And did he?' She met his eyes once more. 'Leave you anything?'

A cynical half smile twisted his mouth as his eyes meshed with hers. 'He left me everything he didn't want for himself.'

She had to look away from the burning heat of his eyes. She stared down at the slice of lemon in her glass. 'It must be very hard for you…just now.'

Jake gave an inward grimace as he watched her toy with her straw, her small neat fingers demonstrating her unease in his company.

The hardest thing he'd ever had to do was to look her up that afternoon. His pride, his damned pride, had insisted he was a fool for doing so, but in the end he'd overridden it for just one look at her.

When he'd seen her mother at the house he'd considered waiting for however long it took for Ashleigh to return, but sensing Mrs Forrester's discomfiture had reluctantly left. He hadn't been entirely sure she would have even told Ashleigh of his call. He could hardly blame her, of course. No doubt Ashleigh had told her family what a pig-headed selfish bastard he'd been to her all the time they'd been together.

But he *had* to see her.

He had to see her to remind himself of what he'd thrown away.

'Yes…it's not been easy,' he admitted, staring into his empty glass.

He felt her shift beside him and had to stop himself from turning to her and hauling her into his arms.

She looked fantastic.

She'd grown into her body in a way few women these days did. Her figure had pleased him no end in the past, but now it was riper, more womanly, her softer curves making him ache to mould her to him as he had done in the past.

If only they had just met now, without the spectre of their previous relationship dividing them. But it wasn't *their* past that had divided them—it had been his. And it was only now that he was finally coming to terms with it.

'Your mother looks the same,' he said, sending her another quick glance, taking in her ringless fingers with immeasurable relief.

'Yes…'

'How is your father?'

'Retired now,' Ashleigh answered. 'Enjoying being able to play with…er…'

Jake swung his gaze back to hers at her sudden vocal stall. 'Golf?'

Ashleigh clutched at the sudden lifeline with relief. 'Yes… golf. He plays a lot of golf.'

'I always liked your dad,' he said, looking back at his empty glass again.

The undisguised warmth in his statement moved her very deeply. Ashleigh's family had come over to London for Christmas the second year she'd been living with Jake, and she had watched how Jake had done his best to fit in with her family. When he hadn't been hiding away at work he'd spent a bit of time with her father, choosing his company instead of the boisterous and giggling presence of her younger sisters, Mia and Ellie, and her trying-too-hard mother. She had been touched by his effort to include himself in her family's activities, his tall, somewhat aloof, presence often seeming out of place and awkward amidst the rough and tumble of the family interactions that she had always taken for granted.

'How are your sisters?' he asked after another little pause.

A small smile of pride flickered on her mouth. 'Mia is trying her best to get into acting, with some limited success.

She was a pot plant in a musical a month ago; we were all incredibly proud of her. And Ellie… Well, you know Ellie.' Her expression softened at the thought of her adopted youngest sister. 'She is still the world's biggest champion for the underdog. She works part-time in a café and spends every other available minute at a dogs' home as a volunteer.'

'And what about you?' Jake asked, looking at her intently.

'Me?' She gave him a startled look, her pulses racing at the intensity of his dark eyes as they rested on her face. His smile had softened his normally harsh features, the simple upward movement of his lips unleashing a flood of memories about how that mouth had felt on hers…

'Yes, you,' he said. 'What are you doing with yourself these days?'

'I…' She swallowed and tried to appear unfazed by his question. 'Not much.' She twirled her straw a couple of times and continued. 'I work as a buyer for an antique dealer.' She pushed her glass away and met his eyes again. 'Howard Caule Antiques.'

He gestured to the barman to refresh their drinks, taking his time to turn back to her to respond. 'I've heard of him.' He picked up his glass as soon as it was placed in front of him. 'What's he like to work for?'

For some reason Ashleigh found it difficult to meet his eyes with any equanimity. She moistened her lips, her stomach doing a funny little somersault when she saw the way his eyes followed the nervous movement of her tongue.

'He's…he's nice.'

Damn it! She chided herself as she saw the way Jake's lip instantly curled. Why couldn't she have thought of a better adjective than that?

'A nice guy, huh?'

She had to look away. 'Yes. He's also one of my closest friends.'

'Are you sleeping with him?'

Her eyes flew back to his, her cheeks flaming for the second time that day. 'That's absolutely no business of yours.'

He didn't respond immediately, which made her tension go up another excruciating notch. She watched him as he surveyed her with those dark unreadable eyes, every nerve in her body jumping in sharp awareness at his proximity.

She could even *smell* him.

Her nostrils flared to take in more of that evocative scent, the combination of full-blooded-late-in-the-day active male and his particular choice of aftershave that had always reminded her of sun-warmed lemons and exotic spices.

'My my my, you are touchy, aren't you?' he asked, the mocking smile still in place.

She set her mouth and turned to stare at the full glass in front of her, wishing herself a million miles away.

She couldn't do this.

She couldn't be calm and cool in Jake Marriott's presence. He unsettled her in every way possible.

'I'm not being touchy.' Her tone was brittle and on edge. 'I just don't see what my private life has to do with you...*now*.'

His continued silence drew her gaze back as if he'd pulled it towards him with invisible strings.

'Ashleigh...' He reached out to graze her cheek with the back of his knuckles in a touch so gentle she felt a great wave of emotion swamp her for what they'd had and subsequently lost.

She fought her feelings down with an effort, her teeth tearing at the inside of her mouth as she held his unwavering gaze.

'I'd like to see you again while I'm here in Sydney,' he said, his deep voice sounding ragged and uneven. 'I'm here for a few weeks and I thought we could—' he deliberately paused over the words '—catch up.'

Ashleigh inwardly seethed. She could just imagine what he meant by catching up; a bit of casual sex to fill in the time before he left the country to go back to whoever was waiting for him back in London.

'I can't see you.'

His eyes hardened momentarily and his hand fell away. 'Why not?'

She bit her lip, hunting her brain for the right words to describe her relationship with Howard.

'Is there someone else?' he asked before she could respond, his eyes dipping to her bare fingers once more.

She drew in a tight breath. 'Yes…yes there is.'

'You're not wearing a ring.'

She gave him an ironic look and clipped back, 'I lived and slept with you for two whole years without needing one.'

Jake shifted slightly as he considered her pert response. Her cheeks were bright with colour, her eyes flashing him a warning he had no intention of heeding.

He knew it bordered on the arrogant to assume that no one had taken his place after four and a half years, but he'd hoped for it all the same. His own copybook wasn't too pristine, of course; he'd replaced her numerous times, but not one of his subsequent lovers had affected him the way Ashleigh had, and, God help him, still did.

'What would you say if I told you I've had a rethink of a few of my old standpoints?' he asked. 'That I'd changed?'

Ashleigh got to her feet and, rummaging in her purse, placed some money on the counter for her drink, her eyes when they returned to his like twin points of angry blue flame.

'I'd say you were four and a half years too late, Jake Marriott.' She hoisted her bag back on her shoulder. 'I have to go. I have someone waiting for me.'

She turned to leave but one of his hands came down on

her wrist and turned her round to face him. She felt the velvet-covered steel bracelet of his fingers and suppressed an inward shiver of reaction at feeling his warm flesh on hers once more.

'Let me go, Jake.' Her voice came out husky instead of determined, making her hate him for affecting her so.

He rose to his full height, his body within a whisper of hers. She felt as if she couldn't breathe, for if she so much as drew in one small breath her chest would expand and bring her breasts into contact with the hard wall of his chest. Dark eyes locked with blue in a battle she knew she was never going to win, but she had to fight regardless.

'I can't see you, Jake,' she said in a tight voice. 'I am engaged to be married.' She took another shaky breath and added, 'To my boss, Howard Caule.'

She saw the sudden flare of heat in his eyes at the same time the pressure of his fingers subtly increased about her wrist.

'You're not married yet,' he said, before dropping her wrist and stepping back from her.

Ashleigh wasn't sure if his statement was a threat or an observation. She didn't stay around to find out. Instead, she turned on her heel and stalked out of the bar with long purposeful strides that she hoped gave no hint of her inner distress.

Jake watched her go, his chest feeling as if some giant hand had just plunged between his ribs and wrenched out his heart and slapped it down on the bar next to the ten dollar note she'd placed beside her untouched drink…

CHAPTER TWO

ASHLEIGH drove back to her parents' house with her bottom lip between her teeth for the entire journey.

It had *hurt* to see Jake again.

It had *hurt* her to hear his voice, to see his hands grip his glass—the hands that had once caressed her and with his very male body brought her to the highest pinnacle of human pleasure.

It had *hurt* to see his mouth tilt in a smile—the mouth that had kissed her all over but had never once spoken of his love.

Damn it! It had *hurt* to turn him down, but what other choice did she have? She could hardly pick up where they'd left off. How could she, with the secret of Lachlan's existence lying between them? Jake had made it clear he never wanted to have children. She could hardly tap him on the shoulder and announce, *By the way, here is your son. Don't you think he looks a bit like you?*

'Mummee!' Lachlan rushed towards her as soon as she opened the door, throwing his little arms around her middle and squeezing tightly.

'Hey, why aren't you in bed?' She pretended to frown down at him.

His chocolate-brown eyes twinkled as he looked up at her.

'Grandad promised me I could show you what we caught first.'

She looked up at her father, who had followed his young grandson out into the hall. 'Hi, Dad. Good day at the bay?'

Heath Forrester grinned. 'You should have seen the ones we let get away.'

Ashleigh smiled and stood on tiptoe to plant a soft kiss on his raspy cheek. 'Thanks,' she said, her one word speaking a hundred for her.

Heath turned to Lachlan. 'Go and get our bounty out of the fridge while I have a quick word with your mum.'

Lachlan raced off, the sound of his footsteps echoing down the hall as Heath turned to his eldest daughter. 'How was Jake?'

'He was…' she let out a little betraying sigh '…Jake.'

'What did he want?'

'I got the distinct impression he wanted to resume our past relationship—temporarily.'

Her father's bushy brows rose slightly. 'Same old Jake then?'

She gave him a world-weary sigh. 'Same old Jake.'

'You didn't tell him about Lachlan?'

Ashleigh hunted her father's expression for the reproach she privately dreaded, but found none and was immensely grateful for it.

'No…' She inspected her hands for a moment. 'No, I didn't.'

'Howard called while you were out.' Heath changed the subject tactfully. 'He said something about taking you out to dinner. I told him you'd call but if you want me to put him off I can always—'

Ashleigh forced her mouth into a smile and tucked her arm through one of his. 'Why don't we go and look at that fish first?'

'What a good idea,' he said and led her towards the kitchen.

An hour later Lachlan was fast asleep upstairs and Ashleigh made her way downstairs again, only to be halted by her

sister Mia who had not long come in from an actors and per-
formers' workshop.

'Is it true?' Mia ushered her into the study, out of the hearing of the rest of the Forrester family. 'Is Jake really back in
Sydney?'

Ashleigh gave a single nod. 'Yes…he's back.'

Mia let out a very unladylike phrase. 'Have you told him
about Lachlan?' she asked.

Ashleigh shook her head. 'No…'

Mia's eyes widened. 'What are you doing? Of course he
has to know now that he's back.'

'Listen, Mia. I've already had this sort of lecture from
Mum, so I don't need another one from you.'

Mia held up her hands in a gesture of surrender. 'Hey,
don't get all shirty with me, but have you actually listened to
that kid of yours lately? All he ever talks about is dad stuff.'

Ashleigh frowned. 'What do you mean?'

Mia gave her a sobering look. 'I read him a story the other
night when you were out with Howard. You know, the one
about the elephant with the broken trunk who was looking
for someone to fix it? Lachlan kept on and on about how if
he could find his real dad he was sure he would be able to fix
everything. How cute, but how sad, is that?'

Ashleigh turned away, her hands clenching in tension. 'I
can't deal with this right now. I have enough to think about
without you adding to it.'

'Come on, Ash,' Mia said. 'What's to think about? Jake
has come home to Sydney and he should be told the truth.
It's not like you can hide it from him. One close look at that
kid and he's going to see it for himself.'

Ashleigh felt the full force of her sister's words like a blow
to her mid-section. Lachlan was the spitting image of his
father. His darker-than-night eyes, his long rangy limbs, his
black hair that refused to stay in place, his temper that could

rise and fall with the weight of a timely smile or gentle caress…

The doorbell sounded and Ashleigh turned and walked down the hall to answer it rather than continue the conversation with her sister.

'Ashleigh,' Howard Caule greeted her warmly, pressing a quick kiss to her cheek as he came in. 'How's my girl?' He caught sight of Mia hovering. 'Hi, Mia, how are the auditions for the toilet paper advertisement going?'

'Great, I'm going to wipe the floor with the competition,' Mia answered with an insincere smile and a roll of her eyes before she walked away.

Ashleigh dampened down her annoyance at her sister's behaviour towards her fiancé, knowing it would be pointless to try and defend him. Mia and Ellie had never taken to him no matter how many times she highlighted his good points. It caused her a great deal of pain but there was nothing she could do about it. Howard was reliable and safe and more or less wanted the same things in life that she did. Her family would just have to get used to the idea of him being a permanent fixture in her life. Lachlan liked him and as far as she was concerned that counted for more than anything.

Once Mia had gone she closed the front door and leant back against it, her eyes going to Howard's. 'We have to talk.'

'Let's do it over dinner,' he suggested. Then, taking something out of his pocket, he added, 'Is Lachlan still awake? I brought him a little present.'

Ashleigh took the toy car he held out to her, her expression softening with gratitude. 'He's asleep but I'll leave it on his bedside table for him. Thank you; you're so good to him.'

'He's a good kid, Ashleigh,' he said. 'I can't wait until we're finally married so I can be a real father to him.'

She gave him a weak smile. 'I'll just tell my folks we're leaving.'

'I'll go and start the car,' he offered helpfully and bounded back out the front door.

Ashleigh spoke briefly with her parents before joining Howard in his car, all the time trying to think of a way to bring up the subject of Jake Marriott.

She had told Howard the barest details of her affair with Lachlan's father, preferring to keep that part of her life separate and distant from the here and now. She hadn't even once mentioned Jake's name. Howard hadn't pressed her, and in a way that was why she valued his friendship so much. He seemed to sense her pain in speaking of the past and always kept things on an upbeat keel to lift her spirits.

Howard was so different from Jake, and not just physically, although those differences were as marked as could ever be. Howard had the typically pale freckled skin that was common to most redheads, his height average and his figure tending towards stocky.

Jake's darkly handsome features combined with his imposing height and naturally athletic build were made all the more commanding by his somewhat aloof and brooding personality.

Howard, on the other hand, was uncomplicated. Mia and Ellie described him as boring but Ashleigh preferred to think of him as predictable.

She *liked* predictable.

She could handle predictable.

She liked knowing what to expect each day when she turned up to work. Howard was always cheerful and positive, nothing was too much trouble and even if it was he didn't let on but simply got on with the task without complaining.

She wished she was in love with him.

Truly in love.

He was worthy of so much more than she could give him but her experience with Jake had taught her the danger of loving too much and too deeply.

'You're very quiet.' Howard glanced her way as he pulled up at a set of traffic lights.

'Sorry…' She shifted her mouth into a semblance of a smile. 'I've got a lot on my mind.'

He reached over and patted her hand, his freckled fingers cool, nothing like the scorching heat of Jake's when he'd touched her earlier.

Her wrist still felt as if it had been burnt. She looked down at it to see if there were any marks but her creamy skin was surprisingly unblemished.

What a pity her heart hadn't been as lucky.

The restaurant he'd chosen was heavily booked and even though Howard had made a reservation they still had to wait for over half an hour for their table.

As Ashleigh sat with him at the bar she couldn't help thinking how different it would have been if it had been Jake with her. There was no way he would have sat patiently waiting for a table he'd pre-booked. He would have demanded the service he was paying for and, what was more, he would have got it.

'What did you want to talk to me about?' Howard asked as he reached for his mineral water.

Ashleigh took a steadying breath and met his light blue eyes. 'I met with Lachlan's father today.'

He gave her a worried look. 'Does he want to see him?'

'I didn't get around to telling him about Lachlan,' she answered. 'We talked about…other things.'

Howard put his glass down. 'You mean he still doesn't know anything about him? Nothing at all?'

'I know it seems wrong not to tell him, but at the time it was the right decision…and now…well…'

'What about now?' Howard asked. 'Shouldn't he be told at some point?'

Ashleigh had thought of nothing else, especially after what Mia had told her about Lachlan. It seemed wrong that her tiny son could never openly acknowledge his father. And yet after seeing Jake again it brought it home to her just what he had missed in knowing nothing of his son's existence. He had not been there for any of the milestones of Lachlan's life. His first smile, his first words and his very first 'I love you'. Jake had missed out on so much and those years could never be returned to him. But she had done what she had thought was right… She still thought it was right. But somehow…

'Lachlan's father hasn't changed a bit.' She gave a deep regretful sigh. 'I was young, far too young to even be in a relationship let alone with someone as intense as him. I lost myself when I was with him. I forgot how to stand up for myself, for what I believed in. I let him take control… It was a mistake… Our relationship was a mistake.'

'Did you tell him about us?' he asked. 'That we're engaged to be married?'

'Yes…'

He frowned as he looked at her bare hands. 'I wish you'd wear my mother's ring. I know you don't like the design but we could get it altered.'

Ashleigh wished she liked it, too. She wished she liked his mother as well, but nothing in life was perfect and she had learned the hard way to make the most of what was on offer and get on with it.

'I'll think about it,' she said. 'Anyway, it's only a symbol. It means nothing.' The words were not her own but some that Jake had used in the past but she didn't think Howard would appreciate that little detail.

'Come on, let's have dinner and forget all about Lachlan's

father for the rest of tonight,' Howard said as the waiter indicated for them to follow him to their table.

Ashleigh gave him a wan smile as she made her way with him to their seats, but even hours later when she was lying in her bed, willing herself to sleep, she still had not been able to drive all thought of Jake from her mind.

He was there.

Permanently.

His dark disturbing presence reminding her of all that had brought them together and what, in the end, had torn them apart.

Ashleigh had not long arrived at the main outlet of Howard Caule Antiques in Woollahra the next morning when Howard rushed towards her excitedly.

'Ashleigh, I have the most exciting news.'

'What?' She put her bag and sunglasses on the walnut desk before tilting her cheek for his customary kiss. 'Let me guess…you've won the lottery?'

His light blue eyes positively gleamed with excitement. 'No, but it sure feels like it. I have just spoken to a man who has recently inherited a veritable warehouse full of antiques. He wants to sell them all—to us! Can you believe it?' He rubbed his hands together in glee. 'Some of the stuff is priceless, Ashleigh. And he wants us to have it all and he's not even worried about how much we are prepared to pay for it.'

Ashleigh gave a small frown. 'There must be some sort of catch. Why would anyone sell off such valuable pieces to one dealer when he could play the market a bit and get top dollar?'

Howard shrugged one shoulder. 'I don't know, but who cares? You know how worried I've been about how things have been a bit tight lately and this is just the sort of boost I need right now.' He reached for a sheet of paper on his desk and handed it to her. 'I've made an appointment for you to meet with him later this morning at this address.'

'But why me?' she asked, glancing down at the paper, her heart missing a beat when she saw the name printed there.

Jake Marriott.

She lifted her tortured gaze to Howard's blissful one. 'I—I can't do this.' The paper crinkled in her tightening fingers.

'What are you doing?' Howard plucked the crumpled paper out of her hand and began straightening it as if it were a piece of priceless parchment. 'He particularly asked for you,' he said. 'He said he knew your family. I checked him out on a few details. I wouldn't allow you to deal with anyone who I thought was unsafe. He knew both your parents' names and—'

'That's because he's Lachlan's father,' she said bluntly.

Howard's eyes bulged. *'Jake Marriott is Lachlan's father?'*

She gave a single nod, her lips tightly compressed.

'Jake Marriott?' His throat convulsed. 'Jake Marriott as in the billionaire architect who's designed some of the most prestigious buildings around the globe?'

'That's the one,' she said.

'Oh, no…' Howard flopped into the nearest chair, the freckles on his face standing out against the pallor of his shocked face.

Ashleigh gnawed her bottom lip, fear turning her insides to liquid.

Howard sprang back to his feet. 'Well, for one thing, you can't possibly tell him about Lachlan,' he insisted, 'or at least not right now. If you do he'll withdraw the offer. I need this deal, Ashleigh.'

'I'll have to tell him sometime…' She let out a painful breath. 'Mia told me Lachlan has been asking about his father. He must have heard the other kids at crèche talking about their dads. I knew he would eventually want to know but I didn't expect it to be this soon.'

'Let's get married as quickly as possible,' he said, taking

both her hands in his. 'That way Lachlan can start calling me his dad.'

She eased herself out of his hold, suddenly unable to maintain eye contact. 'I don't want to get married yet. I'm not ready.'

'Are you ever going to be ready?' His tone held a trace of bitterness she'd never heard in it before.

She turned back to him, her expression wavering with uncertainty. 'It's such a big step. We haven't even…you know…' Her hands fluttered back to her sides, her face hot with embarrassment.

'I told you I don't believe in sex before marriage,' he said. 'I know it's old-fashioned, but my faith is important to me and I think it's a small sacrifice to make to show my loyalty to you and to God.'

Ashleigh couldn't help wondering what Jake would think of Howard's moral uprightness. Jake hadn't even believed in the sanctity of marriage, much less waiting a decent period before committing himself to a physical relationship. He'd had her in his bed within three days of meeting her and if it hadn't been for the prod of her conscience at the time, she knew he would have succeeded on the very first.

She was trapped by circumstances beyond her control and it terrified her. No matter how much she wished her past would go away and never come back she had a permanent living reminder in her little son. Even now Lachlan was a miniature of his biological father and even if a hundred Howards offered to step into his place no one could ever be the man Lachlan most needed.

Besides, she'd seen this played out before in her adopted sister Ellie's life. Ellie pretended to be unconcerned about who her biological parents were but Ashleigh knew how she secretly longed to find out why she had been relinquished when only a few days old. It didn't matter how loving her adoptive parents and she and Mia as her sisters were, Ellie was like a lost soul looking for a connection she both dreaded and desired.

She took the paper out of Howard's hand with dogged resignation. 'All right, I'll do it. I'll buy the goods from him and keep quiet, but I can't help feeling this could backfire on me.'

'Think about the money,' he said. 'This will take me to the top of the antiques market in Sydney.' He reached for the telephone. 'I have to ring my mother. This has been her dream ever since my father died.'

Ashleigh gave an inward sigh and picked up her bag and sunglasses from the desk. Jake had her in the palm of his hand and she could already feel the press of his fingers as they began to close in on her...

The drive to the address in the leafy northern suburb of Lindfield seemed all too short to Ashleigh in spite of the slow crawl of traffic on the Pacific Highway.

She kept glancing at the clock on the dashboard, the minutes ticking by, increasing her panic second by painful second.

The street she turned into as indicated on the paper Howard had given her was typical of the upper north shore, leafy private gardens shielding imposing homes, speaking quietly but unmistakably of very comfortable wealth.

She pulled up in front of the number of the house she'd been given but there was no sign of Jake. The driveway was empty, the scallop-edged blinds at the windows of the house pulled down low just like lashes over closed eyes.

The front garden was huge and looked a bit neglected, as if no one had bothered to tend it recently, the lawn still green but interspersed with dandelion heads, the soft little clouds of seeds looking as if the slightest breath of wind would disturb their spherical perfection for ever.

She walked up the pathway towards the front door, breathing in the scent of sun-warmed roses as she reached to press the tarnished brass bell.

There was no answer.

She didn't know whether to be relieved or annoyed. According to the information Howard had given her, she was to meet Jake here at eleven a.m. and here it was twelve minutes past and no sign of him.

Typical, she thought as she stepped away from the door. When had Jake ever been the punctual type?

She made her way around to the back of the house, curiosity finally getting the better of her. She wondered if this was the house where he had grown up. He had always been so vague about his childhood but she seemed to remember him mentioning a big garden with an elm tree in the backyard that he used to sometimes climb.

She found it along the tall back fence, its craggy limbs spreading long fingers of shade all over the rear corner of the massive garden. She stepped beneath its dappled shade and looked upwards, trying to picture Jake as a young child scrambling up those ancient limbs to get to the top. He wasn't the bottom branches type, a quality she could already see developing in her little son.

'I used to have a tree-house way up there,' Jake's deep voice said from just behind her.

Ashleigh spun around so quickly she felt light-headed, one of her hands going over her heart where she could feel it leaping towards her throat in shock. 'Y-you scared me!'

He gave her one of his lazy half smiles. 'Did I?'

He didn't seem too bothered about it, she noted with considerable resentment. His expression held a faint trace of amusement as his eyes took in her flustered form.

'You're late,' she said and stepped out of the intimacy of the overhanging branches to the brighter sunlight near a bed of blood-red roses.

'I know,' he answered without apology. 'I had a few things to see to first.'

She tightened her lips and folded her arms across her chest crossly. 'I suppose you think I've got nothing better to do all day than hang around waiting for you to show up. Why didn't you tell me yesterday about this arrangement?'

He joined her next to the roses, stopping for a moment to pick one perfect bloom and, holding it up to his nose, slowly drew in the fragrance.

Ashleigh found it impossible to look away.

The softness of the rose in his large, very male, hand had her instantly recalling his touch on her skin in the past, the velvet-covered steel of his fingers which could stroke like a feather in foreplay, or grasp like a vice in the throes of out of control passion.

She gave an inward shiver as his eyes moved back to meet hers.

He silently handed her the rose and, for some reason she couldn't entirely fathom at the time, she took it from him. She lowered her gaze from his and breathed in the heady scent, feeling the brush of the soft petals against her nose where his had so recently been.

'I'm glad you came,' he said after a little silence. 'I've always wanted you to see where I grew up.'

Ashleigh looked up at him, the rose still in her hand. 'Why?'

He shifted his gaze from hers and sent it to sweep across the garden before turning to look at the house. She watched the movement of his dark unfathomable eyes and couldn't help feeling intrigued by his sudden need to show her the previously private details of his childhood.

It didn't make any sense.

Why now?

Why had it taken him so long to finally reveal things she'd longed to know way back? She had asked him so many times for anecdotes of his childhood but he had skirted around the subject, even shutting her out for days with one of his stony silences whenever she'd prodded him too much.

His eyes came back to hers. 'I used to really hate this place.'

She felt a small frown tug at her forehead. 'Why?'

He seemed to give himself a mental shake, for he suddenly removed his line of vision from hers and began to lead the way towards the house. Ashleigh followed silently, stepping over the cracks in the pathway, wondering what had led him home if it was so painful to revisit this place.

There was so much she didn't know about Jake.

She knew how he took his tea and coffee, she knew he had a terrible sweet tooth attack at about four o'clock every afternoon, she knew he loved his back rubbed and that he had one very ticklish hip. But she didn't know what made his eyes and face become almost mask-like whenever his childhood was mentioned.

Jake unlocked the back door and, leaving Ashleigh hovering in the background, immediately began rolling up blinds and opening windows to let the stale, musty air out.

Ashleigh wasn't sure if she should offer to help or not. She was supposed to be here in a professional capacity but nothing so far in Jake's manner or mood had indicated anything at all businesslike.

'I'm sorry it's so stuffy in here,' he said, stepping past her to reach for the last blind. 'I haven't been here since…well…' He gave her a wry look. 'I haven't been here since I was about sixteen.'

She knew her face was showing every sign of her intrigue but she just couldn't help it. She looked around at the sun-room they were in, but apart from a few uncomfortable-looking chairs and a small table and a cheap self-assembly magazine rack there was nothing that she could see of any great value.

'I know what you're thinking,' he said into the awkward silence.

She looked at him without responding but her eyes obviously communicated her scepticism.

'You're thinking I've led you here on a fool's errand, aren't you?' he asked.

She drew in a small breath and scanned the room once more. 'The contents of this room would barely pay for a cup of coffee and a sandwich at a decent café.' She met his eyes challengingly. 'What's this about, Jake? Why am I here and why now?'

'Come this way.'

He led her towards a door off the sun-room which, when he opened it, showed her a long dark, almost menacing, hallway, the lurking shadows seeming to leap out from the walls to brush at the bare skin of her arms as she followed him about halfway down to a door on the left.

The door opened with a creak of a hinge that protested at the sudden movement, the inner darkness of the room spilling out towards her. Jake flicked on a light switch as she stepped into the room with him, her eyes instantly widening as she saw what was contained within.

She sucked in a breath of wonder as her nostrils filled with the scent of old cedar. The room was stacked almost to the ceiling with priceless pieces of furniture. Tables, chairs, escritoires, chaise longues and bookcases and display cabinets, their dusty shelves filled with an array of porcelain figurines which she instinctively knew were beyond her level of expertise to value with any sort of accuracy. It would take days, if not weeks, to assess the value of each and every item.

She did her best to control her breathing as she stepped towards the first piece of polished cedar, her fingers running over the delicately carved edge as if in worship.

'What do you think?' Jake asked.

She turned to look at him, her hand falling away from the priceless heirloom. 'I think you've picked the wrong person to assess the value of all of this.' She chewed her lip for a moment before adding, 'Howard would be much better able to give you the right—'

'But I want you.'

There was something in his tone that suggested to Ashleigh he wasn't just talking about the furniture.

'I'm not able to help you…' She made to brush past him, suddenly desperate to get out of this house and away from his disturbing presence.

'Wait.' His hand came down on her arm and held her still, leaving her no choice but to meet his dark brooding gaze. 'Don't go.'

She dragged in a ragged breath, her head telling her to get the hell out while she still could, but somehow her treacherous heart insisted she stay.

'Jake…' Her voice sounded as if it had come through a vacuum, it didn't sound at all like her own.

His hand cupped her cheek, his thumb moving over the curve of her lips in a caress so poignantly tender she immediately felt the springing of tears in her eyes.

She watched as his mouth came down towards hers and, in spite of her inner convictions, did absolutely nothing to stop it.

She couldn't.

Her body felt frozen in time, her lips waiting for the imprint of his after four and a half years of deprivation. Her skin begged for his touch with goose-bumps of anticipation springing out all over her, her legs weakening with need as soon as his mouth met hers.

Heat coursed through her at that first blistering touch, her lips instantly swelling under the insistent pressure of his, her mouth opening to the command of his determined tongue as it sought her inner warmth.

She felt the sag of her knees as he crushed her close to his hard frame, the ridges of his body fitting so neatly into the soft curves of hers as if made to measure.

Desire surged through her as if sent on an electric circuit from his. She felt its charge from breast to hip, her body singing with awareness as his body leapt in response against her. She felt the hardening of his growing erection, the heat and length of him a heady, intoxicating reminder of all the intimacies they had shared in the past.

Her body was no mystery to him. He had known every crease and tender fold, had explored and tasted every delicacy with relish. Her body remembered with a desperate burning plea for more. She ached for him, inside and out, her emotions caught up in a maelstrom of feeling she had no control over. It was as if the past hadn't happened; she was his just as she had been all those years ago. He had only to look at her and she would melt into his arms and become whatever he wanted her to become...

She jerked herself out of his hold with a strength she had not known she was capable of and, thankfully for her, he was totally unprepared for.

'You have no right.' She clipped the words out past stiff lips. 'I'm engaged. You have no right to touch me.'

His eyes raked her mercilessly, his expression hinting at satire. 'You gave me the right as soon as you looked at me that way.'

'What way?' She glared at him defensively. 'I did not *look* at you in any way!'

His mouth tilted in a cynical smile. 'I wonder what your fiancé would say if he saw how you just responded to me?'

Ashleigh felt as if someone had switched on a radiator behind her cheeks. Guilty colour burnt through her skin, making her feel transparent, as if he could see right through her to where she hid her innermost secrets.

She had to turn away, her back rigid with fury, as she glared at a painting on the wall in her line of vision.

'Oh, my God...' She stepped towards the portrait, her eyes growing wide with amazement, incredulity and what only could be described as gobsmacked stupefaction as re-alisation gradually dawned. Her eyes dipped to look at the signature at the bottom of the painting, even her very fin-gertips icing up with excitement as she turned around to look at him.

'Do you realise what you have here?' she asked, her tone breathless with wonder. 'That painting alone is worth thou-sands!'

He gave the painting a dismissive glance and met her eyes once more. 'You can have it,' he said. 'And everything else. There's more in the other rooms.'

She stared at him for at least five heavy heartbeats. *'What?'*

'You heard,' he said. 'I'm giving it to you to sell; every-thing in this house.'

She felt like slapping the side of her head to make sure she wasn't imagining what she'd just heard. 'What did you say?'

'I said I'm giving you the lot,' he said.

She backed away, her instincts warning her that this was not a no-strings deal. 'Oh, no.' She held up her hands as if to warn him off. 'You can't bribe me with a whole bunch of priceless heirlooms.'

'I'm not bribing you, Ashleigh,' he said in an even tone. 'I'm simply giving you a choice.'

'A choice?' She eyeballed him suspiciously. 'What sort of choice?'

His eyes gave nothing away as they held her gaze.

'I told you I wanted to see you again,' he said. 'Regularly.'

Ashleigh's heart began to gallop behind the wall of her chest. 'And I told you I can't...' She took a prickly breath.

'Howard and I…' She couldn't finish the sentence, the words sticking together in her tightened throat.

He gave her a cynical little smile that darkened his eyes even further. 'I don't think Howard Caule will protest at you spending time with me sorting this house out. In fact, I think he will send you off each day with his blessing.'

Cold fear leaked into her bloodstream and it took several precious seconds to locate her voice. 'W-what are you talking about?'

'I want you to spend the next month with me, sorting out my father's possessions.'

'I can't do that!' she squeaked in protest.

'Fine, then.' He reached for his mobile phone and began punching in some numbers. 'I'll call up another antiques dealer I know who will be more than happy to take this lot off me.' His finger was poised over the last digit as he added, 'For free.'

Ashleigh swallowed as he raised the phone to his ear.

He was giving the lot away? *For nothing?*

She couldn't allow him to do that. It wouldn't be right. The place was stacked to the rafters with priceless heirlooms. She owed Howard this deal for all he had done for her and Lachlan. She couldn't back out of it, no matter what it cost her personally.

'No!' She pulled his arm down so he couldn't continue the call. 'Wait… Let me think about this…'

He pocketed the phone. 'I'll give you thirty minutes to think it over. I should at this point make it quite clear that I'm not expecting you to sleep with me.'

She blinked at him, her tingling fingers falling away from his arm as his words sank in.

He didn't want her.

She knew she should be feeling relief but instead she felt

regret. An aching, burning regret that what they'd had before was now gone…

He continued in an even tone. 'We parted on such bitter terms four and a half years ago. This is a way for both of us to get some much needed closure.'

'But…but I don't need closure,' she insisted. 'I'm well and truly over you.'

He held her defiant look with enviable ease while her pulse leapt beneath her skin as she stood uncertainly before him.

'But I do,' he said.

Her mouth opened and closed but no sound came out.

Jake stepped back towards the door, holding it open as he addressed her in a coolly detached tone. 'I will leave you to make your initial assessment in private. When the thirty minutes are up I'll be back for your decision.'

Ashleigh stared at the back of the door once he'd closed it behind him, the echo of its lock clicking into place ringing in her ears for endless minutes.

A month!

A month in Jake's presence, sorting through the house he'd spent his childhood in.

She turned back around and stared at the fortune of goods in front of her, each and every one of them seeming to conceal a tale about Jake's past, their secrets locked within the walls of this old neglected house.

Why was he as good as throwing it all away? What possible reason could he have for doing so? Surely he would want to keep something back for himself? She knew he was a rich man now, but surely even very wealthy people didn't walk away from a veritable fortune?

Ashleigh sighed and turned, her eyes meeting those of the subject in the portrait on the wall. She felt a little feather of unease brush over her skin, for it seemed that every time she tried to move out of range of the oil-painted sad eyes they continued to follow her.

She gave herself a mental shake and rummaged in her bag for her digital camera. The sooner she got started the sooner she would be finished.

Her stomach gave a little flutter of nerves. There was something about this house that unsettled her and the less time she spent in it the better.

Especially with Jake here with her…

Alone…

CHAPTER THREE

ONCE she'd taken some preliminary photos Ashleigh left the overcrowded room for some much needed air and found herself wandering down the long passage, her thoughts flying off in all directions.

This was Jake's childhood home, the place where he had been raised, but for some reason it didn't seem to her to be the sort of house where a child would be particularly welcome.

This house seemed to be almost seeping with the wounds of neglect; the walls spoke of it with their faded peeling paint, the floorboards with their protesting creaks, as if her very tread had caused them discomfort as she moved across their tired surface. She could sense it in the woodwork of the furniture, the heavy layer of dust lying over every surface speaking of long-term disregard. And she could feel it in the reflection of the dust-speckled glass at the windows, the crumpled drape of the worn curtains looking as if they were doing their best to shield the house's secrets from the rest of the quiet conservative street.

Ashleigh had never considered herself a particularly intuitive person. That had been Ellie's role in the Forrester family, but somehow, being in Jake's childhood home made her realise things about him that had escaped her notice before.

He hated the darkness.

Why hadn't she ever noticed the significance of that before?

He had always been the first one to turn on the lights when they got home, insisting the blinds be pulled up even when the sunlight was too strong and disrupted the television or computer screen.

He'd hated loud music with a passion, particularly classical music. She couldn't remember a time when he hadn't come in and snapped her music off, glaring at her furiously, telling her it was too loud for the neighbours and why wasn't she being more responsible?

What did it all mean?

She opened another door off the hall and stepped inside. Some pinpricks of light were shining through the worn blinds, giving the room an eerie atmosphere, the dust motes disturbed by the movement of air as the door opened rising in front of her face like a myriad miniature apparitions.

The air was stuffy and close but she could see as she turned on the nearest light that it was some sort of study-cum-library, two banks of bookshelves lining the walls from floor to ceiling.

She moved across the old carpet to examine some of the titles, her eyes widening at the age of some of them nearest her line of vision.

Jake's father had sure known how to collect valuable items, she mused as she reached for what looked like a first edition of Keats's poems.

She put the book back amongst the others and turned to look around the rest of the room. The solid cedar desk was littered with papers as if someone working there had been interrupted and hadn't returned to put things in order. She picked up the document nearest her and found it was a financial statement from a firm of investors, the value of the portfolio making her head spin.

She heard a sound behind her and turned to see Jake standing in the frame of the door, his dark gaze trained on her.

Her time was up.

She put the paper back down on the desk, her mouth suddenly dry and uncooperative when there was so much she wanted to ask him before she committed herself to the task he had assigned her.

'Jake…I…I don't know what to say.' She waved a weak hand to encompass the contents of the room, the house and the sense of unease she'd felt as she'd moved through each part but not really knowing why.

'What's to say?' he said, moving into the room. 'My father died a very rich man.'

She gave a small frown as she recalled their conversation at his hotel the day before. 'I thought you intimated he left you nothing in his will?'

His eyes held hers for a brief moment before moving away. He wandered over to the big desk and, pulling out the throne-like chair, sat down, one ankle across his thigh, his hands going behind his head as he leaned backwards.

'He left me nothing I particularly wanted,' he answered.

Her teeth caught her bottom lip for a moment, her eyes falling away from the mysterious depths of his.

'But…we're not talking about a few old kitchen utensils and second-hand books here, Jake. This place is worth a fortune. The house itself on current market value would be enough to set anyone up for life, let alone the contents I've seen so far.'

'I'm not getting rid of the house, just what's inside it,' he informed her.

'You plan to live here?' She stared at him in surprise.

He unfolded his leg and stood up, his sudden increase in height making her feel small and vulnerable in the over-crowded space of the room.

'I have set up a branch of my company here in Sydney. I plan to spend half the year in England and the other half here.'

She moistened her mouth. 'But you told me earlier you've always hated this house.'

'I do.' He gave her another inscrutable look. 'But that's not to say it can't have a serious makeover and be the sort of home it should have been in the first place. I'm looking forward to doing it, actually.'

Ashleigh knew there was a wealth of information behind his words but she wasn't sure she was up to the task of asking him exactly what he meant. After all, hadn't he been the one who'd insisted on living in a low maintenance one-bedroom apartment when they had lived in London? Whatever was he going to do with a house this size, which looked as if it had at least ten bedrooms, several formal rooms, including a ballroom, not to mention an extensive front and back garden with a tennis court thrown in for good measure?

'It seems a bit…a bit big for a man who…' She let her words trail away when he moved towards her.

'For a man who what, Ashleigh?' he asked, picking up a strand of her shoulder-length hair and coiling it gently around his finger.

She swallowed as her scalp tingled at the gentle intimate tether of his finger in her hair, her heart missing a beat as his darker-than-night eyes secured hers.

'You're…you're a c-confirmed bachelor,' she reminded him, her tone far more breathy than she'd intended. 'No wife, no kids, no encumbrances, remember?'

His mouth lifted at one corner. 'You don't think it's possible for people to change a little over time?'

Her heart gave another hard thump as she considered the most likely possibilities for his change of heart.

Perhaps he'd met someone…someone who was so perfect

for him he couldn't bear to live without her and was prepared to have her on any terms, even marriage—the formal state he had avoided so determinedly in the past.

She couldn't get the question past the blockage in her throat, but her mind tortured her by conjuring up an image of him standing at an altar with a beautiful bride stepping slowly towards him, his eyes alight with desire as the faceless woman drifted closer and closer to finally take his outstretched hand...

Jake uncoiled her hair but didn't move away.

Ashleigh tried to step backwards but her back and shoulders came up against the solid frame of the bookshelves. The old books shuffled on their shelves behind her and, imagining them about to tumble down all over her, she carefully edged away a fraction, but it brought her too close to Jake.

Way too close.

'W-what's...what's changed your mind?' she asked, surprised her voice came out sounding almost normal considering she couldn't inflate her lungs properly.

He stepped away from her and, picking up an old gold pen off the desk, began to twirl it in his fingers, his face averted from hers. It seemed to Ashleigh a very long time before he spoke.

'I have spent some time since my father's death thinking about my life. I want to make some changes now, changes I just wasn't ready to face before.' He put the pen down and faced her, his mouth twisted in a little rueful smile. 'It might sound strange to you, but you're the first person I've trusted enough to tell this to.'

Ashleigh felt her guilt claw at her insides with accusing fingers, sure if he looked too closely he would see the evidence of her betrayal splashed over her features.

She had kept from him the birth of his son.

What sort of trustworthiness had that demonstrated?

Jake turned away again as he continued heavily, 'But four

and a half years ago I just wasn't ready.' He raked a hand through his hair. 'I guess I'm only doing it now because my father is dead and buried.' He gave a humourless grunt of laughter and looked back at her. 'It's that closure I spoke of earlier.'

'So…' she ran her tongue over her desert-dry mouth '…have you changed your mind about…marriage?'

'I have given it some considerable thought,' he admitted, his eyes giving nothing away.

'What about the…the other things you were always so adamant about?' At his enquiring look she added, 'Kids, pets, that sort of thing.'

She picked up the faint sound of his breath being released as he turned to look out of the window over the huge back garden, the solid wall of his tall muscled frame instantly reminding her of an impenetrable fortress.

'No,' he said, reverting to the same flat emotionless tone he'd used earlier. 'I haven't changed my mind about that. I don't want children. Ever.'

Ashleigh felt the full force of his words as if he had punched them right through the tender flesh of her belly where his child had been curled for nine months. She hadn't realised how much she had hoped for a different answer until he'd given the one she'd most dreaded.

He didn't want children.

He *never* wanted children.

How could she tell him about his little son now?

Jake turned round to look at her. 'Have you decided to take me up on my offer, Ashleigh?' he asked.

'I—I need more time…'

'Sorry.' The hard glance he sent her held no trace of apology. 'Take it or leave it. If you want to have this stuff then you'll have to fulfil my terms. A month working nine to five in this house—alongside me.'

Panic set up an entire percussion section in Ashleigh's chest, the sickening thuds making her feel faint and the palms of her hands sticky with sweat.

'I—I don't usually work nine to five,' she said, avoiding his eyes.

'Oh, really?' There was a hint of surprise in his tone. 'Why ever not?'

'Howard doesn't like the thought of me working full-time,' she said, pleased with her response as it was as close to the truth as she could get.

'And you agreed to that?'

'I…' She lifted her chin a fraction. 'Yes. It frees me to do… other things.'

'What other things do you like doing?'

Ashleigh knew she had backed herself into a tight corner and the only way out of it was to lie. She averted her gaze once more and inspected a figurine near her with avid intent. 'I go to the gym.'

'The gym?' His tone was nothing short of incredulous.

Her chin went a bit higher as she met his eyes again. 'What are you saying, Jake? That I look unfit as well as fat?'

He held up his hands in a gesture of surrender. 'Hey, did I ever say you were fat?'

She threw him a resentful look and folded her arms across her chest. 'Yesterday when we met you said I'd put on weight. In my book that means you think I'm fat.'

She heard him mutter an expletive under his breath.

'I think you look fabulous.' His dark gaze swept over her, stalling a little too long for her comfort on the up-thrust of her breasts. 'You were a girl before, barely out of your teens. Now you're a woman. A sexy gorgeous-looking woman.'

Who has given birth to your son, Ashleigh wanted to add, but knew she couldn't.

Would she ever be able to?

'Thank you,' she mumbled grudgingly and looked away.

Jake gave an inward sigh.

He'd almost forgotten how sensitive she was. Her feelings had always seemed to him to be lying on the surface of her skin, not buried deep inside and out of reach as his mostly were.

But the Ashleigh he'd known in the past was certainly no gym junkie. Her idea of exercise had never been more than a leisurely walk, stopping every chance she could to smell any flowers that were hanging over the fence. It had driven him nuts at times. He needed the challenge of hard muscle-biting endurance exercise to keep his mind off the pain of things he didn't want to think about.

He still needed it.

'I'm prepared to negotiate on the hours you work,' he inserted into the silence.

Her head came up and he saw the relief in her blue eyes as they met his. 'Is…is ten to four all right?' she asked.

He pretended to think about it for a moment.

She shifted uncomfortably under his scrutiny and he wondered why she felt so ill at ease in his company. He'd expected a bit of residual anger, maybe even a good portion of bitterness, but not this outright nervousness. She was like a rabbit cornered in a yard full of ready-to-race greyhounds, her eyes skittering away from his, her small hands fluttering from time to time as if she didn't quite know what to do with them.

'Ten to four will be fine,' he said. 'Do you want me to pick you up each day?'

'*No!*'

One of his brows went upwards at her vehement response.

Ashleigh lowered her eyes and looked down at the twisting knot of her hands. 'I—I mean that won't be necessary. Besides—' she gave him a little speaking glance '—Howard wouldn't like that.'

'And what Howard wouldn't like good little Ashleigh wouldn't dream of doing, right?' he asked without bothering to disguise the full measure of scorn in his tone.

She clamped her lips shut, refusing to dignify his question with an answer.

'For Christ's sake, Ashleigh,' he said roughly. 'Can't you see he's all wrong for you?'

'Wrong?' She glared at him in sudden anger. 'How can you say that? It was you who was so wrong for me!'

'I wasn't wrong for you; I just—'

'You *were* wrong for me!' She threw the words at him heatedly. 'You ruined my life! You crushed my confidence and berated everything I held as important. I was your stupid plaything, something to pass the time with.'

'That's not true.' His voice was stripped of all emotion.

Ashleigh shut her eyes for a moment to hold back the threatening tears. She drew in a ragged breath and, opening her eyes again, sent him a glittering look. 'God damn you, Jake. How can you stand there and say Howard is all wrong for me when at least I can be myself with him? I could never be myself with you. You would never allow it.'

Jake found it hard to hold her accusing glare, his gut clenching at the vitriol in her words. As much as he hated admitting it, she was very probably right. He wasn't proud of how he had treated her in the past. He'd been insensitive and too overly protective of his own interests to take the time to truly consider hers.

The truth was she had threatened him from the word go.

He had always avoided the virginal, looking for hearth-home-and-cute hound-thrown-in types. He'd shied away from any form of commitment in relationships; the very fact that he'd let his guard down enough to allow her to move in with him demonstrated how much she had burrowed beneath his skin.

Her innocence had shocked him.

He had taken her roughly, their combined passion so strong and out of control he hadn't given a single thought to the possibility that it might have been her first time.

He'd hurt her and yet she hadn't cried. Instead she'd hugged him close and promised it would be better next time.

And it had been.

In fact, making love with Ashleigh had been an experience he was never likely to forget. She had given so freely of herself, the passion he'd awakened in her continually taking him by surprise. No one he'd been with since—and there had been many—had ever touched him quite the way she had touched him. Ashleigh had reached in with those small soft hands of hers to deep inside him where no one had ever been before. Sometimes, if he allowed himself, he could still feel where her gentle stroking fingertips had brushed along the torn edges of his soul.

'Ashleigh…' His voice sounded unfamiliar even to his own ears. He cleared his throat and continued. 'Can we just forget about the past and only deal with the here and now?'

Ashleigh brushed at her eyes with an angry gesture of her hand, hoping he wouldn't see how undone she really was. How could she possibly pretend the past hadn't happened when she had Lachlan to show for it?

'Why are you doing this?' she asked. 'What can you possibly hope to achieve by insisting I do this assessment for you? You say you don't want the money all this stuff is worth…' She drew in a scalding breath as her eyes scanned the goods in front of her before turning back to meet his steady gaze, her voice coming out a little unevenly. 'What exactly do you want?'

'This house is full of ghosts,' he said. 'I want you to help me get rid of them.'

She moistened her bone-dry lips. 'Why me?'

'I have my reasons,' he answered, his eyes telling her none of them.

Her gaze wavered on his for a long moment. This was all wrong. She couldn't help Jake deal with whatever issues he carried from his past. How could she when she had the most devastating secret of all, that at some point he would have to hear?

But he needs you, another voice inside her head insisted.

How could she turn away from the one man she had loved with all of her being? Surely she owed him this short period of time so he could achieve the closure he had spoken of earlier.

It was a risk she had to take. Spending any amount of time with Jake was courting trouble but as long as she stood her ground she would be fine.

She *had* to be fine.

'I think we need some ground rules then,' she said, attempting to be firm but falling well short of the mark.

'Rules?'

'Rules, Jake.' She sent him a reproachful look. 'Those moral parameters that all decent people live by.'

'All right, run them by me,' he said, the edge of his mouth lifted in a derisory smile.

She forced her shoulders back and met his gaze determinedly. 'There's to be no touching, for a start.'

'Fine by me.' He thrust his hands in his jeans pockets as if to remove the temptation right there and then.

Ashleigh had to drag her eyes away from the stretch of denim over his hands. 'And that includes kissing, of course,' she added somewhat primly.

He moistened his lips with his tongue as if removing the taste of her from his mouth. 'Of course.'

She straightened her spine, fighting to remain cool under that dark gaze as it ran over her. 'And none of those looks.'

'Which looks?' he asked, looking.

She set her mouth. *'That* look.'

'This look?' He pointed to his face, his expression all innocence.

She crossed her arms. 'You know exactly what I mean, Jake Marriott. You keep undressing me with your eyes.'

'I do?'

He did innocence far too well, she thought, but she could see the hunger reflected in his gaze and no way was she going to fuel it.

'You know you do and it has to stop. *Now.*'

He sent her one of his megawatt lazy smiles. 'If you say so.'

'I say so.'

He shifted his tongue inside his cheek for a moment. 'Are you done with your little rules?'

She gave him a schoolmarm look from down the delicate length of her nose. 'Yes. I think that just about covers it.'

'You want to hear my rules now?' he asked after a tiny heart-tripping pause.

Ashleigh gave a covert swallow and met his eyes with as much equanimity as she could muster. 'All right. If you must.'

'Good.'

Another little silence coiled around them.

Ashleigh didn't know where to look. For some strange reason, she wanted to do exactly what she'd just forbidden him to do.

She wanted to feast her eyes on his form.

She wanted to run her gaze over all the hot spots of his body, the hot spots she had set alight with her hands and mouth in the past.

She could almost hear the sound of his grunting pleasure in the silence throbbing between them, could almost feel the weight of him on her smaller frame as he pinned her beneath him.

She could almost feel the pulse of his spilling body between her legs, the essence of himself he had released at the moment of ecstasy, the full force of his desire tugging at her flesh both inside and out.

She forced herself to meet his coal-black gaze, her stomach instantly unravelling as she felt the heat coming off him towards her in searing scorching waves.

'I promise not to touch, kiss or even look if you promise to refrain from doing the same,' he stated.

I can do that, she thought. *I can be strong.*

I *have* to be strong.

'Not a problem,' she answered evenly. 'I have no interest in complicating things by revisiting our past relationship.'

'Fine. We'll start Monday at ten.' He took his hands out of his pockets and reached for a set of keys in the drawer of the desk and held them out to her like a lure.

'These are the keys to the house in case you get here before me,' he said.

She slowly reached out her opened palm and he dropped them into it.

'See? No touching.' He grinned down at her disarmingly.

She put the keys in her bag and straightened the strap on her shoulder to avoid his wry look. 'So far,' she muttered and turned towards the door.

'Ashleigh?'

She took an unsteady breath and turned back to face him. 'Yes?'

He held out the blood-red rose he'd picked for her earlier, the soft petals deprived of water for so long, already starting to wilt in thirst.

'You forgot this,' he said.

She found herself taking the four steps back to him to get her faded bloom, her fingers so meticulously avoiding his that she encountered a sharp thorn on the stem of the rose instead.

'Ouch!' She looked at the bright blood on her fingertip and began rummaging in her bag for a tissue, but before she could locate one Jake's hand came over hers and brought it slowly but inexorably up to his mouth.

She sucked in a tight little breath as he supped at the tiny pool of blood on her fingertip, her legs weakening as his eyes meshed with hers.

'Y-you promised…no t-touching…' she reminded him breathlessly but, for some inexplicable reason, didn't pull her finger out of his mouth.

She felt the slight rasp of his salving tongue, felt too the full thrust of her desire as it burst between her legs in hot liquid longing.

'I know.' He released her hand and stepped back from her. 'But you'll forgive me this once, won't you?'

She didn't answer.

Instead she turned on her heel and flew out the door and out of the house as if all the ghosts contained within were after her blood.

And not just one tiny little pin drop of it…

CHAPTER FOUR

LACHLAN flew out of the crèche playroom to greet her. 'Mummy! Guess what I did today?'

Ashleigh pressed a soft kiss to the top of his dark head and held him close for longer than normal, breathing in his small child smell. 'What did you do, my precious?'

He tugged on her hand and pulled her towards the painting room. 'I drewed a picture,' he announced proudly.

Ashleigh smiled and for once didn't correct his infant grammar. He would be four in a couple of months—plenty of time ahead to teach him. For now she wanted to treasure each and every moment of his toddlerhood.

It would all too soon be over.

'See?' He pressed a paint-splattered rectangle of paper into her hands.

She looked down at the stick-like figures he'd painted. 'Who's this?' she asked, bending down so she was on a level with him.

His chocolate-brown eyes met hers. 'That's Granny and Grandad.'

'And this one?' She pointed to another figure, who appeared to be doing some sort of dance.

'That's Auntie Mia,' he said.

I should have guessed that, Ashleigh thought wryly. Mia

was the Forrester fitness fanatic and was never still for a moment.

'And this one?' She knew who it was without asking. The dog-like drawing beside the blonde-haired human figure was a dead give-away but she wanted to extend his pleasure in showing off his work.

'That's Auntie Ellie.' He pointed to the yellow hair he'd painted. 'And that's one of the dogs she's wescued.'

Ashleigh's eyes centred on the last remaining figure who was standing behind all the others.

'Who is that?' she asked, not sure she really wanted to know.

'That's you,' he said, a touch of sadness creeping into his tone.

She swallowed the lump in the back of her throat and stared down at the picture. 'Really?'

'Yes.' He met her eyes with a look so like his father's she felt like crying.

'Why am I way back there?' She pointed to the background of his painting.

His eyes shifted away from hers, his small shoulders slumping as a small sigh escaped from his lips. 'I miss you, Mummy.'

'Oh, baby.' She clutched him to her chest, burying her head into the baby-shampoo softness of his hair, her eyes squeezing shut to hold the tears back. 'Mummy has to work, you know that, darling.' She eased him away from her and looked down into his up-tilted face. 'Aren't you happy at crèche and at the times you have with Granny and Grandad?'

His little chin wobbled for a moment before he got it under control. 'Yes…'

Ashleigh's stomach folded as she saw the insecurity played out on his features. Hadn't she seen that same look on Jake's face in the past, even though, like Lachlan, he had done his level best to hide it?

'I have to work, poppet,' she said. 'I have to provide for us. I can't expect Granny and Grandad to help us for ever.'

'But what about my daddy?' Lachlan asked. 'Doesn't he want to provide for me too?'

I will kill you, Mia, so help me God, she said under her breath. This was surely her sister's doing, for Lachlan had never mentioned anything about his father in the past.

'He doesn't know about you,' she said, deciding the truth was safer in the long run.

'Why not?'

She couldn't meet his eyes.

Was this how it was going to be for the rest of her life, guilt keeping her from looking at eyes that were the mirror image of his father's?

'I couldn't tell him…' she said at last.

'Why not, Mummy?'

She closed her eyes and counted to five before opening them again. 'Because he never wanted to be a daddy.'

'But I *want* a daddy,' he said, his big dark eyes tugging at Ashleigh's heartstrings. 'Do you think if I met him and asked him he would change his mind?'

She looked down at the tiny up-tilted face and smiled in spite of her pain. 'I just know he would. But you can't meet him, sweetie.'

'Why?'

She hugged him close, not sure how to answer.

'Mummy?'

'Mmm?' She bit the inside of her cheek to stop herself from falling apart.

'I still love my daddy even if he doesn't want to see me,' he said solemnly.

Ashleigh felt as if someone had just stomped on her heart.

* * *

Howard couldn't contain his delight at her decision to take on the assessment.

'You mean he wants to give us the whole lot?' he asked incredulously. *'For nothing?'*

She nodded, her expression unmistakably grim. 'That's the deal.'

'But on market value the whole load is probably worth…' He did a quick mental calculation from the notes Ashleigh had already prepared. 'Close to a couple of million, at the very least!'

'I know…' Her stomach tightened another notch. 'But he doesn't want any of it.'

'He's mad,' Howard said. 'Totally out of his mind, stark staring mad.'

Ashleigh didn't answer. She didn't think Jake was mad, just being incredibly tactical.

Howard frowned for a moment. 'Does he…' he cleared his throat as if even harbouring the thought offended him '…does he want something in exchange, apart from you working in the house to document everything?'

'What do you mean?' Ashleigh hoped her cheeks weren't as hot on the outside as they felt to her on the inside.

'Some men can be quite…er…ruthless at times, Ashleigh, in getting what they want,' he said. 'No one but no one gives away a fortune of goods without wanting something in return.'

'He doesn't want to sleep with me, if that's what's worrying you,' she said, wondering why it had hurt to say it out loud.

'He told you that?' Howard's red brows rose.

She nodded.

He let out a sigh of relief. 'You are doing me the biggest favour imaginable, Ashleigh.' He took her hands and squeezed them in his. 'This will secure our future. We can get married in grand style and never have to worry about making ends meet again. Think of it!' His face glowed with delight at this stroke of good fortune. 'My mother is thrilled. She wants you to come to dinner this evening to celebrate with us.'

Ashleigh felt like rolling her eyes. The one sticking point in her relationship with Howard, apart from his deeply ingrained conservatism, was his mother. No matter how hard she tried, she just did not like Marguerite Caule.

'I need to spend time with Lachlan,' she said carefully, removing her hands from his hold. 'He's been missing me lately.'

'Bring him with you,' Howard suggested. 'You know how much my mother enjoys seeing him.'

Seeing him, but not hearing him, Ashleigh added under her breath. Marguerite was definitely from the old school of child-rearing: children were to be seen not heard, and if it could possibly be avoided without direct insult, not interacted with at all.

'Maybe some other time,' she said, avoiding his pleading look. 'I have a lot on my mind just now.'

She heard him sigh.

'Is this all too much for you?' he asked. 'Do you want me to call Jake Marriott and pull out on the deal? I know it's a lot of money but if you aren't up to it then I won't force you.'

Ashleigh turned to look at him, privately moved by his concern. He was such a lovely person, no hint of malice about him. He loved Lachlan and he loved her.

Why, oh, why, couldn't she love him in return?

He had so much to lose on this. His business hung in the balance. It was up to her to save it. She couldn't walk away from Jake's deal without hurting Howard, and hurting him was the last thing she wanted to do.

Besides, it *was* a lot of money to throw away. How could

she live with herself if she turned her back on Jake's offer, no matter what motive had precipitated it?

'No…' She picked up her bag and keys resignedly. 'I'm going to see this through. I think Jake is right.' She gave a rough-edged sigh. 'I need closure.'

'Good luck.'

She gave him a rueful look as she reached for the door. 'Luck has been in short supply in my life. I hardly see it changing any time soon.'

'Don't worry, Ashleigh,' Howard reassured her. 'He's given you the opportunity of a lifetime. Don't let your past relationship with him get in the way of your future with me.'

Ashleigh found it hard to think of an answer. Instead she sent him a vague smile and left the showroom, somehow sensing that her future was always going to be inextricably linked with Jake.

Even if by some miracle he never found out about Lachlan.

The house and grounds were deserted when Ashleigh arrived. Jake's car was nowhere in sight and, although most of the blinds at the windows hadn't been pulled completely down, the house still gave off a deserted, abandoned look.

She walked up the cracked pathway to the front door, feeling as if she was stepping over an invisible barrier into the privacy of Jake's past.

She rang the doorbell just in case, but there was no answer. She listened as the bell echoed down the hall like an aching cry of loneliness, the sound bouncing off the walls and coming back to her as if to taunt her. She put the key into the lock and turned it, the door opening under her hand with a groan of protest.

At least it didn't smell as musty as before.

The movement of air in the hall indicated that Jake had left a window open and she couldn't help a soft sigh of remembrance. Hadn't he always insisted on sleeping with at least one window open, even when it had been freezing cold outside?

She wandered from room to room, taking a host of pictures with a digital camera, stopping occasionally to carefully document notes on the various pieces, her fingers flying over the notebook in her hand as she detailed the estimated date and value of each item.

As treasure troves went, this was one of the biggest she'd ever encountered. Priceless piece after priceless piece was noted on her list, her estimation growing by the minute. Howard's business would be lifted out of trouble once these babies hit the showroom floor.

She lifted the hair out of the back of her top and rolled her stiff shoulders as she finished the first room. She glanced at her watch and saw it was now well after twelve. Two hours had gone past and still no sign of Jake.

Deciding to take a break, she left her notebook and pen on a side table and wandered through to the kitchen at the back of the house.

It wasn't the sort of kitchen in which she felt comfortable. It was dark and old-fashioned, the appliances so out of date she wondered if they were still operational.

She picked up a lonesome cup that someone, she presumed Jake's father, had left on the kitchen sink. It was heavily stained with the tannin of tea, the chipped edge seeming out of place in a house so full of wealth. She ran her fingertip over the rough edge thoughtfully, wondering what sort of man Jake's father had been.

Ashleigh realised with a little jolt that she had never seen a picture of either of his parents, had never even been informed of their Christian names.

She thought of the stack of family albums her mother had lovingly put together. Every detail of family life was framed with openly adoring comments. There were shiny locks of hair and even tiny pearly baby teeth.

What had Jake's parents looked like? She hadn't a clue and yet their blood was surging through her son's veins.

'I'm sorry I'm so late,' Jake said from just behind her.

Ashleigh swung around, surprise beating its startled wings inside her chest. 'I wish you would stop doing that,' she said, clutching at her leaping throat.

'Do what?' He looked at her blankly.

She lowered her hand and gave herself a mental shake. 'You should announce your arrival a bit more audibly. I hate being sneaked up on like that.'

'I did not sneak up on you,' he said. 'I called out to you three times but you didn't answer.'

She bit her lip, wondering if what he said was true. It was certainly possible given that her thoughts had been located well in the past, but it still made her feel uncomfortable that he could slip through her firewall of defences undetected.

She put the cup she'd been holding down and turned away from his probing gaze. 'I've almost finished assessing one room.'

'And?'

Her eyes reluctantly came back to his. 'Your father certainly knew what he was doing when it came to collecting antiques.'

He gave a humourless smile. 'My father was an expert at many things.'

Again she sensed the wealth of information behind the coolly delivered statement.

'Would it help to…to talk about it?' she asked, somewhat tentatively.

His eyes hardened beneath his frowning brow. 'About what?'

'About your childhood.'

He swung away from her as if she'd slapped him. 'No, not right now.'

She bit her lip, not sure if she should push him. A part of her wanted to. She ached to know what had made him the man he was, but another part of her warned her to let well alone. His barriers were up again. She could see it in the tense line of his jaw and the way his eyes moved away from hers as if he was determined to shut her out.

'Which room would you like me to work on next?' She opted for a complete change of subject.

He gave a dismissive shrug and shoved at a dirty plate on the work table in front of him as if it had personally offended him.

'I don't care. You choose.'

'Which room was your bedroom?' she asked before she could stop herself.

She saw the way his shoulders stiffened, the rigidity of his stance warning her she had come just a little too close for comfort.

'I don't want you to go in there,' he said. 'The door is locked and it will stay that way. Understood?'

She forced herself to hold his glittering glare. 'If that's what you want.'

He gave her one diamond-hard look and moved past her to leave the room. 'I will be in the back garden. I have some digging to do.'

She sighed as the door snapped shut behind him.

What had she taken on?

It was well after three p.m. when she decided she needed a break. She had nibbled on a few crackers she'd brought with her and had a glass of water earlier, but her eyes were watering from all the dust she'd disturbed as she itemised the contents of the largest formal room.

She went out the back door, her eyes automatically searching the garden for Jake as she sat down on one of the steps, stretching her legs out to catch the sun.

He was down in the far corner, his back and chest bare as he dug up the ground beneath the shade of the elm tree. She saw the way his toned muscles bunched with each strike of the spade in the resisting earth, the fine layer of perspiration making his skin gleam in the warm spring sunshine.

He stopped and, leaning on the spade, wiped a hand across his sweaty brow, his eyes suddenly catching sight of her watching him.

He straightened and, stabbing the spade into the ground, walked towards her, wiping his hands on the sides of his jeans.

From her seated position on the back step she had to crane her neck to look up at him. 'That looks like hard work,' she said. 'Do you want me to get you a glass of water?'

He shook his head. 'I drank from the tap a while ago.'

She lowered her gaze, then wished she hadn't as she encountered the zipper of his jeans. She jerked upright off the step but her sandal caught in the old wire shoe-scraper and she pitched forwards.

Jake caught her easily, hauling her upright, his hands on her upper arms almost painfully firm.

'Are you OK?'

'I—I'm fine…' She tried to ease herself out of his hold but he countered it with a subtle tightening of his fingers.

She had no choice but to meet his eyes. 'You can let me go now, Jake.'

Tiny beads of perspiration were peppered over his upper lip, a dark smudge of soil slashed across the lean line of his jaw giving him an almost primitive look. Gone was the high-powered architect who had offices in several major cities of the world; in his place was a man who smelt of hard physical work and fitness, his chest so slick with sweat she wanted to press her mouth to his skin and taste his saltiness.

His hands dropped away from her and he stepped backwards. 'I've made you dirty,' he said without apology.

She glanced at each of her arms, her stomach doing a funny little tumble turn when she saw the full set of his earthy fingerprints on the creamy skin of her bare upper arms.

'It's all right,' she said. 'At least I wasn't wearing the jacket. I left it inside it was so…so hot…'

His eyes ran over her neat skirt and matching camisole and she wished she hadn't spoken. She could feel the weight of his gaze as it took in her shadowed cleavage, a cleavage she hadn't had four and a half years ago.

'I'd better get back to work…' she said, waving a hand at the house behind her, her feet searching blindly for the steps. 'There's still so…so much to do and I need to leave on time.'

'If you want to leave early, that's fine,' he said, narrowing his eyes against the sun as he looked back over the garden. 'I'm just about finished for the day myself.'

Ashleigh hovered on the first step. 'What are you going to plant in that garden bed you're digging?'

It seemed an age before his gaze turned back to meet hers, his eyes so dark and intense she felt the breath trip somewhere in the middle of her throat.

'I'm not going to plant anything.'

A nervous hand fluttered up to her neck, her fingers holding the fine silver chain hanging there, her expression clouded with confusion. 'Then what are you digging for?'

His mouth tilted into one of his humourless smiles.

'Memories, Ashleigh,' he said, his tone deep and husky. 'I'm digging for memories.'

Ashleigh watched him, her eyes taking in the angles and planes of his face, wondering what was going on behind the screen of his inscrutable gaze.

He'd always been so adept at concealing his true feelings; it had both frustrated and fascinated her in the past. She knew his aloofness was part of what fed her lingering attraction for him. She felt ashamed of how she felt, especially given her commitment to Howard, but every time she was in Jake's presence she felt the pull of something indefinable, as if he had set up a special radar to keep her tuned in to him, only him. She felt the waves of connection each time his gaze meshed with hers, the full charge zapping her whenever he touched her. His kiss had burnt her so much she was sure if it were to be repeated she would never have the strength to pull away. It wouldn't matter how committed she was elsewhere, when Jake Marriott's mouth came down on hers everyone else ceased to exist.

'You're breaking rule number three,' Jake's voice cut through her private rumination. 'No looks, remember?'

She dragged her eyes away from the amused line of his mouth and met his eyes, her cheeks heating from the inside like a stoked furnace.

'I wasn't *looking*, I was thinking,' she insisted.

'One wonders what was going on in that pretty little head of yours to make you blush so delightfully,' he mused.

'I'm not blushing!' She flung her hair back with a defiant toss of one hand. 'It's hot. You know how I can't stand the heat. You always said I…' She stopped speaking before she trawled up too many dangerous memories. She didn't want him thinking she had stored away every single word he'd ever spoken to her.

'I always said what?'

'Nothing; I can't remember.' She carefully avoided his eyes. 'It was all such a long time ago.'

'Four years is not such a long time.'

'Four and a half,' she said, meeting his eyes with gritty determination. 'Time to move on, don't you think?'

'That's why we're here,' he said. 'So we can both move on.'

'Then let's get on with it,' she suggested and turned towards the house.

'Ashleigh.'

She sent her eyes heavenward with a silent prayer for strength as she turned to look back at him. Because she was on the top step he was now at eye level. This close she could see the curling fringe of his sooty lashes, could even feel the movement of air against her lips when he let out a small breath. Her stomach muscles tightened, her legs going to water at his physical proximity. She had only to tilt her body a mere fraction and she would be touching him.

No touching, she reminded herself firmly.

Rule number one.

Her gaze dipped to the curve of his mouth and she mentally chanted rule number two, over and over again. *No kissing, no kissing, no kissing, no—*

'I want to visit your family,' Jake said, startling her out of her chant. 'I was thinking about coming over this evening.'

'What?' She choked. 'W-whatever for?'

He gave her a long studied look, taking in her flustered features and fluttering nervous hands.

Ashleigh fought her panic under some semblance of control as her mind whirled with a list of possible excuses for putting him off. She straightened her shoulders, controlled her hands by tying them together and forced herself to meet his eyes.

'We're all busy,' she said. 'No one's going to be home.'

'Tomorrow will do just as well.'

'That's no good either,' she said quickly—far too quickly.

He gave her a sceptical look. 'What happened to the happy-to-be-at-home-altogether-every-night Forrester family? I thought your family's idea of a big night out was once a month to the cinema.'

She set her mouth, knowing he was mocking the stable security of her family. 'My parents have regular evenings out and so do my sisters,' she said, not bothering to hide the defensiveness in her tone. 'Anyway, I will be out with Howard.'

'I don't need you to be there,' he said.

No, but if he were to see even a single toy of Lachlan's lying about the house he would begin to ask questions she wasn't prepared to answer. Not to mention all the photographs arranged on just about every surface and wall by her overly sentimental mother. She'd been lucky the first time when he'd called in unexpectedly but she could hardly strip the house of everything with Lachlan's name or face on it.

'All the same, I don't think it's such a good idea.' She bit her lip momentarily as she hunted her brain for a reasonable excuse. 'My parents are…very loyal and since we…I mean… you and I parted on such bitter terms they might not be all that open to seeing you now.'

'Your mother was fine with me the other day,' he said. 'Admittedly she didn't ask me in for tea and scones, but she was openly friendly and interested in how I was doing.'

I will throttle you, Mum, for being so damned nice all the time, she silently vowed.

'I don't think Howard would like the thought of you fraternising with my family,' she put in desperately.

The cynical smirk reappeared at the mention of her fiancé's name.

'We don't have to tell Howard,' he said, adding conspiratorially with the wink of one dark glittering eye, 'it can be our little secret.'

Ashleigh was already sick to death of secrets, her one and only one had caused enough anguish to last a lifetime. She felt as if her heart hadn't had a normal rhythm in days and even now her head was constantly pounding with the tension of trying to avoid a vocal slip in Jake's presence.

'I'd rather not do anything behind Howard's back,' she said.

'Good little Ashleigh,' he drawled with unmistakable mockery.

She ground her teeth and wished she could slap that insolent look off his face, but she knew if she did all three rules would end up being broken right there and then where they stood on the back door steps.

She straightened her spine, speaking through tight lips. 'I'll arrange a meeting for you with my family on neutral ground. A restaurant or something like that some time next week or the one after.'

He inclined his head at her in a gesture of old-world politeness. 'If you insist.'

'I do.'

'Why don't you and Howard join the party?' he suggested.

'I don't think so.'

He gave a soft chuckle of laughter. 'Why? Would he be frightened he might have to foot the bill?'

She sent him an arctic glare. 'Howard is a hard-working man. Sure, he doesn't have the sort of money that you do to throw around, but at least he is honest and up-front.'

'What are you implying? That I came by my fortune by less than honest means?' His eyes were hard as they lasered hers.

'How did you do it, Jake?' she asked. 'When we were living in London you hardly had a penny to your name.'

'I worked hard and had some lucky breaks,' he said. 'No shady deals, so you can take that look of disapproval off your face right now.'

'From living in squalor to billionaire in four and a half years?' she gave him a disbelieving look. 'You should write one of those how-to-be-successful books.'

'I didn't exactly live in squalor,' he said.

'No, not after I moved in and did all your housework for

you,' she bit out resentfully. 'How delightfully convenient for you, a housekeeper and lover all rolled into one.'

Ashleigh felt his continued silence as if it were crawling all the way up her spine to lift the fine hairs on the back of her neck.

She knew she was cornered. Her back was already up against the closed door behind her and his tall frame in front of her blocked any other chance of escape.

She could feel the air separating them pulsing with banked up emotions. Dangerous emotions, emotions that hadn't been unleashed in a very long time…

CHAPTER FIVE

ASHLEIGH could feel the weight of his dark gaze on her mouth, the sensitive skin of her lips lifting, swelling as if in search of the hard pressure of his, her heart fluttering behind her ribcage as his head came even closer.

'Don't even think about it…' she cautioned him, her voice a cracked whisper of sound as it passed through her tight throat.

His lips curved just above hers, hovering tantalisingly close, near enough to feel the brush of his warm breath as he asked, 'Is that to be another one of your little rules?'

She moistened her lips nervously. 'Yes…' She cleared her throat. 'Rule number four: don't think about me in that way.'

'How do you know what way I'm thinking about you?' His dark eyes gleamed with mystery.

'You're still a full-blooded man, aren't you?' she asked with considerable tartness. 'Or is that another one of those changes you insist you've undergone in the last four and a half years?'

He had timed silences down to a science, Ashleigh thought. He used them so tactically. She had forgotten just how tactically.

She held her breath, waiting for him to say something, her head getting lighter and lighter as each pulsing second passed.

'Want to check for yourself?' he finally asked.

'What?' Her indrawn breath half-inflated her lungs and her head swam alarmingly as his meaning gradually dawned on her.

He pointed to his groin, her eyes following the movement of his hand as if they had a mind of their own.

'You're the expert assessor. Why don't you head south to check out if the crown jewels are still in mint condition?'

Her eyes flew back to his in a flash of anger. 'This is all a big game to you, isn't it, Jake? You think this is so funny with your stupid double meanings and sexual hints.' She sucked in a much needed breath and continued, 'I'm not interested. Got that? Not in-ter-est-ed. Do I have to spell it out for you? Why can't you hear what I'm telling you?'

'There seems to be some interference from the transmission centre,' he said.

'Transmiss…' She rolled her eyes. 'Oh, for God's sake! Is your ego so gargantuan that you can't accept that what we had is over?'

'It would be a whole lot easier to accept if you didn't look at me with those hungry eyes of yours,' he said.

'Hungry eyes?' She gaped at him in affront. 'You're the one with the wandering eyes!'

'I said hungry, not wandering.'

'Don't split hairs with me!' she spat back. 'And back off a bit, will you?' She leant back even further against the door behind her until the door handle began to dig into the tender flesh of her lower back. 'I can practically see what you had for breakfast.'

'I didn't have breakfast.'

'Do you think I care?' she asked.

He gave her one of his lengthy contemplative looks. Ashleigh could feel herself dissolving under his scrutiny. She felt as if he could see through her skin to where her heart was beating erratically in response to his closeness.

'See?' He held up his hands as if he'd just read her mind. 'I'm not touching you.'

'You don't have to; just being close to you is enough to—' She clamped her wayward mouth shut and sent him another furious glare.

'Is enough to what, Ashleigh?' he asked, his deep voice like a length of sun-warmed silk being passed over too sensitive skin.

She refused to answer, tightening her mouth even further.

'Tempt you?' he prompted.

'I'm not the least bit tempted,' she said, wishing to God it was true.

'That's what the rules are for, aren't they, Ashleigh?' he taunted her softly. 'They're not for me at all. They're for you, to remind you of your commitment to dear old Howard.'

'He is not old!' she put in defensively. 'He's younger than you. He's thirty and you're thirty-three.'

'How very sweet of you to remember how old I am.'

Damn! She chided herself. She hadn't seen that coming and had fallen straight into it.

'If you don't mind I'd like to get on with what I'm supposed to be doing,' she said, hitching up her chin.

He stepped down a step and her breath whooshed out in relief. He didn't speak, but simply turned away to stride down to the back of the garden to the spade he'd dug into the earth under the elm, lifting it out of the ground and resuming his digging as if the last few minutes hadn't occurred.

Ashleigh tore her eyes away from the sculptured contours of his muscles and, wrenching open the back door, hurried inside where, for once, the dark lurking shadows of the house didn't seem quite so threatening.

Her father was the first person she saw when she got home that afternoon after picking up Lachlan from the crèche.

'I need to talk to you, Dad,' she said, hanging up Lachlan's backpack on the hook behind the kitchen door.

'Where's Lachlan?' Heath Forrester asked.

'He wanted to play outside for a while,' she informed him with undisguised relief. Her young son had been full of energy and endless chatter all the way home from the crèche and it had nearly driven her crazy.

Heath gave her a look of fatherly concern. 'What's on your mind, or should I say who?'

Her breath came out on the back of a deep sigh. 'Jake wants to have a family get-together of all things.'

Heath's bushy brow rose expressively. 'That could be a problem.'

She sent him a speaking glance as she reached for the kettle. 'He wanted to come here tonight but I managed to put him off. I said I'd organise a restaurant for some other evening in a week or two.' She leant her hips back against the bench as the kettle started heating. 'I just wish I didn't have to deal with this. I can't think straight when he's…when he's around.'

'You share a past with him,' her father said. 'It won't go away, especially with Lachlan lying between you.'

'You think I should tell him, don't you?'

Heath compressed his lips in thought for a moment. 'Jake's a difficult man, but not an unreasonable one, Ashleigh. For all you know he might turn out to be a great father if given the chance.'

'But he's always made it more than clear he never wanted to have children,' she said. 'He told me the very same thing again yesterday.'

'He might think differently if he met Lachlan,' Heath said.

Ashleigh smiled sadly in spite of her disquiet. 'You and Mum are the most devoted grandparents I know. Of course you would think that, but I know Jake. He would end up hating Lachlan for having the audacity to be born without his express permission.'

'I understand your concerns but you can't hide Lachlan from him for ever,' Heath pointed out. 'Attitudes have changed these days. He has a legal right to know he has fathered a child.'

'I know…' Ashleigh sighed. 'But I can't do it now. Not like this. I need more time. I need to prepare myself, not to mention Lachlan.'

'Who is going to prepare Jake?' Heath asked.

'That's not my responsibility,' she said.

Her father didn't answer but reached for two cups in silence. Ashleigh dropped two tea bags into the cups he put on the bench in front of her and poured the boiling water over them, watching as the clear liquid turned brown as the tea seeped from the bags into the water.

'I *will* tell him, Dad,' she addressed the cup nearest her, 'eventually.'

'I know you will,' her father answered, taking his cup. 'But I just hope it's not going to be too late.'

Ashleigh stared into the cup in her hands, the darkness of her tea reminding her of Jake's fathomless eyes—eyes that could cut one to the quick or melt the very soul.

'Better late than never…' she murmured.

'That's certainly a well-used adage,' Heath said. 'But I wonder what Jake will think?'

Ashleigh just gave her father a twisted grimace as she lifted her cup to her lips. She spent most of her sleepless nights tortured by imagining what Jake would think.

It wasn't a pretty picture.

'So how is your assessment going?' Howard asked her the next morning.

Ashleigh handed him the notes she'd made so far. 'I've

done one room, mostly the furniture as I think I'll need your help with the figurines. I've looked them up in the journals but I'd prefer your opinion. The painting, however, is certainly an Augustus Earle original. I think there are more but the one I've seen so far is worth a mint.'

'Good work,' Howard congratulated her as he glanced over her descriptions.

'I've taken some initial digital photos but I haven't downloaded them yet,' she said. 'It's a big house and the furniture is virtually stacked to the ceiling in some rooms. It will take me most of the next week to get everything photographed and documented.'

'So how is it working alongside your ex-boyfriend?'

Ashleigh found it hard to meet Howard's gently enquiring gaze. 'It's all right…I guess.'

'He hasn't—' he paused, as if searching for the right word '—made a move on you, has he?'

'Of course not!' she denied hotly.

Howard gave her a slightly shamefaced look. 'Sorry, just asking. You know I trust you implicitly.'

She stretched her mouth into a tight smile that physically hurt. 'Thank you.'

'However, I'm not sure I trust him,' he continued as if she hadn't spoken.

'You've only met him the once; surely that's not enough time to come to any sort of reasonable opinion on someone's character.' She found it strange springing to Jake's defence but it irked her to think her fiancé had made that sort of critical judgement without a fair trial.

'I know the type,' Howard answered. 'Too much money, too much power, not enough self-restraint.'

That about sums it up, she thought to herself, but decided against telling him how close he'd come to assessing her ex-lover's personality.

'I thought you were glad he was giving us this load of goods?' she said.

'I am,' he said. 'More than glad, to be honest. Who wouldn't be? It's a dream come true. Without this input of goods I was going to be sailing a little too close to the wind for my liking. The antiques fair coming up will time in nicely with this little haul. I will make a fortune out of it.'

'If it goes through,' she muttered darkly.

'What do you mean?' Howard looked at her in consternation.

'What if he pulls on the deal?'

'Why would he do that?' he asked. 'He gave us the exclusive. Well, at least he gave it to you.' He glanced at her narrowly. 'You're not making things difficult for him, are you?'

'Why would I do that?'

He gave a shrug. 'You're very bitter about him. Up until the other day you never once mentioned his name in the whole time I've known you.'

'You didn't ask.' She kept herself busy with shuffling some papers on her desk.

'That's because I sensed it was too painful for you,' he said.

Ashleigh looked at him, her expression softening as she recalled the way he had always considered her feelings. He was like the older brother she'd always wanted—caring, considerate and concerned for her at all times.

'I'm hoping he won't pull out of the deal.' She picked up a pen and rolled it beneath her fingers, the line of her mouth grim. 'But who knows what he might do if he finds out about Lachlan?' She stared at the pen for a moment before adding, 'He seems keen to get his father's house cleaned out so he can start renovating it.' She gave a tiny despondent sigh and added, 'I think I'm what you could call part of his clean-up process.'

'What do you mean?'

The pen rolled out of her reach. A small frown creased her brow as she lifted her gaze back to his. 'I can't quite work him out. Sometimes I think he wants to talk to me about his past…I mean *really* talk. You know, tell me every detail. But then he seems to close up and back off as if I've come too close.'

'It's a difficult time when a parent passes away,' Howard said. 'I remember when my father died how hard it was. I was torn between wanting to talk and needing to stay silent in case I couldn't handle the emotion.'

Ashleigh chewed her bottom lip for a moment. 'I could be wrong, but I can't help feeling he isn't exactly grieving his father's passing.'

'Oh?' Howard frowned. 'You mean they didn't get on or something?'

'I don't know…but why else would he be practically giving away everything his father left him?'

Howard let out a breath. 'I guess it wouldn't hurt to listen to him if he ever decides he wants to tell you about it. What harm could it do? You never know, you might come to see him in a totally new light.'

Ashleigh gave him a small wan smile by way of response. She didn't want to see Jake Marriott in a new light.

She didn't want to see Jake Marriott at all.

It wasn't safe.

'Come on!' Mia urged Ashleigh on the cross-training machine at the local gym early the next morning. 'Use those legs now, up and down, up and down.'

Ashleigh grimaced against the iron weight of her thighs and continued, sweat pouring off her reddened face and pooling between her breasts. 'I thought this was supposed to fun,' she gasped in between steps.

'It is once you get fit,' Mia said, springing on to the tread-mill alongside.

Ashleigh watched in silent envy as her trim and toned sister deftly punched in the directions on the treadmill and began running at a speed she'd thought only greyhounds could manage.

'You make me sick,' she said with mock sourness as she clung to the moving handles of the machine, her palms slippery and her legs feeling like dead pieces of wood.

Mia gave her a sweet smile as she continued running. 'It's your fault for fibbing to Jake about going to the gym regularly.'

'Yeah, don't remind me.'

'Anyway, I think it's a great idea for you to get some exercise,' Mia said without even puffing. 'You're so busy juggling work and Lachlan that you don't get any time on your own. You know how much Mum and Dad love to mind him for you so there's no excuse. The gym is a great place to switch off.'

Ashleigh looked at the sea of sweaty bodies around her and seriously wondered if her sister was completely nuts. Loud music was thumping, a row of televisions were transmitting several versions of early morning news shows, and a muscle-bound personal trainer who looked as if he'd been fed steroids from birth was adding to the cacophony of noise by shouting out instructions to a middle-aged man with a paunch, in tones just like a drill sergeant at Boot Camp.

'I can't believe people get addicted to this,' she said with a pointed look at her sister.

Mia grinned. 'It's also a great place to meet people.' She glanced at a tall, exceptionally handsome man who was doing bench presses on the other side of the room. 'Not a bad sight for this time of the morning, is it?'

Ashleigh couldn't help thinking that Jake's muscles as he'd dug the garden the previous day were much more

defined than the man in question; however, she had to accede
that her sister was right. There were certainly worse things
to be looking at first thing in the morning.

'How long do I have to do this for?' she asked after a few
more excruciating minutes of physical torture.

'Five more minutes and then we'll do some stomach
crunches,' Mia informed her cheerily.

Ashleigh slid a narrow-eyed glance her sister's way.
'How many?'

'Three hundred a day should do it,' Mia said determinedly.
'You're not overweight, just under-toned.'

'*Three hundred?*' Ashleigh groaned.

'Come on,' Mia said and, jumping off the treadmill, pulled
over a floor mat near the mirrored wall. 'Down on the floor
and let's get started.'

'One…two…three…four…five…'

When Ashleigh arrived at Jake's house later that morning the
temperature had risen to the late thirties and the air was thick
and cloying with humidity. A clutch of angry, bruised-looking
clouds was already gathering on the western horizon as if in
protest at the unseasonable heat.

She couldn't see Jake's car or any sign of him about the
house or garden so she let herself in and closed the door with
a sigh of relief as the coolness of the dark interior passed over
her like a chilled breath of air.

She lost track of time as she went to work in the second
of the two formal sitting rooms, this one smaller but no less
jam-packed. She ran her hand over a Regency rosewood
and brass-inlaid dwarf side cabinet in silent awe. The
cabinet had a frieze drawer and a pleated cupboard door
decorated with a brass grille and was on sabre supports.
She knew it would fetch a fabulous price at auction and the

very fact that Howard had it in his possession would lift his profile considerably.

Her gaze shifted to a George III mahogany cabinet, and then to a Victorian walnut credenza which was inlaid and gilt metal-mounted, the lugged serpentine top above a panelled cupboard door and flanked by glazed serpentine doors.

The scent of old wood stirred her nostrils as she took photo after photo, edging her body around the cluttered furniture to show each piece off to best advantage.

During her time working with Howard she had seen many wonderful pieces, had visited many stately homes and purchased deceased estates, but nothing in her experience came anywhere near what was in Jake's father's house. She'd completed enough courses by correspondence to recognise a genuine antique when she saw it and this house was practically filled floor to ceiling with them, most of them bordering on priceless.

It only begged the question why someone had collected such expensive showpieces when he'd clearly had no intention of ever showing them off. They were cheek by jowl in an old neglected house that needed more than a lick of paint on the outside and a great deal of it inside as well.

From the unfaded splendour of the furniture she could only assume the blinds at the windows had nearly always been kept down. She couldn't help thinking what sort of life Jake must have had as a young child in this mausoleum-like house. She couldn't imagine her little son lasting even a full minute without touching or breaking something valuable. She looked at a Prattware cat and wondered if Jake had ever broken anything in the boisterousness of youth. Lachlan had recently accidentally toppled over a vase at Howard's house and Marguerite Caule had torn strips off him, reducing him to tears even though the vase hadn't even been so much as chipped.

She gave an inward shudder and left the room.

The closed door of what used to be Jake's bedroom was three doors away down the hall. She looked at it for a long moment, wondering what secrets he kept locked there. She walked slowly towards the door, each of her footsteps making the floorboards creak as if they were warning her not to go any further. Jake had forbidden her to go in, telling her he kept it locked at all times, but she wouldn't be human or indeed even female if she didn't try the handle just the once...

It opened without a sound.

She stared at the open space before her for at least half a minute until the overwhelming temptation finally sent her feet forward, one after the other, until she was inside, the door as her hand left it, shifting soundlessly to a half-open position behind her.

It wasn't as dark as the rest of the rooms in the house. The blinds were not pulled all the way down and, although the sky outside was cloudy, enough light still came through for her to see the narrow single bed along one wall. Compared to the rest of the furniture in the house, Jake's bedroom was furnished roughly, almost cheaply. There was nothing of any significant value, that she could see. The wardrobe was little more than a chipboard affair and the chest of drawers not much better. There was a single mirror on the wall above the chest of drawers but it was cracked and crooked as if someone had bumped against it heavily but not bothered to straighten it again.

The bed was lumpy and looked uncomfortable, the ugly brown chenille spread bald in spots. The walls looked pock-marked, bits of poster glue still visible, although there was not a poster or photograph in sight. Again she thought of her childhood home with the walls covered with loving happy memories. Jake's childhood house was stripped of any such sentimentality. She had asked him once when they lived to-gether to show her a photo of himself as a child but he'd told her he hadn't bothered bringing any overseas with him. She had accepted his answer as reasonable and had thought nothing more about it. But now, in the aching emptiness of this room, she couldn't help wondering if anyone had ever taken one of him and cherished it the way her parents cherished the ones they had collected over the years.

There were no loving memories in this house.

The thought slipped into her head and once it took hold she couldn't erase it. The painful truth of it seemed to be seeping towards her, like a nasty stain that had been hidden for a long time but was now finally coming through the cracked paint on the walls to taint her with its dark shameful secret.

Jake had been abused by his father.

Her stomach clenched in anguish as the puzzle began to fall into sickening place. It all made sense now. No wonder he was getting rid of everything to do with his father. And no wonder he had never wanted children of his own.

Oh, Jake! Why didn't you tell me?

She looked again at the askew mirror on the wall and her stomach gave another painful lurch. Was that blood smeared in one corner?

Her eyes fell away from its mottled secrets and went to the chest of drawers beneath it. Almost of its own volition, her hand began to reach for the first drawer. She knew it was contravening Jake's rule but she had to find out what she could about his background. It was like a compulsion, an addiction she just had to feed, if only for the one time.

The drawer slid uneasily from its tracks as if it too was advising her against prying as the floorboards had seemed to do earlier, the scrape of rough-edged timber sounding like fingernails being dragged down the length of a chalk board.

She suppressed a tiny shiver and looked down at the odd socks tumbled in a heap, no two seemed to match or were even tucked together in the hope of being considered a pair. There was a bundle of underwear that looked faded and worn and a few unironed handkerchiefs not even folded.

The second drawer had a few old T-shirts, none of them ironed, only one or two folded haphazardly. A sweater was stuffed to one side, one of its exposed elbows showing a gaping hole.

Jeans were in the third drawer, only two pairs, both of them ragged and torn. She couldn't help a tiny smile. Both her sisters insisted on buying torn and ragged jeans; it was the fashion and they paid dearly for it, insisting they would *die* if anyone saw them in anything else.

She pushed against the drawer to shut it but it snagged and wouldn't close properly. She gave it another little shove but it refused to budge. She bent down and peered into the space between the second and third drawers but it was hard to see in the half light. She straightened and tugged the drawer right out of the chest in order to reinsert it, to check if anything was stuck behind.

A small package fell to the floor at her feet and, carefully sliding the drawer back into place, she bent down to retrieve it...

CHAPTER SIX

IT WAS an envelope, the edges well-worn as if it had been handled too many times. Ashleigh opened the flap and drew out the small wad of photographs it contained, her breath stalling in her throat as the first one appeared.

It was Jake as a small toddler and he looked exactly like Lachlan at the same age.

'I thought I told you this room was out of bounds.'

Ashleigh spun around so quickly she dropped the photographs, each of them fluttering to the floor around her quaking legs and feet.

'I…I…' She gave up on trying to apologise, knowing it was going to be impossible to get the words past the choking lump in her throat.

Jake moved into the room and she watched in a shocked silence as he retrieved the scattered photographs off the floor, slipping them back inside the old envelope and putting them to one side.

'There is nothing of value in this room.' He gave the room a sweeping scathing glance before his eyes turned back to hers. 'I told you before.'

She moistened her mouth, shifting from foot to foot, knowing he had every right to be angry with her for stepping across the boundary he had set down.

'You always were the curious little cat, weren't you?' he said, stepping towards her.

Ashleigh felt her breath hitch as he stopped just in front of her, not quite touching but close enough for her to feel the warmth of his body. It came towards her in waves, carrying with it the subtle scent of his essential maleness, his lemon-scented aftershave unable to totally disguise the fact that he'd been physically active at some point that morning. It was an intoxicating smell, suggestive of full-blooded male in his prime, testosterone pumped and charged, ready for action.

'The door...it wasn't locked...'

'It usually is, but I decided to trust you,' he said. 'But it seems I can no longer do so.'

She didn't know what to make of his expression. She didn't think he was angry with her but there was a hint of something indefinable in his gaze that unnerved her all the same.

'I was just checking...' she said lamely.

He gave a little snort of cynicism. 'I just bet you were.'

'I was!' she insisted. 'Was it my fault you left the door unlocked?'

'You didn't have to search through my things,' he pointed out.

'You haven't lived in this house for something like eighteen years,' she said. 'I'm surprised anything of yours is still here.'

He gave her an unreadable look. 'Quite frankly, so am I.'

She frowned at his words, her brain grappling with why his father had left things as they were. The room looked as if Jake had walked out of it all those years ago and yet it seemed as if nothing had been removed or changed since.

'Maybe he missed you,' she offered into the lengthy silence.

Jake's dark eyes hardened as they pinned hers. 'Yes, I suppose he did.'

She ached to ask why but the expression on his face warned her against it. Anger had suddenly tightened his jaw, sent fire to his eyes and tension to his hands as they fisted by his sides.

She couldn't hold his look. She turned and found herself looking at her own reflection in the cracked mirror on the wall. It was like looking at a stranger. Her blue eyes looked wild and agitated, her hair falling from the neat knot she had tied it in that morning, her cheeks flushed, her mouth trembling slightly.

She could see him just behind her. If she stepped back even half a step she would come into contact with the hard warmth of his very male body. Her workout in the gym that morning made her aware of her body in a way she had not been in years. She felt every used muscle, every single contraction reminding her of how she used to feel in his arms. Making love with Jake had been just like a heavy workout. He had been demanding and daring, taking her to the very limits of consciousness time after time until she hadn't known what was right and decent any more.

She met his eyes in the mirror and suppressed an inward shudder of reaction. Would she ever be able to look at him without feeling a rush of desire so strong it threatened to overturn every moral principle she had been taught to cling to?

She sucked in a breath as his hands came down on her shoulders, his eyes still locked on hers in the mirror. She did her best to control her reaction but the feel of his long fingers on her bare skin melted her resolve. She positively ached for him to slowly and sensually slide his hands down the length of her arms as he used to do, his fingers curling around the tender bones of her wrists in a hold that brooked no resistance. She wondered if he knew how he still affected her, that her heart was already racing at the solid presence of him standing so close behind her, the knowledge that in the past his hardened maleness, thick with desire, would be preparing to plunge between her legs and send every trace of gasping air out of her lungs.

'Y-you're touching me…' Her voice came out not much more than a croak.

'Mmm, so I am.' His hands moved slowly down her arms, his eyes never once leaving hers.

She moistened her parched lips when his fingers finally encircled her wrists, her breathing becoming ragged and uneven. 'Y-you're breaking the rules, Jake.'

'I know.' He gave her a lazy smile as his thumbs began a sensual stroking of the undersides of her wrists. 'But you broke my one and only rule and now I shall have to think of a suitable penalty.'

She wasn't sure if it was she who turned in his arms or if he turned her to face him, but suddenly she wasn't looking at his reflection in the mirror any more but into his darker than night gaze as it burned down into hers.

His body was too close.

She could feel the denim seam of the waistband of his jeans against her, and when his hands drew her even closer her stomach came into contact with his unmistakable arousal. No one else could make her feel this way. Her body remembered and hungered for what it had missed for so long.

When his mouth came down over hers a tiny involuntary whimper of pleasure escaped her already parted lips, and as his tongue began an arrogant and determined search for hers she gave no resistance but curled hers around his in a provocative dance which spoke of mutual blood-boiling desire.

Ashleigh vaguely registered the dart of lightning that suddenly lit the room and the distant sound of thunder, the low grumble not unlike the sounds coming from Jake's throat as he took the kiss even further, his body grinding against hers. She wound her arms around his neck, her fingers burrowing into his thick dark silky hair, her breasts tight with need as they were crushed against his chest.

Jake sucked on her bottom lip, a bone-melting act he'd perfected in the past, making her feel as if her body and mind were totally disconnected. She no longer felt like someone else's fiancé. She felt like Jake's lover, a lover who knew exactly how to please him. She remembered it all so well! How to make him groan with ecstasy as he spilled himself into her body, her mouth or wherever she chose to tempt him beyond the tight limits of his control.

Now she couldn't help relishing the feeling of power his reaction afforded her. She could sense his struggle to hold back as his tongue thrust back into her mouth, the sexy male rasp inciting her to give back even more. She bit down on his bottom lip, a tantalising little nip that made him growl deep in his throat. She wouldn't release him, supping on him as if she wanted to take him deep inside and never let him go.

She loved the feel of his hard mouth, the way his masculine stubble never seemed to be quite under smooth enough control, the rough scrape of skin against the softness of hers reminding her of all that was different between them.

How had she lived without his touch? This madness of blood racing through veins alight with passion, a frenzy of feeling that would not go away without the culmination of physical union.

And then only temporarily.

When she felt Jake's hands slide beneath her top she did nothing to stop him. She couldn't. Her breasts were aching too much for the cup of his warm hands, hands that in the past her too slim body hadn't quite been able to fill. But it did now.

Her flesh spilt into his hands as he released her simple bra, the stroke of his fingers over the tight buds of her nipples an almost unbearable pleasure. When he bent his head to place his hot mouth on her right nipple she nearly fainted with reaction, the slippery motion of his tongue stirring her into a madness of need that she knew had only one assuagement. He knew it too, for he did the same to her other breast, drawing little agonised gasping groans from her lips, her cheeks flushing with passion, her limbs weakening as she leant into his iron-strong hold.

He pressed her backwards until the backs of her knees came into contact with his narrow single bed. A distant corner of her conscience prodded her, reminding her of her commitment to Howard. But somehow when Jake's long strong body came down over hers and pinned her to the mattress, any notion of resistance disappeared on the tail end of a gasp as his thighs nudged between the quivering silk of hers.

'I have waited so long to do this,' Jake groaned as he lifted her skirt with impatient hands, his eyes like twin torches of fire as he looked down at her desire-flushed features. 'I have dreamt of it, ached for it, planned for it until I could think of nothing else.'

Planned for it? Ashleigh froze as his words sank in. She eased herself up on her elbows, dislodging his weight only because he hadn't expected it. 'What do you mean, *planned* for it?' she asked.

He began to press her back down but she pushed his hand away. 'No, Jake. Tell me what you mean.'

He gave her a frustrated look from beneath frowning brows. 'Do we have to talk *now?*'

'Yes.' She rolled off the bed and quickly rearranged her clothing with as much dignity as she could, and turned to face him determinedly. 'Tell me what you meant. Now.'

He drew in a harsh breath and got off the bed in a single movement, one of his hands marking a rough pathway through his hair. 'I have made no secret of my intention to see you again,' he said. 'I told you that the very first day.'

She gave him a reproachful glare. 'You also told me the following day that you had no intention of sleeping with me, or have you forgotten that little detail?'

His mouth curled up in one corner as he looked down at her. 'I was only responding to the invitation you've been sending out to me from the first moment we met in the hotel bar. You can deny it all you like, but you're as hungry for me as I am for you.'

'I. Am. Engaged.' She bit the words out with stiff force.

His cynical smile tilted even further. 'Just exactly who are you reminding of the fact, me or you?'

Ashleigh had never felt closer to violence in her entire life. Her hand twitched with the desire to take a swipe at the self-satisfied smirk on his darkly handsome face, and in the end only some tiny remnant of her conservative upbringing fore-stalled her.

She clenched her fists by her sides and berated him coldly. 'If you think you can replay our relationship just for the heck of it you're very much mistaken. I know what you're doing, Jake. As soon as you clean up this place you'll be back off to London or Paris or wherever you have some other stupid misguided woman waiting in vain for you to commit.'

'That has always been a sticking point with you, hasn't it?' he said, folding his arms in a casual unaffected pose. 'You don't think a relationship is genuine without some sort of for-mal commitment.'

She found it difficult to hold his very direct look but be-fore she could think of a response he continued, 'Which kind of makes me wonder why you don't wear an engagement ring. Can't poor old Howard even rustle up a second-hand one for you?'

It was all she could do to keep her temper under control.

Rage fired in her blood until she could see tiny red spots of it before her eyes. She so wanted to let fly at him with every gram of bitterness she'd stored up over the years, but instead of a stream of invective coming out of her mouth when she finally opened it, to her utter shock, shame and embarrassment a choked sob came out instead.

Jake stared at her, his own mouth dropping open as she bent her head to her hands, her slim shoulders visibly shaking as she tried to cover the sounds of her distress.

He muttered one short sharp curse and reached for her, pulling her into the shield of his chest, one of his hands cupping the back of her silky head as he brought it down against his heart.

'I'm sorry.' He was surprised it hadn't physically hurt to articulate the words, especially as he'd never said them to anyone before.

She didn't answer other than to burrow a bit closer, but after a moment or two he could feel the dampness of her tears through his thin cotton T-shirt.

He couldn't remember ever seeing her cry before. He'd always secretly admired her for it, actually. His childhood had taught him that tears were for the weak and powerless; he'd disciplined himself not to cry from an early age and, no matter what treatment had been dished out to him, he had been determined not to let his emotions get out of control. He had gritted his teeth, sent his mind elsewhere, planned revenge and grimly stored his anger, and for the most part he'd succeeded.

The only time he'd failed was the day his father had told him his dog had been sent away to the country. Jake had only been about ten and the little fox-terrier cross had been a stray he'd brought home. Her excited yaps when he'd come home from school each day had been the highlight of his young life.

The *only* highlight.

No one else had ever looked that happy to see him since…
well…maybe Ashleigh had in their early days together, her
eyes brightening like stars as he'd walked in the door.

Ashleigh eased herself out from his hold and brushed at
her eyes with the back of her hand, her other hand hunting
for a much-needed tissue without success.

Jake reached past her and opened the top drawer of the
chest of drawers and handed her one of the crumpled handkerchiefs. 'Here,' he said, his tone a little gruff, 'it's more or
less clean but I'm afraid it's not ironed.'

'It doesn't matter,' she said, turning away to blow her nose
rather noisily.

Jake watched her in silence, wishing he could think of
something to say to take away the gaping wound of their past
so they could start again. He knew he didn't really deserve
the chance, but if he could just explain…

He wanted to change. He wanted to be the sort of man she
needed, the solid dependable type, the sort of man who would
be a brilliant father to the children he knew she wanted to have.
But what guarantee could he give her that he wouldn't turn out
just like his father? Things might be fine for a year or two,
maybe even a little longer, but he knew the patterning of his
childhood and the imprint of his genes would win in the end.

He'd read the statistics.

Like father like son.

There was no getting away from it.

He just couldn't risk it.

Ashleigh scrunched the used handkerchief into a ball in
her hand and turned back to meet his gaze. 'I'm sorry about
that…' She bit her lip ruefully. 'Not my usual style at all.'

He smiled. Not cynically. Not sneeringly, but sadly, his
coal-black eyes gentle, the normally harsh lines of his mouth
soft. 'No,' he agreed, 'but everyone has their limits, I guess.'

She lowered her gaze, concentrating on the round neckline

of his close-fitting T-shirt. 'I think it's this house…' She rubbed at her upper arms as if she was suddenly cold. 'It seems sort of…sort of miserable…and…well…sad.'

Jake privately marvelled at the depth of her insight, but if only she knew even half of it! The walls could tell her a tale or two, even the mirror behind her bore the scar of his final fight with his father. He'd been fully expecting to see his blood still splattered like ink drops all over it and the wall but apparently his father had decided to clean up his handiwork, although it looked as if he'd missed a bit in one corner.

He forced his thoughts away from the past and, reaching for the envelope he'd put aside earlier, sat on the bed and patted the space beside him, indicating for her to sit alongside. 'Hey, come here for a minute.'

He saw the suspicion in her blue eyes and held up his hands. 'No touching, OK?'

She came and sat on the bed beside him, her hands in her lap and her legs pressed together tightly.

He opened the envelope with careful, almost reverent fingers and Ashleigh found herself holding her breath as he took out the first photograph.

It was the photo she'd seen earlier. It was the spitting image of Lachlan at the age of eighteen months or so—the engaging smile, the too long limbs and the olive skin the sun had kissed where summer clothes hadn't covered.

She didn't know what to say, so said nothing.

'I was about a year and a half old, I think,' Jake said, turning over the photo to read something scrawled in pencil on the back. 'Yeah…'

'What does it say?' she asked.

He tucked the photo to the back of the pile, his expression giving little away. 'Not much. Stuff about what I was doing, words I was saying, that sort of thing. My mother must have written it.'

Ashleigh felt the stabbing pain of her guilt as she thought about the many photographs she had with Lachlan's early life documented similarly.

Jake took out the next photograph and handed it to her. She felt the warm brush of his fingers against hers but didn't pull away. She held the photograph with him, as if the weight of the memories it contained was too heavy for one hand.

It was a photograph of a small dog.

Ashleigh wished she had her sister Ellie's knowledge of canine breeds but, taking a wild guess, she thought it looked like a fox-terrier with a little bit of something else thrown in. It had a patch of black and tan over one cheeky bright intelligent eye and another two or three on its body, its long narrow snout looking as if it was perpetually smiling.

She glanced at him, their fingers still linked on the picture. 'Was this your dog?'

He nodded and shifted his gaze back to the photograph. She sensed rather than heard his sigh.

'What happened to him?' she asked after what seemed an interminable silence.

'Her,' he corrected, without looking up from the image.

Ashleigh held her breath, instinctively knowing more was to come. Exactly what, she didn't know, but for now it was comforting that he trusted her enough to show her some precious relics of his past. Somehow she knew he hadn't done this before.

With anyone.

Jake tucked the photograph behind the others and closed the envelope. 'I called her Patch. She followed me home from school one day when I was about eight or so.'

'How long did you have her?'

'A year or two.'

'She died?'

He met her gaze briefly before turning away. 'My father sent her to live in the country.'

Ashleigh felt her stomach clench with sympathy for the child he had been and the loss he must have felt. 'Why?'

He gave another small shrug. 'I must have done something to annoy him.' He pushed the envelope away and stood up. 'As punishments went it was probably the best he'd ever come up with, not that I ever let on, of course.'

Ashleigh could just imagine how stoical he had been. His chin stiff, no hint of a wobble even though inside his heart would have been breaking. Hadn't she seen it in Lachlan when Purdy, the family's ancient but much loved budgerigar, had died not that long ago?

'Did you ever get to visit her?' she asked.

'No.' The single word was delivered like a punctuation mark on the subject, effectively closing it.

'Can I see the rest of the photos?' she asked after another stretching silence.

He pushed the envelope into the top drawer of the chest of drawers by way of answer. Ashleigh looked at the stiff line of his back as it was turned towards her, somehow sensing he'd let her past a previously well-guarded barrier and was now regretting his brief lapse into sentimentality. She could almost see the words Keep Out written across his face as he turned to look at her.

'Maybe some other time.' He moved past her to the door and held it open for her. 'Don't let me keep you from your work.'

Ashleigh brushed past him with her head down, not sure she wanted him to see the disappointment in her eyes at his curt dismissal. He'd allowed her into his inner sanctum for a moment, had made himself vulnerable to her in a way she'd never experienced with him before. It made it extremely difficult to use her bitterness as a barrier to what she really felt for him. The feelings she'd locked away for years were creeping out, finding gaps in the fences she'd constructed around herself. Her love for Jake was like a robust climbing vine that refused to die no matter how hard it was pruned or poisoned.

Ashleigh went into the first room she came to rather than have Jake's gaze follow her down the length of the hall. It was a dining room, the long table set with an array of dusty crockery and china, instantly reminding her of Miss Havisham's abandoned wedding breakfast in Charles Dickens's *Great Expectations*.

She reached for the light switch and watched as the ornate crystal chandeliers overhead flickered once or twice as if deciding whether to make the effort to throw some light in the room or not. The delicate drape of spiders' webs only added to the Dickensian atmosphere. She gave herself a mental shake and stepped further into the room to reach for the nearest blind, but just as she took hold of the tasselled cord a big furry black spider tiptoed over the back of her hand.

It was probably her best-ever scream.

Her mother had always said that Ashleigh held the record in the Forrester family for the scream that could not only wake the dead but everybody sleeping this side of the Blue Mountains as well.

The door behind her crashed open so roughly that the delicate glassware on the dining room table shivered in reaction as Jake came bursting in.

'What happened?' He rushed to her, his hands grasping her upper arms as he looked down at her pale face in concern.

'Nothing…' She gave a shaky little laugh of embarrassment and moved out of his hold. 'It was a spider, that's all.'

He frowned. 'I didn't know you were scared of spiders.'

'I'm not.' She rubbed the back of her hand on her skirt. 'I just don't like them using me as a pedestrian crossing.'

He glanced at what she was doing with her hand and grimaced. 'Where is it now?' He swept his gaze across the window-frame before looking back at her. 'Do you want me to get rid of it for you?'

'It's probably long gone,' she said. 'I think I screamed it into the next century.'

He gave her one of his rare genuine smiles. 'I thought you'd seen a ghost. I had no idea anyone so small could scream so loudly.'

Small? One gym workout and he already thought she was smaller? Thank you, Mia!

'I've had a lot of practice over the years,' she said. 'Mia and Ellie and I used to have screaming competitions.'

'Your poor parents,' Jake commiserated wryly.

'Yes…' A small laugh bubbled from her lips before she could stop it. 'The police were called once. Apparently one of the neighbours thought someone was being murdered or tortured at the very least. You should have heard the lecture we got for…' Her words trailed away as she saw the expression on Jake's face. It had gone from mildly amused to mask-like, as if something she had said had upset him and he didn't want to let her see how much.

'Jake?' She looked at him questioningly, her hand reaching out to touch him gently on the arm.

He moved out of her reach and turned to raise the blind.

The angry black clouds had by now crept right over the garden, their threatening presence casting the room in menacing, creeping shadows. The flickering light bulbs in the chandelier over the table made one last effort to keep the shadows at bay before finally giving up as a flash of sky-splitting lightning came through the window, momentarily illuminating the whole room in a ghostly lucency. The boom of thunder was close on its heels, the ominous sound filling Ashleigh's ears.

'Are you afraid of storms?' Jake asked without turning to look at her.

'No… not really,' she said, waiting a few seconds before adding, 'are you?'

She watched as he turned to look at her, the eerie light of the morning storm casting his face into silhouette.

'I used to be,' he answered, his voice sounding as if it had come from a distant place. 'But I'm not anymore.'

She waited a heartbeat before asking, 'How did you overcome your fear?'

It seemed an age before he responded. Ashleigh felt the silence stretching to breaking-point, her mind already rehearsing various phrases to relieve it, when he suddenly spoke, shocking her into vocal muteness.

'My father always used nature to his advantage. If a storm was loud and ferocious enough it would screen his activities from the neighbours.' He gave her a soulless look. 'Of course none of the neighbours called the police. They thought the booms and crashes going on were simply the effects of the storm.'

Ashleigh felt a wave of nausea so strong she could barely stand up. How had Jake survived such a childhood? She almost felt ashamed of how normal and loving her background was. She had been nurtured, along with her sisters, like precious hothouse flowers, while Jake had been consistently, cruelly crushed underfoot like a noxious weed.

'Oh, Jake…' She breathed his name. 'Why didn't you tell me?'

He gave a rough sound that was somewhere between scorn and dismissal. 'I'm over it, Ashleigh. My father's dead and I have to move on. Storms are just storms to me now. They hold no other significance.'

For some reason which she couldn't quite explain, her gaze went to the scar above his right eye. The white jagged line interrupted the aristocratic arc of his eyebrow like a bulldozed fire trail through a forest.

'Your eye…' she said. 'You always said you got that scar in a fight.' She took an unsteady breath and continued. 'Your father did it, didn't he?'

Jake lifted a hand and fingered the scar as if to make sure it was still there. 'Yes,' he said. 'It was the last chance he got to carve his signature on me. I was two days off my sixteenth birthday. I left and swore I'd never see him again.'

'You kept your promise…' She said the words for him.

He gave her a proud defiant look. 'Yes. I never saw him alive again.'

'I wish you'd told me all of this when we…when we were together,' she said. 'It would have helped me to understand how you—'

His lip curled into one of his keep-away-from-me snarls. 'What good would it have done? You with your perfect little family, everyone chanting how much they love each other every night as the night closed in like in all of those stupid TV shows. Do you know anything about what really goes on behind closed doors? Do you even know what it is like to go without a meal?' he asked, his tone suddenly savage, like a cornered neglected dog which had known nothing but cruelty all its life. 'Do you know what it is like to dread coming home at the end of the school day, wondering what punishment was in store if you so much as made a floorboard creak or a door swing shut too loudly?'

Ashleigh's eyes watered and she bit her lip until she could taste the metallic bitterness of blood.

Jake slashed one of his hands through the air like a knife and continued bitterly. 'I had no respite. From the day my mother died when I was three I lived with a madman. Not a day went past when I didn't have fear turning my guts to gravy while he watched and waited, timing his next hit for maximum effect.' He strode to the window once more, the next flash of angry lightning outlining his tall body as he stared out at the garden.

Ashleigh wanted to say something but knew this was not her turn to speak. Jake had been silent for most of his life; it was his turn to talk, to get what he could out of his system and he had chosen her to be witness to it.

He gave a deep sigh and she heard him rub his face with one hand, the slight raspy sound making her weak with her need to go to him in comfort. How she wanted to wrap her arms around him, to press soft healing kisses on all the spots on his body where his father had kicked, punched or brutalised him.

It was almost impossible for her to imagine someone wanting to harm their own child. She thought of Lachlan and how she would gladly give her life for his, had in fact given up so much for him already and not once complained. How could Jake's father have been so heartless? What possible motive could he have had to inflict such unspeakable cruelty on a defenceless child?

Jake turned around to look at her, his expression bleak. 'For most of my life I have done everything possible not to imitate my father. My life's single goal has been to avoid turning into a clone of him.'

She drew in a shaky little breath, hardly able to believe she was finally witnessing the confession she had always longed to hear.

'He remarried more often than he changed his shirts,' he continued in the same flat tone. 'I had a procession of step-mothers come in and out of my life, each of whom left as soon as they found out the sort of man my father was. I decided marriage was never going to be an option for me in case I ended up the same way, leaving a trail of emotional and physical destruction in my wake as my father did.'

'He abused you…didn't he?' Her voice came out on a thin thread of sound.

Jake's eyes shifted away from hers, his back turned towards her as he raised the ragged blind and stared out of the window.

'Not sexually,' he answered after what seemed another interminable pause.

Ashleigh felt her tense shoulders sag with instant relief.

'But he did just about everything else.'

Her stomach clenched, her throat closing over. 'Oh, Jake…'

He turned back to face her, his expression rueful. 'Do you realise you are the first person I've ever told this to?'

'I—I am?'

He gave her a sad smile. 'Every single day we lived together I wanted to tell you, but I thought if I did you would run a mile in case I turned out just like him.'

'You could never be like him, Jake…'

He turned back to the window, effectively shutting her out again.

'I have to go away for a few days,' he said into the silence, his voice sounding gut-wrenchingly empty.

After another little silence he turned around to look at her, the storm raging outside his backdrop. 'I have some things to see to interstate and I won't be back before the weekend.'

'That's OK,' she said softly. 'I can continue with the assessment on my own. There are quite a few things I'll need to do some research on anyway in order to give you some idea of valuation.'

'I don't care what this stuff is worth; I just want it out of here,' he said.

Ashleigh watched as he strode out of the room, his eyes avoiding hers as if he didn't want her to see the residual pain reflected there.

She didn't need to see it, she thought sadly, as the door clicked shut behind him.

She could *feel* it for him.

CHAPTER SEVEN

'But I don't want to go to crèche!' Lachlan whined for the fifth time a few days later on the Friday morning.

Ashleigh's patience was wearing thin. She hadn't slept properly in days, unable to erase the images of Jake's haunted past from her mind. Each day she'd spent in the old house seemed to make it worse, especially as he wasn't coming back until Monday to break the long aching silences. She knew it was disloyal to Howard, but she missed seeing Jake, missed hearing him move about the house and garden. God help her, she even missed his snarls and scornful digs.

'You have to go, Lachlan,' she insisted, stuffing his lunch box in his backpack.

'But I want to come wif you!' His chin wobbled and his dark eyes moistened.

Ashleigh felt the strings on her heart tighten; her son's little speech impediment always returned in moments of stress. She put the backpack to one side and squatted down in front of him, holding his thin shoulders so that he had to look at her.

'What's wrong, darling? Is someone making you unhappy at crèche?'

He shook his head, his bottom lip extended in a pout.

She gently pushed on his lip with the tip of her finger. 'You'll trip over that if you poke it out any further.' She gave him a smile as his lip returned to base. 'Now, what's all this about?'

He shuffled from one foot to the other. 'I just want to be wif you.'

Ashleigh sighed. 'Darling, you know I have to work. We can't live with Granny and Grandad for ever. They need time alone and we need to have our own place too. As soon as Howard and I get married…' She found it strange saying the words and secretly wished she could take them back.

'Can I have a dog when we move to Uncle Howard's?' Lachlan asked hopefully.

She forced her attention back to her son. His desire for a dog had been so strong but her mother's allergy to cat and dog hair had prevented it happening. However, Howard's home with its pristine family heirloom décor was hardly the family home a playful puppy would be welcomed into. She could almost see Marguerite Caule's look of horrified distaste at the first set of muddy pawprints on the pristine white carpet or one of the linen-covered sofas.

'We'll see,' she said and straightened.

'We'll see means no,' Lachlan said with the sort of acuity that marked him as Jake's son if nothing else. 'You always say that, but it doesn't mean yes.'

She sighed and, zipping up his backpack, reached for his hand. 'Come on, I'm late as it is.'

'I'm not going to crèche.' He snatched his hand away.

'Lachlan, I will not tolerate this from you,' she said through tight lips. 'I have to go to…to that house I'm working at and I have to leave now.'

'Take me to the house!' he begged. 'I'll be good. I won't touch anyfing.'

Ashleigh closed her eyes as she pinched the bridge of her nose.

Today of all days, she winced in frustration. Her mother

was out at a fundraising breakfast and wouldn't be back for hours. It was her father's annual heart check-up appointment in town and he'd left early to avoid the traffic and Mia had gone to an audition straight from the gym. Ellie, her last hope, hadn't come home yet from an all night sleep-in-the-park-for-homeless-dogs public awareness stunt that would probably see her on the front page of the morning's paper. It had happened before.

She let out her breath in a whoosh of tired resignation. 'All right, just this once. But if you so much as touch anything or break anything I won't let you watch *The Wiggles* or *Playschool* for a week.'

'Thank you, Mummy!' Lachlan rushed at her and buried himself against her, his arms around her waist, his cheek pressed to her stomach.

She eased him away to quickly scrawl a note for her mother who usually picked Lachlan up from the crèche on Friday afternoons to tell her about the change of plan.

'I love you, Mummy,' Lachlan said as she stuck the note on the fridge with a magnet.

'I love you, too, baby, but you're getting too big for pulling this sort of stunt.'

'What's a stunt?'

She tucked his hand in hers and shouldered open the door. 'Come on, I'll tell you in the car.'

Ashleigh was surprised and more than a little proud of the way Lachlan behaved at Jake's house. He had played quietly by her side as she worked in the library, never once complaining about being bored. He wheeled his little collection of toy cars across the floor, parking them in neat little rows on the squares on the Bakhtiari carpet with meticulous precision.

She knew she was taking a risk having him with her but

couldn't help feeling it had been worth it to see the simple joy on his little face every time she looked down at him.

She knew she was no different from every other working single mother, so often torn between the necessities to provide a reasonable living whilst allowing adequate time to nurture the child she'd brought into the world, but it still pained her to think how short-changed Lachlan was. Of late he'd been increasingly unsettled and clingy and she felt it was her fault. She'd thought her engagement to Howard would have offered him a bit more security but, while he liked Howard, she knew Marguerite intimidated him, although he did his very best not to show it.

'Can I go out into the garden for a while?' Lachlan got up from the floor with his little cars tucked into the old lunchbox container he kept them in, his dark eyes bright with hope.

Ashleigh pursed her lips as she thought about it. The garden, though large, was enclosed and the neighbourhood very quiet. The sun was shining, which it hadn't done properly in days, and she knew that—like most little boys his age—he needed lots of exercise and space.

'As long as you promise not to go through the side gate to the front; I can check on you while I'm working in this part of the house.'

'I promise,' he said solemnly.

A smile found its way to Ashleigh's mouth and she reached out a hand and ruffled his dark hair. 'Thanks for being so good this morning. It's really nice to have some company in this big old house.'

'Who lives here, Mummy?' Lachlan asked.

'No one at the moment,' she answered, fiddling with a gold shield-shaped bloodstone opening seal. 'The person who used to live here has…gone.'

'Did they die?'

It occurred to Ashleigh at that point that Lachlan had recently lost a blood relative, his paternal grandfather. It seemed unfair not to be able to tell her son who had actually lived in this house, when if things had been different he might have visited like any other grandson would have done, maybe even inherited some of the priceless pieces she was documenting.

But telling Lachlan would mean having to reveal the truth to Jake.

She wasn't ready to tell him and, given what she'd heard earlier that week about his childhood, Jake was nowhere near ready to hear.

'An old man used to live here,' she said.

'All by himself?' Lachlan asked, giving the imposing library a sweeping glance, his eyes wide with amazement.

'Yes…but a long time ago he used to live here with someone.'

'Who was it?' Lachlan's voice dropped, the sibilance of his childish whisper making Ashleigh feel slightly spooked.

'His…son.'

'Didn't he have a mummy too?'

'Yes…but she…she went away.' Ashleigh could see the stricken look come into Lachlan's eyes and wished she hadn't allowed the conversation to get to that point. As a child a few months off turning four who had grown up thus far without a father, his very worst nightmare was to have something take his mother away as well. She had always done her best to reassure him but still his fear lingered. She could see it in the way he looked at her at times, a wavering nervousness in his dark brown gaze, as if he wasn't sure if he would ever see her again once she walked out of the door.

She bent down and, tipping up his chin, pressed a soft kiss to the end of his nose. 'Why don't you go and explore the garden and in five minutes I'll join you. I'll bring out a drink and some fruit just like they do at crèche.'

His small smile brightened his features but did nothing to remove the shadow of uncertainty in his eyes. 'OK.'

She took his hand and led him back through the house to the back door, watching as he went down the steps with his car collection tucked under one small arm. He went straight to the elm tree, she noticed. The leafy shade was certainly an attraction on such a warm morning but she couldn't help wondering if it was somehow genetic.

She waited for a while, watching him set out his array of cars on the patches of earth where the lawn had grown thread-bare, parking each of them neatly before selecting one to drive up and down the exposed tree root nearest him.

A pair of noisy currawongs passed overhead and a light warm breeze stirred the leaves of the old elm, making each one shiver.

'I'll be out to check on you in five minutes, poppet,' she called out to him.

He didn't answer, which in a way reassured her. He was happy playing under the tree with the sounds of the birds to keep him company.

After being in the outdoor sunshine it took a moment for Ashleigh's eyes to adjust when she went back to the library. She took a few photos of some Tunbridge Ware book slides and stands and wrote a few notes about each, unconsciously gnaw-ing the end of her pen as her thoughts gradually drifted to Jake.

She wondered where he was and who he was seeing in-terstate. She drew in a painful breath as she thought of him with another lover. Over the years she'd forced herself not to think of him in the arms of other women and mostly she'd been successful. She'd been too busy looking after his little son to torture herself with images of leggy blondes, racy redheads or brunettes with the sort of assets that drew men like bees to a paddock full of pollen.

'You look pensive,' Jake's deep voice said from the door of the library.

Ashleigh nearly swallowed the pen she had in her mouth

as she spun around in shock. 'What are you doing here?' she gasped, the pen falling from her fingers.

He eased himself away from the door frame where he'd been leaning and came towards her, stooping to pick up the pen and handing it to her with a quirk of one dark satirical brow. 'My business was dealt with a whole lot earlier than I expected,' he said. 'I thought I'd surprise you.'

You certainly did that, she mused, even as her stomach rolled over at the thought of him taking a look out of the library window. One look and she would have hell to pay.

She forced her features into impassivity. 'I didn't hear you come in... Which door did you use?'

'The front door,' he answered as he picked up a Tunbridge Ware bookmark and began to turn it over in his hands.

Ashleigh edged towards the window, waiting until she was sure Jake was looking elsewhere before quickly checking on Lachlan. Her heart gave an extra beat when she couldn't see him under the tree. She glanced back at Jake but he appeared to be absorbed in the bookmark. Checking the elm tree once more, she found her son had come back into view. Her heart's pace had only just settled down again as she turned back to look at Jake.

He was watching her steadily, his dark intelligent gaze securing hers.

'So...' She forcibly relaxed her shoulders, a tight smile stretching her mouth as her heart began its rollercoaster run again. 'How was your business trip?'

'It was nothing out of the ordinary,' he responded, his eyes never once moving away from hers. 'How have you been while I've been away?'

'Me?' It came out like a squeak and she hastily cleared her throat and began again. 'I mean...I'm fine. Great, been to the gym and feeling pretty fit and...' She couldn't finish the sentence under his probing gaze. She was rambling but she knew that if she didn't go out to Lachlan soon he would come in to her. She didn't know which would be worse. Maybe she should just come right out and tell Jake now before he set eyes on Lachlan. It wasn't much of a warning for him, but what else could she do?

She straightened her spine and faced him squarely. 'Jake… I have something to tell you that…' She took a much needed breath and continued. '…that I should have told you before, but I just felt it was never the right time, and—'

'Mummee!' A child's voice rang out from the back of the house, closely followed by the sound of little footsteps running down the hall.

Ashleigh swallowed painfully as her son came rushing into the room, her breath stopping completely when he cannoned into Jake's long legs encased in dark trousers.

She watched in stricken silence as Jake's hands steadied Lachlan, his touch gentle but sure as he looked down at the small face staring up at him.

'J-Jake, this is Lachlan,' she said in a voice she hardly recognised as coming from her own mouth. 'Lachlan, this is…Jake.'

Lachlan, with the impulsiveness of youth on his side, got in first. 'Are you the boy who used to live here a long time ago?'

Jake stared down at the little child in front of him for what seemed like endless minutes until he registered that the boy had spoken to him. 'Yes…I am,' he said, hoping his tone wasn't showing how shell-shocked he felt.

Ashleigh had a child.

The child she'd always wanted.

The child he wouldn't give her, *refused* to give her.

He couldn't look at her. He knew if he did she would see his disappointment, his *unjustified* disappointment.

So she'd had Howard's child.

He assumed it was Howard's, although the child in front of him certainly didn't look much like Ashleigh's fiancé, he had to admit. The sick irony of it was that the kid looked more like him. Once the thought was there it tried to take hold but he just as quickly dismissed it, although it surprised him how much it hurt to let it go.

There was no way that kid could have been his. He'd watched Ashleigh take her pills every day; it had been part of their daily ritual. *He* had made it a part of it. She'd never missed a dose and if she had he would have insisted on using an alternative until things were safe.

It was hard to assess the kid's exact age. He'd deliberately avoided everything to do with children for most of his adult life and had very little idea of what age went with what stage in a child's life. On what limited knowledge he had, he thought the boy might have been about three and a half, which meant Ashleigh had dived pretty quickly into Howard Caule's bed, but then, hadn't she done the same with him?

The prospect of fathering a child had always terrified him. He had become almost paranoid about it. The thought of spreading his father's genes to the next generation had been too much for him to bear. How could he ever forgive himself if he turned on his own child the way his father had done to him? Parenting wasn't an easy task. How soon would it have been before a light tap of reproof became a closed-fist punch? How quickly would his gentle chastising tone have turned into full-blown self-esteem eroding castigation? How many unspeakable hurts would he have inflicted before the child was damaged beyond repair?

Nothing had ever been able to convince him it would be desirable to father a child, and yet one look at Ashleigh's little son had rocked his conviction as only flesh and blood reality could do. She'd had another man's child because he had been too much of a coward to confront his past and deal with it appropriately.

A burning pain knifed through him as a sudden flood of self-doubt assailed him. But what if he *hadn't* turned out like his father? What if, in spite of all that had been done to him, he could have rewritten the past and become a wonderful father, the sort of father he had longed for all his life? One who would listen to the childish insecurities that had plagued him, especially after his mother had died. Who would have listened and comforted him instead of berating him and punishing for simply being a lost, lonely little boy.

Other people had difficult backgrounds; there was hardly a person alive who didn't have some axe to grind about their past. Why had he let his take over his life and destroy his one chance at happiness? His father had been violent and cruel and totally unworthy of the role of parent, but in the end the person who had hurt Jake the most had been himself. When Ashleigh had walked out of his life four and a half years ago he had done absolutely nothing to stop her. Instead he had stood before her, stiff and uncommunicative, as she accused him of being unfaithful after she'd mistakenly read one of his e-mails about his recent trip to Paris. He could have told her then and there the real reason for his weekend away but he hadn't, for it would have meant revealing the filthy shame of his past to her. In the end his pride had not been able to stretch quite that far.

'I was going to tell you…' Ashleigh said, taking Lachlan's hand in hers and drawing him close to her.

Jake saw the way the child's eyes were watching him, the sombre depths quietly assessing him. It unnerved him a bit to have a kid so young look at him so intently, as if he were searching for something he'd been looking for a long time.

'It's none of my business,' he said, wishing his tone had sounded a little more detached.

Ashleigh had been waiting for the bomb to drop and found it hard to grasp the context of his words for a moment. She studied his expression and nervously disguised a swallow as his eyes went to Lachlan before returning to hers.

'I know it's probably very sexist of me, but it sure didn't take you long to replace me, did it?' he said.

It took her a nanosecond to get his meaning but she didn't know whether to be relieved or infuriated. Couldn't he see his own likeness standing before him in miniature form?

'I don't think this is a conversation we should be having at this time,' she said, indicating her son by her side with a pointed look.

'You're right,' Jake agreed.

There was a tense little silence. Ashleigh hunted her brain for something to fill it but nothing she wanted to say was suitable with her young son standing pressed to her side, facing his father for the very first time.

She wanted to blame someone.

She wanted to pin the responsibility for this situation on her mother for having a prior commitment, on her father for having a heart condition that needed regular monitoring, on her sister Mia for having an audition and Ellie for having a social conscience that was too big for her. If any of them had been free she wouldn't be standing in front of Jake now with his son, with a chasm of misunderstanding and bitterness separating them.

But in the end she knew there was no one to blame but herself. She should have told Jake four and a half years ago, given him the choice whether to be involved in his child's life or not.

Her mother was right. Even if he had pressed her to have a termination, the final decision would surely have been hers. She had thought she was being strong by walking away but, looking back with the wisdom of hindsight, she had to concede that she'd taken the weakling's way out. She had run for cover instead of facing life head on.

She turned to Lachlan, schooling her features into a serenity she was far from feeling. 'Poppet, why don't you go back out to the garden and we'll join you in a few minutes?'

Lachlan slipped his hand out of hers and scampered away without a single word of protest. He gave one last look over his shoulder before his footsteps sounded out down the hall as he made his way to the back door leading out to the garden.

This time the silence was excruciating.

Ashleigh felt each and every one of its invisible tentacles reaching out to squeeze something out of her but her throat had closed over as soon as Jake's eyes came back to hers.

'He doesn't look much like Howard,' he commented.

'That's because he's not Howard's son.'

'You surprise me.' The cynical smile reappeared. 'I didn't think you were the sleep-around type.'

'I had a very good teacher,' she returned, marginally satisfied when his smile tightened into something else entirely.

'How old is he?' he asked after another tense moment or two.

'Why do you ask?'

He shrugged one shoulder. 'Isn't it the usual question to ask?'

'As you said earlier, it's none of your business.'

'Maybe, but I'd still like to know,' he said.

'Why?'

It seemed an age before he answered.

'Because I need to be absolutely sure he's not mine.' He scraped a hand through his hair and added, 'You would have told me if he was, wouldn't you?'

It was all Ashleigh could do to hold his penetrating gaze. She felt herself squirming under the weight of its probe, the burden of her secret causing her a pain so intense she could scarcely draw in a breath.

'You can take a paternity test, if you'd like,' she said, taking a risk she wasn't sure would pay off. 'Then you can be absolutely sure.'

He gave her a long contemplative look before asking, 'Are you in any doubt of who the child's father is?'

'No,' she answered evenly. 'No, I know exactly who the father is.'

Jake moved away and went to the window she'd guarded so assiduously earlier. 'It was the one thing I could never give you, Ashleigh,' he said with his back still towards her. 'I told you that from day one.'

'I know…'

'I just couldn't risk it,' he said. He took a deep breath and added, 'My father…'

She bit her lip as she heard the slight catch in his voice, knowing how difficult this was for him.

'My father suffered from a rare but devastating personality disorder,' he said heavily. 'It's known to be genetic.'

'I understand…'

Jake squeezed his eyes shut, trying to block out the vision of Ashleigh's child playing underneath the tree he'd spent most of his own childhood sheltering beneath or in.

'No, you can't possibly understand,' he bit out, turning around to face her. 'Do you think I've wanted to have this burden all my life? I wish I could walk away from it, be a normal person for once instead of having to guard myself from having a re-run of my childhood played out in front of me every day.'

'I'm sorry…' She lowered her eyes from the fire of his, unable to withstand the pain reflected in his tortured gaze.

'But I couldn't risk it,' he went on. 'I couldn't put that intolerable burden on to another person. Not you, or whatever children we might have produced. My father was a madman who could switch at any moment. I'd rather die than have any child of mine suffer what I suffered.'

'But it might have skipped a generation…' she offered in vain hope.

'And then what?' His eyes burned into hers. 'I would have to watch it played out in the next or even the one after that but have no control over it whatsoever.' His expression grew embittered as he continued, 'How could I do that and live with myself?'

Ashleigh swallowed painfully. The burden of truth was almost more than she could bear but she knew she couldn't tell him about Lachlan's true parentage now. It would totally destroy him.

She watched as he sent his hand through his hair, his eyes losing their heat to grow dull and soulless as he turned to stare out of the window, the wall of his back like an impenetrable barrier.

'You don't know how much I've always envied you, Ashleigh,' he said after another long moment of silence. 'You have the sort of background that in fact most people today would envy. You have two parents who quite clearly love each other and have done so for many years exclusively, two sisters who adore you and not a trace of ill feeling to cast a shadow over the last twenty-odd years you've spent being a family.' He turned and looked at her, his expression grim. 'I'm sorry for what I couldn't give you, Ashleigh. If it's any comfort to your ego, I was tempted. Damn tempted. More tempted than I'd ever been previously and certainly more tempted than any time since.'

'Thank you…' she somehow managed to say, her eyes moving away from the steady surveillance of his.

She heard him give one of his trademark humourless grunts of laughter.

'Aren't you going to ask me how many lovers I've had over the years? Isn't that what most women would have asked by now?'

'I'm not interested,' she answered.

'How many lovers have you had?' he asked.

'I told you before, it's none of your business.'

'Well…' He stroked the line of his jaw for a moment, the raspy sound of his fingers on his unshaven skin making Ashleigh's toes curl involuntarily. 'One has to assume there have been at least two. Your son's father for one and then, of course, there's dear old Howard.'

Ashleigh felt increasingly uncomfortable under his lazy scrutiny. She kept her eyes averted in case he caught even a trace of the hunger she knew was there. She could feel it. It crawled beneath the surface of her skin, looking for a way out. Even her fingertips twitched with the need to feel his flesh under them once more. Behind the shield of her bra she could feel the heavy weight of her breasts secretly aching for the heat and fire of his mouth and tongue, and her legs were beginning to tremble with the effort of keeping her upright when all they wanted was to collapse so her body could cling to the strength and power of his.

'Tell me, Ashleigh.' Jake's voice was a deep velvet caress across her too sensitive skin. 'Does Howard make you scream the way I used to?'

She stared at him speechlessly, hot colour storming into her cheeks, her hands clenching into fists by her sides.

'How dare you ask such a thing?' she spat at him furiously.

His lip curled. 'You find my question offensive?'

She sent him a heated glare. 'Everything about you is offensive, Jake. You might think handing over your father's goods for free gives you automatic licence to offend me at every opportunity, but I won't allow you to speak to me that way.'

'It's a perfectly reasonable question, Ashleigh,' he said. 'You and I did, after all, have something pretty special going on there for a couple of years way back then. I was just wondering, as any other man would, if your future husband comes up to scratch in the sack.'

She folded her arms and set her mouth. 'Unlike you, Jake Marriott, Howard treats me with a little more respect.'

'You mean he hasn't had you up against the kitchen bench with your knickers around your ankles?' he asked with a sardonic gleam in his dark eyes. 'Or what about the lounge room floor with all the curtains opened? Has he done you there? Or what about the—'

'Stop it!' She flew at him in outrage, her hands flying at his face to stop the stream of words that shamed her cruelly. 'Stop it!'

Jake caught her flailing arms with consummate ease and pulled her roughly into his embrace, his mouth crashing down on hers smothering her protests, her cries, even her soft gasp of pleasure...

His tongue slid along the surface of hers, enticing it into a sensuous, dangerous, tempting dance that sent the blood instantly roaring through her veins, the rush of it making her head swim with uncontrollable need—a need that had lain hidden and dampened down for far too long.

Ashleigh vaguely registered the sound of movement in the hall, but was too far gone with the sensations of Jake's commanding kiss to break away from his iron hold.

So what if Lachlan came in and found her kissing Jake as if there was no tomorrow? The truth was that there was no tomorrow for her and Jake, and this kiss would very probably have to last a lifetime.

But in the end it wasn't Lachlan's voice that had her springing from Jake's arms in heart-stopping shock.

It was her sister's.

CHAPTER EIGHT

'ASHLEIGH, I just thought I'd let you know—' Ellie pulled up short when she came across her sister's stricken look '—that Mum couldn't make it to pick up Lachlan so…so I decided to come and take him off your hands.' She pointed in the general direction of the front door. 'I did try and knock but there was…no answer…'

Jake let his arms fall from Ashleigh and greeted Ellie with his customary somewhat detached politeness.

'Hello, Ellie.' He brushed her cheek briefly with a kiss. 'You're looking…er…very grown up.'

Ashleigh felt like groaning at his understatement. Ellie had the sort of figure that turned heads, male and female, her most attractive feature, however, being that she seemed totally unaware of how gorgeous she looked.

'Hi, Jake!' Ellie beamed up at him engagingly. 'You're looking pretty good yourself.' She glanced about the room and added, 'Wow, this sure is some mansion.' She turned back to look at him. 'I didn't know you had a thing for antiques.'

'I don't,' Jake answered. 'Ashleigh is helping me sort through everything.'

Ashleigh wanted the floor to open up and leave her to the spiders under the house's foundations. Surely it would be better than facing the knowing wink of her cheeky younger sister, who was quite obviously speculating on the interesting little tableau she'd just burst in on.

Ashleigh knew for a fact that Jake certainly wasn't suffering any embarrassment over it. She caught the tail-end of his glinting look, his dark eyes holding an unmistakable promise to finish what he'd started as soon as they were alone, rules or no rules.

'Ashleigh will do a fine job, I'm sure, won't you, Ash?' Ellie grinned. 'She'll have all your most valuable assets in her hot little hands in no time.'

Ashleigh threw her a fulminating look but just then Lachlan's footsteps could be heard coming along the hall.

'Auntie Ellie!' Lachlan came bounding in, instantly throwing his arms around Ellie's middle and squeezing tightly.

'Hi there, champ.' Ellie hugged him back and then bent down to kiss the tip of his nose, 'How did you get out of going to crèche, you monstrous little rascal?'

'I wanted to be with Mummy,' Lachlan answered, his cheeks tinged with pink as he lowered his eyes.

Ellie straightened and, giving his hair a quick ruffle, kept her hand on his little head as she turned to face her sister. 'I saw your note so I thought I would come instead. I took the bus so it will be a bit of a trek back, but Mum met up with an old school friend. I thought it best if I left her to catch up over a long lunch. Besides…' She tucked her spare hand into her torn jeans pocket and tilted her platinum blonde head at Jake. 'I wanted to check out what Jake thought of his son now that he's finally met him.'

Ashleigh felt every drop of blood in her veins come to a screeching, screaming halt. She even wondered if she was going to faint. She actually considered feigning it to get out of the way of the shockwaves of the bomb Ellie had unthinkingly just delivered.

Six sickening heartbeats of silence thrummed in her ears as she forced herself to look at Jake standing stiffly beside her.

'*My son?*' Jake stared at Ellie in stupefaction.

Ashleigh saw the up and down movement of her sister's throat as she gradually realised the mistake she'd just made.

'I—I thought you knew…' Ellie turned to Ashleigh for help but her older sister's expression was ashen, the line of her mouth tight with tension. She swivelled back to Jake's burning gaze. 'I kind of figured that since Lachlan was here at your house…' Her words trailed off, her eyes flickering nervously between the two adults. 'I sort of thought…she must have told you by now…'

'Mummy?' Lachlan piped up, his childish innocence a blessed relief in the tense atmosphere. 'Can I show Auntie Ellie the garage for my cars I made under the tree?'

Ashleigh gave herself a mental shake. 'Sure, baby, take her outside and show her what you've been up to.'

'Come on, Auntie Ellie.' Lachlan took Ellie's hand and tugged it towards the door. 'I made a garage out of sticks and a driveway and a real race track. Do you want to see?'

'I can hardly wait,' Ellie said, meaning it, and giving her sister one last please-forgive-me glance, closed the door firmly behind them.

As silences between them went, this one had to be the worst one she'd ever experienced, Ashleigh thought as she dragged her gaze back to the minefield of Jake's.

'My son?' He almost barked the words at her.

She closed her eyes on the hatred she could see in his eyes.

'*My son?*' he asked again, his tone making her eyes spring open in alarm. 'You calculating, lying, deceitful little bitch! How could you do this to me?'

Ashleigh had no defence. She felt crushed by his anger, totally disarmed by his pain, not one word of excuse making it past the scrambled disorder of her brain.

He swung away from her, his movements agitated and jerky as if he didn't trust himself not to shake her senseless.

She watched in silent anguish as his hand scored his hair, the long fingers separating the silky strands like vicious knives.

'I can't believe you did this to me,' he said. 'I told you from day one this must never happen.' He swung back to glare at her. 'Did you do it deliberately? To force me into something I've been avoiding for all of my god-damned life?'

'I didn't do it deliberately,' she said evenly, surprised her voice came out at all.

His heavy frown took over his entire face. 'You were on the pill, for Christ's sake!'

'I know…' She bit her lip. 'I had a stomach bug when you were in New York that time…I didn't think…I thought it would be all right…'

'Why didn't you tell me, for God's sake?'

She stared at him, a slow-burning anger coming to her defence at long last. 'How could I possibly tell you? You would have promptly escorted me off to the nearest abortion clinic!'

He opened his mouth to say something but nothing came out.

'You were always so adamant about no kids, no pets and no permanent ties,' she went on when he didn't speak. 'How was I supposed to deal with something like an unexpected pregnancy? I was just twenty years old, I was living in another country away from the security I'd taken for granted for most of my life, living with a man who had no time for sentimentality or indeed any of the ethics that had been drummed into me from the day I was born. How was I supposed to cope with such a heart-wrenching situation?' She drew in a ragged breath. 'For all I knew, you would have had me off to the nearest facility to get rid of "my mistake" before I could even think of an alternative. I wanted time to think of an alternative…'

'What sort of alternative were you thinking of?' he asked after a stiff pause.

She met his eyes for a brief moment. 'I couldn't face… getting rid of it…' She turned away and examined her hands. 'I considered adoption, but having seen Ellie go through the heartache of wondering whether to seek out her blood relatives or not, I just couldn't do it. I knew I would spend the rest of my life wondering what my child was doing. Whether his new parents would love him the way I loved him…whether he was happy…' She lifted her head and gave him an agonised look and continued. 'I knew that on his birth date for the rest of my life I would wonder… I would ache… I would want to know how he was… I couldn't go through with it. I had to have him. I had no other choice.'

She stared back down at the tight knot of her hands. 'I knew you wouldn't want to know about his existence, so I decided to go it alone. I knew it wouldn't be easy but my family have been wonderful. They love Lachlan so much…I can't imagine life without him now.'

Jake turned away, not sure he could cope with Ashleigh seeing how seriously he was affected.

A son!

His son!

His father's grandson…

His stomach churned with fear. This is what he had spent his lifetime avoiding and now here it was, inescapable. Ashleigh had given birth to his child without his permission and now he had to somehow deal with it.

'I want a paternity test,' he said. 'I want it done immediately and if you don't agree I'll engage legal help to bring it about.'

Ashleigh felt another corner of her heart break.

'If that's what you need I won't stop you.'

'I want it done,' he said, hating himself for saying it. 'I want it done so at least I know where I stand.'

'I don't want anything from you,' she said. 'I've never wanted anything from you. That's why I didn't tell you. I couldn't bear the thought of you thinking of me as some sort of grasping woman who wanted their pound of flesh on top of everything else.'

'Were you ever going to tell me?'

His words dropped into the silence like a bucket of ice-cold water on flames.

She seemed to have trouble meeting his eyes. He wasn't sure what to make of it but he assumed in the end it was guilt. Her shoulders were slumped, her head bowed, her hands twisting in front of her.

'Answer me, damn you!' he growled. 'Were you ever going to tell me?'

She lifted her head, her eyes glazed with moisture.

'I thought about telling you that first night…at the bar…' Her teeth caught her bottom lip for a moment before she continued raggedly. 'But you were so arrogant about insisting on seeing me again, as if I'd had no life of my own since we broke up. It didn't seem the right atmosphere to inform you of…of Lachlan's existence.'

Jake turned away from her, his back rigid with tension as he paced the floor a couple of times.

He couldn't take it in.

He tried to replay their conversation at the hotel bar, to see if there had been any hint of her well-kept secret, but as far as he could recall she had only met him under sufferance and had given every appearance of being immensely relieved to escape as soon as she possibly could.

'Jake, please believe me,' she appealed to him, her voice cracking under the pressure. 'I wanted to tell you so many times but you seemed so out of reach. And when you finally told me about your father I knew that if I told you it would only cause more hurt.'

'Hurt?' He swung back to glare at her. 'Do you have any idea of what you've done? How much you have hurt me by this?'

She tried her best to hold his fiery look but inside she felt herself falling apart, piece by piece.

'I know it seems wrong now but I thought I was doing the right thing at the time,' she said. 'I didn't want an innocent child to suffer just because his father didn't want to be a father. I thought I'd do my best…bring him up to be a good man and one day…'

Jake slammed his hand down on the nearest surface, the crash of flesh on old wood jarring her already overstretched nerves.

'Don't you see, Ashleigh? If things were different I would have gladly embraced fatherhood.' One of his hands moved over his face in a rubbing motion before he continued, his eyes dark with immeasurable pain. 'If I didn't have the sort of gene pool I have, do you not think I wouldn't have wanted a son, a daughter, maybe even several?'

She choked back a sob without answering.

He gave a serrated sigh and continued. 'I have spent my life avoiding exactly this sort of situation. I even went as far as insisting on a vasectomy but I couldn't find a surgeon who would willingly perform it on a man in his early thirties, let alone when I was in my twenties, especially a man who supposedly hadn't yet fathered a child.'

'I'm so sorry…'

He turned to look at her. 'Does your fiancé know I'm the boy's father?'

Ashleigh raised her eyes to his, her head set at a proud angle. 'His name is Lachlan. I would prefer it if you would refer to him as such instead of as "the boy".'

'Pardon me for being a bit out of touch with his name,' he shot back bitterly. 'I have only just been informed of his existence. I don't even know his birth date.'

'Christmas Eve,' she answered without hesitation.

Ashleigh could see him do the mental arithmetic and silently prepared herself for the fallout.

'You were almost *four months pregnant* when you left me?' he gasped incredulously.

She hitched up her chin even more defiantly. 'It wasn't as if you would have noticed. You were no doubt too busy with one of your other international fill-ins. Who was it now…Sigrid?'

He lowered his gaze a fraction. 'I wasn't unfaithful to you that weekend.'

'Why should I believe you?' she asked. 'I read her e-mails, don't forget. She said how much she was looking forward to seeing you, how much she had enjoyed meeting you that first time and how she hoped your "association" with her would continue for a long time.'

Jake closed his eyes in frustration and turned away, his hands clenched by his sides as he bit out, 'She means nothing to me. Absolutely nothing.'

'That's the whole point, isn't it, Jake?' she said. 'No one ever means anything to you. You won't allow them to. You keep everybody at arm's length; every relationship is on your terms and your terms only. You don't give, you just take. I was a fool to get involved with you in the first place.'

'Then why did you get involved with me?' he asked, turning around once more.

She let out a tiny, almost inaudible, sigh. 'I…I just couldn't help myself…'

Jake straightened to his full height, his eyes clear and focused as they held hers. 'I mean it, Ashleigh, when I say I wasn't involved in any way with Sigrid Flannigan.'

'Why should I believe you?'

'You don't have to believe me, but I would like you to hear my side of it before you jump to any more conclusions.'

'I asked you four and a half years ago and you refused to tell me a thing,' she pointed out stringently.

'I know.' He examined his hands for a moment before re-connecting with her gaze, a small sigh escaping the tight line of his lips. 'Sigrid is a distant cousin of mine. She was conducting some sort of family tree research. To put it bluntly, I wasn't interested. However, she was concerned about some health issues within the family line and I finally agreed to meet her. We met in Paris. She was there on some sort of work-related assignment and, as I was close by, I decided to get the meeting over and done with.'

'And?'

'And I hated every single minute of it.' He dragged his hand through his hair once more. 'She kept going on about how important family ties were and even though we were distantly related we should keep in touch. Apparently I have the questionable honour of being the one and only offspring of Harold Percival Chase Marriott, the last of the male line on that side of the family.' He sent her an accusing look and added, 'Or so I thought.'

'Why didn't you tell me the truth about her?' she asked, choosing to ignore his jibe. 'Why let me believe the worst?'

'I wasn't ready to talk to anyone about my background,' he said. 'I was tempted to tell you a couple of times but I couldn't help thinking that if I told you the truth of my upbringing it would in some way make the differences between us even more marked. Sigrid was an annoying reminder of where I'd come from and I wanted to forget it as soon as I could.'

'So you deliberately let me think she was your lover, even though in doing so it broke my heart?'

He gave an indolent shrug of one shoulder. 'I didn't tell

you what to believe. You believed it without the slightest in-put from me.'

She let out a choked gasp of outrage. 'How can you say that? You deliberately misled me! You were so cagey and ob-structive. You wouldn't even look me in the eye for days on end, much less speak to me!'

'I was angry, for God's sake!' he threw back. 'I was sick to my back teeth with all your tales of how wonderful your family was and how much you missed them. I was sick and tired of being the dysfunctional jerk whose only memories were of being bashed senseless until I could barely stand up-right. Do you think I wanted to hear how your mother and father tucked you into your god-dammed bed every night to read you a happy-ever-after story and tell you how much they loved you?'

Ashleigh had no answer.

She felt the full force of his embittered words like barbs in her most tender unprotected flesh. She had no personal hook to hang his experience on. She had never been shouted out; no one had ever raised a hand to her. Her parents had expressed their love for her and her sisters each and every day of their lives without exception. She was totally secure in their devotion. She had absolutely no idea of how Jake would have coped without such consistent assurances of belonging, no idea how he would have coped with nothing but harsh cruelty and the sort of vin-dictiveness which she suspected had at times known no bounds.

'Is this a good time to interrupt?' Ellie spoke from the doorway, for once her usually confident tone a little dented.

Jake recovered himself first and turned to face her, his ex-pression giving away nothing of his inner turmoil.

'Sure, Ellie.' He stretched his mouth into a small smile. 'Do you need a lift back into town? I'm just about to leave.'

'No,' Ellie insisted. 'I've already promised Lachlan a ride on the bus. He's looking forward to it.'

'So you haven't got your licence yet?' he asked.

Ellie gave him a sheepish grin. 'I've failed the test ten times but I haven't entirely given up hope.'

Jake couldn't help an inward smile. Same old delightful Ellie.

'Is there an instructor left in the whole of Sydney who'll take you on?'

Ellie pretended to be offended. 'I'll have you know I've been with the very best of instructors but not one of them has been able to teach me to drive with any degree of safety.'

'Tell me when you're free and I'll give you a lesson,' he offered. 'After driving in most parts of Europe I can assure you I can drive under any conditions.'

Ellie grinned enthusiastically. 'It's a date. But don't tell me I didn't warn you. Ashleigh will vouch for me. She gave up on lesson two when I ploughed into the back of a taxi.'

Jake swung his gaze to Ashleigh. 'What did she do, rattle your nerves?'

No more than you do, Ashleigh felt like responding. No, she would much rather have Ellie trying to drive in the peak hour any day than face the sort of anger she could see reflected in his dark eyes.

'I have learnt over time to recognise when I am well and truly beaten,' she said instead. 'Ellie needs a much more experienced hand than mine.'

'I don't know…' He rubbed his jaw for a moment in a gesture of wry speculation. 'Seems to me you're pretty experienced at most things.'

Ellie interrupted with a subtle clearing of her throat, Lachlan standing silently by her side, his small hand in hers.

'Excuse me, but we really need to get going if we're going to make the next bus.'

'Are you sure you don't want a lift?' Jake asked again, his glance flicking to the small quiet child at her side.

Before Ellie could answer, Lachlan piped up determinedly, 'I want to go on the bus.'

Jake met the dark eyes of his son, the sombre depths staring back at him sending a wave of something indefinable right through him.

He knew a paternity test was going to be a complete waste of time. This was his flesh and blood and there was clearly no doubt about it. Even the way the boy's hair grew upon his head mimicked his. It was a wonder he hadn't recognised it from the first moment but his shock in discovering Ashleigh had a child had momentarily distracted him. He had still been getting used to the idea of her carrying someone else's progeny when Ellie had dropped her bombshell.

'Don't hurry home.' Ellie filled the small silence. 'You two must have lots to catch up on. I can mind Lachlan tonight. I'm not going out.'

'That won't be necess—'

'That's very kind of you, Ellie.' Jake cut across Ashleigh's rebuttal. 'Your sister and I do indeed have a lot of catching up to do.'

Ellie sent Ashleigh an overly bright smile. 'Well, then... Come on, Lachlan, let's go and get that bus. We'll leave Mummy and Daddy to have a chat all by themselves.'

'Daddy?' Lachlan stopped in his tracks, his expression confused as he looked between his mother and aunt and back again.

Ashleigh sent her sister a now-see-what-you've-done look before bending down to her son.

'Lachlan...'

'Is he my daddy?' Lachlan asked in a whisper, his glance going briefly to the tall silent figure standing beside his mother.

Ashleigh swallowed the lump of anguish in her throat. 'Yes... Jake is your daddy.'

Lachlan's smooth little brow furrowed in confusion. 'But you told me he didn't want to ever know about me.'

'I know…but that was before and now…' She couldn't finish the sentence as her emotions took over. She bit her lip and straightened, turning away to try to pull herself together.

'Lachlan…' Jake stepped into the breach with an out-stretched hand. 'I am very pleased to meet you.'

Lachlan slipped his hand out and touched Jake's briefly, his eyes wide with wonder. 'Are you going to live with Mummy and me now?' he asked.

Jake wasn't sure how to answer. He had never really spoken to a child this young before. How did one go about explaining such complicated relationship dynamics to one so young?

'No,' Ashleigh put in before he could speak. 'Remember I told you? As soon as you go to big school we are going to live with Howard and Mrs Caule.'

Lachlan's shoulders visibly slumped and his bottom lip began to protrude in a pout. 'But I don't like Mrs Caule. She scares me.'

'Lachlan!' she reprimanded him sternly. 'She will be like a pretend granny for you, so don't let me ever hear you speak like that again.'

Ellie tactfully tugged Lachlan towards the door, 'Time to leave, mate.'

Ashleigh opened her mouth to call them both back but caught Jake's warning glance. She let out her breath in a whoosh of frustration and flopped into the nearest seat, dropping her head into her hands.

Jake waited until he heard the front door close on Ellie and Lachlan's exit before he spoke.

'You cannot possibly marry Howard Caule.'

She lifted her head from her hands to stare up at him. *'Excuse me?'*

He met her diamond-sharp gaze with steely determination.
'I won't allow it.'

She sprang to her feet, her hands in fists by her sides.

'What do you mean, you won't allow it?' She threw him
a blistering look. 'How the hell are you going to stop me?'

The line of his mouth was intractable as his eyes held
hers.

'You cannot possibly marry Howard Caule because you
are going to marry me instead,' he said. 'And I will not take
no for an answer.'

CHAPTER NINE

ASHLEIGH stared at him for several chugging heartbeats.

'I'm asking you to marry me, Ashleigh,' Jake said into the tight silence.

'Asking me?' she shot back once she found her voice. 'No, you're not. You're demanding something you have no right to demand!'

'Don't speak to me of rights,' he bit out. 'I had a right to know I'd fathered a child and you kept that information from me. This is payback time, Ashleigh. You either marry me or face the consequences.'

What consequences? she thought with a sickening feeling in the pit of her stomach. Exactly what sort of consequences was he thinking of?

Jake was a rich man.

A *very* rich man.

How could she even begin to fight someone with his sort of financial influence? The best lawyers would be engaged and before she knew it she would be facing custodial arrangements that would jeopardise her peace of mind for the rest of her life. How would she cope with seeing Jake every second weekend when he came to collect his son on visitation access? How indeed would she cope if he were to gain full custody of Lachlan?

'How long do you think such a marriage would last?' she asked, hoping her panic wasn't too visible, even though her insides were turning to liquid.

'It will last for as long as it needs to last,' he said. 'Every child needs security and, from what little I've seen so far, that little kid is insecure and in need of a strong father figure.'

He'd seen all that in one meeting? His perspicuity amazed her but she didn't let on.

'He's not yet four years old,' she said. 'I would have thought it was a little early to have him written off as an anxious neurotic.'

He gave her a hardened look. 'What did you tell him about me?'

She faced him squarely. 'I told him the truth. I told him his father had never wanted to be a father.'

Jake opened his mouth to berate her but snapped it shut when he saw the defiant glitter in her eyes. He turned away, his stomach clenching painfully as he mentally replayed every conversation he'd had with her in the past on the subject.

No wonder she hadn't told him of the pregnancy.

She was right.

He would have very likely packed her off to the nearest abortion clinic, railroading her into a procedure he had never until this moment given the depth of thought it demanded. Seeing Lachlan this afternoon had made him realise that a foetus was not just a bunch of cells. It had the potential to become a real and living person.

Lachlan was a real and living person.

And he was *his* son.

'I can't change the past, Ashleigh,' he said after another lengthy silence. 'I never wanted this sort of situation to occur but it has occurred and I realise now you probably had little choice in the matter.' He took a steadying breath and continued. 'Given the sort of background you've had, I can see how you would be the very last person to rush off to have a pregnancy terminated. And, as you said earlier, given Ellie's situation, I guess adoption wasn't an option you would have embraced with any sense of enthusiasm.'

Ashleigh witnessed the play of tortured emotions on his face as he spoke and wished she could reach for him and somehow comfort him. They shared the bond of a living and breathing child and yet it seemed as if a chasm the width of the world divided them.

He was devastated by the knowledge of his son's existence; it was his biggest nightmare come true in stark, inescapable reality. It didn't matter how sweet Lachlan was or how endearing his personality, for in Jake's mind there was no escaping the fact that, along with his genetic input, Harold Marriott's blood also flowed through his son's veins.

'I'm sorry, Jake…' she said. 'I don't know what else to say.'

'You can say yes,' he said. 'You can agree to marry me and then this situation will be resolved.'

'How can it be resolved?' she asked. 'How can we pretend things are any way near normal between us?'

'I would hazard a guess that things between us will be very normal. Once we're married we will resume our previous relationship.'

She gaped at him in shock. 'You mean a physical relationship?'

'But of course,' he answered evenly.

'Aren't you forgetting the little but no less significant detail that I already have a fiancé?'

He gave her a cynical look. 'I don't consider Howard Caule your fiancé. He hasn't even convinced you to wear his ring and I can tell by that hungry look in your eyes that he hasn't yet convinced you to share his bed.'

'There are still some men in the world who have some measure of self-control,' she put in with a pointed glare his way. 'Howard has faith. I respect that, even though I don't necessarily share it.'

'Faith?' He let out a scathing snort. 'He would need more than faith to live with you. You are the devil's own temptation from the tip of your head to your toes. I've wanted to throw you onto the nearest flat surface from the first moment I walked into the bar and saw you sitting there twirling your straw in that glass with your fingers.'

His words shocked her into silence. She could feel her skin lifting in physical awareness, tiny goose-bumps breaking out all over her and the pulse of her blood stepping up a pace as her breathing rate accelerated.

'I am engaged.' She finally found her voice but she knew it sounded even less convincing than previously. She looked down at her ringless fingers and repeated, as if to remind herself, 'I am engaged to be married to Howard.'

Jake plucked his mobile phone from his waistband and held it out to her. 'Tell him it's off. Tell him you're marrying me instead.'

Ashleigh stared at the phone as if it were a deadly weapon set to go off at the merest touch.

'I can't do that!'

'Do it, Ashleigh,' he commanded. 'Or I'll do it for you.'

'You can't make me break off my engagement!'

'You don't think so?' he asked, his lip curling sardonically. 'How about if I call dear old Howard and tell him the deal is off?'

Her throat moved up and down in a convulsive swallow.

'There are any number of antique dealers who would gladly snatch up this little load,' he continued when she didn't speak, sending his free hand in an arc to encompass the priceless goods in the room.

'You think you can persuade Howard to release me with such a bribe?' she asked.

'Why don't you call him and find out?' he suggested and pushed the phone towards her again.

She took the phone, her fingers numbly pressing in the numbers.

'Howard?'

'Ashleigh!' Howard's tone was full of delight. 'How was your day?' He hardly paused for her to respond before he went on. 'Do you remember that consignment from Leura that I'd thought we'd lost to the opposition? Well, you'll be thrilled to know that the family of the deceased have decided to give us the deal after all. Isn't that wonderful news? With the consignment you're getting from Jake Marriott we'll be the toast of the town come the antiques fair!'

'Howard…Jake has met Lachlan.'

'My mother, of course, is beside herself,' Howard rambled on excitedly. 'She and my father never imagined the heights I would aspire to, but I have you to thank for that, for without your—'

'Howard—' she interrupted him '—Jake knows about Lachlan.'

'I know it is early days but it will be in all the papers. Howard Caule Antiques will be the premier…' Howard took a small breath. 'What did you say?'

Ashleigh's eyes avoided Jake's as she said into the phone, 'Jake knows Lachlan is his son.' She took an unsteady breath and continued, 'He has asked me to marry him.'

There was a tiny beat of silence before Howard asked, 'What answer did you give him?'

'How do you think I answered?'

Howard let out a long sigh. 'Ashleigh, I know you've done your very best to hide it from me, but I've known for a long time now that you don't really love me.'

'But I—'

'It's all right, Ashleigh—' he cut through her protest '—I understand, I really do. You still have feelings for—'

'Is this about the consignment?' she asked sharply.

'How could you think that of me, Ashleigh?' The hurt in his tone was unmistakable. 'I would gladly let them go to someone else if I thought by insisting you marry me instead of Jake you would be happy. You are never going to be happy until you sort out your past with Jake and we both know it.'

Ashleigh clutched the phone in her hand with rigid fingers, annoyed that Jake was quite clearly hearing every word of her fiancé's.

'You'll have to go through with it,' Howard insisted. 'If not for Lachlan's sake, then for mine.'

'What do you mean?' she asked, her heart plummeting in alarm.

'Jake has a prior claim. He's the child's father, after all. I could never stand in his way; it wouldn't be right. It wouldn't be decent. It wouldn't be moral.'

'But what about us?' she asked in an undertone, turning her back on Jake's cynical sneer.

'Ashleigh.' Howard's voice was steady with resignation. 'You know how much I care for you, but I've known for a long time you don't really feel the same way about me. My mother has been concerned about it for ages. We could have been married months ago, but you wouldn't commit. Doesn't that tell you something?'

She found it difficult to answer him. She *had* been stalling, almost dreading the day when her life would be legally tied to his, in spite of her very real gratitude for all he'd done for her both professionally and personally.

Ashleigh chanced a glance in Jake's direction and noted the self-satisfied curl of his lip with a sinking feeling in her belly.

She turned her back determinedly and spoke to Howard once more. 'I'm sorry about this, Howard…I didn't mean to hurt you like this. You've been so good to me and Lachlan.'

'Don't worry,' Howard said. 'We will always be friends. Anyway, it's not as if we won't see each other. You do still work for me, remember?'

'Yes…'

Jake reached across and took the phone out of her hand and spoke to Howard. 'Caule, Jake Marriott here. Ashleigh won't be working for you once this consignment is delivered to your showroom. I have other plans for her.'

'Oh…I see… Well, then, I wish you all the best, both of you, and Lachlan, too, of course…' Howard's words trailed off.

'We should have this deal stitched up in the next week. It's been good doing business with you, Caule,' Jake said.

'Yes, yes, of course…marvellous to do business with you, Mr Marriott. Absolutely marvellous. Goodbye.'

'What a prick,' Jake muttered as he clipped the phone back on his belt.

Ashleigh stood stiff with rage, her eyes flashing with sparks of fury.

'You arrogant jerk!' She pushed at his chest with one hand. 'How dare you take over my life? "I have other plans for her" indeed! Who the hell do you think you are?'

Jake captured her hand and held it against the wall of his chest.

'I am your son's father and as soon as I can arrange it I will be your husband.'

'You can't cancel my job just like that!'

'I just did.'

'Exactly what plans have you in store for me?' she sniped. 'Licking your boots every day?'

He gave her mouth a sizzling glance before raising his eyes back to her flashing ones.

'No. I was thinking of you going a little higher than that.'

She was incensed by his blatant sexual invitation, her cheeks flaming as a flood of intimate memories charged through her brain.

'I don't want to marry you! I hate you!'

His hand tightened as she tried to remove herself from his hold.

'You don't hate me, Ashleigh,' he said, tugging her even closer, the hard wall of his body shocking her into silence. 'You want me. That's why you've been constructing all those silly little barriers of no touching and no looking and so on because you are so seriously tempted to fall into bed with me. You know you are. It's always been the same between us. From the very first day we met in London, the chemistry between us took over. Neither of us had any chance of holding it back.'

'Your ego is morbidly obese!' she threw at him. 'I have no desire to fall into bed with you.'

'Do you think if you say that enough times you will eventually convince yourself?' he asked. 'Don't be a fool, Ashleigh. I can feel your desire for me right here and now; it's like a pulse in your blood, the same pulse that is beating in mine.' He pressed the flat of her palm over his heart. 'Can't you feel it?'

Ashleigh's eyes widened as his drumming heartbeat kicked against her palm, her mouth going dry as his coal-black eyes glinted down at her with undisguised desire.

She could feel his strong thighs against hers, her soft stomach flattened by the flat hard plane of his, the heat and throb of his growing arousal reaching towards her tantalisingly, temptingly and irresistibly.

Her eyes flickered to his mouth and her breath tripped in her throat as his head came down. She felt the brush of his breath over her mouth just before he touched down, the gentle pressure of his mouth on hers so unlike the hectic passion-driven kisses of the past. For some reason it made it all the more difficult for her to move away. It felt so wonderful to have her lips tingle and buzz with sensation as his caressed hers in a series of barely there kisses.

She felt the intimate coiling of their mingled breaths inside her mouth as he deepened the kiss, the sexy rasp of his tongue sliding along hers, rendering her legs useless.

Her tongue retreated and then flickered tentatively against his, a hot spurt of arrant desire shooting upwards from between her thighs, making her stomach instantly hollow out. She felt the smooth silk of desire anointing her inside as his hardened erection burned into her belly with insistent pressure. Her body remembered how he filled her so completely, privately preparing itself for the intimate onslaught of his passion-driven body surging into her with relentless clawing need.

Her thoughts and memories were in the end betraying her. She had been so determined to push him away. She had wanted to clutch at whatever rag of pride she could to cover herself but it was hopeless. He was right; the chemistry they felt was far too strong to ignore. The air almost crackled with it every time they were in the same room, let alone in each other's arms as they were now.

Jake scooped her up just as she thought her legs were going to fail, and carried her through to his childhood bedroom, coming down hard on the mattress with her, his weight on her a heavy but delicious burden.

He fed off her mouth like a man who had been starved for too long, his lips greedy, ravenous and relentless. Ashleigh kissed him back with the same grasping desperate hunger, her lips swelling beneath the pressure of his, her hands already tearing at his clothes. She tugged his T-shirt out of his jeans and he shrugged himself out of it and sent it hurling across the room, drawing in a ragged gasp as she went for the waist-band of his jeans.

Her eyes drank in the sight of him, the fully engorged length of him, as she pulled away the covering of his tight-fitting underwear. His sharp groan of pleasure as her fingers ran over him lightly sent another burst of liquid need between her legs.

He pushed her hand away and lifted her top, pushing her bra off her straining breasts without even stopping to unfasten it properly. She sucked in a scalding little breath as his mouth closed around one tight aching nipple, the sensation of his teeth scraping her making her hover for a moment in that sensual sphere located somewhere between intense pleasure and exquisite pain.

He left her breasts for a moment while he shucked himself out of his jeans, his shoes thudding to the floor, coming back over her with determined hands to deal with the rest of her clothes. She heard the sound of a seam tearing but was way beyond caring. His hands were on her naked flesh, hot and heavy, rough almost, unleashing yet another trickle of sensual delight right through her.

Feeling his naked skin on hers from chest to thigh was almost too much sensation for her to deal with at once. Her brain was splintering with the electrifying pulse of his body on hers, the probing, searching thickened length of him between her legs.

Suddenly he was there, the force of his entry arching her back as she welcomed him without restraint, her body so ready for him she had trouble keeping her head. She wanted to linger over the feel of him, draw in the scent of their combined arousal to store away for private reflection, but his pace was too hard and fast and she got carried along with the tidal wave of it. She felt the tightening of her intimate muscles, the swelling of her most sensitised point rising to meet each of his determined thrusts.

As if sensing she was close he backed off, withdrawing slightly, his mouth lightening its pressure on hers.

She dragged her mouth from under his and clutched at his head with both of her hands, her eyes searching his face. 'Don't stop now,' she begged in a harsh whisper. 'You can't possibly stop now!'

His mouth twisted into a rueful grimace and he sank into her warmth again, the tightly bunched muscles of his arms either side of her as he supported his weight indicating the struggle he was undergoing to keep some measure of control. 'I shouldn't even be doing this,' he said, his voice tight with tension. 'I'm not wearing a condom.'

'It's all right,' she gasped as he sank a little deeper, her hands going to his buttocks, digging in to hold him where she most wanted him.

'Are you on the pill?' he asked, stilling for a moment.

The pill? Oh, God, when was the last time she'd taken the pill? What was today…? Friday… Surely she had taken it some time this week? She had become a little careless… It wasn't as if Howard had ever…

'Are you on the pill?' he repeated.

'Yes,' she said, mentally crossing her fingers.

'I'll pull out just in case,' he said.

'No!' She grasped at him again, her eyes wild with need. 'You don't have to do that.'

He gave her a sexy smile. 'There are other ways of dealing with it, don't you remember?'

She did remember.

That was the whole trouble.

She remembered it all; the poignant intimacy of taking him in her mouth to relieve him whenever there hadn't been enough time to linger over the preliminaries.

His eyes burned into hers as he began his slow sensuous movements again, each surge and retreat pulling at her with exquisite bone-melting tenderness.

His mouth came back to hers and she sighed with relief,

her legs gripping him tightly, not giving him another chance to pull away.

She felt each and every deep thrust of his body, even felt him nudge her womb where his son had been implanted with his seed, and a great wave of overwhelming emotion coursed through her.

She loved this man.

He was her world. Her life had started the day she'd met him and the only reason it had continued after they'd broken up was because she had carried a part of him away with her.

They were forever joined by the bond of their child and no matter how much he hated being a father and was only offering to marry her out of a sense of duty, she still loved him and knew she would do so until the day she drew her very last breath…

Jake gritted his teeth as he tried to hold back his release. He closed his eyes and counted backwards, trying to think of something unpleasant to focus on instead, but it was no good. The pressure building in him was just too strong. He felt like a trigger-happy teenager with Ashleigh, instead of a thirty-three-year-old man who was always in control.

Always.

'Oh, God!' He felt himself tip over, the emission of pleasure sending shockwaves of shivering ecstasy right through him, great deep racking shudders of it, until he collapsed in the circle of Ashleigh's arms.

He waited for five or so heartbeats of silence.

'I'm sorry.' He eased himself up on his arms to look down at her. 'That was so selfish and crass of me.'

Ashleigh reached up and touched the line of his lean jaw where a tinge of red was already pooling.

'No…don't apologise.'

'I couldn't hold back,' he said, his breathing still a little choppy. 'You have this weird effect on me. I feel about sixteen when I'm near you. All out-of-control hormones, no finesse, no foreplay, just full-on selfish lust.'

'You're not selfish…' She traced her fingertip over the line of his top lip lingeringly.

He took her finger into his mouth and sucked on it, hard.

Her eyes glazed over with unrelieved need and he released her finger, pressing her hand back to the mattress beside her head.

She knew what that look in his eyes meant and her stomach folded over as he moved down her body.

'You don't have to…*oh!*'

He lifted his head for a moment and sent her a spine-loosening look. 'I do have to, baby. I owe you.'

'I…I…' She gave up when his tongue separated her, hot bursts of pleasure sending every thought out of her brain.

She was mindless under his touch, a touch her body remembered like a secret code. Her senses leapt in acute awareness, her pleasure centre tightening to snapping point, each sensitive nerve stretched beyond endurance until it was beyond her capacity to contain it. She felt the rising waves go over her head, crashing all around her, fragmenting her consciousness until she was a mindless, limbless melting pool of nothingness…

Ashleigh wasn't sure how long the silence continued.

She lay with her eyes closed, not sure she was quite ready to meet Jake's penetrating gaze. She knew she had let herself down terribly. Falling into his arms like a desperado was hardly going to give her the ground she needed to maintain her pride.

What a mess!

She gave a painful inward grimace. The irony of it all was gut-wrenching to say the very least. Four and a half years ago all she had wanted was a marriage proposal from him, a promise of security and a future family they could nurture together in the same wonderful way her parents had done for her sisters and her. Instead, she had left him, pregnant, terrified and alone, knowing she had no future with him while she carried his child.

Had he ever cared for her?

He had never said the words. Those three simple words that had been uttered every day of her life in her family: I love you.

No. Jake had never said he loved her. He told her he desired her, he had overwhelmed her with the physical demonstration of his need for her, but he had not once said he loved her.

She felt the shift of the mattress as he got off the narrow bed and opened her eyes, not all that surprised to encounter the stiff line of his back turned towards her as he reached for his clothes.

'How long do you think it will take to get this place clear of all of this stuff?' he asked, zipping up his jeans and turning to face her.

Ashleigh had to fight not to cover herself. Some remnant of pride insisted she pretend she was totally unaffected by what had just transpired. She crossed her ankles and, releasing her hair from behind her neck, met his dark, unreadable eyes.

'I can get the house cleared within a few days,' she said. 'I haven't finished assessing it all, but that can be finalised in Howard's showroom.'

'Good,' he said, reaching for his discarded T-shirt. 'I want to get started on renovating so we can move in as soon as we are married.'

She took immediate offence at his assumption that she was simply going to fall in with his plans. 'Aren't you assuming a little too much?' she asked. 'I don't remember agreeing to marry you.'

His scooped up her clothes from the floor and tossed them towards her, his eyes sending her a warning. 'Get dressed. I want to meet with your family tonight to discuss the wedding arrangements.'

She flung herself off the bed and threw her clothes to one side, beyond caring that she was totally naked.

'You can take a running jump, Jake Marriott,' she snapped at him furiously. 'Do you think my parents are going to go along with your plans? I think I know them a little better than you do.' She folded her arms across her heaving breasts and added bitterly, 'Besides, I can't see my father giving his permission.'

'You're twenty-four years old, Ashleigh,' he pointed out neatly, his eyes flicking briefly to the upthrust of her breasts. 'I hardly think we need to have anyone's permission to get married.'

'I can't believe you want to go through with this. You've always been so against the institution of marriage. The fact that we share a child doesn't mean we have to get married.'

'No, but I have decided that I want to marry you and marry you I will.'

She sent him a caustic glare. 'Well, for one thing, your proposal certainly needs a little polish.'

'Yeah, well, I've never done it before so I'm sorry if it's a bit rough around the edges,' he said with an element of gruffness.

She turned away to step into her clothes, her fingers totally uncooperative under his silent watchful gaze. She bit back a curse as the zip on her skirt nicked the bare skin of her hip, the sudden smarting of tears in her eyes frustrating her. Why couldn't she be more in control around him? Why did he always reduce her to such a quivering emotional wreck?

She turned around at last, determined to have the last word, but he'd already gone. She stared at the wood panel of the door for endless moments, the scent of their recent lovemaking lingering in the air until she felt as if she was breathing the essence of him into her very soul...

CHAPTER TEN

ASHLEIGH drove away from Jake's house with a scowl of resentment distorting her features, her emotions in such disarray she could barely think.

She knew it was unreasonable of her, but a part of her felt intensely annoyed that Howard hadn't fought for her. She knew it was because of the sort of person he was, principled and self-sacrificing, the very qualities she'd been drawn to in her desperate quest for security. But he had caved in to Jake's demands without a single whimper of protest. And it totally infuriated her that Jake had borne witness to it; every time she recalled that self-satisfied smirk on his face her rage went up another notch.

She was far too angry to go home to face her family. She knew Ellie would hold on her promise to mind Lachlan for the evening, so instead of taking the turn to her parents' house, she drove on until she came to Balmoral Beach, a sheltered bay where she'd spent most of her childhood playing in the rock pools and swimming in the jetty enclosure.

She kicked off her shoes and walked along the sand until she came to Wyargine Reserve at the end of the beach, standing at the edge and looking out to sea, the evening breeze ruffling her hair.

After a while the breeze kicked up a pace and her bare

arms started to feel the slight nip in the evening air. She turned and went back the way she'd come, stepping over the rocky ground with care, her shoes still swinging from her hand.

Walking back along the Esplanade, she saw a slim figure jogging towards her and stopped as she recognised her sister Mia.

'Hey there, Ashleigh,' Mia chirped without a single puff. 'I thought you'd be home preparing for the celebrations tonight.'

Ashleigh frowned. 'Celebrations…celebrations for what?'

Mia gave her a rolling-eyed look. 'Your marriage, of course! Jake is around there now. He's brought French champagne. Loads of it. Mum and Dad are thrilled to bits.' She jogged up and down on the spot and continued. 'It was *so* romantic. Jake asked for a private meeting with Dad. How sweet is that? No one but no one asks a woman's father for her hand in marriage any more. Dad was really impressed. Mum was howling like an idiot, of course, and Lachlan has his chest out a mile wide.'

Ashleigh just stared at her, unable to think of a single thing to say. Her family had fallen in with Jake's plans without even consulting her to see if it was what she wanted.

'Is something wrong, Ash?' Mia stopped bouncing from foot to foot to peer at her. 'You do want to marry him, don't you? I mean Howard was all right, but he doesn't exactly ooze with sensuality the way Jake does.' She gave a chuckle of amusement, her grey-blue eyes sparkling cheekily. 'I could never quite imagine Howard dropping his trousers and going for it up against the kitchen bench. In fact, I can't imagine him doing it at all.'

'You are so incredibly shallow sometimes,' Ashleigh bit out and began to stalk back to her car.

'Hey!' Mia grabbed her arm and swung her around to face her. 'What's going on, Ash? Jake wants to marry you. *Hello?*'

She snapped her fingers in front of her older sister's face. 'Isn't that what you've always wanted, to be married to Jake and have a family?'

'He doesn't love me, Mia,' she said bitterly. 'He's only doing it because he found out about Lachlan.'

'I heard about Ellie's little clanger,' Mia said with an expressive little grimace. 'But, all things considered, he's taken it extremely well, don't you think? I mean, a lot of men would refuse to ever speak to you again and try and wriggle their way out of maintenance payments, not to mention insisting on a paternity test.'

'He did insist on one.'

'Oh…' Mia looked a little taken aback. 'Well…I guess that's understandable. I mean, you haven't seen him for years; Lachlan could easily have been someone else's kid.'

Ashleigh sent her a quelling look.

'I mean if you were any other sort of girl…which, of course, you're not,' Mia amended hastily.

They fell into step as they continued along the Esplanade and Mia tucked her arm through her sister's affectionately. 'You know something, Ashleigh, this is like a dream come true. Lachlan now has a father—his real father. I can already see how happy it has made him. Sure he's a little shy around Jake, but he keeps looking up at him with this big wide-eyed look of wonder and it just makes my heart go all mushy.'

Ashleigh kept walking, not trusting herself to respond.

'Jake even brought him a present,' Mia continued. 'It's one of those digging trucks. He said he could help him in the garden at Lindfield.'

He had it all planned, Ashleigh thought bitterly. She wasn't being considered in any part of this; even her family had succumbed to his plan to take over her life as if she had no mind of her own.

'Why are you frowning like that?' Mia asked. 'You love him, don't you, Ashleigh? You've always loved him.'

There didn't seem any reason to deny it.

'Yes, but that's not the point,' Ashleigh said, searching for her keys.

'Then what is the point?' Mia asked as they came to a halt beside Ashleigh's car.

Ashleigh shifted her gaze out to sea once more, a small sigh escaping before she could stop it. 'I have always loved Jake. From the moment I met him I felt as if there could never be anyone else who could make me feel that way. When we parted and I came back to Australia, I sort of drifted into a relationship with Howard, more out of a need for security than anything else. I thought if I settled down with some nice decent man I would eventually forget all about Jake.'

'Jake is not exactly the forgettable type,' Mia remarked wryly.

'Tell me something I don't already know.' Ashleigh gave her a twisted smile.

'Have you slept with him yet?'

Ashleigh felt her face start to burn and turned to unlock her car.

'*Ohmigod!*' Mia crowed delightedly. 'I knew it! You have! Look at your face—you're as red as anything!'

Ashleigh threw her a withering glance. 'One day, Mia, I swear to God I'm going to strangle you.'

Mia just laughed. 'I'll see you at home,' she said with her usual grin. 'I just want to run to the point and back again. Unlike you, my heart rate hasn't gone through the roof today.'

Ashleigh got into the car without another word.

Ashleigh had barely got in the door when Lachlan rushed towards her, his little face beaming.

'Look what Daddy gave me!' He held up the shiny truck for her to see.

She gave him an overly bright smile and bent down to kiss the top of his raven-dark head. 'I hope you said a big thank you,' she said.

'He did,' Jake said, stepping out into the hall from the lounge, his eyes instantly meshing with hers.

'I…I need to have a shower…' she said, making her way past him.

'Wait.' His hand fastened on her arm, halting her.

He turned to his son, who was watching them both with large eyes. 'Lachlan, give me five minutes with Mummy and I'll be up to read that story to you I promised earlier.'

Lachlan's face threatened to split into two with his smile. 'You mean just like a real daddy does?' he asked.

'You betcha.'

'And will you tuck me in and get me to blow the light out?'

Jake turned a quizzical glance Ashleigh's way.

'It's a little thing we do,' she answered softly so Lachlan couldn't hear. 'I put my hand on the light switch and as soon as he puffs a breath out I turn it off. It makes him think he's blown it out like a candle.'

'Cute.'

Jake turned back to the hovering child. 'Better get your lungs into gear, mate. That light might prove a bit difficult unless you start practising right now.'

Lachlan scampered off, the bounce in his step stirring Ashleigh deeply.

'He's a nice little kid,' Jake said into the sudden silence.

She raised her eyes to his, catching her bottom lip for a moment with her teeth.

'You left without saying goodbye,' he said. 'I was worried about you. Where have you been?'

'I needed some time alone. I went for walk on the beach.'

'I've told your family of our plans.'

'*Our* plans?' She sent him an arctic look. 'Don't you mean

your plans, meticulously engineered so that I have no way of extricating myself?'

'You know, Ashleigh, I don't quite see what all this fuss you're making is about. You were desperate for marriage all those years ago and now I'm offering it you want to throw it back in my face. What is it with you?'

'You're not marrying me for the right reasons.'

'What do you expect me to do?' he threw back. 'I come back to Australia to tie up my father's estate and suddenly find I have a nearly four-year-old son to a woman who is hell-bent on marrying a man she doesn't even feel a gram of attraction for.'

She blew out a breath of outrage, her hands fisting by her sides as she glared at him. 'What gives you the right to make those sorts of observations? You know nothing of my feelings for Howard.'

'Are you telling me you're in love with Howard Caule?'

'What difference would it make if I told you yes or no? You're still going to force me to marry you.'

'If he was truly in love with you he wouldn't have exchanged you for a houseful of useless antiques,' he said.

'He did not exchange me for the stupid consignment! He cares about me so, unlike you, he put his personal feelings aside so I could be free. It's called self-sacrifice, in case you aren't familiar with the term.'

Jake gave another one of his snorts of cynicism. 'It's called being a prick. If he was man enough he would have been round here by now knocking my teeth out.'

'But then Howard is not a violent man with no self-control,' she said with a pointed look.

She saw the flare of anger in his dark eyes and the sudden stiffening of his body.

'I have never laid a rough hand on you and you damn well know it,' he ground out.

'Yet,' she goaded him recklessly.

His mouth tightened into a harsh line of contempt. 'I see what you're trying to do. You're trying to push me into being the sort of man my father was. But you can't do it, Ashleigh. I am not going to do it. You can goad me all you like, throw whatever names and insults my way you want, but nothing will make me sink to that level. Nothing.'

'Er…' Ellie popped her head around the door, champagne bottle in hand, juggling two glasses in the other. 'Anyone for a drink?'

Jake gave Ashleigh one last blistering look and, excusing himself, informed Ellie he was going upstairs to put his son to bed.

Ashleigh stood rooted to the spot, her legs refusing to move.

'Trouble in paradise?' Ellie came to her, holding out a glass of champagne.

Ashleigh stared at the rising bubbles in the glass she took off her sister and, taking a deep breath, tipped back her head and downed the contents.

'Way to go, Ash!' Ellie grinned. 'God, he's gorgeous when he's angry. How in the world do you resist him?'

How indeed? Ashleigh thought. That was the whole damn trouble. She couldn't resist him. Her pathetic show of last-minute spirit was all an act. She had no intention of refusing to marry him, but her pride insisted she make him think otherwise.

'I'm going to have a shower,' she said, handing her sister her empty glass.

'Will I tell Jake to join you?' Ellie asked impishly.

'You can tell him to go to hell,' she muttered as she pushed past.

'Isn't that where *you've* been all these years?' Ellie said.

Ashleigh didn't answer. She didn't need to. Her baby sister knew her far too well.

* * *

Ashleigh took her time showering, trying to prolong the moment when she would join the rest of the family downstairs, champagne glasses in hand, wide smiles of congratulations on their lips.

She decided against dressing for the occasion and slipped into a pink sundress she'd had for years, not even caring that it was too tight around her bust. She dragged a brush through her still wet hair and, ignoring her make-up kit and perfume, left her room.

She was just about to go in and kiss Lachlan goodnight when she heard the murmur of voices in his room, Lachlan's higher pitched childish insertions once or twice, and the deep burr of Jake's as he finished the story he was reading. She stopped outside the open door, despising herself for eavesdropping but unable to stop herself.

'I love stories about dogs,' Lachlan was saying. 'I've always wanted a puppy but Granny has al…al…'

'Allergies?' Jake offered helpfully.

'Yes, I think that's what it's called. She sneezes all the time and has to have a puffer thing.'

'I had a dog once…a long time ago now,' Jake said. 'Her name was Patch.'

'That's a funny name.' Lachlan chuckled.

'Yeah…I guess…'

'What was she like?'

Ashleigh heard the sound of the mattress squeaking as Jake shifted his weight on the edge of the bed.

'She was the best friend I ever had.'

'Do you still miss her?'

'Sometimes…' Jake sighed and the mattress made another noise as he stood up. 'I should let you get some sleep.'

'Daddy?'

Ashleigh felt her breath lock in her throat and, before she could stop herself, she turned her head so she could see into the room to where Jake was standing looking down at his little son lying in the narrow bed.

'Yes?' Jake asked.

Lachlan's fingers began to fidget with the hem of his racing car sheet, his eyes not quite able to meet his father's.

'Have you changed your mind about wanting to be a daddy?'

It seemed a very long time before Jake answered, Ashleigh thought, her heart thumping heavily as she counted the seconds.

'I've changed my mind about a lot of things, Lachlan,' he said at last. 'Now go to sleep and we'll talk some more tomorrow.'

Jake took a couple of strides towards the door.

'Daddy?'

He turned to look at his son, something inside him shifting almost painfully when he saw the open adoration on the little guy's face.

'I love you, Daddy,' Lachlan said.

Jake swallowed the tight constriction in his throat but, no matter how hard he tried, he just couldn't locate his voice.

'I loved you even when I didn't know who you were,' Lachlan went on. 'You can ask Mummy, 'cause I told her. I've always wanted a daddy.'

Ashleigh hadn't been aware of making a sound but suddenly Lachlan saw her at the door and sent her a big smile.

'Mummy! Can I blow the light out now?' he asked.

'Not until I give you a big kiss goodnight,' she said and, moving past the silent figure of Jake, gathered her son in her arms and squeezed him soundly before kissing the tip of his nose, both his cheeks and each and every one of his little fingertips.

She straightened and went back to the door where the light switch was but as she put her hand out to it Jake's came over the top of hers and held it there.

'On the count of three, Lachlan,' Jake said, his voice sounding even deeper than usual. 'One…two…three!'

The light was extinguished on Lachlan's big puff of breath and he giggled delightedly as he burrowed back into his bedclothes.

Ashleigh slipped her hand out from under Jake's and met his eyes. She'd thought she had seen just about every emotion in those dark depths in the past but never until this moment had she seen the glitter of unshed tears.

'Jake?'.

He reached around her to close Lachlan's door softly, his eyes moving away from hers.

'Come on, your parents are waiting to congratulate us,' he said and, without waiting for her, moved down the hall.

Ashleigh watched his tall figure stride away, the set of his broad shoulders so familiar and yet so foreign. She had shared his body that afternoon and yet he did not want to share his heart.

Did he even have one?

Or was it too late?

Had his father destroyed that, along with every other joy he should have experienced as a child?

'Darling!' Gwen Forrester swept her daughter into her arms as soon as she came into the lounge. 'Congratulations! We are so very thrilled for you and Jake.'

Her father came over and hugged her tightly and Ashleigh buried her head into his shoulder, wondering if he knew how confused she really was.

'Jake.' Gwen started bustling about with her usual motherly fuss. 'Come and sit down and have a drink. Mia? Get your brother-in-law-to-be some champagne, or would you prefer a beer?'

'Champagne is fine,' Jake said.

'When are you going to get married?' Ellie asked.

'In a month's time,' Jake answered. 'It takes that long to process the licence.'

'Wow! A month isn't very long,' Mia said. 'Can I be bridesmaid?'

'Me, too!' Ellie put in.

Ashleigh stretched her mouth into a smile but inside she felt her anger simmering just beneath the surface.

'Will you have a big wedding?' Gwen asked.

'No, I don't think—' Ashleigh began but Jake cut her off.

'No point getting married if you don't do it properly.' He sent her a smile. 'After all, Ashleigh has always wanted to be a bride, haven't you, darling?'

She gave him what she hoped looked like a blissful smile although her jaw ached with the effort.

'How did Howard take the news?' Ellie asked, twirling her champagne glass in one hand.

Jake didn't give Ashleigh the chance to respond. His smile encompassed everyone as he said, 'He was a true gentleman. He wanted what was best for Ashleigh and wished us both joy.'

Ashleigh was sure her dentist was going to retire on the work she'd need done after this. She ground her teeth behind her smile and downed the contents of her glass, her head spinning slightly as she set it back down on the nearest surface.

'How soon will you be able to move into the house at Lindfield?' Heath asked.

'It will take most of the month, I'm afraid. I'm starting work on it this weekend,' Jake answered. 'In fact, I was hoping Ashleigh and Lachlan would come with me. It will be our first weekend as a family.'

Ashleigh knew she would look a fool if she said she had other plans so stayed silent.

'Are you sure Lachlan won't be in the way?' Mia gave her sister a mischievous wink.

'I'd like to spend some time with him,' Jake said. 'I won't let him come to any harm. The workmen won't arrive till Monday to do the major renovations, so it will be quite safe.' He turned to Ellie. 'I was hoping to take Ashleigh out tonight to celebrate on our own. Is your offer to babysit still on?'

'Sure!' Ellie beamed. 'Go out and have a good time. In fact, why don't you take her to stay out all night at your hotel? Lachlan won't wake up till morning and it's Saturday tomorrow so there's no rush to get him to crèche or anything.'

'But I—'

'I wouldn't want to impose…' Jake said before Ashleigh could get her protest out.

'Rubbish!' Gwen joined in heartily. 'Go on, the two of you, have some time to yourselves. After all, four and a half years is a lot of time to catch up on.'

'Thank you,' he said and turned to face Ashleigh. 'How long will it take you to get ready, darling?'

How about another four and a half years? she felt like retorting.

'Five minutes,' she said and left the room.

'You're very quiet,' Jake commented once they were on their way to the city a short time later.

She swivelled in her seat to glare at him. 'How could you do that to me?'

'Do what?' He flashed a look of pure innocence her way.

'Act as if you're the devoted fiancé who can't wait to get me all alone.'

'But I can't wait to get you all alone.'

She sucked in a shaky breath as his words hit home, her stomach doing a crazy little somersault.

'That's beside the point…' She floundered for a moment.

'You had no right to pretend everything is perfectly normal, that we've patched things up as if the past didn't happen. Quite frankly I'm surprised my family couldn't see through it.'

'I had a long talk with your father before you came home,' he said. 'I told him I'd changed my mind about marriage and that I wanted to be a real and involved father to Lachlan. I also told him that I would look after you, provide for you and protect you.'

She folded her arms crossly and tossed her head to stare out of the passenger window. 'No doubt you threw in a whole bunch of lies about loving me, too, just for good measure.'

The swish of the tyres on the bitumen was the only sound in the long stretching silence.

Ashleigh silently cursed herself for revealing her vulnerability in such a way. What was she thinking? He hadn't even been able to utter the words to his three-year-old son. What hope did she have of ever hearing them directed at her?

'I saw no reason to lie to your father,' Jake said evenly.

She frowned, trying to decipher his statement, but before she had any success he spoke again.

'Your family want what is best for you, Ashleigh. They know that you haven't been happy for a long time, and to their credit they are prepared to put any past prejudices they may have held against me to one side in order to welcome me into the family.' He sent her a teasing little glance. 'Besides, both your sisters think I'm a much better deal than dear old Howard.'

'I wish you wouldn't speak of him in that way.'

'I still can't believe you were considering marrying him.'

'Yeah? Well, at least he had the decency to ask me,' she threw at him resentfully.

Jake's hands tightened on the wheel as her hard-bitten words hit their mark. He gritted his teeth against the surge of anger he felt. What did she expect? Some promise of blissful happy ever after, when all he could promise was to…*was to what?*

He dragged in a prickly breath and tried to concentrate on the line of traffic ahead, watching as each car edged closer and closer together, as if to nudge the red light signal into changing. His foot hovered on the accelerator, biding his time to go forward, his fingers drumming the steering wheel in increasing agitation.

All he could promise was to what?

CHAPTER ELEVEN

ASHLEIGH was so determined she wasn't going to say another word to Jake for the rest of the journey, if not the rest of the evening, that it took her a quite a while to realise that he hadn't directed a single word her way for several minutes. She cast him covert glances every now and again as he negotiated the city traffic, but his eyes didn't once turn her way and the stiff line of his mouth clearly indicated that he had no desire to engage in conversation with her.

OK, so he hadn't appreciated her little dig about his forceful proposal.

Fine.

She could handle his stonewalling. It would make for a long and tense evening, but why should she always be the one to smooth things over? Besides, he was the one who'd steamrollered her into committing to a marriage she knew he would never have been insisting on if it wasn't for Lachlan's existence.

How was that supposed to make her feel? He hadn't even tried to pretend to have any feelings for her, other than displaying his usual rampant desire which he no doubt felt for any woman between the ages of nineteen and forty.

Admittedly, he'd somehow convinced her family that things were now all rosy and romantic between them, but she knew that was probably because Howard had always seemed to them to be not quite the right partner for her. Her parents, of course, had known better than to say so out loud, but Mia and Ellie hadn't abided by any such polite boundaries. The open joy on their faces as they'd toasted her engagement to Jake that evening was testament to their relief that she had finally come to her senses. But exactly what was sensible about marrying a man who not only didn't love her but loathed the whole notion of marriage and family life?

The hotel valet parking attendant greeted Jake by name as he drove into the reception bay. Ashleigh stepped out of the car when one of the uniformed bell boys opened her door for her and stood waiting for Jake, who was exchanging pleasantries with another staff member.

'I'll have the young lady's luggage brought up to your room immediately,' the young man said as he took the keys from Jake.

Ashleigh gave an audible snort. Her small tote bag could hardly be described as luggage; she'd barely put a thing in it besides her cosmetics purse and her oldest, most unflattering, nightgown. If Jake thought he was in for a hot night of passion with her in his hotel bedroom he could think again.

'Will you require a reservation for dinner in the restaurant this evening or will you be ordering room service, Mr Marriott?' The concierge asked as they approached reception for Jake to collect his mail.

'Room service will be fine,' Jake answered without even consulting Ashleigh. 'Were there any messages left for me today?'

The concierge handed him two or three envelopes. 'That's all so far. Is there anything else we can do for you, Mr Marriott?'

'Yes.' Jake's mouth tilted into a smug sort of smile. 'Have the bar send up a bottle of your very best champagne and two glasses.'

'Right away, Mr Marriott.' The concierge's eyes went to Ashleigh, standing rigidly to one side. 'May I ask, are we celebrating something special this evening?'

'Yes. Ms Ashleigh Forrester and I are celebrating our engagement and forthcoming marriage,' Jake said and, tucking the envelopes in his back pocket, added, 'Oh... and could you also contact the press and make a formal announcement on my behalf?' He took one of the gold pens off the reception counter and, reaching for a hotel notepad, quickly wrote down what he wanted to appear in the following day's paper and handed it back to the concierge.

'Consider it done, Mr Marriott. And on behalf of the hotel management and staff may I offer you our most sincere congratulations.' He turned towards Ashleigh and gave her a polite smile. 'Nice to meet you, Ms Forrester.'

Ashleigh mumbled something in reply and stumbled after Jake as he led her by the elbow towards the bank of lifts.

Once they were out of earshot of the reception area she tugged herself out of his hold and dusted off her elbow as if to remove something particularly nasty from it before sending him a furious glare. 'You've got a dammed hide!'

Jake pressed the call button without answering and, folding his arms across his chest, leaned indolently against the wall.

Ashleigh felt like stamping her foot in frustration.

'You know what the staff are all thinking, don't you?' she hissed at him. 'They think we're going to hole ourselves up in your room for a night of raunchy sex, fortifying ourselves with champagne and bloody room service!'

Jake's eyes were still and dark as they met her flashing ones. 'Is that a problem for you?'

She let out a whooshing breath. 'Of course it's a problem for me! This time yesterday I was engaged to Howard Caule. What will everyone think when they see tomorrow's paper and hear that you are now my fiancé?'

The lift doors opened and Jake stood back to allow her to enter first. The door hissed shut behind them before he responded smoothly. 'They will think the best man won.'

She let out another infuriated breath. 'This is all a game to you, isn't it, Jake? All this talk about winning and losing, as if I'm some sort of prize that everyone's been bidding for.'

She caught her lip with her teeth and looked away from the glint of satire in his dark eyes. 'I don't want to even be here with you, much less sleep with you,' she said, privately hoping she had the strength of will to follow through on her rash words.

'You know you don't mean that, Ashleigh, so don't go making me get all fired up just so I have to prove it to you.'

She felt a flicker of betraying need between her thighs at his statement, the smouldering fire in his challenging gaze threatening to consume her on the spot.

The lift doors opened and she almost fell out in relief, her lungs dragging in air as if she'd been holding her breath for hours instead of a mere few seconds.

She suddenly felt faint, light-headed and disoriented, the carpeted floor rolling up towards her, the swirling colours getting all mixed up in a stomach-churning pattern that seemed to make the floor unstable beneath her feet…

'Are you all right?'

She heard Jake's voice as if he was speaking to her through a long tunnel, the words rising and falling like an echo, here one second, gone the next.

'I…I think I'm going to… She wobbled, one of her hands clutching at mid-air until she found something strong and immovable to keep her upright.

Jake held her tightly against him as he swiped his key card

to his room and, shouldering open the door, scooped her up and carried her inside, the door clicking shut behind him.

'I…I…I'm going to be sick…' Ashleigh gasped as she put a shaky hand up to her mouth.

'The bathroom is just through—'

Too late.

Ashleigh threw up the contents of her stomach all over his chest.

Jake managed to salvage the cream carpet by tugging his shirt out of his trousers to act as a sort of bib-cum-scoop as he led her to the bathroom. He set her down on the edge of the bath, one hand still holding the contents of his T-shirt as he frowned in concern at the pallor of her face.

'Oh, God…'

She swayed for a moment and then lunged for the toilet bowl. He winced as she threw up again, each harsh tortured expulsion of her throat reminding him of the weeks after she'd left him in London when a daily bottle of Jack Daniels had been his only comfort.

He gingerly removed himself from his T-shirt, leaving it in the bottom of the shower stall, and reaching for one of the hand towels, wet it under the cold tap before applying it to her shockingly pale face.

'Hasn't anyone ever told you never to drink champagne on an empty stomach?' he said, gently mopping her brow.

She gave him a withering glance and looked as if she was about to throw a stinging comment his way when her face suddenly drained of all colour once more and she lurched towards the toilet bowl again.

Jake waited until she was done before handing her the re-rinsed towel again.

Ashleigh buried her face in its cool, refreshing, cleansing folds, wondering if this was some sort of omen for the rest of their future together.

'When was the last time you ate?' Jake asked.

Ashleigh groaned into the towel. *'Please* don't talk about food!'

'How many glasses of champagne did you have at your parents' house?'

'I don't know…two…maybe three…'

'Too many, if you ask me.'

'I didn't ask you.'

'That reminds me,' Jake said, helping her to her feet, his hands on her upper arms gentle but firm. 'It has occurred to me that I haven't actually asked you to marry me.'

Ashleigh stared at him, her stomach still deciding on its next course of action, her throat raw and her eyes and nose streaming.

'You were right to be angry with me,' he continued. 'I didn't ask you, I just told you that we were going to get married. I didn't even give you a choice.'

She opened her mouth and just as rapidly closed it, not sure if words or something a little less socially appropriate was still intent on coming out.

'Ashleigh…' He cleared his throat, his eyes dark and steady on hers. 'Will you marry me?'

Jake stepped backwards as she lunged for the toilet bowl again and flinched as she gave another almighty heave.

She was right after all, he thought wryly as he rinsed out the hand towel yet again.

Maybe he *did* need a little polish on his proposal.

Ashleigh crawled into the shower a few minutes later, way beyond the point of caring that Jake was standing watching her shivering naked under the warm spray. She closed her eyes and let the water run over her, trying to concentrate on staying upright instead of sinking to the floor and disappearing down the drain, which her body seemed to think was a viable option.

'You don't look so good,' Jake said.

She opened one bloodshot eye. 'Thanks…just what a naked woman wants to hear.'

He smiled and reached for a big fluffy white bath sheet, holding it to one side as his other arm brushed past her breast to turn off the shower rose.

Ashleigh stepped into the soft towel he held out and didn't even try and take over the drying of her body herself. Instead she stood like a helpless child as he gently dried her, the softness of the towel and his soothing, caress-like touch making her throat threaten to close over with emotion.

'Do you want me to dry your hair for you?' he asked once he'd wrapped her sarong-wise in a fresh dry towel. 'There's a hairdryer on the wall next to the shaving outlet. I've never done a blow job before but who knows? Like someone else I know, I might prove to have a natural flair.'

She rolled her eyes at him and then wished she hadn't. 'I think I might just lie down for a while…my head hurts.'

He pulled back the bed covers and she climbed in, closing her eyes as soon as her head found the feather-light pillow.

Jake stood watching her for endless moments, wondering if he should have called a doctor or something. But then he remembered what a hopeless head for alcohol she'd had in the past. One drink and she was practically under the table.

His conscience gave him a sharp little prod of recollection which he wanted to push away but couldn't. She had held him off for two dates but on the third he had been so determined to have her that he hadn't thought much beyond getting her clothes off any way he could…

He gave a rough-edged sigh and, before he could stop himself, gently brushed the back of his hand across the velvet softness of her cheek, the feel of her skin under his work-roughened knuckles reminding him of the smooth cream of silk. She mumbled something he couldn't quite catch and, curling up into an even smaller ball, nestled her cheek further into the pillow.

He reached for the bedside chair and sat in it heavily, his head dropping to his hands, his fingers splaying over his forehead.

It was going to be a long night.

Ashleigh woke sometime during the night, her head feeling surprisingly clear but her stomach instantly clamouring for food.

'Did you say something?' Jake's voice came out of the darkness from the other side of the huge bed.

'No...that was my stomach,' she said, her insides giving another noisy rumble.

She felt the slight tilt of the mattress as he reached for the bedside lamp, her pupils shrinking a little when the soft light washed over her.

'What did it say?' he asked, his mouth curving into a small smile.

Don't look below his neck, she warned herself.

'It said it wants some food,' she said, fiddling with the edge of the sheet that only just covered her breasts.

'What sort of food?' Jake got up from the bed and stretched. 'Soup and toast or what about something greasy for a hangover cure?'

'I don't have a hangover,' she said a little tightly.

She sensed rather than saw his smile as he reached for the phone.

'Jake Marriott here, suite fourteen hundred,' he said. 'Can we have some bacon and eggs with a double side of fries?'

Ashleigh threw him a filthy look and he added, 'No, no champagne with that order. We haven't started on the other bottle yet.' He hung up the phone and gave another big stretch, his biceps bulging as he raised his arms above his head, his stomach muscles rippling like rods of steel under a tightly stretched satin sheet.

'Do you have to do that?' she said irritably.

'Do what?' He rolled his shoulders and dropped his arms, his look totally guileless.

She pursed her mouth and edged the sheet a little higher. 'You could at least put something on.'

'You've seen me naked before,' he pointed out. 'Besides, I fell asleep in the chair a little earlier and it made me a little stiff.'

Her eyes went to his pelvis, her cheeks instantly filling with heat. She wrenched her gaze away and fiddled with the sheet to distract herself from his tempting form.

'You know something? You never used to be such a little prude,' he commented. 'I hope Howard hasn't given you a whole lot of hang-ups about sex.'

'I don't have any hang-ups…' She chewed her bottom lip for a moment. 'It's just that…' She paused, not sure it was exactly wise to go on.

'Just what?' he asked.

She raised her eyes to his. 'It's just it's always been such a very physical thing…for you, I mean.'

'And it's not for you?' he asked, holding her gaze.

'Yes, yes, of course it is…but…' She lowered her eyes and began to tug at a loose thread on the sheet, wishing she hadn't drifted into such deep water.

'I don't like the sound of that "but",' he said after a short silence. 'What are you trying to say? That you're still in love with me after all this time?'

She stared at him for five heavy blood-clogging heart-beats.

'Ashleigh?'

There was a discreet tap at the door and their eyes locked for a moment.

'Room service,' a young male voice called out.

Jake reached for his jeans where he'd left them hanging over a chair, stepping into them, zipping them up and running a rough hand through his hair before he moved across to open the door.

Ashleigh hitched the sheet right up to her chin and watched as Jake tipped the young man who carried in the tray of food, waiting until he'd gone again before turning back to her.

'Come on, let's get some food into you, then we can continue that little discussion we were having on sex,' he said.

She propped herself up in the bed with pillows as he carried the tray over. He set it across her lap, giving her a little wink as he snitched a French fry and popped it in his mouth.

She gave him a guilt-stricken look as she suddenly recalled how the evening in his room had started. 'You must have missed dinner…I'm sorry.'

He gave her another one of his wry smiles. 'To be quite frank with you, sweetheart, I didn't feel all that much like food after your little bathroom routine.'

She grimaced and speared a chip with her fork. 'Don't remind me.' She gave a little shudder. '*Yeeuck.* I am never going to drink champagne again. *Ever.*'

He laughed and took another fry. 'You never could handle alcohol. One drink and you are anybody's.'

Her fork froze halfway to her mouth, her eyes slowly meeting his.

His smile faded. 'You know, I didn't actually mean that quite the way it sounded.'

'Yes, you did.' She pushed the food away in disgust.

'No!' He rescued the tilting tray and set it to one side before coming back to untie her hands from where she'd crossed them tightly over her breasts.

'Hey.' He gave her fists a little squeeze. 'I didn't mean to insult you. The truth is, I have never forgotten what it was like that first time...' His throat moved up and down in a swallow. 'I've tried to, believe me, but it just won't go away.'

She tossed her head to one side. 'You've probably had hundreds of lovers since then who have imprinted themselves indelibly on your sexual seismic register.'

'Maybe—' he gave a shrug of one shoulder '—but, as far as I recall, no four point fours.'

Her eyes came back to his, her look indignant. *'Four point four?* Is that all I rated?'

He tapped her on the end of her nose, the edges of his mouth tipping upwards sexily. 'Thought that would get a rise out of you.'

She reached past him for the tray of food and scooped up a rasher of bacon without the help of cutlery and stuffed it in her mouth, her blue eyes flashing sparks of fire as she chewed resolutely.

'You know something, Ashleigh,' he said, spearing a French fry with her abandoned fork. 'You're really something when you're all fired up.'

'Stop pinching my fries.' She slapped his hand away. 'I want them all to myself.'

He laid the fork down and, moving the tray just out of her reach, kissed her hard upon the mouth.

Ashleigh blinked up at him when he lifted his mouth off hers.

'What was that for?' she asked.

He picked up a French fry and held it near her tightly clamped lips. 'Open.'

She opened.

'That's good.' He smiled as she chewed and swallowed. 'Now we're getting somewhere.'

Ashleigh wasn't sure she wanted to know exactly what he meant. Besides, her stomach was still screaming out for food and he seemed perfectly happy to pass it to her, morsel by morsel. All she had to do was chew and swallow and avoid his probing gaze.

She opened her mouth on a forkful of easy-over egg and wickedly fattening bacon and closed her eyes.

Heaven.

CHAPTER TWELVE

ASHLEIGH woke the next morning to find Jake sitting fully dressed in one of the chairs near the bed, his dark gaze trained on her, his expression thoughtful.

'Hi,' he said, a small smile lifting the edges of his mouth.

'Hi.' She eased herself upright, securing the sheet around her naked breasts, wondering what was going on behind those unreadable eyes.

'I've been doing some thinking while you were sleeping,' he said after a little silence.

She gave him a wary look without responding.

He ran a hand through his hair and continued. 'I realised during the night that from the very first day I met you in London I fast-tracked you into a physical relationship. I did it to you again recently.' He held her gaze for a moment or two. 'I want to prove to you that I'm serious about making our marriage work by being patient, a quality you're not used to seeing in me.' He drew in a breath and added, 'In the next four weeks leading up to our wedding I promise not to kiss you, touch you or even look at you in a sexual way when we are alone.' He paused as if waiting for her reaction to his announcement but when she remained silent he shifted his gaze and, getting to his feet, walked over to the window and looked down at the street below, his back turned towards her. 'I want to get to know my son and start to build the sort of family structure I missed out on as a child.'

'I see...'

He turned back to face her, his expression giving nothing away. 'Four weeks isn't all that long when you consider we'll have the rest of our lives together, don't you agree?'

Ashleigh wasn't sure how to answer. She had spent four and a half miserable years missing him and now that he was back, four minutes without him touching her hurt like hell. How would she ever get through it?

'If that's what you want...' Her eyes fell away from the intensity of his.

He eased himself away from the window sill where he'd been leaning and reached for the room service menu. 'Let's have breakfast and get going. I want to spend the day with Lachlan. He's probably wondering where we both are.'

Ashleigh sat on the back step at Jake's house and watched as Lachlan helped his father complete the tree-house they'd been building in the elm tree.

Almost four weeks had passed and Jake had stuck to his promise; not once had he touched her while they were alone.

She gave a twisted little smile.

With all the rush of wedding preparations they'd had precious little time by themselves and she couldn't help wondering if he'd planned it that way to make it easier on himself. As for herself, she had ached for him relentlessly, her body tingling with awareness whenever his dark as night eyes rested on her.

Now, with a day to go before they were officially married, she could barely contain her nervous anticipation. Her legs felt weak and shaky whenever he smiled at her, the slightest brush of his hand against hers stirring her into a frenzy of clawing need.

'What do you think, Ashleigh?' Jake asked as he strode

towards her with Lachlan's small hand tucked in his. 'Do you think it'll do?'

She smiled at the pure joy on Lachlan's grubby face as he gazed up at his father. Her son had blossomed in a matter of days as he'd soaked up the presence of Jake. He had clung to him during every waking hour as if frightened he might suddenly disappear. It had made Ashleigh's heart swell to witness the sheer devotion on his little face and she knew that no matter what happened in her relationship with Jake in the future, Lachlan would always want to be in contact with his father and she would do nothing to come between them.

'It looks wonderful,' she said.

Jake helped her to her feet, his work-roughened palm sending a riot of sensations through her fingers to the centre of her being as his eyes meshed with hers.

'This time tomorrow,' he said on the tail-end of an expelled breath.

She didn't trust herself to answer without betraying herself.

Jake's eyes left hers to look at the house, his small sigh of approval speaking volumes. 'It looks like a real home now, doesn't it?'

Ashleigh followed the line of his gaze. The house had been painted inside and out, the threadbare blinds replaced with the soft drape of curtains and the floors polished, with new rugs laid out here and there for comfort and cosiness. The furniture was all modern and comfortable, all except for one small writing desk that Jake wanted to keep because it had been his mother's. The rest of the antiques had gone along with the outdated appliances in the kitchen; it was now newly appointed and the bathrooms beautifully refurbished as well.

The front and back gardens had been tidied, Jake doing a lot of the physical labour himself with Lachlan faithfully by his side.

'Yes,' she agreed. 'It looks like a real home.'

'Can I play with my cars now, Daddy?' Lachlan asked, tugging on Jake's hand.

'Sure,' Jake said, ruffling his hair. 'Thanks for helping me. I couldn't have done that last bit without you.'

Lachlan's proud grin threatened to split his face in two. 'I love you, Daddy.' He hugged the long legs in front of him. 'I love you *this* much!' He squeezed as hard as he could, the sound of his childish little grunt of exertion making tears spring to Ashleigh's eyes.

She blinked them back as she watched Jake bend down to his son's level, his voice gruff with emotion. 'I love you, too, mate. More than I can say.' His eyes shifted slightly to meet Ashleigh's over the top of their son's dark head. 'Sometimes words are just not enough.'

Lachlan scampered off but Ashleigh hardly noticed. She'd never heard Jake say those three little words to anyone before, not to her certainly, and not even to Lachlan until now, even though Lachlan had said it to him many times over the last four weeks.

She ran her tongue over her dry lips as Jake straightened to his full height, his body so close to hers that she could feel the heat of it against her too sensitive skin.

He gave her a small rueful smile. 'I promised myself a long time ago that I'd never say those words again.'

'Why?' Her voice came out soft as a whisper.

There was a small but intense silence as his eyes held hers.

'Remember I told you about my dog?'

She nodded.

'I really loved that dog,' he said after another little pause. 'But as soon as I said those words to her my father heard me and got rid of her.'

'Oh, Jake…' She bit her lip to stop it from trembling.

He took something out of his pocket and silently handed it to her.

She looked down at the decayed strip of red-coloured leather lying across her hand, the small silver buckle jangling against something metal attached to it. She turned the tiny name tag over to see the name Patch engraved there.

'He didn't send her to the country after all,' Jake said. 'He killed her and buried her in the garden. I found her body, or at least what was left of it, and her collar a few days ago.'

Ashleigh lifted her gaze to his, tears rolling down her cheeks as she saw the raw emotion etched on his face.

'Jake…'

'Shh.' He pressed a finger against her lips to stop her speaking. 'Let me get this out while I still can.' He took a deep breath and let the words tumble out at last. 'I love you. I guess I've wanted to tell you that from the first moment I met you but I was too cowardly to do so. Instead, I hurt you immeasurably, wrecking my own life in the process, robbing myself of the precious early years of my son's life. Can you ever forgive me for the pain I've caused you?'

She was openly blubbering by now but there was absolutely nothing she could do to stop it. 'There's nothing to forgive…I love you…I've loved you for so long…I…I…'

Jake crushed her to him, his face buried in the fragrant cloud of her hair. 'I don't deserve you…I don't deserve Lachlan either. You're both so incredibly beautiful…I feel like I'm going to somehow spoil your life now that I am in it again.'

'No!' Ashleigh grasped at him with both hands, holding his head so his eyes were locked on hers. 'Don't *ever* think that. I have spent four and a half of the unhappiest years of my life without you. I don't think I would survive another day if you were to leave me now. You are the most wonderful person. I know that. I know it in my heart. You are nothing like your father. Look at the way Lachlan loves you; how can you doubt yourself? I certainly don't. I *know* who you are, Jake. You might bear your father's name but you don't have anything else of him inside you. I just know it.'

His dark eyes were bright with moisture as he looked down at her. 'I didn't realise loving someone could be so painful,' he said. 'When I saw you at the bar that night I could barely breathe. I was so determined that I could handle seeing you again but one glimpse of you turned me inside out with longing.'

'Oh, Jake…' She looked up at him with shining eyes. 'What a silly pair of fools we were. I was feeling exactly the same way! I had to stop myself reaching out to touch you to make sure you were really back in my life after all that time. I loved you so much and was so scared you'd see it and make fun of me.'

His eyes grew very dark and his voice husky and deep with emotion. 'Promise me you'll keep telling me you love me, Ashleigh. I'm not sure if my mother ever told me because I was so young when she died, but you're the first person I can remember ever saying those three little words. You have no idea how wonderful they make me feel.'

'I promise.'

He brushed the crystal tears spilling from her eyes with a gentle finger. 'I love you.'

'I know…I can hardly believe it's true…'

'You'd better believe it because I'm going to say it about ten times a day to make up for all the times I should have said it in the past.'

'Only ten times a day?' She gave him a little teasing smile. 'What else are you going to do with your time?'

His eyes glittered as they held hers. 'You know all those kitchen benches that were recently fitted inside?'

She gave a little nod as her stomach flipped over itself in anticipation. 'I did wonder why you wanted such a lot of bench space. Have you suddenly developed an intense passion for cooking?'

He gave her a bone-melting look and brought her even closer. 'I'm not much of a cook but I'm sure between the two of us we'll think of something to do with all that space. Don't you agree?'

Ashleigh just smiled.

EPILOGUE

Eight months later…

ASHLEIGH was in one of her nesting moods again. Ever since she'd found out she was pregnant she'd been fussing about the house, rearranging things to suit her ever changing whims; now with only a month to go she was virtually unstoppable.

Jake smiled fondly as she instructed him to shift yet another piece of furniture, her swollen belly brushing against him as she moved past him.

He still found it hard to believe he was married with a son and a little daughter on the way. His life had changed in so many ways but each one was for the better. His bitterness about the past had gradually faded to a far off place which he rarely visited now. Ashleigh's love had healed him just as surely as his son's devotion, which still brought a clogging lump to his throat every time he looked into those dark eyes that so resembled his own.

'No…I think it looks better back over there,' Ashleigh said, turning around to look at him. 'What do you think, darling?'

His eyes ran over her, lingering for a moment of the full curve of her breasts before meshing with her blue gaze. 'If I told you what I was thinking right now you'd probably blush to the very roots of your hair.'

She smiled one of her cat-that-swallowed-the-canary smiles. 'What exactly are you thinking?'

He gently backed her up against the writing desk, his hand going to her belly, his open palm feeling for the movement of his child. 'That you are the sexiest mother I've ever seen and if it wasn't for Ellie and Mia bringing Lachlan back any minute now I would have my wicked way with you.'

Ashleigh felt her legs weaken and grasped at the writing desk behind her to steady herself. The fragile timber gave a sudden creak and part of the front panelling of the top drawer came away in her hand.

'Oh, no!'

'Did you hurt yourself?' Jake's tone was full of concern as he steadied her.

She shook her head, turning to look at the damage she'd done to his mother's desk.

'No, but—' She stopped as she stared at the small compartment that had been hidden behind the panelling she'd inadvertently removed. In the tiny thin space was an envelope.

She took it out, turning it over in her hands, her eyes briefly scanning the feminine writing and the name written there before she handed it to Jake.

'I think it's a letter of your mother's,' she said. 'It's addressed to someone in New Zealand. She mustn't have been able to post it before she died…'

Jake opened the envelope and read through the pages one by one, his dark eyes absorbing each and every word, the only sound in the room the soft rustle of paper that hadn't seen the light of day in close to thirty years.

'What does it say?' Ashleigh asked softly as she saw the sheen of tears begin to film over his eyes.

Jake drew in a deep breath and looked at her. 'You were right, Ashleigh. You knew it all along.'

'Kn-knew what?' Her voice wobbled along with Jake's chin as she watched him do his best to control his emotion. 'W-what did I know?'

'This is a letter to my father,' he said, wiping a hand across his eyes. 'My *real* father.'

'You mean…?'

'Harold Marriott was infertile.' He looked down at the words he'd just read as if to make sure they hadn't suddenly disappeared. 'He had testicular cancer as a young man and after the treatment was unable to father a child.'

'So you're not…' She couldn't get the words past the sudden lump in her throat.

'My mother was five months pregnant when she married him,' he said. 'She hadn't told my real father of my existence because he was already married, but when she knew she was dying she decided to write to him…but, probably due to her sudden decline in health, the letter was never sent.'

'Oh, Jake…'

Jake pulled her to him and hugged her tightly, his head buried into her neck. 'You were right, Ashleigh. You were right all along. I am *not* my father's son.'

Ashleigh looked up at him, her eyes brimming over. 'I would still love you even if you were his son. I'm happy for you that you're not but it makes absolutely no difference to me. I love you and I always will, no matter what.'

No matter what. Jake breathed the words deep into his soul, where Ashleigh's love had already worked a miracle of its own.

THE UNEXPECTED PREGNANCY

Catherine George

Catherine George was born in Wales and early on developed a passion for reading, which eventually fuelled her compulsion to write. Marriage to an engineer led to nine years in Brazil, but on his later travels the education of her son and daughter kept her in the UK. And, instead of constant reading to pass her lonely evenings, she began to write the first of her romantic novels. When not writing and reading she loves to cook, listen to opera and browse in antiques shops.

Don't miss *The Power of the Legendary Greek,* the exciting new novel by Catherine George, available from Mills & Boon® Modern™ romance in June 2010

CHAPTER ONE

HARRIET let herself into the still, empty house, but instead of making her usual nostalgic tour went straight to the kitchen to make a pot of the expensive coffee brought along for brain fuel. It was crunch time. She had to get to grips right away with the problem she'd taken a week's holiday leave to solve. Before she went back to London a decision had to be made about her legacy. Her grandmother had made it very clear in her will that End House and its contents were to be left to Harriet to dispose of exactly as she wished. But what she *wished*, thought Harriet fiercely, was that her grandmother were still alive, and that any minute she'd come in from the garden with a bunch of herbs in her hand, demanding help to make supper.

When the coffee-pot was empty Harriet took her bags upstairs and, because this might be the last time she ever slept here, put them in her grandmother's room for the first time instead of her own. She ran a caressing hand over the brass rails of the bed, hung up some of her things in the oak armoire, and folded the rest away in the beautiful Georgian chest. Olivia Verney had disapproved of clothes flung down on chairs. Harriet grinned as she made up the bed. A good thing her grandmother had never seen her flatmate's bedroom. Dido Parker was a good friend, and good at her job, but tidy she was not.

After supper Harriet made some phone calls to announce her arrival, watered the array of plants in the conservatory, and had just settled down to read in the last of the evening light when she heard a car stop outside. She got up to look, and dodged back in dismay when she recognised the driver.

But there was no point in hiding behind the sofa. Tim had probably told his brother she was here.

When the knock came on the door, Harriet counted to five before opening it to confront the tall figure of James Edward Devereux.

She gave him a cool smile. 'Hello. I'm afraid Tim's not here. I came on my own.'

'I know that. May I come in?'

As if she could refuse, she thought irritably, and showed him into the small, elegantly furnished sitting room.

Her visitor was silent for a moment as he looked at his surroundings. 'It's months since your grandmother died, but here in her house it seems only right to offer my condolences again, Harriet.'

'Thank you. Do sit down.'

'I liked your grandmother very much,' he said, choosing Olivia Verney's favourite chair. 'I was deeply sorry I couldn't make it to the funeral. I went down with some virus at the time.'

'I heard.' She perched on the edge of the sofa, feeling edgy. She'd known Tim's brother since she was thirteen years old, and lately she'd even run into him in London once or twice, but they'd never been alone together before. What on earth was he doing here?

'It must have been a shock when she left you so suddenly,' he said with sympathy.

Harriet nodded soberly. 'A shock for me, but great for her.'

'True.' James Devereux became suddenly businesslike. 'Right, then, Harriet, I'll get to the point. Did Mrs Verney tell you I'd approached her about selling the house to me?'

She stared at him blankly. '*This* house?'

'Yes. The others in the row already belong to Edenhurst—'

'You mean to you.'

'Yes, Harriet, to me,' he said patiently. 'I need more staff accommodation, and End House would be ideal.'

'Sorry,' she said instantly. 'It's not for sale.'

His eyes narrowed. 'Tim told me you were spending a week here to come to a decision.'

'I am.'

'So when did you arrive?'

'A couple of hours ago.'

'And the decision's already made?' His smile was mocking as he got to his feet. 'Tell me, Harriet. If someone else had made the offer would you have accepted?'

'It's nothing personal,' she said, lying through her teeth. 'I just don't want to sell End House right now.'

'But Tim said you'd had it valued.'

'On his advice, yes,' she said curtly, making a note to have strong words with Tim Devereux.

He looked at her thoughtfully. 'If I offered slightly more than the estimate, would that change your mind?'

'It most certainly would not!' Her eyes flashed. 'And Tim had no right to discuss the price with you.'

'He didn't. I asked the estate agent who sold me the other three.'

'You needn't have bothered. End House is not for sale.'

'Before I go, enlighten me, Harriet,' he said, following closely as she marched out into the hall. 'Why are you always so damned hostile towards me?'

She turned a scornful smile on him. 'It's no mystery. You make it pretty obvious lately that you disapprove of my relationship with Tim.'

'You surely realise why?'

'I've never given it a thought,' she told him, amazed that her nose failed to grow a couple of inches at the lie.

'Then think about it now,' he said crisply. 'I've had to be father, mother *and* brother to Tim since he was ten. I don't want to see him hurt.'

She bristled. 'You think *I'm* going to hurt him?'

'Yes.' His eyes held hers. 'Tim's a one-woman man, but I know that you have other men in your life. I'd say the odds on Tim getting hurt are fairly high.'

Not for the first time in their acquaintance Harriet wanted to punch James Edward Devereux on his elegant nose. Instead she opened the door wide to speed him on his way. 'Tim's perfectly happy with the fact that I have friends of both sexes.'

'In the same situation I couldn't be happy with that.'

'You and Tim are two very different people,' she said coldly.

'True. Everyone loves Tim. Goodnight, Harriet.' James Devereux glanced back as he reached his car. 'The offer will stay on the table for a while. Ring me if you change your mind.'

Harriet closed the door, rammed the bolts home and stormed to the kitchen to make a pot of coffee black and strong enough to counteract the effect James Devereux invariably had on her.

She'd met his brother Tim in the village post office when she first came to live with her grandmother in Upcote, and the two orphaned thirteen-year-olds had taken to each other on sight. Tim had raced back to End House with Harriet right away to ask Olivia Verney's permission to take her granddaughter fishing in the stream that ran through Edenhurst grounds. And afterwards he'd taken Harriet off to meet his brother, who was twelve years Tim's senior, and possessed of such striking good looks he'd seemed like a god from Olympus to the youthful Harriet.

Tim so openly worshipped his brother that for a while Harriet had found it natural to follow suit. Unlike her friends at school, who had crushes on rock stars and football players, Harriet Verney's naive form of hero-worship had centred on James Edward Devereux. Tall, self-assured, with glossy dark hair and the tawny Devereux eyes, he was the archetypal Corsair to a teenager just introduced to Byron's poetry.

During that first summer vacation with her grandmother, Harriet had come to terms with her first experience with grief. The double loss of her parents in a storm on a sailing holiday had broken her world in pieces, and it had taken all her grandmother's loving care to put it back together again. The meeting with Tim accelerated the healing process. That summer Harriet spent most of her daylight hours with him. Totally comfortable in each other's company, they ate at the kitchen table at End House with Olivia Verney, or ran free on the acres of land belonging to Edenhurst, the beautiful, but increasingly dilapidated home of the Devereux brothers.

By that time both Devereux parents had been dead for some time and life had become difficult for the heir to the estate. Crippling inheritance tax, plus school fees for Tim and wages for even the bare minimum of staff required to keep Edenhurst going had all been a huge burden for a young man only just qualified as an architect. Through Tim Harriet had learned that some of the antique furniture and the more valuable family paintings had to be sold. With the proceeds as back-up James Devereux had taken a gamble, and with a partner set up a company to convert derelict warehouses into expensive riverside apartments.

The gamble paid off, the apartments sold like hot cakes, and riding high on the success of the enterprise James Devereux eventually went on to transform Edenhurst into the first of a series of hotels with integral health spas. He married an established star in the modelling world, and the only cloud on the dynamic young entrepreneur's horizon had been his brother's flat refusal to join the company.

Tim Devereux insisted on taking a fine art degree instead, and went straight from college to work in a London gallery owned by Jeremy Blyth, an art dealer highly respected in his field. None of Tim's choices had been influenced by Harriet, but James made it plain he blamed her for all of them, even though Tim was adamant that nothing would have persuaded him to go into property developing. The new job suited him down to the ground. Jeremy Blyth was charming, witty, openly gay and knew all there was to know about the art world. The job would provide invaluable experience, also allow spare time for Tim's own painting. He shared a house with two friends from art college and he had Harriet. What else could he want in life?

'His lordship's blessing?' she'd said bluntly.

'I don't know why you're always so down on Jed.' Tim had given her a coaxing smile as he put an arm round her. 'Come on, Harry. Get if off your chest at last. You and I don't have secrets, remember. What is it with you and my brother?'

He'd kept on about it until at last, desperate to shut him up, Harriet finally told him that one Sunday afternoon she'd stopped to stroke the dog outside the open kitchen door of Edenhurst, overheard James lecturing Tim, and suffered the usual fate of eavesdroppers.

'He felt great sympathy for my situation, but thought you should see something of the lads from the village as well, instead of spending all your time with a girl—even one who looked just like a boy with such close cropped hair and a gruff little voice.' She growled at the memory, which still burned. 'I wanted to kill him with my bare hands!'

Tim had roared with laughter. 'You've changed a bit since then, tiger. The hair grew, the girl equipment arrived, and that voice of yours could earn a fortune these days on one of those sexy chat lines—ouch!' he howled as she hit him. 'And now he's shackled to the fair Madeleine surely you feel *some* sympathy for Jed.'

'Not a scrap! He's far too overbearing and sure of himself to merit any sympathy from me.'

From that day on Harriet never thought of or referred to James Edward Devereux as Jed, as he was known to family and friends. And she never told a soul that her teenage self-esteem had been dealt such a blow that summer afternoon it had taken years afterwards for her to think of herself as even passably attractive.

Harriet rang Dido early next morning to say she'd received an offer for End House. 'Tim's brother wants to add it to the Edenhurst estate, but I just can't face giving the house up yet, so I turned him down.'

'Good God, are you mad?' said Dido, shocked. 'I know your grandma left money to keep the place going for six months, but from now on you'll have to pay running costs yourself.'

'I know all that. But it's been my home for the past ten years, remember. I just can't bear to part with it yet. In fact,' added Harriet, bracing herself, 'I thought I might even live here myself for a bit, Dido.'

There was a pause. 'You work in London,' Dido reminded her, sounding close to tears.

'I could look round for something in this area instead— Cheltenham, maybe.'

'You really want to desert me?'

Harriet felt a guilty pang. 'You earn serious money these days. Couldn't you manage the mortgage on your own?'

'I don't care about the beastly mortgage. I just want you here with me. Besides, what about Tim?'

'We can see each other at weekends.'

'I think you're making a huge mistake, Harriet. Please don't make any snap decisions.'

Harriet spent some time reassuring her friend, then walked to the village shops to buy a newspaper, stopped to chat with a couple of people she knew, and, because it was such a beautiful day, took the longer route back along the small tributary that formed the boundary to Edenhurst. She paused as she reached the stepping stones she'd hopped across so often with Tim in the past, and on impulse took off her sandals to see how far she could get. Halfway across she discovered that the water was faster and deeper than she remembered. She turned to retrace her steps, wobbled precariously as she hung on to her sandals, but lost her newspaper to the current when she spotted James Devereux in the shade of the willow hanging over the far bank.

'Want some help?' he asked, grinning broadly.

'No,' she said through her teeth.

To her annoyance he kicked off his shoes and strolled across the stones towards her, sure-footed as a panther. 'Give me your hand,' he ordered.

Harriet hesitated, almost lost her balance, and James grabbed her hand and hauled her across the stream straight up the bank into Edenhurst territory.

'Now I've saved you from a ducking I claim a reward,' he said, collecting his shoes. 'Have lunch with me, Harriet. No wedding or conference this weekend. It's fairly peaceful here for once.'

Harriet eyed him in astonishment as she thrust damp feet into her sandals. 'If this is a ploy to win me over about End House it won't work.'

'Certainly not. I just think it's time you and I tried to get along better, for Tim's sake.' His lips twitched. 'Besides, when I'm bent on persuasion—of any kind—I tend towards champagne and caviare.'

'I detest caviare.'

'I'll make a note of that.' He smiled persuasively. 'But right now a humble sandwich is the only thing involved. So what do you say?'

She looked at him for a moment, then gave a reluctant nod. 'All right.'

His lips twitching at her lack of enthusiasm, James rang the house to order a picnic lunch in the folly. 'I remember the days when you ran wild round here, Harriet,' he commented as they began climbing the steep, winding path. He glanced at her fleetingly. 'You've changed out of all recognition since then. The clothes are not much different, I suppose, but the resemblance ends there, full stop. At one time it was hard to tell you from Tim, whereas now—'

'Whereas now,' she cut back at him, 'my hair's long and you can tell exactly what sex I am. But I'm stuck with the voice.'

He stopped dead at a stile blocking the path, comprehension dawning in his eyes. 'Is this something *I* said?'

'I once overheard you trying to persuade Tim to spend less time with me and more with the village boys.' Harriet smiled sweetly. 'If you were trying to turn him off me it didn't work.'

'Quite the reverse! Tim's been crazy about you since he was fourteen years old.'

'Thirteen,' corrected Harriet.

'Unlucky for some,' James said lightly, and startled her considerably by picking her up to deposit her on the other side of the stile.

By the time they reached the mock-Grecian temple where she'd once played endless games with Tim, their lunch was waiting on the stone bench girdling the interior. The tray held fresh fruit, a covered silver dish of sandwiches and an opened bottle of red wine.

James poured a glass for Harriet, and sat down beside her on the bench to remove the cover from the platter. 'Definitely no caviare,' he assured her.

'Quite a choice just the same,' she said, impressed. 'Is

that how things work for you all the time, James? You just wave a wand and—what have I said?'

'You actually allowed my given name to pass your lips!' He raised his glass in mocking toast. 'To truce, Harriet, long may it last. Now, what would madam like? Ham, smoked salmon, and, yes, I do believe there's good old cheese as well.'

'Very good old cheese,' she said, tasting it.

Harriet took a long, affectionate look at the house while they ate in surprisingly comfortable silence for a minute or two. Edenhurst's limestone architecture was typical of the area, with dips built into the steeply pitched roof to keep the tiles in place, and small-paned casement windows protected by stone mullions and drip-courses. But Harriet felt a sudden, sharp stab of nostalgia. Now it was restored and renovated as a luxury hotel, with park-perfect gardens, Edenhurst wore an air of affluence very different from the shabby charm of the past.

'What are you thinking?' said James.

'That in some ways I preferred the house the way it was when I first came here.'

He smiled wryly. 'A romantic viewpoint! To me it was an endless juggle of resources in those days, to decide which repair to do next.'

'Tim told me that.' Harriet cast a glance at him as she took another sandwich. 'My grandmother was deeply impressed by the way you tackled the problem.'

'So she told me. She was a very special lady.' His mouth turned down. 'It went against the grain to part with any family possessions, but I had no choice. Then I had a stroke of luck when a college friend put some capital in with mine to found the company.' He shook his head reminiscently. 'God, how we worked—twenty hours a day in the beginning.'

'It certainly paid off. The rest is history.' Harriet smiled crookedly. 'You know, it amazes me that this is happening.'

'You and me, alone, breaking bread together?'

'Exactly.'

His eyes glinted as he refilled her glass. 'Even though I'm the wicked squire trying to evict you from your home?'

'Trying to tempt me out of it with an inflated offer!'

'Not inflated at all. End House possesses a larger garden than its neighbours, remember, plus a conservatory.'

Harriet sighed. 'My friend thinks I'm mad to refuse such a good offer, but it's hard to part with the house. It's been my home for a long time. Besides, selling it is too much like a final break from my grandmother—who was a practical soul, and would laugh me out of court for being so sentimental.'

'I see your point.' James looked at her searchingly. 'But if selling is out of the question are you thinking of letting it instead?'

'I did consider that, but a solicitor friend of mine pointed out some of the drawbacks of being a landlord.' She sighed. 'If I thought I could get work in the area I'd live at End House myself.'

'You might find life in Upcote a little quiet after London, so think it over very carefully before you make a decision,' he advised.

'I came down here to do just that. But it means a week less for my holiday in Italy with Tim later on,' added Harriet with regret.

'Tim told me he's persuaded you to go to La Fattoria at last.' James frowned. 'Doesn't he mind that you're cutting the holiday short?'

'Only my part of it.' Harriet shrugged. 'Tim's going on ahead for the first week. He doesn't mind.'

'Because where Tim's concerned you can do no wrong.' She put her glass down on the tray with a click. 'You just don't understand my relationship with Tim. We don't live in each other's pockets. If he wants to do something independently I'm perfectly happy with that, and the reverse also applies.'

James shook his head. 'I'd be anything but happy in the same circumstances.'

'Really?' said Harriet sweetly. 'If that was your attitude with Madeleine no wonder she took off.'

He got up, his handsome face suddenly blank as he stacked the remains of their lunch on the tray. 'You know nothing about my marriage, young lady.'

'No, indeed—I beg your pardon.' Harriet jumped to her feet, her face hot. 'I'd better go.'

'Why? What's so pressing at End House that you can't stay for coffee?' He smiled a little, his eyes warming again. 'You know how easy it is to get service round here. I just wave my wand.'

Harriet shook her head. 'No, thanks.'

'Then I'll walk you home.'

'Unnecessary.'

James raised an eyebrow. 'Truce over already?'

'Of course not. It's only practical to keep on civil terms.' She gave him a direct look. 'If only for Tim's sake.'

'Point taken. By the way,' he added, 'Tim's been throwing out hints about a wedding.'

'It's far too soon to talk about that.'

James shrugged. 'He'll tell me soon enough when you name the day. He couldn't keep a secret to save his life. He'll be pleased that we had lunch together,' he added.

'I'm sure he will.' She smiled politely. 'Thank you. It was delicious.'

'My pleasure. I take a walk round the grounds every morning when I'm here, but I've never been lucky enough to meet a fair maiden in need of rescue before.'

'At one time I could hop across those stones with no

trouble at all.' She pulled a face. 'My sense of balance was better when I was thirteen.'

He smiled ruefully. 'I apologise for trying to turn Tim off you all those years ago, Harriet. I just wanted to give him some back-up with the village lads when you weren't around. Without you he was always like a lost soul.' The familiar tawny eyes, so like and yet so unlike Tim's, held hers. 'Am I forgiven?'

'Of course,' she said lightly. 'Goodbye.'

Harriet chose the more formal route home via the main gates in preference to getting her feet wet again, called in at the village stores to buy another newspaper, and walked back to End House deep in thought. The unexpected picnic had by no means been an ordeal. For most of the time the atmosphere over lunch had been relatively amicable. And Tim would be delighted that she'd thawed even a little towards his brother. Not that she was likely to see more of James while she was here. She knew from Tim that to keep his staff on their toes James made brief unheralded visits to all his properties and at Edenhurst the stable block had been converted into private quarters for the Devereux brothers. But James was the only one to use them. Tim had taken to metropolitan life like a duck to water and kept well away from Edenhurst now it was a hotel.

The two brothers, thought Harriet, could hardly be less alike. Tim was slight and fair, with boyish good looks and a natural charm that made women yearn to mother him. Her lips curved in a cynical smile. Of all the emotions James Devereux stirred up in the opposite sex, maternal leanings probably never made the list.

CHAPTER TWO

HARRIET found a note pushed through the door when she got back to End House.

'Harriet, if you're here for the week will you want me on Monday as usual? Regards, Stacy.'

Harriet was more than capable of looking after one small house for a week, especially on her own, without the mayhem Dido created in their London flat. But because Stacy Dyer was a single parent who needed the money Harriet rang to ask her to come in as usual.

After spending the rest of the day in the sunshine in the back garden Harriet had an early night, and next morning, in contrast to the hectic rush of London routine, she read in bed for a while before getting up to enjoy a leisurely bath. But as she lingered over breakfast later she felt a touch of panic. What was she going to do for the rest of the day, let alone the rest of the week? After all her fine talk about living here it was a bit of a blow to find she'd had enough of it already. Living alone here on a permanent basis was very different from odd weekends away from London.

Harriet faced the truth as she washed her breakfast dishes. Her knee-jerk reaction to James' offer had been ill-advised. She might never get another as generous. And, painful though it was to part with End House, she needed the money as security now she was alone in the world. She would stay until the weekend to save face, and then sell End House to James Devereux.

Harriet found an old cagoule in the closet, put money in the pocket and went off with an umbrella to the village

18

stores to buy a Sunday paper. By the time she got back the sun was out, and she could hear Livvie's voice reminding her that a garden needed weeding whether she was selling the house or not. Armed with fork and trowel, and a large waste bag for the weeds, Harriet prepared to do battle. End House gave directly onto the street in front, but owned a sizeable garden at the back, with apple trees and flowering shrubs. The laurel hedges were still reasonably neat, courtesy of the man who'd always helped her grandmother, but now Harriet could no longer afford to keep him the lawn needed mowing, and the herbaceous borders were fast getting out of hand.

Harriet got to work, but after only half an hour or so she was sweating and grubby, her neck ached, and only a discouragingly small portion of border was weed-free. She went indoors, gulped down a glass of water, and then set to it once more, determined to clear at least as much ground again before she took another breather. One thing was certain, she found, panting as she tugged and pulled, she'd hit on a sure way to kill time. Gardening looked a lot easier on television. She got to her feet at last to stretch her aching back, and groaned silently in frustration when she saw James Devereux strolling along the side path towards her.

'Hello, Harriet.'

'Hi. You're still here, then.' Oh, well done, Harriet. Top marks.

'Interviews this week,' he said briefly. 'Am I interrupting?'

'No, I've just finished. Did you want something?'

He looked at her levelly. 'I just called in to say hello.'

Or to put pressure on her about the sale, more likely. Reminding herself that this was a good thing now she'd made her decision she smiled brightly. 'Come inside. I'll just dispose of this stuff first.' Harriet put her gardening tools away and led her visitor into the kitchen. 'Would you like a drink, or some tea?'

'Tea would be good.'

Harriet washed her hands and filled the kettle, wishing that her shorts were longer and less encrusted with mud and sweat. 'Do sit down,' she told him as she hunted out teapot and cups.

James took one of the rush-seated chairs at the table, watching her objectively as she laid a tray and put tea bags in the pot. 'You were the same height at thirteen. I remember those long legs of yours.'

She glanced up in astonishment as she filled the teapot and splashed boiling water on her wrist in the process.

James leapt from his chair at her anguished gasp. 'Did you scald yourself?' he demanded, seizing her hand.

'Not much,' she said faintly. 'It's just a drop or two.'

James turned the cold tap on in the sink and held her wrist under the water. 'You're trembling,' he said gently, and put his arm round her. 'Shock, probably.'

If so he was making it a whole lot worse. She could feel the heat of his body through the thin shirt, a faint aura of citrus and spice mingled with the scent of warm male skin—and he's Tim's *brother*, she reminded herself in horror, limp with relief when James released her and turned off the tap.

'That's better. Sit down, Harriet.' He put the lid on the pot, poured tea, passed a cup to her, and sat down at the table. 'Why didn't Tim come down with you for the weekend before going off to Paris?'

'I needed time on my own to make my mind up about the house,' she told him gruffly, utterly floored by the discovery that James Devereux was a man she was attracted to. At least, her body was. Her brain flatly refused to believe it.

James eyed her downcast face thoughtfully. 'If you

change your mind and sell the house to me, Harriet, you could buy a flat of your own. Tim tells me you're tired of sharing with your friend.'

Tim, she thought irritably, should keep his big mouth shut. 'It's a tempting prospect,' she agreed.

James leaned forward. 'But frankly it astonishes me that you and Tim haven't set up house together long before this. Are you waiting to get married first?'

Harriet paused for a heartbeat, and then raised dark, demure eyes to his. 'I'm old-fashioned that way.'

James sat back again, frowning. 'And how does Tim feel about that?'

'He agrees with me.'

'This time you really do amaze me! No wonder he's talking about a wedding soon.'

She looked him in the eye. 'Frankly I'm surprised you're such a keen advocate of marriage.'

'Don't be put off by my example.' His face shadowed. 'You and Tim are soul mates. Madeleine and I were not. But I apologise for snapping at you on the subject yesterday, Harriet. Tim would create hell if he knew I'd upset you in any way.'

'You didn't,' she assured him. 'Have some more tea.'

James shook his head and got up. 'I must go. How is your hand now?'

'Fine.'

'Good. Be more careful in future.'

And to Harriet's surprise he took himself off, leaving her mystified as to why he'd come to see her again. Surely not just to apologise for a remark he'd had every right to make! He'd made no further attempt to persuade her into selling, and if his aim was to sound her out about wedding plans he was out of luck. She smoothed her reddened wrist, reliving her physical reaction to James Devereux's touch. At the mere thought of it a shiver ran through her entire body, right down to her toes, but she shook it off angrily. He was Tim's brother, for heaven's sake.

During the evening Tim rang up for a chat before his departure for Paris on business, astonished when she told him she'd seen his brother on three occasions so far, one of which had entailed a picnic lunch in the Edenhurst folly.

'Which reminds me,' she said, militant because she felt guilty for a sin not even committed, 'in future don't discuss my personal affairs with all and sundry.'

'I do nothing of the kind,' he said indignantly. 'But if you mean End House, Jed asked about it so I told him.'

'He wants it as staff accommodation for Edenhurst.'

'Pretty urgently if he's popping in on you all the time.'

'Thanks a lot!'

'You know what I mean, Harry.'

'I do know. By the way, *dearest*, he asked why you and I aren't living together right now.'

He whistled. 'And what did you say to to that?'

'I made it clear I disapprove of cohabiting before marriage,' she said primly.

'You're kidding me!' Tim gave the uproarious laugh that always had Harriet joining in. 'I do love you, Harry.'

'I love you, too. Enjoy yourself.'

Harriet put down the phone, unsurprised that Tim had no idea how miserable she felt under all the banter. Their relationship was unique and very special to them both, but secretly it was very different from the one they made it out to be. Usually she had no problem with this, but today she had experienced James Devereux's touch for the first time. And found it was a dangerously inflammable sensation never experienced before with any man, including Tim. Especially Tim. Yet in the circumstances she had to try and forget it had ever happened. If she could.

*   *   *

Stacy Dyer arrived at nine on the dot the following morning, complete with black eye and a baby boy fast asleep in a pushchair.

'I had to bring Robert with me today,' she said anxiously. 'Do you mind?'

'Of course I don't mind!' Harriet smiled down at the sleeping child. 'He's gorgeous, Stacy. Have some coffee before you start. How did you get the shiner?'

Stacy wheeled the pushchair inside and sat down at the kitchen table. 'His dad did it,' she said, flushing.

Appalled, Harriet added a dollop of cream to a mug of strong coffee and passed it to Stacy.

'Thanks.' The girl stirred sugar into the steaming liquid and sipped it gratefully. 'Yummy! I love real coffee.'

Harriet gave her a searching look. 'What happened, Stacy?'

'Greg came round last night when Mum was out, wanting to see Robert. He'd had a drink, so I wouldn't let him. We had a bit of a struggle when he tried to get past me and he caught me on the cheek with his elbow. So I told him to get lost.'

'I'm not surprised!'

'He didn't mean to hit me. He's not like that.' Stacy sighed, depressed. 'But I won't let him come near Robert if he's had a drink. I had enough of that with my own father. Not that Greg drinks much, he can't afford it, but he gets frustrated because he can't get a full-time job, and I won't get a place with him until he does.'

'How old is he?'

'Same age as me. I fell for Robert while Greg and I were still in school.' Stacy shrugged philosophically. 'At the moment cleaning is all I can do, but I go to computer classes two evenings a week, so by the time Robert starts nursery school I'll be able to try for office jobs.'

'How about Greg? Is he trained for anything?'

'He's got a couple of A-levels, but he likes to be out-doors, so he does whatever garden jobs he can get.'

'It's not easy for either of you, then,' said Harriet. 'Look, Stacy, there's no need for you to do any cleaning today—'

The girl eyed her in dismay. 'But I want to. *Please!* I'm sorry I had to bring Robert, but I couldn't leave him with Mum in case Greg came back. She'd have given him what for over my eye, and Robert gets terrified when people shout.'

'Bring Robert any time you like,' Harriet assured her. 'But for pity's sake take it easy. If you feel rough at any point pack it in.'

Robert woke up while his mother was finishing the sitting room. Stacy changed his nappy with swift efficiency, but when she fastened her son back in the buggy the move met with heartbroken protests.

'Why don't I take him out in the garden?' suggested Harriet. 'Would he like to sit on a blanket for a bit in the sun?'

'He'd just love it,' said Stacy, and kissed her son's wet cheeks as she popped a floppy cotton hat on his fair curls. 'Thanks, Harriet. I brought some toys for him to play with.'

There was a sticky moment when Stacy left her son with his new playmate, but Robert soon decided that he liked sitting on a rug in the sunshine. His tears dried like magic when Harriet began building a tower with plastic bricks. He scooted nearer, demolished them with chuckles of delight, and made imperious demands for a repeat performance. Harriet obeyed, laughing, time and time again, and felt quite sorry when Stacy came out at last to say she'd finished for the day.

'We've had a great time, Mummy.' With reluctance Harriet gave Robert to his mother. 'Are you going home now?'

'No, I'm due at the vicarage first.'

'Can you take Robert there with you?'

'I don't normally, but I'll just have to for once. I just hope the vicar isn't writing his sermon today.' She gave Harriet an uncertain smile. 'Would you mind if I gave Robert his lunch here, first?'

'Of course not. In fact,' added Harriet on impulse, 'why not leave him here with me afterwards?'

'I can't do that! It's taking advantage.'

'No, it's not. If he gets restless I'll take him for a walk in his buggy.'

'If you're really sure, that would be great,' said Stacy thankfully. 'I've got my phone, so just ring me if there's a problem.'

When his young mother left later Robert showed a moment of lip-trembling doubt when she kissed him goodbye, but he cheered up when his new friend took him back into the garden. Harriet built brick towers again for a while, but when the blue eyes began to droop she laid the little boy down on the blanket with his teddy, opened an umbrella to shade him from the sun, then stretched out beside him, content just to watch over the child as he fell asleep.

'Mum, Mum?' he sobbed when he woke up, and Harriet picked him up, cuddling him close.

'She won't be long, my darling,' she assured him. 'How about some juice?'

Blessing efficient Stacy for leaving a beaker of his favourite tipple ready in the kitchen, Harriet took the tearful little boy inside to find it, and cuddled him on her lap, deeply relieved when he stopped crying to drink.

'What a good boy you are,' she said fervently, and then sniffed at him in deep dismay. 'Now this,' she told him, 'is where you make allowances for an amateur, Robert Dyer. I've never changed a nappy before.'

He gurgled, and clutched a lock of her hair as she bent over him, but made no objection to lying on the changing mat his mother had left ready. Harriet had watched closely when Stacy changed her son, but in actual practice found that, like gardening, the process wasn't as easy as it looked. Due to much chuckling and wriggling it seemed a very long time before Robert was clean, fragrant and put back together again. Flushed with success, Harriet praised him extravagantly, balanced him inexpertly while she washed her hands, then sat him on her lap and gave him a biscuit.

'Where's Stacy?' demanded a voice from the open doorway.

Harriet jumped up in fright, clutching the child protectively at the sight of a thin, furious youth she'd never seen before.

Robert beamed, and the boy darted forward, arms outstretched.

'Hand him over!' he yelled.

Robert burst into tears at the loud noise, and burrowed his face against Harriet's neck.

'Who are you?' she demanded, her arms tightening round the child. 'What are you doing in my house?'

'I'm Greg Watts, Robert's dad. Give him to me!' He tried to snatch his child, but Robert held onto Harriet, sobbing piteously when he dropped his biscuit.

'Don't be an idiot, man,' she said, standing her ground. 'Can't you see you're frightening Robert to death? Stacy left him in my charge so I'm holding onto him until she comes back.'

'You've no right. I'm his *father*,' he said, his voice cracking, but as he made another lunge for the child James Devereux strode through the open door, seized Greg by the scruff of his neck and marched him outside, then came back to check on Harriet.

'Are you all right?' James demanded.

'I'm fine, but Robert's very upset.' She kissed the sobbing baby and cuddled him close. 'Oh, sweetheart, don't cry. I'll ring Mummy and ask her to come right now. James, you didn't hurt the boy, did you?' she said anxiously.

'Of course not. Greg says the child is his, but who's the mother?' he added.

'Stacy Dyer, my cleaner.'

'Give me the number and I'll ring her. Then I'll get Greg back in here and read the Riot Act.'

James' lecture was so effective Greg Watts was trying to choke back tears when Stacy raced in, wild-eyed and distraught.

'Greg, what on earth have you done?' she wailed.

The young man stared in horror at her bruised eye. 'Oh, God, Stace, did I do that? I'm *sorry*! You know I wouldn't hurt you for the world. I just wanted to see Robert.'

Much to Harriet's surprise the child had fallen asleep on her shoulder. 'He's fine,' she assured the girl, handing him over with care. 'He was a bit frightened by all the fuss, that's all.'

'Miss Dyer should really call in the police,' James told the boy sternly. 'You obviously intended to abduct the child.'

'*No!*' The boy stared at him in utter dismay. 'I just wanted to take Robert home to my mother for a bit, Mr Devereux. Stacy wouldn't let me near him last night.'

'If you behave like this I never will, either,' she snapped, glaring at him over her son's damp curls.

'Don't involve the police, love, *please*,' he pleaded. 'I'll never have a drink again if you let me see more of Robert. I'm not like your dad, Stacy, honest. I would never hurt you or my boy.'

She nodded slowly. 'I know that, Greg.'

There was silence for a moment while the young pair gazed at each other, oblivious of the other two.

'You can load the buggy in the car and I'll drive you

home, Stacy,' said Harriet at last, but the girl shook her head firmly.

'No way, Harriet. I'll wheel Robert, and Greg can carry my things.'

The boy's eyes lit up. 'Can I give Robert his tea?'

'Yes. And his bath, if you like.' She fastened her sleeping son in his pushchair, and turned to Harriet. 'After all this fuss do you still want me on Thursday?'

'Of course I do.'

'Thanks.' She eyed Harriet's pallor anxiously. 'You look shattered. I'd better make you some tea before I go.'

'No need, I'll do that,' said James quickly.

Stacy smiled shyly at him. 'OK, Mr Devereux. Come on, then, Greg.'

The boy looked at Harriet in remorse. 'I'm really sorry. I know Stacy works here on Mondays so I came round to apologise for last night. I didn't expect to find Robert here. When I saw him on your lap I just lost it.'

'Because Stacy left your son with a stranger instead of with you,' Harriet said with understanding.

'Which gave you no right to terrorise Miss Verney, my lad,' said James sternly.

'I know that, Mr Devereux.' Greg pulled a face. 'When Dad hears about this I'll probably get a shiner to match Stacy's.'

'He won't hear it from me,' James assured him, relenting.

When the young pair had finally departed with their son James drew out a chair. 'You look exhausted, Harriet. Sit down. Is there anything to drink in the house?'

'Wine in the fridge.'

'No brandy?'

'There might be some in the cabinet in the other room.' She got up, but James pushed her down again.

'I'll look.'

Surprised by an urge to lay her head down on the table and howl once she was alone, Harriet combed her fingers through her untidy hair, brushed soggy biscuit crumbs from her T-shirt, and managed a smile when James returned with a bottle of cognac and two crystal brandy snifters.

'My grandmother's emergency kit,' she informed him.

'I think we can definitely class this as an emergency.' He poured a small quantity into each glass and handed one over.

Harriet took a cautious sip from hers, shuddering a little as the fiery heat hit her. 'Thank you for coming to my rescue. Greg gave me rather a shock.'

James nodded. 'I know. That's why I was so rough with the kid.'

'It probably taught him a lesson.' Harriet smiled ruefully. 'When Stacy said the child's father had hit her I visualised some bruiser with fists like sledgehammers, so Greg came as something of a surprise. It was sad, really. Robert was delighted to see his daddy until Greg frightened him by yelling at me. How do you know Watts Senior, by the way?'

'You probably know him as Frank. He's the head gardener up at the house. I've known young Greg all his life.'

'His father must be good at his job. It all looked very perfect when I was up there the other day.' Harriet sighed. 'Poor Greg. I'm glad Stacy relented towards him.'

'Talking of relenting,' said James lightly, 'did you tell Tim you had lunch with me?'

'Yes. For once he was lost for words.' She grinned. 'I was pretty surprised myself.'

'That you shared a meal with the ogre and survived?'

Harriet flushed. 'I don't think of you as an ogre.'

'Liar!'

'All right, a bit, maybe. When I was young.'

'You're young now, Harriet.'

'Older than I was. You don't scare me any more.'

He frowned. 'Did I scare you in the past, then?'

'Of course you did!' She drained her glass. 'You blamed me every time Tim disobeyed your orders.'

'Because I knew he was obeying yours instead.'

'Mine were always suggestions, not orders.' Harriet gave him a straight look. 'And Tim only fell in with them when they appealed to him. You must surely know by now that he goes his own sweet way.'

'I do.' He got up. 'But in spite of that, or maybe because of it, I still feel protective towards him.'

'And you're convinced I'm going to hurt him in some way.' She looked at him challengingly. 'Do you really believe I'm sneaking into other men's beds behind Tim's back?'

His eyes flared dangerously for an instant. 'Are you?'

They stared at each other in taut silence for a moment.

'I don't have to answer to you, James,' she said hoarsely, and turned away.

He moved round the table and turned her face up to his. 'Tears, Harriet?'

She jerked her head away, blinking hard. 'Would you go now, please?'

'Harriet, I'm sorry. I've no right to question your private life,' he said wearily.

'No, you haven't.' Harriet reached blindly for a sheet of kitchen paper to mop herself up, and James caught her in his arms, pressing her face against his chest as he smoothed her hair.

'Don't cry, little one,' he said, in a tone that brought the tears on thick and fast. For a few blind, uncaring moments Harriet sobbed with abandon, but as she calmed down she grew aware of James' heart thudding against her own, and pulled away in panic.

'It's just reaction to all the drama,' she said thickly,

knuckling the tears away. 'Go away. I'd rather cry in private.'

'I'd rather you didn't cry at all,' he said huskily. 'Particularly when I'm to blame.'

She turned to face him, careless of tousled hair and swollen eyes. 'The man you saw with me at the theatre is an old college friend, and Tim was perfectly happy about it. It's absolutely none of your business, James Devereux, but just for the record I don't sleep around. Now let's drop the subject.'

For once James looked at a complete loss. 'Harriet—'

She held up an imperious hand. 'Look, I'm tired. Could you just go now?'

On his way to the door he paused, and turned to look at her. 'On an entirely different subject, Harriet, I need an assistant gardener to help Frank Watts. If I offered the job to his son, my bar manager could move here to End House and young Greg could take Stacy and the boy to the garage flat,' he added. 'Think about it. I'll be in touch.'

She stood utterly still for a while after he'd gone, staring at the door James had closed so gently behind him. Clever devil, she thought resentfully, then gave a wry little laugh. He might think he was persuading her in the one way certain of success, but he'd actually given her the perfect, face-saving way out of a dilemma. She could now sell End House at a very good price without revealing her change of heart. And no one need know that living alone there on a permanent basis had lost its appeal after only a day or two.

CHAPTER THREE

THE drama of the afternoon left Harriet with no enthusiasm for a trip to Cheltenham to see a film, as she'd intended. Instead she stretched out on the cane sofa in the conservatory after supper, trying to read. But, restless for reasons she refused to analyse, she gave up after a while and went out to water the flowers in the herbaceous borders instead. She spotted a gap in the hedge she hadn't noticed before, made a note to point it out to James and, reluctant to go back indoors on such a beautiful evening, she fetched her phone and sat on the rustic seat at the end of the garden to ring Dido.

'About time,' her friend said indignantly. 'Don't you ever look at your messages?'

'I've had distractions.' With suitable drama Harriet described her adventures of the afternoon.

'Wow!' said Dido, awed. 'You must have been scared to death.'

'Not really. He was only a kid. Anyway Tim's brother came charging to the rescue—'

'Are we talking the famous *Jed* here?'

'That's the one! He's down here doing staff interviews for Edenhurst.'

'And he just happened to be on hand in your hour of need? How come?'

'No idea. He was just passing, I suppose. What's new with you?'

In triumph Dido announced that she'd been given a pay rise, and told Harriet to be back in good time on Saturday.

'I'm in a party mood, so I've asked some people round to celebrate. Make sure Tim comes, too.'

After she'd rung off Harriet sat staring down the garden, not too thrilled about going back to plunge straight into one of her friend's parties. The flat would be filled to overflowing with glossy, perfectly groomed people who worked for the same famous cosmetics house as Dido. No one would leave until the small hours, and before getting to bed there would be an argument, as usual, when Harriet insisted the mess had to be cleared up first.

Then something Dido said came back to Harriet. Why *had* James appeared at her back door at just that particular moment? She curled a lock of hair round her finger as she tried to think of him objectively. If she'd met James Edward Devereux for the first time this week as a stranger, would she have been attracted to him on a purely man/woman basis? She bit her lip. She might have hero-worshipped him when she was a child, but she'd never thought of him in that way before, and right now the worrying answer was yes. Tim would laugh his head off when she told him—not that she would tell him. He wouldn't understand. Nor would she blame him. She didn't understand, either.

Harriet was on her way to bed when the phone rang, and because only one person ever rang her that late she chuckled as she lifted the receiver.

'Some people keep respectable hours, Tim Devereux.'

'Wrong brother, Harriet,' said James coolly.

'Oh—sorry. Hello.'

'I had a word with Frank Watts and told him that if Greg wanted a job I'd see him tomorrow afternoon. I made no mention of accommodation, obviously.'

'Will you give Greg the job even if I don't let you have End House?'

'Of course I will!' said James impatiently. 'I'm ringing

at this hour because it would obviously help if I knew your decision about the house before I see him, Harriet. Think about it overnight. I'll call round in the morning for your answer.'

Harriet locked up and went upstairs to lean out of the open bedroom window, the nostalgic, summer scent of roses reminding her that her grandmother would have strongly approved of James Devereux as the purchaser for End House. Olivia Verney had been very fond of Tim, but Harriet knew she'd had enormous respect for the brother who'd worked so hard to provide security for him.

Next morning Harriet was up early. After a shower she creamed her skin with one of the free samples that often came her way from Dido, brushed her hair until it shone, and instead of tying it back left it to cascade in loose waves to her shoulders. As the final touch she made her face up in City style, instead of the sole smear of moisturiser it had made do with since her arrival. Once she agreed to sell End House to James Devereux she might not see him again for ages and sheer pride urged her to leave him with a better impression than the tear-stained creature of yesterday.

The best Harriet could do from the limited choice of clothes she'd packed was a short ecru denim skirt and jacket and a vest top in a caramel shade that toned well with her hair. And instead of meekly waiting in for whenever James deigned to arrive she went on her usual trip to the shops to buy a paper and her daily pint of milk. She walked back slowly through sunshine that had a heavy, sultry feel to it, and found James, as she'd hoped, waiting on the rustic seat at the end of the garden, formal in a lightweight dark suit. He got up to take her carrier bag, and gave her a look that made all the primping and fussing worthwhile.

'Good morning, Harriet. You're obviously going some-where.'

'I'm off to Cheltenham later on. I intended to yesterday, but after all the commotion I didn't feel like it. Do come in.' Harriet unlocked the door, switched on the kettle and motioned him to a seat at the table. 'I take it you'd like some coffee?'

'Thank you. How do you feel this morning? Any ill effects from yesterday's episode?'

'No.' This time she was ultra-careful as she poured boiling water into the cafetière. 'I'll leave the coffee to mature a bit,' she said, putting the tray on the table. 'But I'll get to the point right now. I accept your offer for End House. Your moral blackmail worked perfectly.'

The striking eyes narrowed as they met hers. 'Blackmail?'

She smiled cynically. 'You know exactly the right buttons to push, James Devereux. You knew I'd cave in once you brought Stacy and the baby into the equation.'

He made no attempt to deny it. 'But Greg may not accept the job,' he warned, 'and even if he does, Stacy may not join forces with him.'

'But my bank balance will look a lot healthier.' She looked at him thoughtfully. 'Why are you so keen to buy End House?'

'If you sold to someone else it might not be maintained to Edenhurst standards. I approached your grandmother about it some time ago,' he added, 'but she told me to wait until the house was yours.'

Harriet nodded sadly. 'She told me she was leaving it to me, but I couldn't bear to talk about it. When did she tell you?'

'I spotted your grandmother leaning against a farm gate at the entrance to Withy Lane one day when I was driving into the village. She accepted a ride with such relief I was worried. She was breathless and very pale, so I insisted on coming in the house with her. I wanted to call a doctor, but she wouldn't hear of it. She put a pill under her tongue, and after fixing me with those big dark eyes you inherited, she admitted that she had a heart problem, but threatened to come back and haunt me if I told anyone about it.'

Harriet stared at him, arrested. 'She knew she was ill as long ago as that?'

James nodded. 'She had such a fright that day she took me into her confidence. I learned that your parents had died too young to make much provision for you, but at least End House and its contents would be yours to dispose of as you wished one day, along with enough funds to keep it going for six months to give you time to decide what to do with it.'

'So you've known all along that the house would come to me,' said Harriet quietly.

He nodded. 'I knew the time was up about now, so once Tim told me you were spending the week here to make your decision I arranged the job interviews for the same time.'

'I see. But if you're in the middle of interviews how were you able to materialise at just the right moment yesterday?'

'I was next door, checking on repairs needed to the roof. When I heard shouting and a baby crying, I barged through the hedge to see what was going on.'

'So that's why there's a hole in it. I was going to report on that.' She looked at him curiously. 'Don't you employ people to inspect your property?'

'Of course I do. And in the others I leave the various estate managers to deal with it. It's different here on my home territory. I prefer a hands-on approach at Edenhurst.' James paused. 'Has Tim ever shown you the apartment I converted from the stable block?'

'No. On the rare occasions he's come down here with me he won't go near the house.'

James gave her a grim smile. 'If he wouldn't with you

for company, he never will with me. I suppose I should be grateful he likes my flat in London.'

'So much he could bore for Britain on the subject!'

'You never come there with him, Harriet, no matter how often I invite you. I suppose I can guess why.'

She flushed. 'Something else always seems to crop up.'

He smiled sardonically. 'No need to fudge, Harriet. Tim told me you weren't comfortable about coming to the ogre's lair.'

'He said that?'

'No, the choice of phrase is mine.' James gave her a straight look. 'Now we've agreed to a truce, will you come with him next time I ask?'

'All right.' Harriet hesitated for a moment. 'Look, James, if I ask you a question, will you tell me the truth, not just what you think I should know?'

'If I can,' he said warily.

'Tim said you were here in Upcote when my grand-mother died.'

'Yes, I was.'

She looked at him in appeal. 'I've never liked to ask you before, but do you know what actually happened? I was on holiday in Scotland. My flatmate's parents own a cottage there. When I made it back here the vicar and his wife were very kind, but I had the feeling they were keeping some-thing from me.'

His eyes softened. 'Then I can set your mind at rest. I was next door with Alec Price, the estate manager, when I saw your grandmother in the garden and went out to talk over the hedge about her problem with moles. She was concerned about a cough I'd developed and told me to go home and take a hot toddy. She breathed in sharply mid-sentence, said she felt dizzy, and quietly fainted. Or so I thought. I vaulted over the hedge in my rush to get to her, and Alec called an ambulance. But when the paramedics arrived they couldn't revive her. She'd gone.' James reached for Harriet's hand, his eyes warm with compassion. 'She died in exactly the place she'd have chosen,' he said gently. 'One minute she was right here in the garden she loved, the next she was with the angels.'

'Thank you,' said Harriet gruffly, when she could trust her voice. 'It's a relief to know the truth.'

James looked at his watch and dropped her hand. 'Damn. I'd better run.'

Harriet got up quickly. 'Hang on a minute. What must I do to get the ball rolling about the sale?'

'Come up to the house this evening. We can discuss it over dinner.'

She shook her head. 'No, thanks. Could you just pop back here for a few minutes?'

His eyes frosted. 'As you wish, Harriet, but it may be late.'

'Whenever.'

Harriet felt a twinge of remorse after James left. She knew she'd offended him, but sheer vanity had prompted her refusal. For a formal place like the Edenhurst dining room she had nothing suitable to wear. Unless, she thought suddenly, he'd meant supper alone with him in the stable flat.

Harriet caught a bus to Cheltenham for lunch and window-shopping, bought a cuddly lion for Robert and, because her finances would be in good shape once James Devereux paid her for End House, had a look round the sales and bought a dress to put her in the mood for Dido's party.

Tim rang when she got back.

'Hi,' said Harriet. 'How's gay Paree?'

'Fabulous! After I sorted the business part with my artist we visited loads of galleries, including the Louvre, of course, and did tourist things together like the Eiffel Tower, and a boat trip along the Seine, and much wining and dining and so on. Anyway, enough about fascinating *moi*, how's life in peaceful Upcote?'

'Not all that peaceful.' Harriet related her adventures with baby Robert and his parents, and surprised Tim by her description of James' way of dealing with the situation.

'Did he beat the bloke up?' said Tim, dumbfounded.

'Of course not. He just took him by the collar and frog-marched him outside.'

'And how, my angel, did Jed just happen to be on hand to rescue you?'

'He was next door and heard the noise. The boy was shouting and the baby was crying—'

'Stop! Go back to London at once. It's obviously far too dangerous in Upcote. Anyway, I want you waiting with open arms to greet the returning wanderer.'

'Of course. By the way,' she added casually, 'I've sold the house. Your brother's bought it as digs for the Edenhurst bar manager.'

'Has he really?' said Tim slowly. 'At one time you clammed up and went all hoity-toity if I even mentioned big brother's name, but if you've let him have the house you've obviously thawed towards him quite a bit.'

'He thought you'd be pleased.'

'I am, in a way.' There was a pause. 'But for obvious reasons don't get *too* chummy with Jed.'

'Of course I won't,' she said scornfully. 'You have nothing to fear, Timothy Devereux.'

'Good.' He sighed. 'I miss you, Harry.'

'I miss you, too. Have fun, I'll see you soon—must go, there's someone at the door. Bye.'

Her visitors were Stacy and Greg, their faces incandescent with excitement as they gave her their news.

'We just had to come and tell you, Harriet,' said Stacy breathlessly.

'The garage flat goes with the job!' Greg added. 'We're going to live together at last, and be a proper family for Robert.'

Harriet congratulated the jubilant young pair and saw them off, glad that something rather wonderful had come from her decision to sell End House.

It was after nine by the time James arrived, looking a lot more approachable in thin cotton trousers and rolled-up shirtsleeves.

'Sorry I'm late. I got held up.' He handed her a chilled bottle. 'I brought some champagne to celebrate our deal. Or have you changed your mind since I saw you last?'

'Of course not. Stacy and Greg came round earlier.' Harriet smiled as she produced glasses. 'They were so happy, it scotched any doubts I had about parting with End House.'

James chuckled as he eased the cork from the bottle of champagne. 'I thought young Greg was going to pass out from excitement when I told him a flat went with the job.'

'You must have felt like God!'

'Not quite.' He shot her a look. 'If I had even a trace of that kind of power I'd have organised some things in my life very differently, my marriage included.'

Harriet pulled a face as she accepted a glass of champagne. 'The last time that subject was mentioned you changed it pretty sharply.'

'And spoilt our surprisingly amicable lunch,' he agreed. 'But as you know, Harriet, my wife left me for the all-too-common reason that she met someone else.'

'Tim was delighted about that. He didn't care for her at all.'

'Poor Madeleine. She believed that her looks were all she had to offer. When new young faces began to replace hers on magazine covers the punishing diet and constant beauty treatments weren't enough any more. When she started on cosmetic surgery I blew the whistle, so she left me.' James drank his champagne down and refilled both glasses.

'That's my limit,' warned Harriet. 'Any more and I'll be telling you the story of my life.'

'That's only fair in return for mine.' His lips twitched. 'Although I know most of yours already.'

Not everything, thought Harriet thankfully. 'Is Madeleine happy with the new husband?'

'No idea. After she walked out all communications were made through lawyers.'

'Talking of lawyers, what happens next about the house?'

James spent a few minutes discussing the opening moves in the transaction, and then asked to see over the house to assess any work needed.

'I'm not quite sure what I should do about the furniture,' Harriet told him when they went into the sitting room. 'I want things like the porcelain for keepsakes, obviously, but I can't see the furniture fitting in anywhere I'm likely to live.'

'No,' James agreed. 'Tim's taste runs to the strictly contemporary. I suggest you make a list of the things you really like, and I'll send the rest to Dysart's Auction House in Pennington.'

'That's very kind of you,' said Harriet, wincing when lightning flashed as she went ahead of him up the narrow stairs.

'I *can* be kind,' he said dryly.

'Greg and Stacy can testify to that.'

'I meant to you, Harriet.'

She turned away to show him the smaller bedroom, which had been furnished specifically for her when she was thirteen. The only thing missing was the battered teddy bear she'd left behind in London.

'I decided to sleep in my grandmother's bed this time in

case I never had the chance again,' Harriet told James as she took him into the main bedroom. 'The armoire would be a bit overpowering in a flat, but I'll keep the brass bed and the Georgian chest. It's beautiful, isn't it?' she added wistfully.

'This must be very painful for you, Harriet,' said James with sympathy.

'A bit, but it has to be done.' She blinked hard. 'Sorry. Champagne makes me emotional. And I'm not terribly keen on storms, either.'

Harriet gave a stifled little squeak as thunder cracked overhead, and James took her in his arms. 'Nothing to be afraid of,' he said soothingly.

He was wrong. Just to be held close to him like this was terrifying because she liked it so much. Hardly daring to breathe, Harriet stood utterly still as his arms tightened round her. Her palms grew damp and her breath caught in her throat when she looked up to meet shock in James' eyes. He stared down at her for a breathless interval, as though he'd never seen her before, and Harriet stared back, mesmerised, as he slowly bent his head to kiss her. When their lips met, hers parted in a gasp, his arms tightened, his tongue slid into her mouth and he held her hard against him, kissing her with such sudden, explicit hunger her knees buckled and she collapsed on the bed. James followed her down, his mouth and hands undermining her resistance so completely it took a crack of thunder to bring Harriet down to earth. She gave a smothered choke of disbelief and tore herself from his arms to stand at the far side of the bed, head averted, clutching at the carved brass finial of the bed as she tried to get her breath back.

Eyes tight shut, Harriet willed James to go away, but he moved round the foot of the bed to raise her face to his.

'Open your eyes! I'm not going to attack you again.'

She raised her lids to half-mast and heaved in a deep breath. 'It was just a kiss.'

'It felt like a hell of a lot more than that to me.' He stared down at her in dazed disbelief.

'It was just a kiss,' she insisted.

His eyes narrowed dangerously. 'Like this?' he said through his teeth, and caught her in his arms again. Harriet struggled for an instant, but he held her still and the fight went out of her, replaced by something that surged through her entire body, and frightened her to death. Pure, unadulterated lust was something new in her life, but in response to James Devereux's relentless hands and mouth she shook and burned with it, and felt answering heat scorch from his body into hers before he thrust her away with a groan of self-loathing.

'What the hell am I *doing*?'

'Conducting an experiment, maybe?' Harriet spat at him, shaking her hair back.

The heat faded from his eyes. 'What do you mean?'

She heaved in a deep, unsteady breath. 'I told you I didn't sleep around. Maybe you were putting me to the test.'

All expression drained from James Devereux's face. 'No,' he said slowly. 'Tests imply conscious thought. I just wanted you, Harriet. God help me, I still do.'

She rubbed a hand across her damp forehead, feeling her resentment evaporate at his honesty. '*Why?* We don't even like each other very much.'

He smiled bleakly. 'Our hormones obviously don't believe that.' The smile vanished suddenly. 'Will you tell Tim?'

Harriet shuddered. 'I most certainly will not. Will you?'

'Hell, no! I was the one spouting fine words about shielding Tim from hurt.' His mouth twisted. 'We just forget it ever happened.'

'Right.'

His eyes held hers. 'I'm not sure I can do that.'

Harriet wasn't sure she could, either. 'It probably wouldn't have happened normally, but you were talking about Madeleine, and I was tearful about this place, and the storm didn't help—'

'None of which is anything to do with it. With you in my arms I forgot everything and everyone, including Tim. Laugh if you like,' he added savagely.

She shivered. 'I don't feel like laughing.'

'Neither do I. For God's sake let's get out of here, away from this bed.' He held the door open for her and Harriet brushed past, trying not to touch him as she made for the stairs.

In the kitchen, with the table between them and the storm retreating now in the distance, she felt marginally calmer as she faced the tall, haggard man who had just turned her life upside down.

'I'll ring my grandmother's solicitor tomorrow.'

James nodded brusquely. 'If you'll give me the number I'll pass it on to my lawyer.'

'And until the sale is official I'll keep paying Stacy to clean the house,' said Harriet, determinedly matter-of-fact.

James shook his head. 'I'll see to that. She can carry on working here after the house changes hands. I'll talk to the Edenhurst housekeeper, too. There may be something Stacy can do up at the hotel on a regular basis.'

'Thank you. That would be a great help for her.'

Rain hammered against the window, and thunder cracked and rolled, but neither of them noticed the elements as silence fell that neither of them was willing to break. Harriet waited, nerves jumping, half wanting James to go and half wanting, quite desperately, for him to stay.

At last he gave her a look that turned her heart over.

'Tell me the truth, Harriet. If you and I were unconnected in any way, would you have let me stay tonight?'

'I would have wanted to,' she said honestly.

His eyes lit with triumph for an instant before the shutters came down. 'But because of Tim it will never happen.'

Harriet glared at him. 'I don't want to talk about Tim right now.'

'Let's talk about us instead, then.'

'There *is* no us, James.'

He moved round the table. 'So we simply delete the episode from our minds, forget it ever happened.'

'Yes,' she said gruffly, backing away. 'That's exactly what we do.'

James looked down at her for a moment, then caught her by the shoulders and kissed her so hard she was shaken and breathless when he thrust her away from him at last. 'Something else to delete,' he said savagely and went out into the rain, slamming the door behind him.

CHAPTER FOUR

NEXT morning Harriet rang Stacy with a change of plans. 'I'm leaving today after all. I've sold the house to Mr Devereux, and he'll be paying you from now on. Thank you for all your good work for me, Stacy. Would Greg see to the garden in his spare time until the property changes hands? I'll pay him the going rate.'

'Of course. He'll be only too glad to, Harriet. Will you come down here again?'

'Possibly. I'm not sure. By the way, I bought a little present for Robert yesterday, and in all the excitement forgot to give it to you last night. I've left it on the kitchen table. Give him a big kiss for me.'

'That's so sweet of you, Harriet. Thank you. Please come back and see us sometime.'

Harriet promised she would, then sent text messages to Dido and Tim, saying she'd be returning that day. She checked the house to make sure she'd left nothing behind, locked the familiar door and took her belongings out to the waiting taxi. As it drove away she looked back at End House with a sudden, sharp pang of misgiving, hoping she'd made the right decision.

When she let herself into the flat at lunchtime it was quiet, and remarkably tidy. Impressed, she took her bags into her room and unpacked the cushion bought in Cheltenham as a present for her friend. She went into Dido's room to leave it on the bed, and dodged out again in a hurry. Her friend was still in bed, and she had company.

Harriet sighed. She was fond of Dido, but this particular

aspect of sharing with her had its drawbacks. It was embarrassing, but not unusual, to run into one of Dido's men friends outside the bathroom of a morning, but normally only at weekends. Sleepovers before a working day were a first. Harriet retreated to her room to unpack, then curled up with the daily paper bought on the way and had finished the crossword by the time Dido tapped on the door.

'You can come out now. He's gone.'

Her face wan under a fall of silky fair hair, Dido smiled guiltily when Harriet joined her in the tiny kitchen. 'It's been lonely without you. Welcome back. Shall I throw some lunch together?'

'Sure you're not too tired?' Harriet batted her eyelashes. 'Sorry I disturbed love's young dream. I backed out in a hurry—honest.'

But there was no answering smile from Dido as she buttered bread. 'I didn't expect you back so early. Not that it matters, you know it wasn't Tim—not that I'd ever try to poach on your preserves,' she added hastily.

'Whose *were* you poaching on, then?'

'Nobody's as far as I know. Louise from Regional Sales brought her brother to the pub to meet the rest of us for her birthday bash last night. He gave me a lift home, and it's my day off today—'

'So he stayed the night,' said Harriet, resigned.

'Why not?' said Dido, flushing. 'It's different for you. You've got Tim.'

'I go out with other men occasionally.'

'But you don't sleep with them. For you there's only Tim. I don't have anyone like that in my life.'

'Oh, come *on*, you know loads of men.'

'No one who matters—' Dido's head flew up in consternation as the buzzer sounded.

'Don't worry. If it's your mystery lover back for seconds I'll see him off. Hide in the bathroom.'

Harriet picked up the receiver and pressed the release button, and smiled, delighted, when she heard a familiar voice. Tim came in like a whirlwind, brandishing a carrier bag, grinning all over his face.

'Great—you're here already. I come with gifts, angel. Will you feed me, or are you entertaining a lover behind my back?'

'Not today,' said Harriet, engulfed in a bear hug. 'I didn't expect you so early. Have you come straight from Waterloo?'

'I sure have, and I'm hungry.'

'What a surprise! Ask Dido nicely and she'll probably let you have something.'

'And where is the fair Dido?' asked Tim, wolfing a piece of bread.

'In the bath, I think.'

He went to hammer on the bathroom door. 'Come out, Dido. I've brought you a present, and I'm starving.'

'Be gentle with her,' said Harriet when he rejoined her. 'She's just got out of bed.'

He grinned. 'Don't worry, I shall handle her with kid gloves—or maybe not. She might like it too much.'

She laughed, admiring the new jacket and stylish haircut. 'You look good. You obviously had a great time?'

'The best. How did you survive your stay in Upcote?'

'By leaving in a hurry.'

'As bad as that?' The familiar Devereux eyes narrowed on hers. 'You shall tell me all later—ah!' He turned as Dido, fully dressed and face perfect, rushed in to kiss him.

'So what did you get up to in Paris, then, Tim Devereux?' she demanded.

'I'll tell you over lunch if you'll give me some food.' He smiled coaxingly as he handed her a package. 'I brought you some perfume guaranteed to send men wild with lust.'

Tim lifted Dido's mood, as usual, but after the meal she bestowed a valiant little smile on him and got up to go.

'I know you want to catch up with Harriet so I'll pop out to do some shopping. See you later.'

'What's up with Goldilocks?' asked Tim, after she'd gone.

Harriet sighed. 'A man stayed the night.'

'Not that unusual for Dido?'

'It was someone she'd just met. Again. She worries me lately. She's so desperate to find a man like you.'

'Like *me*?'

'I mean someone special in her life. She's been detoxing, botoxing, having her teeth whitened, eyelashes dyed, and heaven knows what else.'

Tim eyed her closely. 'You don't do her kind of thing, do you?'

'Invite strange men to stay the night?'

'I meant the drastic beauty stuff.'

'A bit of basic maintenance, otherwise what you see is what you get.' She wagged a finger. 'But don't play the innocent. You know perfectly well that Dido's got a crush on you.'

'And you know perfectly well why she's on a losing wicket.' Tim drew Harriet down on the sofa, eyeing her sternly. 'Don't beat yourself up over Dido. It's her life.'

'I know.' She grinned at him. 'Now tell me what you really got up to on your trip.'

Half an hour later, when he was on the point of leaving, Tim remembered to ask what else had happened in Upcote.

'Nothing much,' she said casually, her stomach churning at the lie. 'I had a couple of lazy days down there, then sold End House to your brother.'

'At a cracking good price, I hope.'

'Since you ask, yes.' Harriet sighed. 'I didn't need much

time to sort things out, after all. It's a pity I docked a whole
week from the Italian trip.'

'You'll still have a fortnight.'

'Can't wait!'

Tim smiled at her in approval. 'You obviously got on a
bit better with Jed if you let him have your beloved house.'

'We agreed to a truce. But he strongly disapproves of
my friendships with other men.' She looked him in the eye.
'He's afraid I'll hurt you.'

Tim shrugged. 'Jed just can't help feeling protective,
love. Besides, I know you'll never hurt me.'

'Try telling your brother that,' she said tartly.

Tim tapped her cheek with his forefinger. 'Why is he
always *my brother*? Can't you force yourself to say his
name?'

'I'm never going to call him Jed. But I try to manage
his given name now and then. It's part of the new peace-
keeping treaty. Which I agreed to solely to make you
happy,' she added, not quite truthfully.

'You always make me happy.' He held out a hand to
pull her to her feet and held her close. 'I missed you,
Harry.'

'I missed you, too.' She held her face up for his kiss.
'I'm glad you had a good time.'

'I know you are.' He stroked her hair gently.

She smiled and patted his cheek. 'Now go home and get
to bed early, you look tired. By the way, Dido's throwing
a party next Saturday. You're invited.'

'Of course I am. Tell her I accept with pleasure.' Tim
clapped a hand to his forehead, and took a package from
his holdall. 'I almost forgot. I brought boring scent for
Dido, but for you something special.'

Harriet tore open the wrappings to find sexy wisps of
underwear, with a label that made her mouth water. 'Tim,
you extravagant thing, they're gorgeous, *and* the right size!

Thank you. I'll wear them under my new dress at Dido's soirée.'

But after Harriet had been through Dido's strict cleanse/tone/moisturise routine before the party a few days later it was James she thought of as she made up her face. The caramel brown of her long, waving hair was natural, the shape under her new dress was all her own, and the effect was satisfactory even to her own critical eyes. She blew a kiss of approval to her reflection. He wouldn't be there to notice, but even by James Devereux's exacting standards the ugly duckling was quite a presentable swan these days.

Tim was still missing by the time the flat was packed to the doors with Dido's guests.

'Where is he?' muttered Dido impatiently as they opened more bottles in the kitchen.

'He'll be here soon,' Harriet assured her.

But when Tim finally put in an appearance he had company.

'Hi, gorgeous,' he said, kissing Harriet. 'Jed called in to see me just as I was leaving, so he gave me a lift.'

'Why, hello,' said Harriet, wanting to clout Tim with one of the bottles he was carrying. 'This is a delightful surprise. I'll fetch Dido.'

'I'll do that.' Tim gave her a guilty look, and plunged into the crowd with his offerings like a criminal bent on escape.

As well he might, thought Harriet, simmering.

'I can leave right now, if you like,' offered James dryly, but Dido raced up to gush over him, and press him to a drink.

'How lovely to meet you at last,' she cried. 'I've heard so much about you.'

'And I about you,' he said, smiling down at her in a way that won him such a delighted, flirtatious response only the arrival of more guests forced Dido to tear herself away.

James moved close to Harriet at once, like a hunter closing in for the kill. 'Tim insisted I come in for a minute to say hello.'

'Surely you've got better things to do,' she muttered.

'I wanted to see you,' he said in a fierce undertone. 'I called round to End House next morning but the bird had flown.'

'It seemed like a good idea. This,' she added rapidly, 'is a bad one.'

'I need to talk to you.'

Harriet backed away. 'If it's about the house—'

'What are you two arguing about?' demanded Tim, putting an arm round her shoulders.

'We're discussing End House,' she told him.

'I was just asking Harriet to meet me sometime to go over the details regarding furniture, and so on,' said James casually.

'Good idea,' agreed Tim, delighted. 'The three of us could have lunch together tomorrow.'

'Come to the flat,' James said promptly. 'I'll organise a meal.'

'All right with you, love?' said Tim eagerly.

'Fine,' she assured him, resigned.

'I'll see you tomorrow, then, about one,' said James. 'Say my goodbyes to the hostess, Tim. Harriet, perhaps you'd see me out.'

She went out into the hall, and closed the door on the uproar in the flat. James stood close in silence, his eyes so like and yet so unlike Tim's, holding hers captive for a moment before he said the last thing she'd expected to hear. 'You look beautiful, Harriet.'

'Why, thank you.' She smiled challengingly. 'You like my swan outfit, then.'

'You were never an ugly duckling,' he said instantly. 'Robert loves the lion, by the way.'

'You've seen him?'

'Stacy brought him with her when she came to see the garage flat.' He moved closer. 'We need to talk alone, Harriet. Just tell me where and when and I'll meet you somewhere.'

She shook her head. 'No need. I'll just come to your place a few minutes early tomorrow.'

He raised a disbelieving black eyebrow. 'Ah, but will you break the habit of a lifetime and actually turn up this time?'

'Yes,' she said curtly.

'Good. I'll be waiting. Goodnight, Harriet.'

James gave her a formal, unsmiling bow and left, taking Harriet's zest for the party with him. Feeling oddly flat, she went to rescue Tim from a trio of Dido's colleagues, and agreed gratefully when he suggested taking food and a bottle of wine to her room to enjoy their own private party. But when they stole away with their feast they found Harriet's bed occupied.

'That does it,' said Harriet savagely, slamming the door shut. 'I just have to get a place of my own.'

'We could go back to mine,' suggested Tim, once he'd stopped laughing.

She shook her head. 'It's late and I'm hungry. Let's just sit out in the back area to eat this lot, and hope it doesn't rain!'

As Tim was leaving, Harriet reminded him about their lunch date next day. 'But there's no point in your trekking here to pick me up tomorrow. I'll meet you at your brother's place.'

Tim eyed her accusingly. 'Does that mean you're going to duck out of it as usual?'

'Certainly not. I have things to discuss with your—'

'For God's sake call him by his name,' he said irritably.

'All right, crosspatch. Go home to bed.'

Tim grinned penitently and gave her a hug. 'Goodnight, love. See you tomorrow.' He kissed her, drew back to yawn, and trudged off to the main entrance. He turned to look at her. 'By the way, did I tell you that you look pretty damn scrumptious tonight, Harry?'

'No, you didn't. But others did!'

It was three in the morning before the last reveller had left, and for once Dido began tidying up without argument.

'Tim left very early tonight,' she complained, emptying ashtrays into a bin bag. 'By the way, the famous Jed's a bit gorgeous! Why didn't he stay?'

'No idea. By the way, Tim and I are having lunch with him tomorrow.'

Dido gave her a cynical look. 'But are you actually turning up this time?'

'We've got a few loose ends to tie up over End House, so I have to.' Harriet yawned. 'Right, I'll leave you to the rest while I change my sheets for the second time in one day. I took Tim off to my room to eat our supper in peace, and walked in on a couple writhing about on my nice clean bed.'

'Oh, God, that's horrible!' Dido shuddered. 'What did you do?'

'Nothing. We shut the door on them and took our supper outside. It could have been worse. It's a fine night.'

'I'm so sorry!'

'Not your fault.'

Dido sighed as she began thumping sofa cushions. 'I suppose that settles it, especially now you've sold your grandma's house. You want a place of your own right away.'

'Yes, I do,' admitted Harriet. 'Can you manage the mortgage yourself, or will you get someone else to share?'

'I'll be fine now I've had a pay rise.' Dido collected a

few glasses, her face still averted. 'Are you and Tim going to move in together, then?'

'Not yet. I quite fancy being on my own for a while.'

'When you could be sharing with Tim? You're mad!'

The prospect of lunch next day gave Harriet another of the restless nights plaguing her lately. Seeing James Devereux, unexpected and out of context, had shaken her badly, and he'd known it.

It was raining hard next morning, which gave Harriet the perfect excuse to dress down in khaki combats and black ribbed cotton sweater, to make it clear she didn't look on the occasion as special. From the first day of James' move, Tim had driven her mad with constant descriptions of his brother's flat, which overlooked the Thames and occupied two floors of a redbrick Victorian warehouse James Devereux and his partner Nick Mayhew had transformed into luxury apartments.

Harriet paid off the taxi and dashed through the rain into the foyer to take the lift to the fourth floor. By the time she reached it she had her smile firmly in place when James, in jeans and chambray shirt, opened his door.

'So you actually came, Harriet. Welcome.' He stood aside to let her in. 'Let me take your umbrella.'

Harriet's tension vanished at first sight of the apartment. The glazed brickwork and great arched windows of the original building housed an interior that looked like a film set for a science fiction movie. Semi-circular white sofas were grouped with glass tables and steel lamps to face a huge plasma-screen television with free-standing speakers, the white, steel and glass theme continued in a kitchen and dining area dominated, like the entire, light-filled living space, by panoramic views of the river.

'Are you going to say something soon?' said James, amused.

'It's not a lot like Edenhurst.'

'True,' he agreed. 'What's your verdict?'

'For once Tim wasn't exaggerating,' she said obliquely, and walked to one of the windows to look at the spectacular view. 'Isn't it a bit like living in a goldfish bowl?'

'I had fine-slat blinds fitted in the bedroom—though only a passing seagull could look in. Let me give you a drink,' said James. 'I've got champagne on ice—'

'No, thanks,' she said, so vehemently he took her by the hand and turned her to face him.

'Relax, child.'

Harriet shook her head. 'I'm not a child any more.'

'No. It would be much simpler if you were.' He dropped her hand. 'So what can I offer you?'

She took a glass of fruit juice with her as he showed her the rest of the apartment. In the sparsely furnished bedroom Harriet gave a fleeting glance at the huge white-covered bed and looked round curiously. 'Where's your bathroom?'

'Through here.' James slid back an opaque glass panel behind the bed to reveal a mosaic-tiled shower, oval bath, and custom-made units in the glass, white and steel of the rest of the apartment. 'Would you like to stay here by yourself for a moment?' he asked tactfully.

'No, thanks,' she said, red-faced again, and splashed fruit juice down his chest in her haste to get away.

James grabbed a towel to blot his shirt, rolling his eyes. 'Harriet, for God's sake stop this sacrificial lamb act. I am not about to throw you on the floor and ravish you.' He gave her a sudden smile. 'Not that the idea lacks a certain appeal.'

Harriet let out a shamefaced little laugh. 'Sorry! Have I ruined your shirt?'

'No. Have a look at the rest of the flat, then we'll have this talk of ours before Tim gets here.' He looked at his

watch. 'He can't be too much longer.' But while James was
showing her the gadgets in his kitchen the phone rang.

'Tim? What's up? You sound rough.' James listened
closely, his face inscrutable. 'In that case,' he said at last,
'take some pills and stay in bed to get in shape for work
tomorrow. I'll hand you over to Harriet.'

'Hey,' she said, heart sinking. 'What's wrong?'

'I rang the flat but Dido said you'd left. I tried your
phone, but no luck. Did you forget to charge it?' demanded
Tim.

'I must have. Sorry.'

'Anyway, now I've tracked you down I'm grovelling. I
feel like death. I had a drink or three with the others when
I got home last night. Bad move. I told Jed I had a migraine, but for your ears only it's the father of all hang-
overs. Sorry, angel. I just can't make it today.'

'OK. Drink plenty of water, and get some sleep,' she
said, resigned. 'Take care. I'll ring you tonight.'

'Shall I call a cab, or can I persuade you to stay to
lunch?' James asked.

Harriet thought about it. 'I'll stay. But just for lunch.'

'Not for the orgy afterwards?' he said affably.

'Or maybe I'll stick with the cab,' she said, glaring at
him.

He held up a hand. 'Let me give you lunch first.'

They sat at the table with the view to eat cold roast
guinea fowl, served with a green salad and hunks of coarse,
crusty bread.

'I kept it simple. This is the food I'd originally planned
for my own lunch,' James told her, and filled their wineglasses. 'And it's just a New Zealand Sauvignon, not champagne.'

Harriet shot him a rueful look as she buttered her bread.
'This is funny, really. Tim not turning up, I mean. It's usually me.'

James' eyes gleamed. 'Come clean, Harriet. Tim's migraine is really a hangover, right?'

Harriet grinned. 'Afraid so. I suppose he thought big brother would be angry if he told the truth.'

'Most people get hung-over sometime. Why should I be angry?'

'Because I turned up at last and he didn't. Tim feels guilty.'

'So do I.'

'Why?'

He looked her in the eye. 'Because I'm enjoying the unexpected treat of lunching alone with you. A stupid thing to admit, because you'll probably go rushing off right away.'

Harriet shook her head. 'We're supposed to talk,' she reminded him. 'It's my reason for coming here.'

'Right up to the moment I opened my door to you I was sure you wouldn't,' he told her.

'So was I,' she said frankly. 'But I promised Tim.'

'Why else?' he said, resigned, and refilled their glasses. 'You haven't told me yet what you think of the apartment.'

'It's not exactly cosy,' she said warily.

'It's not meant to be. It's a showcase, designed to demonstrate to prospective clients exactly what can be achieved with this kind of conversion. But go on,' he added. 'Tell me the worst.'

'It's not my cup of tea,' she said, turning to look at him. 'I admire it enormously as a concept. But it's too hard-edged for me. I couldn't live in it.'

'Tim would move in tomorrow.'

'So he's told me—ad nauseam.'

James laughed as he got up to take their plates. 'It's reassuring to know that you two don't agree on everything.' He put cheese and fruit on the table and sat down again. 'Right, then, Harriet. Let's talk furniture. I suggest you sim-

ply list what you want from End House, and I'll buy the
rest from you.'

Harriet's eyes widened. 'For your bar manager?'

'No, he'll move his own things in. Have you decided
what you want?'

'Just the Georgian chest and the china cabinet and its
contents, and the brass bed,' she said, keeping her eyes on
the orange she was peeling.

'The armoire and the lacquer fire screen would look perfect in my flat at Edenhurst, so I'll keep them myself,' said
James, 'and I'll let Stacy and Greg have the rest. Is that
agreeable to you?'

'It's a brilliant idea!' Harriet smiled at him warmly. 'My
grandmother would be very pleased.'

'Are you?'

She nodded. 'Yes.'

'I'll give you a fair price—'

'Have everything valued first and then tell me what the
professional thinks is a fair price,' she said firmly.

His eyes narrowed dangerously. 'Are you afraid I'll cheat
you?'

'Of course not,' she said impatiently. 'I'm afraid you'll
pay me over the odds, out of charity, like the offer for
End House.'

'I'm a businessman. I don't deal in charity. My offer was
exactly what the house is worth,' said James brusquely.
'And if you doubt my word about the furniture get the
valuation done yourself.'

CHAPTER FIVE

HARRIET looked at James in dismay for a moment, then abandoned her orange and stood up.

'You're offended. I'm sorry. I was trying to say I don't expect any special treatment because—'

'Of what happened between us at End House?' he demanded, jumping to his feet. 'You think I'm finding a way to pay you money for that? It was something to forget, you told me, not something to pay for.'

'You know I didn't mean that,' Harriet said furiously. 'I meant my connection to Tim!'

'My brother,' said James, stalking round the table, 'is nothing to do with it.'

'Of course he is. I wouldn't be here otherwise,' she snapped, and stood her ground.

'You think I don't know that?' He stopped dead, inches away from her.

They stood erect and bristling, glittering tawny eyes boring down into resentful dark ones. Then James sighed, and gave her a wry smile.

'This is ridiculous. I just want you to have the best price possible, Harriet.'

'So that Tim and I can set up house together?'

He frowned. 'You said that wasn't in the cards yet.'

'It's not.'

'Good.'

Harriet raised a suspicious eyebrow. 'Why is it good?'

James took her by the hand and led her over to one of the curved white sofas. 'Let's sit down for a moment, Harriet, while we discuss certain inescapable facts of life.'

She tensed. 'What do you mean?'

'We both love Tim,' he stated.

'Yes.'

'But you do realise that he's the eternal Peter Pan?'

'Of course I do,' said Harriet, relaxing slightly. 'After all, he's only twenty-three.'

'So are you.'

'The female of the species matures faster than the male.' She smiled. 'Don't worry. I've no intention of trying to make Tim settle down yet. I just want a place of my own for a while. Particularly after last night.'

'What happened?'

Harriet explained, keeping her eyes on St Paul's in the distance, then turned to him wrathfully. 'You may well sit there grinning, but I'd only just changed the bed.'

'The last straw!' he agreed.

'It was the ultimate embarrassment as well.'

'I can imagine. The act of love is not a spectator sport.'

'We didn't stop to watch!' Suddenly Harriet's sense of humour revived. 'Tim thought it was hilarious,' she admitted, and they laughed together for a moment.

'I'm sorry I barked at you about the money, Harriet,' said James eventually. 'But when it comes to pushing buttons you're no slouch yourself.'

'I know. Sorry.'

'I promise I'll send you an itemised copy of Adam Dysart's valuation.'

'Thank you.' She held out her hand. 'Shall we shake on it?'

James took the hand in his, but instead of shaking it he raised it to his lips, and Harriet leapt up as though he'd scorched her.

'Hell, Harriet,' he growled, 'will you stop it?'

She flushed. 'Sorry. I'm just—tired. We spent hours tidying up after the party.'

'If your friend entertains on a regular basis I see why you want a place of your own,' he said dryly. 'I'll make some coffee.'

'Thank you.'

While they drank it Harriet gave James a brief account of her work as assistant to the junior director of a City head-hunting firm, smiling as she told him that Giles Kemble had been reluctant to let her have that particular week off for her trip to Upcote.

'Giles lives in a flat with a view of the London Eye. He thought I was raving mad to bury myself in the country on my own for even a day, let alone a week.'

'You ran away long before the week was up,' James reminded her.

Her chin lifted. 'I did not run away. Once the sale of End House was settled there was nothing to keep me there.'

'Of course you ran away. You were afraid I'd come back to take up where we left off.'

'Certainly not,' she lied. 'I knew you wouldn't do that.'

'I wish I shared your conviction.' His eyes held hers. 'I wanted to, Harriet. But I didn't, for obvious reasons. Not that you would have let me in. Last night you made it clear that you'd rather not set eyes on me again.'

'I'm sorry if I was rude.' She bit her lip. 'Although Tim wouldn't have noticed anything unusual. He thinks I dislike you.'

James raised an eyebrow. 'And do you?'

She glowered at him. 'As was pretty obvious during the storm I don't any more, otherwise it—that—would never have happened.'

'It happened,' he said deliberately, 'because after spending even a short time with you in Upcote I discovered that Tim's little friend had matured into a woman who appeals to me so much I lost my head that night. But don't worry,

Harriet. As agreed, we just put it behind us, forget it ever happened, and Tim doesn't get hurt.'

Her feelings didn't matter, obviously. 'Right,' said Harriet briskly. 'That's it, then.'

He got up. 'I'll call you a cab.'

She thanked him stiffly, kicking herself for not suggesting it first.

While James was on the phone Harriet stood at one of the windows to gaze at the view, wondering why on earth she felt like crying. 'Thank you for my lunch,' she said politely when he brought her umbrella.

'Thank you for staying to share it. Let me know when you find a new flat and I'll arrange to have your things sent there.'

Harriet's instinct was to insist on paying for her own haulage, but something in his face decided her not to go there. Besides, she needed a favour. 'James, could you possibly store my things in some corner at Edenhurst for a while? I'd like to rent something furnished until I find exactly what I want.'

'Sensible lady.'

'Not always.'

His jaw clenched. 'The fault was mine.'

'It takes two.'

'In your case more sinned against than sinning.'

'We didn't really sin very much.'

His eyes held hers. 'Sins start in the mind, Harriet.'

She smiled bleakly. 'In our case the best place for them.'

When the taxi arrived James escorted Harriet to the lift, pressed the button and stood well back, as though he had no intention of touching her again in this life. 'I'll hold onto your furniture for as long as you want, but I'll let you know the valuation as soon as I get it. Goodbye, Harriet. Take great care of yourself.'

'Goodbye.' Harriet stepped into the lift, feeling as if a

chapter in her life had ended when the doors closed to block James Devereux's face from view.

The following month was a period Harriet looked back on afterwards with wonder that she actually made it to Italy. She had no contact with James other than communications through solicitors, and a letter from some minion with a list of valuations from the Dysart Auction House for the rest of the furniture, along with a cheque for the items James had bought. Harriet paid the cheque into her bank during a lunch hour, wrote a brief letter of thanks on her computer and heard nothing more from James Edward Devereux.

Her usual source of information on the subject was unavailable because Harriet had to warn Tim to stay well away for a while, due to the streaming cold she woke up with the day after her lunch with James. And with no hope of time off straight on top of a week's holiday she was forced to soldier on at work. Giles Kemble had never been ill in his life, and had no qualms about risking Harriet's germs. In an effort to avoid passing them on to Dido, Harriet went to bed the minute she got back to Bayswater every night, and persuaded her friend to go out as much as possible to avoid infection.

After plying the invalid with hot soup and fresh lemonade to wash down a new wonder cold cure she'd found, Dido reluctantly went out with friends, consoled by the fact that Harriet's flat-hunting had to be put on hold for a while. 'I'll miss you terribly when you go,' she said mournfully.

'I'm not exactly emigrating,' said Harriet, coughing. 'We'll see each other just the same.'

'But not so much. I won't see Tim so much, either,' said Dido, refusing to be comforted. 'You look *awful*. I'd better stay.'

Harriet vetoed that firmly. 'You really don't want this cold. In a heatwave it's bad news, believe me.'

Tim rang at regular intervals, as did Alan Green and Paddy Moran, the 'other men' James Devereux had disapproved of so strongly. But there were no phone calls from James, which, she tried hard to convince herself, was a good thing. But when she closed her eyes she could still feel his body against hers, the scent and touch and taste of him. And not for the first time railed against a fate that had landed her in such an impossible situation.

By the end of the week Harriet's cold had improved enough for her to spend social time with Dido. Tim was busy with the French artist whose pictures were about to be shown at the gallery, and he begged for a rain check when offered supper with two females to wait on him hand and foot.

The two females went out on the town instead. When they got back, a little earlier than usual in deference to the convalescent, Harriet was making for bed when Dido suddenly remembered James Devereux's flat.

'You were in bed when I got in that night,' she reminded Harriet. 'Then you went down with your cold, and never said a dicky-bird about the apartment Tim's always banging on about.'

'It's just as amazing as he said, very twenty-first century,' said Harriet, yawning widely.

'You don't sound terribly keen,' commented Dido.

'It's not my kind of thing at all. Everything in the place is white, glass or steel—no carpets, no curtains, and just two blobs of colour on the walls.'

'Are those the paintings Tim talked about?'

'Incessantly.' Harriet chuckled. 'But to be fair they look exactly right. It's no place to hang a Constable.'

'And not your kind of place at all, obviously.' Dido regarded her thoughtfully. 'Funny, really. Tim would move in there tomorrow, given the chance.'

'He won't get it. James is unlikely to vacate his flat just because Tim fancies it.'

'You seem a tad friendlier towards him these days, though,' said Dido.

'It's a move towards better relations between us,' said Harriet firmly.

Dido looked unconvinced. 'Now I've actually met the man in the spectacular flesh I think you'd better take care the relations don't get closer than they should be, my girl. Tim could get hurt.'

Harriet's eyes flashed. 'You know, Dido, you'd be surprised what enormous lengths I go to just to make sure that nothing's allowed to hurt Tim, ever,' she said tartly, and went off to bed.

Flat-hunting was a process Harriet found frustrating. Whenever she found something even remotely suitable Dido, invited on viewings with Tim to keep her in the loop, invariably dismissed it as impossible. But eventually Harriet found a sixth-floor studio flat with City views in Clerkenwell, well within walking distance of the agency where she spent her working day.

Tim helped Harriet with the move, and next day flew off to Italy to stay in the Tuscan farmhouse James had bought years before. Wishing she could have gone with him as planned, Harriet spent the following week putting her new flat to rights in the evenings, and by day worked even harder than usual to make up for her forthcoming absence. And for the first time in their working relationship Giles Kemble astonished her by rewarding her with an early dinner in an expensive restaurant not far from her new flat. Harriet was about to leave the restaurant with Giles when her heart leapt as she saw James arriving with a trio of men. He shot a look at her companion, gave her a frosty, unsmiling nod and, suddenly stricken with acute indigestion, Harriet thanked Giles and trudged home to the flat to pack.

When Dido arrived later she looked unconvinced when Harriet insisted nothing was wrong. She helped with the packing, insisted on staying the night, and next morning even accompanied Harriet on the underground for the journey to Heathrow. When Harriet finally boarded the plane for Pisa later she settled back in her seat with a sigh of pure relief as the plane took off, determined to let nothing spoil the holiday she'd been looking forward to since winter.

When James Devereux had first set eyes on it La Fattoria had been on the verge of crumbling into ruin, but its rose-tinted stone walls and high square tower endeared the ancient farmhouse to him on sight. He went straight ahead with the purchase and immediately began the expensive, painstaking process of restoration, which was slow, due to business commitments that kept him from making all the supervising trips to Italy he would have liked. The restoration was only half finished when he met Madeleine, but her take on an Italian holiday was a five-star hotel in Positano. Whenever James proposed a visit to show her La Fattoria there was always some fashion shoot or social occasion that made it impossible for her to go. And by the time La Fattoria was ready for occupation, complete with swimming pool, the marriage was over and James spent his holidays there with Tim, or with friends, or alone.

Harriet had been invited to accompany Tim there often enough, but this was the first time she'd said yes to a visit to La Fattoria. When she landed in Pisa she was full of anticipation as she boarded the train for Florence, happy to sit gazing, delighted, at the passing scenery until the train drew into Santa Maria Novella station, where she had to wait for a while until another train drew in and Tim, suntanned, his hair bleached to ash fairness by the Tuscan sun, alighted from it and raced towards her along the striped marble concourse. After hugs and kisses and apologies for being late, he took charge of the heavier bags and hurried her out of the station.

'We have to walk a bit to get your hire car,' he informed Harriet, 'but it's not too far.'

He was right. But the sun was hot, the picturesque streets of Florence thronged with slow-moving crowds, and by the time they'd taken possession of the car Harriet was only too glad to let Tim take the wheel. Once out of the city he took the scenic route, which wound past the famous wine estates of Chianti. But eventually Tim turned off on a narrower road which, he said, with pride in his increasingly fluent Italian, was one of the *strade vicinali*, the local roads that meandered, sometimes aimlessly, all over the Italian countryside.

'But this one leads straight to La Fattoria because the place was a working farm back in the mists of time—not that you can call this straight, exactly,' he added as the car ascended in swooping curves lined with pointing fingers of cypress. Harriet already knew the house by sight from the countless photographs Tim had taken to show her, but when he drove through an archway in the restored outer wall her first actual sight of La Fattoria took her breath away. Green creeper wreathed part of the lower walls, but the square stone tower looking down on the courtyard glowed cinnamon and gold in the afternoon sun.

Tim leapt out to open Harriet's door, grinning in delight at her expression. 'Cool, isn't it?'

'Cool!' She gave him a scornful look as she got out. 'It's like something out of a fairy tale.'

'And you're in the tower room, princess, for the best view. We'll stow your gear, then have a swim.'

Unlike James Devereux's London flat, the interior of La Fattoria matched the outside, with a high-beamed ceiling, glowing rugs on the cool tiled floor, and supremely comfortable, dateless furniture.

'Jed's got great taste,' said Tim with pride.

'It's lovely,' said Harriet, so quietly he shot her a searching glance.

'You're disappointed?'

'Of course not. How could I be? It's perfect.' She smiled at him. 'But I need a shower and a drink of some kind, and then that swim.'

A winding stone staircase led up to the room in the tower. The bed was wide, with crisp white covers and a headboard carved from the dark wood of the settle beneath the window, and an armoire not unlike the one at End House. Filmy curtains stirred languidly at windows that looked down on the courtyard, and beyond to a blue swimming pool set in a terrace with breathtaking views of olive groves and vineyards against a backdrop of rolling, wooded hills. Harriet gazed out in rapturous silence for a moment before smiling at Tim.

'For once, Tim Devereux,' she said, kissing him, 'you were not exaggerating. But, to make my day complete, does that door lead to a bathroom?'

After a good night's sleep to get over her flight, Harriet was happy to fall in with Tim's plan of as much exploration of local Tuscany as possible. With his encouragement she climbed all five hundred and five steps to the top of the bell tower alongside the Palazzo Pubblico in Siena to look down on the great fan-shaped square, and the view of what appeared to be all of Tuscany beyond. But in Florence next day, after hours of standing in line to see the paintings in the Uffizi and the Pitti Palace, she rebelled.

'That's it. I saw Michelangelo's David years ago when I came here with my school, thank God, so if you can't leave here without looking at him again for the umpteenth time I'm going shopping. I've overdosed on culture, Timothy Devereux. No more pictures, no more *duomos*. From now on I just want to chill.'

The caretakers James employed were away on their annual holiday, but their married daughter came in from the village for an hour or two each morning to tidy up, and bring fresh bread and vegetables. Lunch each day consisted of melon with Parma ham, or a simple salad of tomatoes with basil and mozzarella. Afterwards there were short, leisurely explorations of the countryside in the car, and in the evenings a simple pasta dinner in the courtyard. It was a relaxing, unwinding routine Harriet enjoyed to the full until a little after midnight halfway through her holiday.

Surprisingly tired after a day of doing very little at all, Harriet had been deeply asleep until something disturbed her. She stirred, surfaced slowly and opened her eyes to see James standing in a shaft of moonlight at the end of the bed. She smiled at him drowsily for a moment, and then shot upright in shock. It was no dream. He was here, in the flesh.

'I frightened you,' said James tersely. 'I'm sorry, Harriet. I didn't expect to find you here.'

She pulled the sheet up over the heart banging against her ribs. 'But you knew I was coming to La Fattoria.'

'I meant here in my room.'

'Oh.' She heaved in a shaky breath. 'I didn't know it was your room. Tim didn't tell me.'

He cast a glance at the bathroom door. 'Where is Tim?'

Too tired and dazed to think up some story, Harriet told him the truth. 'He's in Florence.'

'What the hell is he doing there?' demanded James, in a tone that made her want to duck under the covers and hide.

'He's meeting an artist he thinks Jeremy might exhibit at the gallery.'

'Why didn't he take you with him?'

'I preferred to stay here.'

'When did he go?'

'A few days ago,' she said reluctantly.

'A few *days* ago!' James stared at her in furious disbelief. 'And when, exactly, is Tim coming back?'

'I'm not sure. He'll ring me tomorrow.'

His eyes glittered angrily. 'Are you telling me that he left you alone here, miles from anywhere in a strange country, and you have no idea when he'll be back?'

She stared at him mutinously. 'I've got the hire car and my phone, and this place is so idyllic I'm perfectly happy on my own.'

James took in a deep breath, very obviously fighting to control his temper. 'Go back to sleep,' he said brusquely. 'We'll talk in the morning.'

Harriet slumped back on the pillows when the door closed behind him, her heart still thumping from the shock of finding a man in her room. Only it wasn't just a man, it was James. And it wasn't her room, either. It was the master bedroom, and the master had not been at all pleased to find it occupied.

She slid out of bed, and then snatched at her dressing gown as the door flew open and James strode in again.

'Some of Tim's belongings are in his room. And not from the last time he stayed, either. Have you two fallen out?'

'No.'

'Then why are you in separate rooms?'

'I refuse to answer such a personal question,' she snapped, taking the war into the enemy's camp.

'I insist that you do, Harriet,' he rapped at her.

'I won't.' She shook back her hair defiantly. 'If you want answers, ask Tim.'

'I want them from you. If Tim's done something to upset you, I want to know.'

'He's done nothing at all to upset me!'

James eyed her grimly. 'He invites you here for a holiday, then takes off and leaves you alone in a place as remote as this, and you call it *nothing*?'

'I've been fine,' she snapped. 'At least I was until I woke up to find a man in my room.'

'I've explained the reason for that,' he said curtly.

'But not why you're here at La Fattoria,' Harriet reminded him. 'Tim didn't say you were coming.'

'He didn't know.' He paused, as though choosing his words. 'I spent the weekend in Umbria at the Mayhews' villa, but this evening I decided to leave a day early and call in here before my flight back tomorrow.'

'Quite a surprise!'

'Obviously not a pleasant one,' he said, moving nearer.

Harriet backed away. 'Men don't normally appear in my room in the middle of the night.'

'So you keep telling me.' He took her hands. 'I want the truth, Harriet. Has Tim hurt you in any way?'

'That's a change,' she said scornfully. 'Normally I'm the one accused of hurting Tim.'

His eyes locked on hers. 'I keep thinking of something you said at End House, that Tim always goes his own sweet way. Does that mean regardless of your feelings in this instance, Harriet?'

She shook her head. 'Tim would never deliberately hurt me, James.'

'That doesn't answer my question.' His grasp tightened. 'Did you know about the stay in Florence before you arrived here?'

'No more questions, James.'

His face was expressionless in the moonlight. 'Just one. Who was he?'

She frowned. 'Who do you mean?'

His grasp tightened painfully. 'You know damn well! The man I saw you with last week.'

She glared at him, and wrenched her hands away. 'It was Giles Kemble, the man I work for.'

'And do you enjoy regular cosy dinners with your boss?'

'Not that it's any business of yours, but that was the first. I'd worked overtime the entire week, and it was his way of showing appreciation.'

'A damn sight too much appreciation from where I was standing.' James recaptured her hands, a glitter in his eyes that rang alarm bells in her head. 'For a split second when you first woke up tonight you looked utterly delighted to see me. Were you?'

Harriet bit her lip. 'That's not fair.'

'Were you?' he persisted, drawing her closer.

'Yes,' she said gruffly. 'But I thought I was dreaming.'

'This is no dream. We're both flesh and blood, and God help me, I want you so much I'm going insane,' he said, in a tone that made her tremble.

The moonlight cast such a dreamlike quality over the shadowy tower room Harriet's will to resist was almost non-existent even before James drew her close. When she breathed in the scent of warm, aroused male Harriet's last defences crumbled, and sensing it he held her close against him, pressing kisses all over her face. By the time his mouth settled on hers they were on fire for each other and he kissed her until her head reeled, his lips and tongue so demanding that hot, unadulterated need short-circuited something in Harriet's brain. She helped instead of hindering when he ripped her nightgown away, and surrendered to the rapture of his skilled, unerring hands as they sought secret places that reacted with such wanton delight her knees gave way when his mouth streaked down her throat to graze on erect, quivering nipples. She gave a husky little moan, and James pushed her down on the bed and plunged his fingers into tight wet heat, rendering her mindless before he surged between her thighs, his mouth on her throat as they came together in such perfect rhythm it rushed them all too quickly to a climax that overpowered them and left them staring, dazed and breathless, into each other's eyes.

Harriet was first to recover as she scrambled away to hunt out her dressing gown. No point in looking for the nightgown he'd torn from her. A great shiver ran through her as she yanked the sash of her robe round her and tied it viciously tight. She made for the bathroom and stood under the shower, holding her face up blindly to the beat of the water as long as she could bear it, then wrapped a towel round her wet hair, shrugged into her dressing gown, and ventured a look at herself in the mirror. Face flushed, mouth a little swollen, a few tell-tale red marks on her throat, but otherwise she looked much the same as usual. Harriet collected a hairbrush, and went into the bedroom to find James standing motionless at the open window. He'd pulled on his jeans but his chest was bare. He was staring down at the moon's reflection in the pool, so still he could have been one of the marble statues Tim had taken her to see at the Bargello in Florence.

He turned to her, his face in shadow as he stood with his back to the moonlight. 'I don't know what the deal is with you two, but I wish to God Tim had been here.'

Oh, right. Not, Thank you, Harriet, for some terrific sex, then. She said nothing, switched on the lamp beside the bed, sat down on the edge and removed the towel to rub at her hair.

James sat down beside her, staring at his bare feet. They were good feet, thought Harriet, long and slim with straight toes. Not a male feature she'd ever thought of as attractive before—or thought of at all.

'What are you thinking?' he asked.

'That you have rather nice feet.'

He gave a choked sound that was almost a laugh. 'No one's ever told me that before.'

'I thought someone with your looks would be used to compliments.' She took up the hairbrush, looking at him searchingly as she drew it through her hair. 'You obviously regret what happened just now.'

'How could I? That was the nearest thing to perfection two people can achieve together.' He cleared his throat, sounding more like an awkward teenager than the supremely self-confident man she was used to. 'After I saw you with that man the other day I couldn't get you out of my head. I was jealous, for God's sake. I know I don't have a right to be. I accepted the invitation to the Mayhews' just to have an excuse for coming here. It was no impulse visit on the way back. I needed to see you. Though God knows this wasn't my intention. I had no idea Tim was missing. But when I found you were alone here I lost it so completely I never even gave a thought to protection.'

'I take the pill,' she said wearily, 'so you don't need to beat yourself up about that, at least. For the rest we just add this to the list of things we keep from Tim.'

'You don't intend telling him, then?'

'No. My relationship with Tim is a pretty hardy plant. It would survive if it were any other man. But because it's you I won't take the chance.'

'Thank you. Tim would forgive you anything, but if he knew about this he'd never forgive *me*.' James got up, stood looking down at her for a moment, then said goodnight and left her alone.

Not even a goodnight kiss, she thought bitterly.

*   *   *

When Harriet woke next morning full recall of the night swamped her for a moment. She shivered, and went to the window to see James powering along the pool as if he had demons after him. She washed and dressed hurriedly, thrust her feet into flip-flops and raced down the winding stairs at breakneck speed to arrive in the kitchen just before Anna came in with her laden basket. With the usual mixture of phrase-book Italian and hand-waving Harriet managed to inform her that there were two for breakfast.

Anna beamed, assuming Tim had come back, but visibly sprang to attention when Harriet informed her that it was Signor Devereux this time. In minutes coffee was scenting the air, rolls were heating in the oven, and the table ready with several kinds of preserves and a pitcher of freshly squeezed orange juice. When James came in, damp about the head, Anna smiled in shy delight as he thanked her in fluent Italian.

'So you're a linguist, too,' said Harriet as the girl went off to do the household chores.

'I had to learn Italian fast when I first bought this place,' he said, taking the chair opposite. He looked at her closely. 'How are you this morning, Harriet?'

'Tired,' she said, and poured juice for him. 'I didn't sleep much. I wasn't looking forward to facing you this morning.'

'Why?' James buttered a roll and passed it to her, a small service she found oddly touching.

Hormones out of kilter, she told herself, which was no surprise after the events of the night. 'You know exactly why, James Devereux. Last night—'

'We need to do some very serious talking about last night,' he interrupted, and frowned as her phone rang. 'If that's Tim don't tell him I'm here.'

She checked the caller ID, nodding at James in confirmation. 'Hi, Tim.'

'Hi, gorgeous. Are you all right?'

'Yes.'

'That's my girl. I'll be with you sometime this evening. So what have you been doing?'

'Swimming, sunbathing, nothing much,' said Harriet, colouring as she met the eyes fixed on her face. 'See you later, then.'

'If you blush like that when Tim arrives,' remarked James as he poured coffee, 'he can't fail to know something's wrong.'

'No more than he'd expect. Tim will take it for granted I'm not happy about having a visitor.'

'You mean this particular visitor.'

'Exactly.' Harriet frowned. 'But if Tim's not coming until tonight you won't see him before you leave.'

'I've postponed my flight. I need a serious talk with my little brother,' said James grimly. 'You'll have to put up with my company for another night.'

'There's a whole day to get through before then.'

'You don't have to spend it with me. I can take myself off somewhere and come back later. But first we talk. Come out and sit by the pool.'

For the past few days Harriet had enjoyed reclining under a canopy on one of the cushioned steamer chairs, with a cold drink, a radio-cassette player, a pile of books on the table beside her and the occasional swim in the pool to cool her down. Determined not to let James spoil her routine, she stripped down to the bikini under her halter and shorts, smoothed on sunblock, put on dark glasses and stretched out on one of the chairs.

'So what shall we talk about?' she asked.

James tore his eyes away from the expanse of sun-gilded skin and took the other chair. 'I want some answers, Harriet. I've done a lot of thinking since we met in Upcote.'

'About what?'

'Tim.'

Harriet controlled herself with difficulty. 'Don't you ever think about anything, or anyone, else?'

'God, yes. I think about you a damned sight too much. Which is why I turned up here last night. I drove miles out of my way to see *you*, not Tim.' He turned to look at her. 'I was jealous of the man I saw you with that day, but here comes the real joke. I'm also jealous of my own brother. And because Tim thinks the world of you, Harriet, I can't do a damned thing about it.'

'I'm not a pound of tea! Don't I have something to say on the subject?' she demanded.

James nodded impatiently. 'Of course you do, which is where the questions come in.' He was silent for a while, but at last he swung his feet to the ground and sat on the footrest of his chair. 'Last night I found that you and Tim are not sharing a room here. Take those glasses off,' he added. 'I can't talk to a mask.'

With reluctance Harriet put them on the table beside her.

'And living together is not an option, you told me, until after the wedding. So tell me the truth, Harriet. After last night I've a right to know. Are you and Tim no longer lovers?'

She was silent for a while, tempted to lie through her teeth, but at last gave it up. Enough was enough. 'Tim and I have never been lovers,' she said flatly, and met his astounded eyes head-on. 'We're not just good friends, either. It's a much closer relationship than that. I suppose to me he's the brother I never had,' she added, watching James' body relax, muscle by muscle, before her eyes.

'And do you feel like Tim's sister?' he said guardedly.

Harriet grinned. 'More like his mother sometimes.'

He pounced, eyes gleaming. 'So tell me, little mother. What is Tim really doing in Florence?'

This time Harriet had a well-rehearsed answer ready.

'He's practising his powers of persuasion on an artist he wants to come to London.'

His eyes narrowed. 'Why don't I believe you?'

She lifted a bare shoulder. 'I'm telling the truth, James.'

'I still think there's something you're keeping from me.' He seized one of her hands. 'So here's the question I wouldn't ask another soul, Harriet. To my knowledge Tim's never had a close relationship with any woman but you. So if you and Tim are not lovers, is there something else I should know?'

'What are you asking?'

'You know damn well. I'm asking if Tim's gay.'

She gave him a long, hard look. 'Would it make any difference to you?'

'None,' he said, with such utter conviction she believed him. 'Tim is Tim. Now I know he's not your lover, Harriet, I can cope if he's gay.' He smiled at her crookedly. 'But if he's involved with Jeremy Blyth I don't want to know.'

'He's not,' Harriet assured him, chuckling. 'Jeremy is his employer, pure and simple.'

'There's nothing pure or simple about Jeremy Blyth!'

'I wouldn't know about that.' She looked at James steadily. 'And Tim's sexual preferences are not something I'm prepared to discuss. You'll have to ask him yourself.'

'I can't do that!'

'Then forget about it. Take Tim as he is, warts and all. In my book that's what loving someone means.'

'You're right,' James said slowly, and gave her a slow, transforming smile that melted her bones. 'Do you have any idea how good I feel right now?'

'Even without your questions answered?'

'You gave me the answer I wanted most. If you're not Tim's lover there's nothing to stop you from being mine,' he said, with such casual certainty Harriet felt her hackles rise.

'Only my own choice,' she pointed out.

'You had a choice last night.' He leaned forward urgently. 'As far as I'm concerned you made it.'

'And soon regretted it.'

James shot upright. 'I disappointed you?'

'Yes,' she said, pleased when she saw colour flare in his face. 'Afterwards, not during,' she added kindly. 'The sex was utterly wonderful. But your attitude later rather took the shine off it.'

He scowled. 'Surely you understood? I felt guilty as hell because I'd just made love to my brother's future wife.'

Harriet glared back. 'If I had been I wouldn't have let you near me.'

'But you did,' he said swiftly. 'Why?'

'For obvious reasons.'

'They're not obvious to me.'

Her chin lifted. 'I'd spent several days alone in the most romantic setting anyone could ask for, and suddenly there you were in my moonlit tower room, the perfect answer to a maiden's prayer.'

'So I might not have been so lucky on a wet night in Clerkenwell,' he said, in a tone that brought colour to her face.

'You've heard about my move, then,' said Harriet, and retaliated by stretching like a cat, her hands clasped behind her head in a way that threatened the security of her bikini.

James flung away, swallowing, to stare at the pool. 'Tim told me before he left. Not the exact address,' he added. 'So let me have it before I go.'

Right between the eyes if he asked like that, thought Harriet resentfully, and sat up to put on her shirt. 'I must go and find Anna. She's brought food for supper tonight, but I assume you'll be here for breakfast tomorrow. I'd better put in an order for more supplies.'

'What do you normally do for lunch?' said James, getting to his feet.

'I eat tomatoes and mozzarella, mainly, and in the evening I throw pasta in a pot and heat whatever sauce Anna has brought for me. I told her yesterday that Tim might be back tonight, so she's brought extra today.' Harriet smiled magnanimously. 'You can share both meals, if you like.'

'I'd rather take you out to dinner.'

'No, thanks. We'd better be here for Tim.'

'Then I accept your offer. With the greatest of pleasure,' James added deliberately.

In the kitchen Anna smiled shyly and indicated a large round tin containing a hazelnut torte and told them about the pudding she'd put ready in the refrigerator, as well as the usual pan of fragrant sauce waiting on the stove.

Harriet thanked her warmly and gave her a list of provisions needed for next day. 'Anna's husband brings her each morning, but I drive her home,' she told James. 'You can do that today.'

While they were gone Harriet went upstairs, chuckling when she looked into Tim's room. The bed had been made up with fresh linen, and Tim's belongings moved to the smaller room next door. If the master couldn't sleep in the master bedroom, Anna obviously felt he should at least have the larger of the two guest rooms.

The tower room was so immaculate Harriet was almost convinced that the bliss she'd experienced there in the night was imaginary. But at the mere thought of it inner muscles tightened and her pulse raced, confirming it had been all too real. And utterly wonderful. She sighed as she looked at her tanned, glowing reflection. Before it could happen again James had to forget any hang-ups from the past and see her as a person in her own right, not as part of a team with Tim.

Harriet swapped her bikini for shorts and yellow halter,

and went back downstairs to find that the house felt empty without James. She shook her head in derision. She'd been on her own for days, other than the early mornings when Anna was there. Yet James had been here only a few hours and already she felt lonely without him. She tried hard to concentrate on her book, but it seemed like hours before he returned to find her in her usual place by the pool, reading under the canopy. She looked up with a smile as he strolled towards her.

'You've been a long time.'

'People know me now in the village. I stopped to chat, and did some shopping.' He frowned as he noticed her clothes. 'Why did you change?'

'I dressed for lunch,' she said, getting up. 'Do you want it out here or indoors?'

'In the kitchen,' he said promptly, and held out his hand. 'Come inside, it's too hot for you out here.'

When they reached the kitchen Harriet discovered why James had insisted on eating indoors. The kitchen table wore a fresh cloth laid with wineglasses and silverware and the blue ceramic pot of pink geraniums Anna had put there at breakfast time. A central platter held creamy slices of mozzarella and red, juicy tomatoes, rolls steamed invitingly in a basket, and Harriet gave James a smile so radiant he bent to plant a swift kiss on her mouth.

'I deserve that,' he informed her.

'You certainly do. This is lovely.'

'But not difficult. You gave me the menu, and the ingredients were to hand. I put this in to chill before I drove Anna home.' He took a bottle of prosecco from the fridge and filled their glasses. 'And,' he added smugly, 'I tore basil and drizzled oil over the tomatoes in true Michelin-star fashion.'

Harriet sat in the chair he pulled out for her, very much aware that things had changed between them. Now James knew the truth about her relationship with Tim his attitude towards her was different, that of a man on equal footing with a woman he found attractive in the normal way of things, rather than a man trying to resist forbidden fruit. When she told him this, his eyes lit with a gleam that sent a shiver down her spine.

'Perceptive creature. Those were my exact feelings when I found that the schoolgirl had suddenly changed into a woman.'

'I didn't "suddenly change" into anything,' she said tartly, helping herself from the platter. 'The process happened in the usual way. You just didn't notice.'

'I didn't see enough of you to notice once you went off to college. When I was in Upcote it was a rare occasion that you came anywhere near me with Tim.' James tore a roll in half with sudden force. 'Then not so long ago I went to see an Ibsen play at the National and saw you with some man in the bar in the interval.'

'I noticed you.' Harriet smiled. 'I was with Paddy Moran. He's very keen on Ibsen. Personally I find him a tad gloomy—'

'Don't change the subject.' James gave her a wry look. 'It took me a minute or two to realise who you were.'

She smiled provocatively. 'Probably because I was wearing one of my swan outfits.'

'If you mention ugly ducklings again I'll turn you over my knee,' he said forcibly.

Her eyes danced. 'Is that a threat or a promise, James?'

'Both—stop trying to divert me.' He took in a deep breath. 'I saw you with this man and felt angry on Tim's behalf, then not long afterwards I saw you coming out of a cinema with a different man.'

'Did you? I didn't notice you that time,' said Harriet, surprised.

'I was in a taxi waiting for the lights.'

'It must have been Alan Green. We both love the buzz of going to the cinema. Tim prefers to hire a video to watch at home.'

'So do I. Then last week I saw you with someone else. And this time I was angry on my own behalf, nothing to do with Tim.' James gave her a savage look. 'But I was with some clients, which meant I couldn't snatch you away from him.'

'Bad for business,' agreed Harriet, secretly thrilled by the idea.

James was quiet for a moment as he went on with his lunch. 'Once I get things sorted out with Tim,' he said eventually, 'you and I could do that kind of thing together.'

'What kind of thing?'

'Theatre, dinner—anything you want.'

Harriet pushed her plate away. 'I'm not ready for a relationship with you.'

His eyes speared hers. 'Why the hell not?'

'Until quite recently you were someone I actively disliked. I admit I feel quite differently now—'

'How *do* you feel?'

Harriet drank some of her wine. 'I like you much better than I ever thought I would. In the past it was a touch of the Dorian Grays, I suppose. You are beyond question the most attractive man I've ever laid eyes on, but because you trampled on my teenage ego I stored this horrible picture of you in my mental attic. It grew uglier and uglier, until my recent stay in Upcote when I discovered that my grandmother had been right about you all along and I was wrong.' She bit her lip. 'It wasn't the only thing I discovered.'

James reached out a hand to take hers. 'Tell me.'

She gave him a crooked little smile. 'You remember the day I scalded myself? When you put your arm round me, my body was delighted even though my brain told it to behave.'

'The feeling was mutual, as you discovered later.' He frowned suddenly and released her hand. 'I felt guilty as hell afterwards, that night of the storm. But *I* had good reason to. You didn't, Harriet. If you and Tim have never been lovers, why did you push me away?'

'You'll have to ask Tim that.'

'You can count on it. I'm going to ask Tim a whole lot of things,' he promised. 'In the meantime you look tired, Harriet. I'll stow this lot in the dishwasher while you take off to the tower room. Sleep if you can.'

How on earth did he expect her to sleep? But when Harriet reached the cool, welcoming room, the prospect of a nap was so inviting she stripped off her clothes, slid into the bed Anna had made up with fresh sheets, and fell instantly asleep. When she woke James was sitting on the edge of the bed.

'You've been up here for more than two hours,' he said quietly. 'I came to see if you were all right.'

Harriet smiled sleepily. 'I'm fine. I was more tired than I thought.'

James took her hand. 'I was tempted to kiss Sleeping Beauty awake.'

She stretched luxuriously. 'She would have liked that.'

His eyes darkened. He leaned over her to thread his hands through her hair, and bent to kiss her, gently at first, but soon with such hunger Harriet's response was openly ardent. She clasped her hands behind his head to hold him even closer, her lips and tongue eager as they answered his. The sheet fell back and James gave a ragged groan when he found she'd slept nude. He leapt to his feet to shed his clothes, then tossed the sheet away and Harriet felt her nipples harden in response to the look that was as tactile as a caress as he gazed at her for a long moment, before he let himself down beside her and took her into his arms. He slid a hand down her spine to draw her close against him, and Harriet's lips parted against his, damp heat pooling low inside her at the feel of his erection hard and ready against her. His mouth roamed over her damp skin, grazing on it with lips and tongue and teeth, then lingering on her nipples long enough to drive her crazy with longing before moving on down over her waist and the slight swell below until he reached the apex between her thighs. She shut her eyes tightly as she felt the brush of his hair on her skin, followed by a piercing dart of sensation as his seeking tongue found the little bud waiting for his caress and she arched, gasping, and he slid back up her body and entered it all in one movement, and they lay joined and motionless for a moment. James looked deep into her eyes and began to move inside her and her body answered his in perfect rhythm as he took her slowly at first, then gradually faster, towards the glory that throbbed and burned just out of reach as she strove with him to find it. She bit back a scream as the rush of hot release engulfed her at last, and he collapsed on her, spent and panting, smiling down at her with the all-conquering, satisfied look of a man who had just given his woman the ultimate experience of pleasure.

Harriet grinned at the sheer effrontery of the smile, and he laughed and kissed her, then turned over on his side and drew her close with her head on his shoulder, and she sighed and curved against him, her last thought one of faint surprise because she needed to sleep again.

The room was dimmer and the shadows longer when Harriet stirred. She tried to free herself from the arm holding her close, but even in sleep James refused to slacken his grip, and she looked up into the sleeping face, free to take her time over it. The glossy black hair was wildly untidy for once, the eyes hidden beneath closed, thickly lashed lids. Her caressing eyes moved down over the straight nose to the wide, positive mouth—then she tensed, her heart thudding. Awkwardly, because of the arm holding her tightly against the hard bare chest, she turned her head to find, for the second time in twenty-four hours, a man standing at the foot of the bed.

CHAPTER SIX

TIM DEVEREUX stood transfixed, his eyes blank with disbelief.

Harriet stared back, horrified, and yanked on the arm constraining her. With a mutter of protest James yawned, opened his eyes and shot bolt upright when he saw his brother.

'About time!' he accused. 'What the hell do you mean by going off and leaving Harriet alone here? Anything could have happened.'

'And obviously did,' retorted Tim, and turned accusing eyes on Harriet as she tugged the covers up to her chin. 'You and *Jed*? How the devil did that come about?'

'I'm not saying a word until I'm dressed,' she said, crimson to the roots of her hair.

James slid out of bed to gather up his clothes. 'You could obviously do with a drink, Tim. We'll join you in ten minutes.'

Harriet shook her head. 'Twenty. I want a shower.'

'Right,' said Tim, still shell-shocked. 'See you later.'

When he'd gone James smiled wryly. 'A spectator sport after all.'

Harriet glared at him, for the moment quite unable to see the funny side of the situation. 'Just go, please.'

'Are you that embarrassed?'

'Embarrassed doesn't begin to cover it,' she retorted. 'Will you please go *away*?'

'It's a little late for maidenly modesty,' he pointed out.

'I'm not getting out of this bed until I'm alone,' she said through her teeth.

'I'll be back for you in fifteen minutes.' James bent to ruffle her hair and strolled from the room.

Harriet wrapped her hair in a towel and rushed through the fastest shower of her life. To boost her morale she put on the outrageously sexy underwear Tim had brought her from Paris and the dress worn at Dido's party, needing all the armour she could muster for the forthcoming confrontation. Tim had never been the slightest put out by her friendships with any other men, but finding her in bed with his idolised brother was another thing entirely. She turned from adding final touches to her face in an ancient gilt-framed mirror to see James watching her from the doorway.

'Ready?' he said, and took her in his arms, but she stood tense in his embrace.

'Ridiculous, I know,' she said, 'but I'm nervous. I keep telling myself it's just Tim.'

James shook her gently. 'Nothing could ever change his feelings towards you. I'm the one who should be worrying.'

'Tim idolises you—'

'Probably not any more, now he's discovered my feet of clay. Let's get it over with.'

On the way down the winding stair Harriet tried in vain to think up something to say to Tim, but when James opened the door to the living room her mind went blank. Tim had company. He faced them proudly, his possessive arm round a strikingly beautiful woman with a mass of black curling hair, her dark eyes fixed on James in appeal.

'Francesca?' he said in astonishment.

'*Come stai*, James?' said the woman, because woman she was, Harriet saw with misgiving.

'And this, darling, is Harriet,' said Tim. 'Harry, I want you to meet my fiancée, Francesca Rossi.'

The silence that followed this announcement was deafening.

'Fiancée?' drawled James at last. 'Is this true, Francesca?'

The look on his face filled Harriet with foreboding. Tim had left certain important details out regarding his Francesca—not only her age, but the fact that James obviously knew her. And possibly in the biblical sense as well as the social one, thought Harriet darkly, newly sensitive to such things after the afternoon she'd just spent.

'Yes, James, it is true,' said Francesca, smiling bravely. 'Will you not give us your blessing?'

From the closed, hard look on James' face the possibility of this seemed remote. 'When did this happen?'

'Last week,' said Tim defiantly.

James turned on Harriet, eyes blazing. 'Did you know about this?'

'No, she didn't,' said Tim at once.

'Did you, Harriet?' repeated James, ignoring him.

'I knew about Francesca,' she admitted reluctantly, 'but not about the engagement.'

The woman smiled nervously. 'Do not discuss me as though I was not here, James. Tim and I have known each other for many years. You know that. You introduced us,' she reminded him.

'I remember. Tim was just a kid at the time. And you were a married woman,' he added deliberately.

Francesca gave him an imploring look. 'But you know that Carlo is dead, James. I am *vedova* now.'

'Not a widow for much longer, darling,' said Tim, gazing down at her possessively. 'You'll soon be my wife.'

'Yes, *tesoro*,' she said, patting his cheek with a hand adorned with a large emerald ring.

'By the way, I've persuaded Jeremy to exhibit some of Francesca's paintings,' Tim told the others triumphantly.

Harriet held her breath as the two men stared at each other with animosity new in their relationship. Tim's eyes were hard and defiant as he faced his brother, with no attention to spare, noted Harriet with sudden heat, for the friend who'd gone to such lengths to keep his love affair secret. James, on the other hand, looked like a volcano about to erupt, which made her decide on escape as the most sensible move.

'I'd love to see your work sometime, Francesca,' Harriet said, smiling brightly, 'but forgive me if I rush off right now. I really must do something about dinner.'

Harriet beat a hasty retreat to the peace of the kitchen, enveloped herself in Anna's apron, opened two bottles of red wine and set to work. She looked up with a scowl when Tim came to join her.

'You're angry with me, I suppose,' he said morosely.

'Is it any wonder?' she retorted. 'You might have told me the truth about Francesca.' She filled a large pan with water, put it to heat then turned on him. 'You not only misled me about her age, you forgot to mention that Francesca and your brother knew each other.'

He shrugged, unrepentant. 'That was the reason for the secrecy. I wouldn't have brought her tonight if I'd known James was here. My plan was to marry her first and tell him afterwards when it was too late for him to do anything about it. Why didn't you warn me on the phone?'

'James wanted to talk to you. Besides, you didn't say a word about bringing Francesca.'

'It was supposed to be a surprise for you.'

'It was certainly that,' said Harriet dryly. 'It was to James, too.'

Tim's mouth twisted. 'An unpleasant one at that. I knew he'd disapprove.'

'I can see his point,' said Harriet, lighting the gas under Anna's sauce. 'Marrying a woman so much older than you was hardly likely to meet with his approval.'

Tim gave her a suspicious look. 'Did you know Jed was coming here?'

'Of course I didn't,' she said scornfully. 'It was a shock when he turned up out of the blue, believe me.'

He gave her a significant look. 'Nothing like the shock I got when I found him in bed with you, my girl.'

Harriet reddened, but returned to the attack. 'He obviously doesn't like this at all, Tim. I just hope Francesca doesn't cause a permanent rift between you.'

Tim took a cloth from a drawer and covered the table, his face set in lines new to Harriet. 'You mean he might stop my allowance.'

Her eyes narrowed. 'What allowance?'

'How do you think I pay for my share of the house in Chelsea? My salary isn't exactly astronomical.'

'It seems there are a lot of things I don't know.'

'No need to look down your nose.' Tim gave her a look that brought colour rushing to her face again. 'I found you naked in my brother's arms, remember. You're in no position to disapprove. Neither is he. What did Jed think he was playing at? As far as he knew, you were my property.'

'I'm nobody's property!' Her chin lifted. 'I told James the truth today.'

'So he promptly rushes you off to *bed*? I thought you two disliked each other. God knows you've always behaved as if you did!'

'When I was in Upcote I discovered a few things which changed my mind,' said Harriet. 'He was very kind to my grandmother, for one thing, and to the young couple I told you about. He was kind to me, too.' And unknown to Tim, his brother was the first man in her life to fill her with lust at the mere touch of his hand.

'A damn sight more than kind if he got you into bed with him!' Tim looked suddenly embarrassed. 'As far as I know, you don't normally go in for that kind of thing, do you, Harry?'

'Not lately! How could I when I was supposed to be marrying you sometime soon? At least my social life should improve again now the truth's out about you and Francesca.' She paused, eyeing him unhappily as she steeled herself to speak her mind. 'Look, are you really sure this will work out, Tim? Francesca's beautiful, and I know you have the art side of things in common, but she's years older than you. Lord knows *I* feel like your mother sometimes, and I'm only twenty-three.'

For the first time in their relationship Tim gave her a look so coldly hostile her heart contracted. 'Age difference didn't keep you out of my brother's bed, did it? And in case you're worried, my relationship with Francesca has nothing to do with Oedipus,' he added, in a tone she'd never heard from him before. 'Not that it's any business of yours, but after her husband died we became lovers in the full, normal sense of the word. If you don't approve, tough. After all,' he added, twisting the knife deeper, 'it's my brother's approval I need, not yours.'

Harriet stared at him, stricken, then turned away to take pasta from a cupboard. She swallowed hard, keeping her back to Tim while she poured the pasta into boiling water. She added salt and olive oil, took a look at her watch, and turned to face Tim with her feelings under control. 'Dinner will be ready in ten minutes…'

But Tim had already gone, and Harriet was left gazing, devastated, at the door slammed shut behind him.

Dinner parties had never featured much in Harriet's life, and she would have given much not to be part of this one. There was no dining room at La Fattoria, but the kitchen was large enough for a table and six chairs under the window looking out on the courtyard. Gleaming crystal and silverware, and candles in white pottery holders on a red cloth, gave an air of festivity very much at odds with Harriet's frame of mind. When the kitchen door opened she pinned on a smile that died abruptly when James came in with a face like thunder.

'Why the hell didn't you tell me Tim was involved with Francesca Rossi?' he demanded.

'Oh, so I'm to blame again!' said Harriet furiously. 'Tim made me promise *not* to tell you, of course. And now I've met Francesca I can see why. He deliberately gave me the impression that she was too young to marry, not too old. You were her lover at one time, too, I assume?' she added, carrying the war into the enemy's camp.

James glared at her in distaste. 'Certainly not. I met her when I bought La Fattoria from her husband. Carlo Rossi was a wealthy man with influential connections in this part of the world. He was deeply interested in my plans for the restoration here, and put me in touch with the people I needed to get things done.'

'So you know Francesca well, then?' she said, deflated.

'Not as well as I knew Carlo. He was a cultured, erudite man and I was lucky enough to enjoy Rossi hospitality on several occasions.' His eyes glittered coldly. 'Even if I had been attracted to Francesca she was married to a man I liked and respected, therefore doubly off limits as far as I was concerned. Tim obviously doesn't suffer from the same scruples. She was still very much married when I introduced her to him in Florence five years ago.'

Harriet sighed. 'I remember. He came back from Italy with stars in his eyes, saying he'd fallen madly in love.'

'He was a teenager with rampant hormones. It was lust, not love.'

Harriet shrugged. 'Whatever they are, his feelings haven't diminished in any way. And Lord knows he's seen enough of Francesca over the years to know his own mind.'

James' eyes narrowed. 'And how, exactly, has he managed that?'

'She joins him on the trips he takes for Jeremy Blyth, including Paris recently. And when he's supposed to be here on holiday he spends most of the time in Florence with Francesca. He asked me to come this time just so I could meet her.' Harriet eyed him unhappily. 'He really does love her, James.'

His mouth twisted. 'If it's lasted this long I suppose he does. Though God knows what Francesca thinks she's playing at.'

'Maybe she feels the same about him.'

'I doubt that, but forget Francesca for a minute,' he commanded. 'Let's talk about *your* role in all this. I suppose you and Tim thought it was utterly hilarious to con me with your cute little double act. You most of all, Harriet, with your talk about waiting to marry before living together!'

Harriet's chin lifted. 'I was actually quoting Tim, but in some ways I have similar views.'

'Really?' He smiled sardonically. 'If so I doubt you'll find another man to share them.'

Feeling thoroughly fed up with the Devereux brothers by this time, she shrugged indifferently. 'Then I'll live alone for the rest of my life. A prospect,' she added with sudden passion, 'which strongly appeals to me right now. Will you call the others, please?'

The sauce was deliciously piquant, the pasta perfectly al dente and the wine mellow, but a meal with two of the diners trying desperately to keep the conversational ball in the air, and the other pair barely civil to each other, made for a trying evening. Harriet was desperate to escape by the time she'd served Anna's luscious berry pudding. The two glasses of Barolo downed like medicine had done nothing to make the evening more bearable. Instead the wine gave

Harriet a headache which grew worse when Tim brought up the subject of sleeping arrangements.

'Francesca will share with me, of course, so you two can keep to your bed in the tower room. James, I moved your things back out of my room,' he told his brother defiantly. 'Francesca was in such a state of nerves when I told her you'd turned up, I didn't tell her I found you in bed with Harriet.'

Francesca looked from Harriet to James in astonishment. 'You are lovers? But Tim says you don't like each other.'

Harriet smiled sweetly. 'Ah, but it's unnecessary to *like* a man to fancy some sex with him, Francesca.' She put the torte on the table, enjoying the various reactions on the three faces. 'If you want coffee with this, please make some, but forgive me if I say goodnight and leave the rest of you to clear away. Anna made up the bed in the other guest room for you, James,' she added, and walked out with her head in the air.

Harriet's fleeting triumph had given way to deep depression by the time she reached the tower room. She could have wept as she leaned at the open window to breathe in the cool night air. The holiday she'd been looking forward to for so long was utterly ruined. Even if James caught the next available flight back to England, as she fully expected, she hated the very thought of staying on here with the other two.

The night was no more restful than she'd expected it to be. Harriet read determinedly until her eyes grew hot and itchy, but sleep stayed out of reach. She felt utterly miserable as she watched a beam of moonlight creep slowly over the floor. For months she'd played along with the stupid deception, just to keep James in the dark about the real love of Tim's life. Yet now, for the first time in all the years she'd known him, Tim had turned on her in fury, just for daring to voice an opinion about his relationship. She frowned suddenly. Francesca had been wearing a very impressive ring. If Tim's finances had to be augmented by James, where had the money come from for a rock like that?

But it was nothing to do with her any more, James Devereux included. Tears leaked from the corners of her eyes. After the bliss of his lovemaking he'd cut her to pieces with his furious accusations. As though she were to blame, not Tim. But no wonder he was angry. Until recently Francesca Rossi had been the wife of a man James deeply respected and looked on as a friend. This was the pill James found too bitter to swallow, not her age. What a gullible fool I've been, thought Harriet wearily. But good luck to Francesca. She had a young, adoring lover who not only brought romance and travel into her life, but had even arranged a London exhibition of her paintings. What more could a woman ask?

Next morning Anna took over the task of providing breakfast for all the guests. Harriet thanked her gratefully and took herself off to the pool before the others came down, but to her annoyance found James there before her.

'Good morning,' he said formally.

Harriet ignored him, took off her shirt and shorts, applied sunblock and, with sunglasses firmly in place, stretched out to enjoy the early morning sun.

'I've managed to get a cancellation on a flight out of Pisa today,' he informed her.

'Splendid.'

'You're glad to see me go?'

'Euphoric.'

'When do you fly back?'

'Sunday. Thank you so much for allowing me to stay here.' She smiled sardonically. 'It's been *such* a memorable holiday.'

He shot a morose look at her. 'What the hell am I going

to do, Harriet? I can see where Francesca's coming from. She was married to a man old enough to be her father, so of course she likes having a young stud like Tim lusting after her. But that's the problem where he's concerned. He's not thinking with his brain.'

Harriet shrugged. 'What you do about it is entirely up to you. I'm no longer involved.'

He stared incredulously. 'You can't mean that. You're too close to Tim to wash your hands of him entirely.'

'Here's a suggestion.' She took off her sunglasses and turned cold eyes on him. 'Tim is pretty sure you'll cut off his allowance. Francesca might change her mind if you do.'

James shook his head. 'Carlo Rossi was seriously wealthy and she inherited everything. Apparently her work sells well, too, so as far as Tim's concerned money's not her object.'

'Why, exactly, are you so dead against the marriage?' she asked curiously. 'Is it just the age difference or are there a lot more things I don't know?'

He was silent for a moment, his face set. 'I was married to someone older than me,' he said eventually. 'One of the reasons for the breakdown was Madeleine's refusal to have children. The age gap between Francesca and Tim is a hell of a sight bigger than it was in my marriage, so she probably won't want children, either, which Tim is bound to regret one day.'

'I'm a little short on concern for Tim right now,' Harriet said flatly. 'I uttered one little word of caution last night and ten years of friendship went straight down the drain.' She gave James a resentful glare. 'You were quick to put the knife in, too. Frankly, I've had it up to here with both of you. As far as the Devereux brothers are concerned I don't give a damn any more.'

'Where I'm concerned, Harriet, I can well believe it, but not with Tim, surely. You've always been so close. Which brings me to one of the many things that kept me awake last night,' he added, his eyes locking on hers. 'Tell me the truth, Harriet. Was it really just friendship between you and Tim?'

'Yes, it was,' she said stonily. 'So now you can devote all your energies to the problem of Tim and Francesca and forget about me.'

James gave her a long, hard look, as though trying to gauge what was going on in her brain. 'Is that a roundabout way of saying you want nothing more to do with me?'

'Exactly.'

'I see.' He got to his feet. 'It's a longish drive. I'd better get started. Are you all right?' he added, eyeing her closely. 'You ate very little last night.'

'How could I in that atmosphere?' She shuddered. 'I'll just wait to see what Tim's plans are, then take off in the car out of the way. No way am I playing gooseberry to a pair of lovebirds.'

'Stand up, Harriet,' he ordered.

'Why?'

'Just do it.'

As soon as her feet touched the ground James pulled her into his arms and kissed her until her head was reeling.

'A little something to remember me by,' he said roughly. *'Arrivederci!'*

Harriet lay very still for a long time after he'd gone, bitterly regretting the pride that had made her cut off her nose to spite her face, as Livvie used to say. It had forced her to lie to James about not wanting him in her life. Now she had the rest of the week alone to regret it, or maybe not alone if Tim and his *innamorata* were staying until she left.

A miserable hour went by before Tim came strolling round the side of the pool to wish her good morning.

Harriet gave him a frosty nod and went on reading.

'Where's Jed?' he asked.

'He left for Pisa an hour ago.'

'He's keeping to it, then.'

She looked up wearily. 'To what?'

'Opposition to my marriage.' Tim gave her a hopeful smile. 'Could you put in a good word for me when you see him next?'

She stared at him incredulously. 'After the way you turned on me last night? Not a chance!'

'I didn't mean it,' he said, flushing.

'I'm not stupid, Timothy Devereux! You meant every word. Not that it matters. I can't help you with James because I won't be seeing him again.'

Tim's eyebrows shot to his hair. 'You mean that was just a one-off I interrupted yesterday?'

'It's not against the law! Now I'm not playing your stupid game any more I'm free to do that kind of thing as much as I like,' she reminded him. 'Where's Francesca?'

'She's getting ready to face Jed. We thought he was still in bed. I'd better go and tell her he's gone. Then we're going back to Florence. You'll be all right here on your own, will you?' he said, as such an obvious afterthought Harriet almost pushed him in the pool.

'I dare say I'll manage,' she snapped.

'Good,' Tim said absently, all his attention on the woman coming towards them.

Francesca was dressed to impress in an exquisitely plain linen dress, delicate kid sandals and cosmetics applied with a skill Harriet could appreciate from long association with Dido.

'Good morning,' said Harriet politely.

'*Buongiorno,*' said Francesca, and looked nervously at Tim. '*Caro*, where is your brother?'

'On his way to catch a plane to London,' said Tim, kissing her.

'You did not talk to him this morning?'

'No. He left early, darling.'

Francesca looked deeply relieved. 'Then we may leave also.' She turned to Harriet with a warm smile. 'It was so good to meet you at last. Next time you come, you must make a visit to my house and see my paintings.'

After the farewells were over Harriet watched the pair leave, finding their body language very illuminating. Tim was quite right about their relationship, she admitted reluctantly. Francesca Rossi's feelings for her young lover were in no way maternal. His passion was returned in full.

Once she heard the car leave Harriet went indoors to clear up after the late breakfast, waving aside Anna's objections when she came running into the kitchen with an armful of bed linen. Harriet insisted on loading the dishwasher and putting things away, and with much hand waving and smacking of lips complimented Anna on the torte and pudding eaten at dinner the night before. Later, she thought with satisfaction, she could console herself by pigging out on the remains of both in peace.

She was in the courtyard after a solitary dinner that evening when her phone rang.

'I'm back,' said James.

'Oh, hello,' she said coolly, her hostility flaring up again the moment she heard his voice.

'Is Tim there?'

'No. He went back to Florence with Francesca. She seemed relieved that you'd left without saying goodbye.'

'I'm not surprised. I had a pretty blunt talk with her last night. She knows damn well I disapprove.'

'It won't make a scrap of difference. You'll just have to bite the bullet and accept her as a sister-in-law.'

'It worries the hell out of me.'

'It's Tim's life.'

'I know you're right, but it goes against the grain to stand

by and let him make a mess of it.' He paused. 'So you're
on your own, then, Harriet, just as you wanted.'

'Yes.'

'You don't mind?'

'No. In a beautiful place like this it's sheer bliss.'

'With no more intruders in your bedroom to spoil it.'

'You said it.'

'Harriet, listen to me—'

But she disconnected deliberately, taking petty satisfaction in cutting him off.

Harriet drove back to Florence at the weekend, left the car
with the hire firm and took the train to Pisa in pensive
mood. There had been no more phone calls from James,
but Tim had rung the night before to say he'd wheedled a
couple of extra days' holiday out of Jeremy Blyth, and
wouldn't be seeing her until he got back to London. He
told her to leave the key with Anna, wished her a safe
journey home and promised to call in to see her as soon as
she got back.

'Don't bother.'

'What?'

'I don't want to see you, Tim. I need some space.'

'You're *that* mad at me?'

'Not mad. Hurt. I need time to lick my wounds.'

'If you ask him nicely, maybe Jed will lick them for
you,' he snapped, and rang off.

Harriet sat staring through the train window, seeing very
little of the passing scenery on the return journey. She
couldn't blame Tim for being crude. Finding her in bed
with James would have been a shock to his system. It was
still a shock to her own every time she thought of it, which
was most of the time. She sighed. She was fed up with Tim
right now, but she still cared enough to hope that the affair
with Francesca wouldn't end in tears. Harriet shrugged the

thought away impatiently. It was high time she concentrated on her own life and stopped mollycoddling Tim Devereux. At least one good thing had come out of it all. James knew beyond doubt that his brother wasn't gay.

CHAPTER SEVEN

HARRIET had dreaded telling her friend that Tim was engaged to someone else, and went straight to Bayswater from Heathrow to get it over with. She did her best to break the news gently, but just as anticipated, Dido was utterly devastated.

'I can't believe it! You two were stringing me along all this time just because Tim's involved with someone older than him?' she said, on the verge of tears.

'It's not like that, Dido. Francesca may be older than Tim, but she's a beautiful woman, and a talented artist. And he's madly in love with her.'

'But you seem so calm about it!'

'It's not a shock to me, love. I've known about Francesca for ages.'

'That's what really hacks me off.' Dido glared at her. 'You could have trusted me, Harriet. Why on earth didn't you *tell* me?'

Harriet sighed. 'I wanted to, believe me, but Tim swore me to secrecy, in case James found out and tried to put a stop to it.'

'Does James disapprove of this Francesca person so much, then?'

'Yes. He knew her first, even introduced Tim to her in the first place.' Harriet pulled a face. 'He regrets that now.'

'Why?'

'Until recently the love of Tim's life had a husband.'

'Good grief,' said Dido, looking sick. 'No wonder James is upset.'

Harriet nodded. 'He's convinced that Tim's heading for

disaster. But I think Francesca's just as mad about Tim as he is about her. And why shouldn't she be? Her husband was much older than her. Tim's young and fun to be with, nice to look at, he loves her to bits and he's probably good in bed, too.'

'*Probably?*' Dido stared, flabbergasted. 'Are you saying you've never found out?'

'Never have, never will. I love Tim, but not in that way.'

'You know that I do,' said Dido forlornly.

Harriet nodded sympathetically. 'But give it up, love. It's never going to happen.'

Dido sighed despondently, and then eyed Harriet in sudden suspicion. 'You seem remarkably clued up about his brother's views on the subject.'

'James made a flying visit to the villa on his way home from Umbria,' said Harriet and diverted her friend by producing the handbag she'd bought for her in Florence.

It was strange to leave later and go on to the flat in Clerkenwell, but Harriet breathed a sigh of relief when she shut her new door behind her at last. She unpacked the clothes Anna had insisted on laundering, made a snack from supplies Dido had bought for her, and when she went to bed later made a conscious effort to put both Devereux brothers from her mind.

By the end of her first, frantically busy working day, Harriet felt she'd never been away. But over supper in the new flat that evening it gradually became clear that she couldn't live with the cobalt blue of the walls. At the weekend paint would be on her shopping list.

When Harriet got home on the Friday evening she found Tim waiting for her, clutching a bunch of flowers.

'I've given you space,' he informed her.

'Not much of it!' She unlocked the entrance door, utterly delighted to see him, but unwilling to let him know how much yet. 'Are those for me?'

'No.' Tim grinned. 'They're the latest accessory for us trendy guys. Jeremy carries a nosegay around with him all the time.'

'I can well believe that,' she said, and shrugged, resigned. 'Oh, all right. Come up, then. When did you get back?'

'This morning.' When they got to the flat Tim put the flowers down and caught her in a hug. 'I'm sorry for the things I said. To you, of all people, Harry. I was completely out of order.'

'You certainly were, you pig. But I had no right to lecture you, either,' she said, her voice muffled against his jacket. Then she looked up. 'Though you should have been straight with me about Francesca.'

'I know,' agreed Tim penitently. 'But if I had, you wouldn't have agreed to the con.'

'You're dead right,' she said with feeling.

'Friends again, then?' he said, his eyes so anxious Harriet smiled affectionately.

'Friends,' she agreed. 'Officially friends now, thank heavens. Masquerading as your significant other had certain drawbacks.'

'Bad for your sex life,' Tim agreed as she arranged the lilies in a vase. 'Talking of which—'

'Let's not, please!'

'If you mean Jed we can't forget he exists.' Tim pulled a face. 'He gave me absolute hell for not taking better care of you.'

Harriet snorted inelegantly. 'He can talk! He gave me hell, too.'

'About Francesca?'

'That, too. But strangely enough I think our cute little double act infuriated him most.'

Tim nodded sagely. 'Nothing strange about it. Jed wants

you bad, my pet. But what's going on? He says you refuse to see him any more.'

Harriet slumped down on the sofa. 'That was my stupid pride talking. I didn't enjoy the row he gave me.' She gave him a wry little smile. 'And between you and me, I didn't care for his high-handed assumption that he could automatically take your place in my life as my, um—'

'Lover? You looked pretty comfortable with the idea when I found you in bed with him,' said Tim slyly, sitting beside her.

She reddened. 'That just sort of happened. Like an avalanche happens. But in normal circumstances I require some creative courtship before letting things get that far with a man, James included.'

'Shall I tell him that?'

Harriet gave him a menacing glare. 'One word and you die!'

'Whatever you say, angel.' Tim smiled at her hopefully. 'I don't suppose you've got any food?'

'Lord, you're predictable. No, I haven't got any food. No time for shopping. Does Francesca know you eat like a horse?'

'Yes. She's got a great cook, thank God.' Tim paused. 'By the way, Harry, Francesca was nervous as hell about meeting you.'

'Really? Why?'

'She's a tad jealous.' Tim smiled fondly. 'She just can't believe that I prefer her to someone young and delicious like you. She says that I'll tire of her, and it won't last.' He sobered. 'But it will. Until death do us part.'

Harriet smiled at him, touched. 'But where on earth did you get the money to buy that ring she was wearing?'

He grinned. 'Are you kidding? It's her mother's. Normally she wears it on the other hand, but I made her swap it over when I found James there.'

'Talking of James, has he stopped your allowance?'

Tim looked sheepish. 'Surprisingly enough, no. I went to see him as soon as I got back, pretty sure he'd cast me off with the proverbial shilling now he knows about Francesca. But he was quite mellow about it, even when I told him I'm going to share her studio after the wedding, and get down to some serious painting at last.'

'Mellow, was he?' Harriet's eyes flashed dangerously. 'So that stupid charade of ours was unnecessary after all.'

'I disagree there.' Tim tapped his nose. 'He was so bloody relieved when he found *you* weren't going to marry me it took the heat right off Francesca.'

She sniffed. 'He's made no effort to contact me since I got back.'

'Are you in love with him?' asked Tim bluntly.

About to deny it hotly, Harriet stared at him, arrested, as the truth hit her between the eyes. The reason for her current lack of joy in life was suddenly obvious. For the first time in her life she was in love. Deeply, desperately in love. And, fool that she was, had demonstrated how much she cared by ordering James out of her life. She groaned in despair. 'Of course I'm in love with him—for all the good it'll do me.'

Tim looked troubled. 'Can't I help things along somehow?'

She shook her head. 'No, thanks. Love unsought is better and all that.'

'Whatever you say.' He gave her a hug. 'Right, then, friend. If you won't let me play Cupid let me feed you instead. Chinese, Indian, or fish and chips?'

Feeling more at peace with the world after making it up with Tim, Harriet went out shopping for paint next morning. She gave in to Dido's pleas to hit the sales with her in the afternoon, but resisted all her friend's coaxing to join her in a spending spree, and went straight back to Clerkenwell afterwards instead of going to a party thrown by one of Dido's friends.

'I must be up bright and early to start painting,' Harriet said firmly.

'Do you have to start right away? Let me treat you to lunch somewhere nice on the river tomorrow instead,' coaxed Dido as they parted at the underground, but Harriet shook her head.

'It's very sweet of you, but I've just got to make a start on those walls.'

Next morning, arrayed in shorts and vest and ancient pink basketball boots, Harriet opened all the windows and moved the furniture to the middle of the room. She pushed her hair up under a baseball cap, veiled the furniture with towels in lieu of dust-sheets, and wrenched her new folding stepladder into position. She filled her new pan with white emulsion, armed her new roller and set to work, but soon found that painting a ceiling took a lot longer than expected because she was obliged to hop on and off the ladder far too often for speed. Wishing vainly that she were taller, with a longer reach, she shifted furniture round from time to time to get better access. Ignoring a crick in her neck, she carried on doggedly, determined not to stop until the ceiling was finished, and only then took time off for a sandwich and a cold drink.

Lunch over, she carried on with the undercoat for the walls, and soon found that the smell of paint had not combined well with her tuna sandwich. She was queasy, sweating, her eyes stinging and her roller arm aching by the time she'd finished the last wall, and said something very rude when the doorbell rang. Dido, she thought, resigned. But when she heard a familiar male voice over the intercom her heart missed a beat, then resumed with a sickening thump.

'May I come up, Harriet?' asked James.

No! Not now, when she was looking such a mess! But instead of banging her head in frustration against her newly painted wall Harriet consented politely and pressed the release button.

When she opened her door to James she stared at him in despair. He was everything she was not. Black hair glossy, olive-skinned jaw newly shaven, casual shirt and khakis immaculate, and above all *clean*. He stood utterly still at the sight of her, his face rigid with the effort to keep it straight.

'I've obviously come at a bad time.'

'You could say that,' she agreed, pretty sure she had a smudge of paint on her nose. 'I can't even ask you to sit down.'

'Could I come in just the same, Harriet? I won't keep you long.'

Without a word she stood aside and motioned him through. 'Wait a moment while I rinse the roller.' She escaped into the tiny cupboard of a kitchen, held the roller under running water until it ran clear, took a despondent look at her paint-splashed face as she washed her hands and decided to stay with the baseball cap rather than struggle with sweat-soaked hair.

'Sorry about that,' she said brightly, returning to James.

'How are you, Harriet?' he asked.

'As you see, busy. What brings you to this neck of the woods?'

'To see you, what else?' He looked at her steadily. 'Tim came round to my place today. He says you've relented towards him.'

She nodded, resigned. 'It's hard to stay angry with Tim for very long, but this time it took a bit longer than usual. I dislike being conned, even by Tim.'

'I felt the same about you,' said James grimly. 'Did you really agree to Tim's idiotic scheme just to make sure I didn't stop his allowance? Am I such a petty tyrant, for God's sake?'

'I knew nothing about the money until that evening at La Fattoria,' snapped Harriet. 'I agreed to the stupid charade because Tim said you disapproved of Francesca. I realise why, now,' she added darkly. 'Tim said it was the age gap, so I took it for granted she was too young for him, not the other way round.'

'Frankly I'm tired of the whole affair. I've taken your advice. From now on Tim can do as he likes, which, as you once tried to tell me, is exactly what he does, anyway.' James shrugged. 'I've no intention of stopping his allowance. He can go and live with Francesca tomorrow as far as I'm concerned.'

'He wants to marry her first.'

'So I gather. Now I've given my blessing I suppose he'll rush her into it as soon as he can.' James paused. 'Tim told me something else today.'

'Oh?'

His eyes took on a gleam Harriet viewed with disquiet. 'He thinks you may also have thawed towards me. Is that true?'

All the answers Harriet thought of stuck in her throat so long James turned to go. 'I dislike the role of mendicant,' he said tersely.

'Don't go!' she said urgently. 'Or better still come back sometime when I'm clean.'

He turned back, the sudden leap of heat in his eyes sending her backing away in alarm. 'You don't want me to touch you?' he said softly, stalking her round the furniture.

'Of course I don't. I'm hot and filthy and I probably smell,' she said despairingly.

His deliberate, relishing sniff sent a wave of scarlet to join the paint streaks on her face. 'You do, Harriet, of your own irresistible blend of pheromones. A pity there's no space to throw you on the floor and ravish you.' He laughed at the shock on her face, and stood back. 'You don't fancy the idea?'

'Not right now, no,' she lied.

'I should have rung first as Tim advised,' he said with regret.

She stared. 'You, taking advice from Tim?'

'On the subject of Harriet Verney he's an expert, he tells me.'

'In his dreams!'

James grinned. 'One thing he said made sense. Subtlety and finesse are vital, according to Tim, if I want to make any headway with you.'

'Tim, preaching subtlety and finesse?' said Harriet, dizzy with euphoria at the mere thought of James wanting to make headway.

'In this case he has a point. So in accordance with his instructions I shall leave you in peace right now, and let you get into that bath you're obviously desperate for, on condition that you have dinner with me tomorrow evening.'

'Sorry, I can't tomorrow, I already have a date.'

'Tuesday then,' said James firmly.

Pride salvaged, she inclined her head graciously. 'Tuesday's good.'

'I'll come for you at eight,' said James.

Harriet closed the door, wishing she had space to dance for joy. Thank you, Tim, she thought gratefully.

When he arrived on the stroke of eight James was wearing a pale, lightweight suit of masterly cut, his slightly darker shirt open at the collar in deference to the hot summer evening, and Harriet could have flung herself into his arms there and then to relieve the tension of getting ready too early in the terracotta linen dress he'd seen twice before.

'Nothing's changed,' said James, looking her up and

down, 'I still feel the urge to throw you on the floor and ravish you, even now you're clean.'

'Not enough space for that,' she said, pulse racing.

'I would have brought you flowers, as Tim instructed,' he informed her as they went down in the lift, 'but it seemed best to wait until you've finishing painting.'

'Sensible,' she approved, and grinned up at him. 'James, I can't believe you're acting on Tim's instructions.'

'Every step of the way,' he assured her earnestly.

To her surprise James took her to the restaurant she'd dined in with Giles Kemble.

'To make up for the last time we ran into each other here,' he said, once they were seated.

Harriet smiled. 'You were so hostile I had indigestion on the way home!'

He reached out a hand to take hers. 'And I invited myself to the Mayhews' place in Umbria the following weekend just so I could call in at La Fattoria to see you again. Doesn't that tell you something, Harriet?'

'What do you mean, exactly?'

James released her hand as a waiter interrupted to pour wine, but once they were alone again he leaned forward, his eyes urgent. 'That night in Tuscany was a revelation. And not just because we made love for the first time, though God knows that was wonderful enough. But learning the truth about you and Tim changed everything. From now on I want you in my life, Harriet.'

James sat back as their first course appeared, and Harriet, still trying to take in what he'd said, stared blankly for a moment at the exquisite arrangement of antipasti in front of her.

To her relief James kept to less emotive subjects during the meal. He asked her about her working day, told her about his own, teased her about her home decorating, and Harriet eventually relaxed, enjoying the evening she'd been looking forward to from the moment he'd left her forty-eight hours before.

'I put the first coat of primrose on last night,' she told him.

He raised a sardonic eyebrow. 'I thought you were going out last night.'

She smiled demurely. 'My date was a pot of paint. Tomorrow I roll on another coat, and with a bit of luck that should do.'

'What was the original colour?'

'A murky sort of blue.'

'Not your taste, obviously. Unlike the colour of that dress.' His eyes moved over her bare arms like a caress. 'Did I mention that you look good enough to eat tonight?'

'No, you didn't. Thank you, kind sir. I wore the dress,' she added, 'because the colour reminds me of the flower-pots at La Fattoria.'

'So your memories of the place aren't all unpleasant, then.'

'No.' She looked at him squarely. 'As I said at the time, my holiday there was memorable. My vacations don't normally provide such extraordinary value for money.'

James raised an eyebrow. 'I didn't charge you any money.'

'I know. Thank you.'

'But I think I deserve *something* in return.'

'What would you like?'

'I'll tell you on the way home.'

This, Harriet found, involved a taxi ride to James' home, not a short walk to hers.

'You might have asked me first,' she said as he gave the address to the driver.

He slid an arm round her. 'It's only a little after ten, there's no space to stand up in your flat, let alone sit down, so another hour of your company in comfort at my place is my fee for letting you stay at La Fattoria. Reasonable?'

'I suppose so,' she conceded, secretly thrilled with the idea. Sitting close to him in the taxi, she was filled with delicious anticipation by the scent and warmth of his body. James might not have said so in so many words, but after all his talk of ravishing she had no doubt he was taking her home to bed to make love to her, a prospect that sent her blood racing through her veins.

When they arrived at the familiar redbrick building James paid off the taxi, and held her hand as they went up in the lift to his floor. He unlocked his door, switched off the alarm and pressed a switch to bring a pair of lamps to life alongside the white crescent-shaped sofas. Certain she would be swept into a passionate embrace the moment they were through the door, Harriet was rather taken aback when James led her to one of the sofas instead.

'Sit down, Harriet, and I'll make some coffee, or would you prefer wine?'

She regrouped hurriedly. 'Tea, perhaps?' she said, crest-fallen.

James switched on spotlights in the kitchen area, slung his jacket over a chair and made two mugs of tea he carried over on a tray that had been laid ready, and even included a container of biscuits. 'You didn't eat enough dinner,' he commented. 'Do you take milk in your tea?'

'Yes, please,' said Harriet, thoroughly deflated. Tea and biscuits seemed an unlikely overture to red-hot sex on that great bed of his in the other room.

'Have a biscuit,' he ordered. 'You've lost weight.'

'Paint is quite an appetite depressant.' Harriet nibbled obediently on a biscuit. It was easier than arguing.

'When Tim marries Francesca, will you go to the wedding?' James asked.

She shook her head. 'Probably not.'

'Why?'

It was hard to tell a man of James' financial situation that she couldn't afford another trip to Italy. One of the great benefits of the holiday at La Fattoria had been that it came free. All she'd had to do was save up for her flight. Tim had paid for the food she ate there, by way of appreciation for her help with his romance. But in Florence she'd bought a handbag for Dido, and pretty coin purses for her friends at the office. James' cheque for the furniture had gone on the deposit on the new flat, and a few basic necessities for it, but now, after the outlay on home decorating equipment, her finances were at an all-time low.

James turned to look closely at her. 'You're taking a long time to answer.'

'If I get an invitation—'

'Of *course* you'll get an invitation. Tim will probably want you to be bridesmaid at the very least!'

Harriet pulled a face. 'Francesca won't want that.'

'Why not?'

'She's jealous of me, according to Tim. Only because of my age,' she added.

'I can think of other reasons,' said James dryly.

Harriet braced herself. 'Without sounding horribly mercenary, could I ask how soon I can expect the money for End House?'

'Any time now, I should imagine.' He gave her a searching look. 'Are you saying that without it you can't afford a trip to Florence?'

'Yes,' she said baldly.

'For God's sake, Harriet, I'll pay for your flight and anything else you need, including a new dress—'

'No, thanks,' she said quickly. 'I can't let you do that.'

'Why the hell not?'

'Pride,' she said simply.

James leaned nearer and took her hand. 'So you let me have End House because you really needed the money?'

She nodded unhappily. 'I just have what I earn. Livvie didn't have much cash to leave. She'd used most of her capital on my education.'

'So why did you turn me down when I first asked you to sell me the house?'

'Two reasons. One because it was you,' she said bluntly. 'At the time you were my least favourite person, if you recall.'

'Vividly!'

'And secondly I just couldn't bear to part with it. When my parents died my grandmother sold the big London house we'd all lived in together and took me to live in Upcote where she grew up. From the time I was thirteen years old End House was my home.' Her eyes shadowed. 'But now Livvie's gone it's not the same. Without her I don't belong there any more. So in the end I sold it to you.'

James was quiet for a moment. 'If the money means so much to you, Harriet, why did you move out of your friend's flat?'

'The rent on the new one is less than my share of Dido's mortgage, and I can walk to work now, so financially I'm better off. And Dido won't see so much of Tim, too, which is all to the good, because she's in love with him,' explained Harriet.

'Good God, how does he do it?' said James in amazement. 'Does every woman he meets fall for him?'

She laughed. 'It's a trait worth thousands to Jeremy Blyth. When a woman comes to look round at the gallery Tim invariably makes a sale.'

'Tim told you that?'

'No, Jeremy did. Interestingly enough,' added Harriet, 'Jeremy was never taken in for a moment about Tim and me. He told Tim I was the wrong wife for him.'

'Probably wants to marry Tim himself,' said James acidly. 'But he was right about you.'

Harriet got up to put her mug on the tray. 'Time I was going, James.'

'Why not stay here tonight?' he said, and took her hand to lead her past the kitchen and dining area towards what Harriet had assumed to be a blank wall. 'I didn't show you this last time.' He touched a discreet button and a section of wall slid back to reveal another bedroom. 'This is where Tim sleeps when he stays here. A bathroom's concealed behind that glass panel, and on this side you get another view of the Thames.'

Harriet smiled politely to mask her fierce disappointment. Instead of sharing a bed with James a night in the spare room appeared to be the only thing on offer. 'Very nice, but I'd better get back.'

'Sure?' he said gently.

'Positive. Will you ring for a cab, please?'

James made the phone call, and turned to take her in his arms. 'Harriet, what's wrong?'

'Nothing.' She smiled up at him. 'Thank you for dinner.'

'Will you tell me something?'

'If I can.'

'Are you in pressing need of this money?'

She stiffened. 'Why?'

'I just want you to know you can come to me if you have a problem. Of any kind,' he added with emphasis.

'James, I'm fine, honestly,' she assured him. 'I want the money as an investment to give me the security of an additional monthly income to add to my salary. Which is quite respectable, by the way, so you really don't have to worry about me.'

'I'll try not to make a career of it. But I suppose this means you won't take up my offer on Florence,' he said, resigned.

'I appreciate it, but no, thanks—and there's the doorbell.
My taxi's here.'

This time James went down in the lift with Harriet, and
the moment the doors closed on them he swept her into his
arms at last, his mouth on hers in a kiss that lasted until
they reached ground level. He smiled into her startled eyes
as he raised his head. 'If I'd done that upstairs I couldn't
have stopped. And you're obviously not ready for that yet.'

How wrong could a man be? thought Harriet irritably as
James handed her into the waiting taxi.

'I'll ring you,' he said, and bent to kiss her again before
handing a banknote to the driver.

Her phone rang five minutes after she got in.

'You're home, then,' said James.

'Is this what you meant when you said you'd ring me?'
she asked, laughing.

'Yes. It may have slipped your mind, but I made certain
overtures about the future before dinner. I want a response,
Harriet Verney. Do you like the idea?'

'Yes, James. I do. I like it a lot.' Harriet wished he'd
mentioned it again at the flat so she could have shown him
exactly how much she liked it.

'Thank God for that! I'll see you on Friday.'

'Are we meeting on Friday?'

'Of course we are. Only this time you stay over and we
spend Saturday and Sunday together to give your walls a
chance to dry out.'

Harriet blinked. 'I thought you were proceeding step by
step, like Tim said.'

'I am. But I'm taking them two at a time.'

CHAPTER EIGHT

BY SEVEN on Friday evening Harriet had changed her clothes twice and repacked her weekend bag more than once, wishing she had some idea of what James had in mind so she could have chosen her weekend gear accordingly. They'd talked on the phone twice, but last night she had been out when he left a message, and when she rang him back she'd had to do the same. And now she was at a fever pitch of anticipation.

This excitement over a man was new in her life. Except for one brief, disastrous encounter, her relationships with men other than Tim had been relaxed, undemanding affairs. With James it was different. Dido was madly in love half the time, and for the duration of each affair became blind to all faults in the man in question. Harriet saw James very clearly, but had no doubt at all that she was in love with him. And would probably stay that way for the rest of her natural life.

She had been waiting for half an hour that seemed twice as long as that by the time her doorbell rang. She snatched up the receiver to hear James' voice and moments later he was at her door, smiling as he handed her a white hydrangea in a yellow porcelain pot.

'Step two,' he said, looking so smug Harriet couldn't help laughing.

'Why, thank you, James,' she said, batting her eyelashes as she took it from him. 'What a lovely surprise.'

He looked round in approval. 'This looks a lot better than on my last visit. You've worked hard. Do you intend painting your bedroom as well?'

Harriet smiled at him pityingly. 'This is my bedroom. It's a studio flat, which is a posh name for a bedsitter. The sofa turns into a bed at night, and the kitchen and bathroom are shoe-horned into a sliver of space behind those doors over there. But it's very convenient for my job, and now my walls are sunnier I think it looks rather good.' She put the plant down on a small wicker table between the two windows, and stood back to admire the effect.

James moved close behind her, sliding his arms round her waist. 'You're supposed to kiss people who give you presents,' he reminded her, his breath warm against her neck.

Harriet twisted round, and reached up to put her arms round his neck. 'So I've heard.' She brought his head down to hers and kissed him with warmth he responded to in kind. 'You weren't in when I rang back last night,' she said gruffly when he raised his head.

'I had dinner with the Mayhews. By the time I picked up your message it was late and it seemed a shame to wake you. Were you out with Dido when I rang?'

'No, with Paddy Moran. He's the Ibsen fan you saw me with one night. We met for a coffee. Paddy's a financial adviser. I rang him to ask for his advice on the best way to invest the money for End House, and he suggested we meet near his bank for a chat before he caught his train home.'

James smiled wryly. 'It didn't occur to you to ask *my* advice?'

'Of course it did. But you've done so much for me already over End House I was determined not to impose on you again.'

'In future impose on me as much as you like.' James took her in his arms and kissed her at length, then raised his head to smile down into her flushed face. 'Last night

Nick Mayhew gave me the key to his house in the Cotswolds. Do you fancy a break from the city?'

As long as James took her with him Harriet didn't care where they went. 'I'd like that very much,' she said sedately. 'Thank you for my present,' she added and reached up to kiss him again.

'You've thanked me once already,' he said huskily, when he finally released her. 'Not that I'm counting.'

'Such a beautiful plant is surely worth more than one kiss,' she said demurely.

'In that case I'll bring orchids next time!'

She shook her head. 'I don't like orchids.'

'What a difficult woman you are. No orchids, no caviare, no champagne.'

'You should be grateful I'm so economical!'

Instead of the sleek, elegant car that she'd first seen outside End House, James drove Harriet to the Cotswolds in a chunky four-wheel drive.

'What happened to the Italian job you drove to Upcote?'

'This chap is better for the terrain we're heading for. Once we get out of this traffic,' added James as they crawled their way from one set of traffic lights to the next. 'We should have waited until Friday rush hour was over.'

'I don't mind,' said Harriet, and meant it. Feeling secure in her high perch in the solid vehicle, she couldn't have cared less about the noise and traffic and heat, simply because she was with James. Maybe this was what being in love was really about. Not just the sex and the excitement, but just being together. But by the end of the trip along the motorway and the more tortuous journey along country roads after it she was glad when James told her there was only a short distance to go. He took a minor road after Burford to a small village a couple of miles farther on until he reached a lane just past a church. He cruised down it slowly until he found a pair of open gates, and turned into a tree-lined drive that led to a house that looked more like a scaled down Edenhurst than the country cottage Harriet had expected.

'I was expecting something smaller,' she said when he swung her down.

'It was a rectory two centuries ago, connected by a path from the back garden to the church we passed back there. Nick bought the house quite recently, so it's still in process of renovation, with not much furniture to speak of.' James smiled at her as he unlocked a beautiful wooden door set in a stone arch. 'But apparently we have curtains, a kitchen, and somewhere to sit and sleep.'

'Perfect! Can I explore?'

'You can do anything you like. Lydia's instructions were to make ourselves at home. They've just spent the odd weekend here with the girls so far, but Nick intends retiring down here one day.'

All the rooms had the same panelling as the square hall, but the only one in use was a large sitting room with triple-light latticed windows looking out on a garden in urgent need of attention.

'Nick isn't much of a gardener,' said James, eyeing his surroundings with a look of nostalgia.

'Do you wish you'd been able to keep Edenhurst on as a home?' she asked with sympathy.

'Of course I do. But it's so much bigger than this it was never an option.' He shrugged philosophically. 'Have a look at the rest of it while I unpack the car.'

The large kitchen and the solitary upstairs bathroom had been modernised, but only two bedrooms were furnished. Harriet looked round with a smile as James joined her in the smaller room.

'This is obviously where your friend's daughters sleep.'

'Do *you* want to sleep here?' he said bluntly.

'No,' she said, equally direct. 'I took it for granted I'd share with you. Isn't that why we came?'

He touched a hand to her cheek. 'I'd be lying if I said it wasn't part of it. But there were other reasons. You looked so tired after your interior decorating I thought you needed a rest.' He smiled wryly. 'You don't like my London flat very much. And for obvious reasons I didn't think you'd fancy a weekend in the one at Edenhurst. I could have taken you to a hotel somewhere, but when Lydia suggested this place last night I was pretty sure you'd prefer it.'

'I do. It's lovely. Have you brought anyone else here?' she added casually.

'No. I've never been here before. Why?'

'Just curious.'

'Let's eat,' said James firmly, and led her down to the kitchen, where a large hamper kept company with a cool box on the table.

Harriet helped him unpack the food, her eyes widening as they stored away enough for the weekend with some left over.

'I put the wine to chill first of all,' he informed her.

'I hope it's not Barolo,' she said, laying the table.

James looked appalled. 'Certainly not. Only a barbarian would chill Barolo. Why don't you like it?'

Harriet pulled a face. 'Our delightful dinner party at La Fattoria put me off it for life.'

'For me it was the only thing bearable about the entire meal. You were so hostile towards me the food stuck in my throat. Your parting shot was the last straw,' James added as he carved a succulent joint of ham. 'Did you mean it?'

'I don't remember what I said,' she muttered, feeling her face grow hot.

'Oh, yes, you do,' he said, brandishing the carving knife

at her. 'You informed the company at large that it's unnecessary to like a man to want sex with him. Were you
speaking from past experience, or just alluding to me?'

'I was hitting out at you.' Her chin lifted. 'Between you
and Tim I felt cut to pieces that night, James Devereux.'

'You cut me back,' he said, and waved a dramatic hand
at his chest. 'Right to the heart.'

'Then I'd better kiss it better,' said Harriet, her eyes
gleaming as she strolled towards him. Greasy from the ham,
he flung his hands wide as she slid one arm round his waist
and began undoing his belt buckle and shirt buttons with
the other.

'Harriet, that's not fair,' he said, breathing raggedly.

'All's fair in love and war,' she informed him, and kissed
the taut, warm skin over his thudding heart.

'Which—is—this?' he said with difficulty.

'Both?' Harriet warmed to her task, teasing his bare back
with her fingernails while her open mouth and flicking
tongue moved up his chest to caress his flat nipples, then
changed direction and moved slowly downwards until they
reached the top button of his Levi's. She heard the sharp
hiss of his breath as he sucked in his stomach muscles, and
released him to stand back, her smile triumphant. 'You can
wash your hands now.'

James let out the breath he'd been holding, his eyes blazing into hers for a moment before he turned away to lean,
head bowed, over the sink, breathing hard as he ran hot
water and detergent over his hands, then held his wrists
under the cold tap. When he turned round he gave Harriet
a smile that sent shivers down her spine. 'I'm hungry, otherwise I'd retaliate right now,' he informed her, buttoning
his shirt. 'Instead I shall defer it to another time.'

'If you didn't like it I won't do it again!'

'You know damn well I liked it,' he growled. 'But I'd

like it a lot better with my hands free.' His eyes gleamed. 'So would you.'

They stared at each other for a long, sexually charged moment, then James smiled and she smiled back, and suddenly they were laughing, and bumping into each other in their rush to get the meal together.

For the first time since starting to paint her room Harriet felt hungry. Suddenly she was ravenous, and James nodded in approval as he cut thick slices of bread.

'That's better. It's time you started eating properly.'

'It was the paint. I didn't know I'd hate the smell of it so much. My grandmother had any decorating done while I was away in school.' She smiled at him happily, and then stopped dead, halfway through slicing a tomato.

'What is it?' he demanded.

Harriet looked at him in wonder for a moment. 'I just realised that for the first time since my grandmother died I feel utterly and completely happy.'

He sat very still. 'Why?' he said at last.

'Because I'm here with you,' she said simply.

James got up and walked round the table to pull her up into his arms and kiss her with tenderness she responded to with delight. 'I'm happy, too,' he said, raising his head, 'for the same reason.' He trailed a finger down her glowing cheek. 'Now finish your dinner like a good girl.'

'I'm always a good girl,' she said, sitting down, and then grinned at him. 'Well, mostly.'

To Harriet's surprise James gave her a parcel to open after dinner, when they were settled on the sofa in the sitting room.

'What is it?' she said, tearing paper aside to find half a dozen brand new novels from the best seller lists. 'Oh, James, how wonderful!'

'Have you read any of them?'

'Only the reviews,' she said, inspecting the titles. 'I wait until they come out in paperback.' She leaned up to kiss him, her eyes sparkling. 'You obviously don't intend boredom to be a problem this weekend.'

'You've got it all wrong. The books are to take home with you. While you're here with me I demand all your attention,' he informed her, and pulled her onto his lap. 'All of it. Starting now,' he whispered.

In Italy their lovemaking had been a tidal wave that swept over them without warning. Here, in this half-empty lamp-lit room, with the curtains drawn to enclose them in their own special world, the magic was different, but no less potent than in the moonlit tower where they'd first made love. This time James was in no rush, and Harriet melted against him with a murmur of pleasure as he kissed and caressed her with restraint all the more exciting because she knew that fire was held in check behind it. Fire, she knew, that would flare up and engulf them both in time, but for the moment just burned steadily, with a glow that permeated her entire body. Suddenly it flamed higher as his tongue found hers in a substitute penetration that triggered off immediate desire for the physical union they both yearned for with equal intensity.

James set Harriet on her feet and stood up, held her close for a moment, then took her hand and led her in silence up the dimly lit stairs to the dark bedroom. He reached out for a light switch but she stayed his hand, afraid that the sudden glare of the overhead light would destroy the magic.

He picked her up and walked in darkness to the bed, where he set her down with care, and leaned over her.

'There's a wall light here,' he whispered. 'I want to see you as we make love.'

Harriet kissed him by way of consent, and smiled at him when the intimate light of a rose-shaded lamp revealed the taut, beautiful male face above her, his eyes alight with an emotion she wanted so much to believe was love, not just the basic desire of a man desperate to mate.

James kissed her as he began to undress her, and she kissed him back as she helped him, and suddenly they were clumsy, panting and laughing as they fought with buttons and zips until at last their naked bodies were in contact, and the laughter died away. They held each other close until just holding was no longer enough, and James began tantalising her with swift, sweet, drinking kisses that moved from her mouth in a grazing, slow descent that filled Harriet with such unbearable expectation that at last she could bear no more.

'Please,' she gasped, but he held her still and continued on his downward path until his tongue penetrated her innermost hot recesses to find the hidden bud that sprang erect in response to his caress. Harriet moaned and tried to push him away, writhing in anguish because she didn't want this to happen yet, but it was coming and coming and she was helpless against the hot, delicious throbbing as he brought her to the climax she experienced alone.

Face flaming, Harriet scrambled away and turned her back on him, but James slid his arms round her and pulled her against him. He kissed the back of her neck, his hands cupping her breasts and caressing her nipples, rolling them between his fingertips, and she gave a smothered moan, and felt his erection nudge her and to her amazement found she was ready for him again. James flipped her over onto her back, slid his hands beneath her bottom and raised her, holding her there for a moment, then sheathed himself to the hilt, the look of fierce possession in his eyes heightening her pleasure as he withdrew slowly and thrust home again, and repeated the skilled manoeuvre again and again, each time a little faster and deeper, the frenzied rhythm culminating at last in release so overwhelming Harriet wondered if she'd died of it, until James kissed her to confirm she was alive before pulling up the covers to hold her in close embrace as she fell asleep.

For weather it was the worst weekend of the summer. For Harriet it was the best weekend of her life. The rain came down in torrents, and for two whole nights and days she never left the house except for a quick dash round the garden under an umbrella with James as a gesture to getting some fresh air. James went out both mornings for the daily paper to read together over the breakfast Harriet made while he was out. They did the crossword, drank coffee, then went back to bed to make love again and sleep until the need for food woke them up. And after a disgracefully late lunch the first day Harriet decided it was time to get a few things straight between them.

'James, about this relationship of ours—'

'Hallelujah!' he said in triumph. 'You actually admit that we have a relationship.'

'Of course I do.' She eyed him warily. 'But I'm not clear about the exact nature of it. You said you wanted me in your life—'

'Surely I've made that plain enough!' He paused, frowning. 'I assumed you wanted me in yours.'

'You assumed right,' she said impatiently. 'I thought I'd made that plain enough, too.'

James leaned across and took her hand. 'So what's the problem, darling?'

'You have a life of your own and so do I. Quite apart from Tim and Dido, I have friends I'm very fond of.' She looked at him in appeal. 'Even if you and I spend time together on a regular basis I still want—need—to go on seeing them.'

'Why on earth shouldn't you?' he said, surprised. 'My work takes me away from London quite a bit, so I don't expect you to sit at home at night, languishing until my return. As long as I get the lion's share of your time when I'm in town, of course,' he added.

'That goes without saying.' Harriet smiled at him luminously. 'Good. I'm glad that's settled. After all, I may need my friends one day.'

'And what day is that?' he demanded.

'When you and I are no longer in this relationship of ours.'

His eyes narrowed. 'You're so sure it won't last?'

Harriet smiled sadly. 'In my experience people I care for disappear from my life all too often.'

James frowned. 'I may be older than you, Harriet, but I'm not going to die just yet, I promise.'

'No. But you might tire of me.' She looked at him squarely. 'These things happen.'

'That's so unlikely it isn't worth discussing,' he said scornfully. 'But let's get something straight. You're happy to have me in your life, but you don't want to live with me. Am I right?'

'Try to see it from my viewpoint.' Harriet braced herself. 'I need time to get used to the idea of sharing my life with someone like you.'

'Someone like me,' James repeated. 'What do you mean by that?'

She sighed. 'I've had boyfriends in the past, until my double act with Tim ruled that out for a while, but I've never had a lover.'

He smiled as his hand tightened on hers. 'You've got one now.'

'I know.' She breathed in deeply. 'But it's hard to come to terms with that. I've never felt like this about anyone before.'

James got up, drawing her up with him. 'Maybe we should continue this on the sofa.' He put his arm round her as they crossed the hall to the sitting room, and kept it there as he drew her down to sit on his lap. 'Now tell me exactly how you feel.'

Harriet curled up against him as she tried to find the necessary words. 'I don't think I can be in love with you,' she said honestly.

His eyes narrowed. 'Why not?'

'Because Dido's been in love quite a lot—'

'With men other than my irresistible brother?'

Harriet nodded ruefully. 'She's always searching for someone like him.'

'She won't succeed,' James assured her. 'Hopefully there's only one Timothy Devereux.'

'Amen to that. Anyway, while she's in love with the current Mr Wrong she's so starry-eyed, she's blind to faults which seem all too apparent to me.' Harriet smiled apologetically. 'I don't feel like that about you.'

'You mean my faults are glaringly obvious?'

'I have good reason to know that you're kind and generous, but you're also impatient and autocratic sometimes. I can see all that clearly, but it doesn't alter the way I feel.'

'For God's sake, Harriet,' he said with sudden impatience. 'How do you feel?'

'Happy when I'm with you, and as though half of me is missing when you're not...' The rest of her words were smothered by a kiss that went on so long both of them were gasping for air when he let her go.

'I've known you since you were thirteen years old,' he said huskily, his hands in her hair to keep her looking up at him. 'I always disapproved of your relationship with Tim, but it was only when we met in Upcote that I realised why.' He smiled slowly, looking deep into her eyes. 'I wanted you myself.'

Harriet knew perfectly well that James Devereux wanted her. His way of showing it thrilled and delighted her. But she needed more than that before committing herself to a long-term relationship. Or even a short one. 'Are you in love with me, James?' she asked bluntly.

He looked at her in silence for a while, as though memorising her every feature. 'Yes,' he said at last. 'Utterly and completely and for as long as we both shall live.'

CHAPTER NINE

HARRIET gradually began to believe James meant every word, even during his absences, which were more often than either of them wanted. He went away regularly on his usual spot-check inspections at his properties, but spent the majority of his time at a new project his company was developing, which meant that sometimes a week, and even a fortnight, passed when Harriet didn't see him at all. But the time apart only made their reunions all the more passionate, their pleasure marred solely by the one main bone of contention between them.

When Harriet remained obdurate about moving in with him James finally came up with a suggestion. If his minimalist modern flat was the stumbling block he would buy her a house.

'I'll keep this flat as a showpiece,' he said as they sat together on one of his crescent-shaped sofas. 'In the meantime we'll look for something more to your taste.'

'It's not only the flat.' Harriet eyed him in appeal. 'I just feel it's too soon for us to live together anywhere quite yet.'

'Too *soon*!' James eyed her in exasperation. 'We've known each other for years, ten of them if you're counting.'

'But it's only recently that you've thought of me as anything but Tim's little chum,' Harriet reminded him.

'Tim's bride-to-be,' he corrected. 'Talking of brides, let's get this out in the open, Harriet. I have an idea that the real stumbling block for you is my take on marriage. Try to understand, darling. After my experience with Madeleine I'm superstitious about it. For me, and for her, too, it was the cure for love.' He cupped her face in his hands. 'I will love and cherish you for the rest of my natural life, I swear. Repeating that in a church won't make any difference.'

'You think I'm holding out for a wedding ring?' demanded Harriet, glaring at him.

'I seem to remember you stating certain views on the subject.'

'I was talking about commitment, not marriage.'

James sighed impatiently. 'And just what do you think I'm talking about? I'm offering you a home, financial security, and my humble self on a permanent basis. What else do you want?'

'Time.' Harriet gazed at him in appeal. 'This is too new. I'm still not used to the fact that you, well, that you—'

'I think love is the word you're looking for,' he said silkily. 'Pay attention. I love you, Harriet Verney.'

'I love you, too, James Devereux. But I'd rather leave any talk about a house until I'm sure.'

'Sure of your own feelings or mine?' he demanded.

'Neither. I just need to be sure it—this—won't end in tears.'

James smiled wryly. 'I probably will make you cry some time. Who knows, you may make me cry, too. But I'll also try my utmost to make you happy, darling.'

'You don't have to try. You just have to be with me to do that,' she assured him. 'Let's go on the way we are for a while,' she pleaded, when he'd stopped kissing her enough for her to speak. 'I couldn't care less about a wedding ring. But I like your version of courtship so much I just want to enjoy it a little longer before we actually live together.'

'When you smile at me like that I suppose you think I'll do anything you want,' he said, resigned, and pulled her on his lap. 'How long are you going to keep me waiting?'

Harriet snorted. 'I don't keep you waiting at all. You rushed me to bed tonight as soon as I got here.'

James gave her cheek an admonishing tap. 'I'm not talking about *making* love, great and glorious though it was just now. I have this desire, by no means unusual, to come home to you at night.'

'Don't expect me to have your slippers warming!'

He grinned. 'I don't wear slippers. To make me happy you just have to be here for me.'

'I work late sometimes.'

'Then I'll be here, waiting impatiently, for you.' James tipped her face up to his, his eyes gleaming triumphantly. 'Besides, when you give up that so-called studio flat of yours just think of the money you'll save on rent.'

'Oh, well!' Harriet laughed, and held up her hands in surrender. 'Why didn't you say that before? Let's start house-hunting tomorrow!'

The house-hunting had to be deferred for a while until James returned from troubleshooting at one of his hotels in Scotland. While he was away Harriet invited herself to supper in Bayswater to tell Dido her news, happy to kill two birds with one stone when Dido begged her to bring Tim along.

Dido was so delighted to see Tim she even managed to congratulate him on his forthcoming wedding. 'You've broken my heart, you monster,' she teased, and gave him a sisterly peck, then turned to hug Harriet. 'It's so lovely, with the three of us together again.'

Dido was right, thought Harriet as she kissed her friend. It was good to be back, now she didn't have to live here any more. Even with Tim talking non-stop about Francesca and his forthcoming nuptials over the meal.

'I expect you both to be there to hold my trembling hand,' he informed them.

'Try keeping me away!' said Dido happily, piling more food on his plate.

When the meal was over Harriet got to her feet, wine-glass in hand. 'Listen up, folks, now Tim's drawn breath for a moment I have an important announcement of my own to make…' She stopped dead, eyes wide in sudden panic and, to the utter horror of the other two, collapsed at their feet.

Harriet came round to the sound of Dido in tears, imploring her to wake up, and opened her eyes on Tim's desperately anxious face as he patted her cheek to bring her round.

'That's my girl,' he said soothingly. 'Up you come.' He helped her to her feet and settled her on the sofa, Dido fussing round them like a mother hen.

'Have some water, or wine, or something, Harriet,' she begged. 'I haven't got any brandy. Lord, you frightened us. What happened? You hardly drank anything.'

Harriet took in an unsteady breath. 'The room started spinning—then I suppose I passed out.'

Tim breathed in deeply, holding her hand. 'How do you feel?'

'Not very wonderful at the moment.' She smiled reassuringly at Dido. 'I'd love some tea.'

Dido leapt into action. 'Right away, love.'

When she was out of earshot in the kitchen Tim gave Harriet a searching look. 'Are you cooking up for some virus? You look hellish peaky.'

'I feel peaky.' She shivered. 'I've never fainted before.'

'I'd be grateful if you never do it again in my company, either! When's Jed coming back?'

'Tomorrow or Saturday, he's not sure yet.'

'Make sure you take it easy this weekend.' He grinned. 'I'm sure Jed won't mind if you want to spend most of it in bed.'

'Bed is exactly where I want to be right this minute,' she said shakily, wishing a magic wand could waft her to her own, there and then.

'Dido will want you to spend the night here,' he warned.

He was right. Dido was loud with protests when Harriet insisted on going back to Clerkenwell.

'I'm fine now,' she assured her anxious friend.

'Don't worry, Dido,' said Tim, utterly serious for once. 'I shall make sure the invalid is safely tucked up in bed with her phone before I go off to my place.'

He was as good as his word. When they got back to the flat he made tea while Harriet undressed in her bathroom, and then saw her into bed.

'Just before you passed out,' he reminded her, 'you were about to make an announcement, one of some import, I fancy.'

Harriet's eyes lit up. 'So I was. James and I are going to live together, Tim. I don't like his flat so he's going to buy a house, and I get to choose it.'

Tim hugged her in delight. 'You're going to be my sister-in-law!'

She detached herself gently. 'No, Tim. I'm moving in with James, not marrying him.'

His expressive face fell. 'Why the hell not?'

'Madeleine,' she said tersely.

'She's history. Why should you be worried about *her*?'

'I'm not. James is. After marriage with Madeleine he's sure it's the cure for love.'

Tim frowned. 'Do you agree with that?'

'No. But I can see his point.'

'How about you, pet? Would you *like* to marry Jed?'

'No,' said Harriet, so positively Tim looked taken aback.

'Oh, right, as long as you both feel the same.' He bent to kiss her goodnight. On his way to the door he turned, wagging a finger. 'If you feel strange again, ring me, and I'll drop everything and rush to the rescue, *ventre á terre*.'

She laughed. 'Nice thought, but you need a horse to race belly to the ground.'

Tim didn't smile back. 'Seriously, I meant what I said. Take care, Harry. Please.'

Harriet felt tearful when he'd gone, overcome by a sudden longing for her grandmother's practical, comforting presence. But because Olivia Verney had disapproved of tears Harriet blew her nose, dried her eyes and settled down early to the sleep she seemed to need so much of lately.

Next morning she slept later than usual, and woke feeling perfectly normal. She rushed off to work without breakfast, but coped with her usual busy day at the agency with a zest remarked on by her colleagues. Teased about the new man in her life, Harriet gleefully hugged her secret to herself. Her man wasn't new at all. But at thirteen she'd had no idea that one day James Devereux would be the most important thing in her life. Euphoric at the thought of seeing him later, she worked flat out all day so she could leave in time to go shopping for a celebration dinner, then hurried home to the message she knew would be waiting for her.

'I'll be with you sometime this evening, as soon as the traffic allows,' James informed her. 'I've missed you, darling. Have you missed me?'

Oh, yes. Her eyes gleamed as she thought of ways to show him later exactly how much she had missed him.

The disadvantage of living in one room meant constant vigilance to keep it tidy, and she'd left in such a rush first thing there was work to be done before James arrived. Harriet whirled like a dervish through some household chores before her shower. While her hair dried she scrubbed potatoes and sliced green beans, mixed a spoonful of horseradish into clotted cream and left it to chill alongside the poached salmon waiting in the fridge. She finished off her hair with a hot brush, made up her face and sprayed herself with perfume, and after a moment's indecision pulled on white cotton drawstring trousers and the caramel vest top she'd worn the first time James had kissed her.

Harriet was searching for shoes when James knocked on her door.

'Someone was leaving the building as I arrived,' he called. 'Let me in.'

Harriet threw open the door, smiling at him in such radiant welcome James dumped down his briefcase, kicked the door shut and swept her off her bare feet to whirl her round a couple of times, then kissed her until her head reeled. When he put her down at last Harriet gave a despairing little moan and crumpled into the arms that shot out to catch her.

When she came round she was lying on the sofa looking up into James' shocked, haggard face.

'Darling,' he said hoarsely, and touched a shaking hand to her cheek. 'What happened?'

'I've been rushing, and then you spun me around,' she said faintly. 'Hold me tight, please.'

James carefully lifted her onto his lap and held her close. 'Have you been going without food while I'm away?' he accused.

'No. And before you ask I've been to bed early every night except Tuesday when Dido asked me to supper. Tim came, too.'

'Brave man. Did he manage to escape unscathed from her clutches?' he asked, relaxing a little.

Harriet smiled. 'Dido's finally come to terms with the fact that he's well and truly spoken for.' But she made no mention of the previous faint. James looked worried enough as it was. There was no point in worrying him even more.

'Are you feeling better now?' he asked, kissing her hair.

'Much better. I must see to dinner.'

'To hell with dinner. We'll pick something up on the way home.'

'No,' said Harriet, and despite his violent protests got to her feet, and stayed on them without mishap. 'I just have to cook a few vegetables.'

'Then I'll just have to stand over you while you do,' said James inexorably.

He was as good as his word, and hovered over her until in the end Harriet told him to go and sit down before she did him an injury.

'This is no place for two people to work together.'

'Or even for one person to live in,' he said, surveying the room with a pejorative eye. 'We spend the rest of the weekend at the flat, and no arguments, please.'

'OK,' said Harriet, with a docility that won her a look of deep suspicion. 'What?' she demanded.

'You must be feeling worse than I thought.'

'I'm fine. And I'm perfectly happy to spend the weekend at your place.' She gave him a look that brought him to his feet again. 'I've missed you so much, James, I don't care where we are as long as we're both in the same place.'

He started towards her, then stopped and stepped back, his eyes glittering. 'If I show my thanks in the time-honoured way, darling, the dinner might spoil. And after the episode just now some food is a good idea for you. Me, too,' he added, and smiled. 'To quote Tim, I'm hungry.'

James rang for a cab after the meal, and told Harriet to get her things together. 'I'll do the washing up,' he informed her, grumbling at the lack of a dishwasher. 'And there's no point in buying one because you won't be living here much longer.'

'Not so fast! If I give the flat up at this stage I won't get my deposit back.'

James shrugged impatiently. 'What does that matter? I'll cover any loss.'

'No.' She shook her head as she zipped up her bag.

'Why not?'

'I won't accept money from you.'

He took the bag from her and picked up his briefcase as the bell rang. 'When we live together, Harriet, you won't have much option.'

'Maybe not. But that's in the future.'

'Not too far in the future,' he assured her. 'Give me one good reason why we should waste time apart?'

When they arrived at his apartment Harriet waited until James switched on the lights, then went straight to the far wall and pressed the button that slid the panel back to reveal the spare room.

'Are you making some kind of statement?' demanded James, close behind her.

'No, I had this bright idea while you were away,' she said absently, studying the room. 'I have a suggestion to make.'

'You want to sleep here tonight?'

Harriet turned to surprise open dismay in his eyes. 'No, of course not,' she said impatiently. 'I want to sleep with you.' She smiled with deliberate invitation. 'After you've made love to me half the night, of course.'

James caught her in his arms. 'I might if you're good! So tell me about this request.'

'If we don't find somewhere else to live for a while, could I use this room when I move in here? If I had a sofa and a small television I could use it as a sort of snug when you're away. Your living room is just too big and minimalist for me to feel comfy.'

'If you're willing to move out of that dump you call a flat and in here you can have anything you want,' he assured her.

'Only until we find a house,' she reminded him, and laughed suddenly.

'What now?'

'In one breath I was refusing your money, and in the next happily splurging it on extra furniture and a new house. Am I illogical or what?'

'I like illogical women. Come to bed.'

'Your seduction technique could use some work,' she informed him as he hustled her through the big, uncluttered room. 'I thought we might watch television for a bit,' she complained as they passed the huge plasma screen.

'We can do that later—much later,' said James, and as if his patience had suddenly run out he picked her up, strode into the other room and deposited her in the middle of his bed.

Harriet lay watching him as he shrugged out of his jacket and tore off his tie. 'I love you, James,' she said quietly, and he stopped dead halfway through unbuttoning his shirt.

'I love you, too, my darling.' He discarded the shirt and knelt on the bed to draw her up against him. 'You frightened the hell out of me tonight. Don't do that again, please.'

'I'll try,' she said against his bare chest, and listened to his heart thudding against hers as he held her closer.

With an effort he put her away from him. 'You know I want to make love to you, but—'

'No buts. I want it, too,' she said fiercely.

'Are you up to it after fainting like that?'

'Yes. Are you?' she whispered and stroked a caressing hand down over his chest and lower still, to the place where lightweight grey fabric covered the exact extent of his readiness. 'If you're not,' she added, 'maybe I can persuade you.' She slid from the bed, undid the drawstring and stepped out of the trousers, then stripped off the vest top and dropped it on the floor. She saw James swallow hard, and smiled as she slowly revolved in front of him. 'The underwear was a present. Do you like it?'

James drew in a deep, shuddering breath, and showed his appreciation by tossing her on the bed and removing the present with ungentle hands. 'Who gave it to you?' he growled as the rest of his clothes hit the floor.

'One of my gentlemen friends,' she said rashly, then gasped as he dived on her and swept her hands wide.

'Which one?' he demanded, his eyes blazing into hers.

'Tim, of course.'

'Why the hell should my brother give you underwear?' he said, incensed.

'It was a *present*. Francesca picked it out for him in Paris.' Harriet swallowed. 'James, kiss me.'

He released her hands at once and his eyes glittered.

'Where?'

'All over,' she sighed, and stretched in invitation against him.

They slept late next morning, and lingered over breakfast before they went shopping for furniture.

'I rang Whitefriars Estates while you were in the bath,' said James. 'I told them we need a reasonable garden and plenty of space and so on. They'll send me some brochures.'

Harriet gave him a warning look as they got in the car. 'I want something more on the lines of End House than Edenhurst, James Devereux.'

'*We*,' he corrected her, 'need a home. And soon. In the meantime let's look at furniture.'

If Harriet had harboured any doubts about sharing her life with James Devereux so soon, they were gone for good by the end of the day. Up to that point their time together had been purely social, but shopping with him, for furniture and a television first, and food later, delighted her by being such fun. They got back to the flat at last, laden with bags, still laughing about the elegant young man who'd given them an unnecessarily hard sell about the sofa Harriet set her heart on the moment she set eyes on it.

'*Exquisitely* comfortable, adjustable to several angles, and in such *butter*-soft leather,' said Harriet, giggling. 'This shade is perfect for madam's hair. Black is *so* last year.'

James laughed and kissed her hair in passing as he stored food away. 'I admit that your choice surprised me.'

'It gave you heart failure, you mean, at that price, especially when you insisted on the chair and that cute footstool thing to go with it.'

'A small price to pay to tempt you into my lair.' He smiled a little. 'But I did expect you to go for something more traditional.'

'And clash with all this stark elegance? Certainly not.'

James took her by the shoulders. 'If you want flowery chintz, or feel a desperate urge for girly cushions, I don't care a damn as long as you come here to live with me. And be my love,' he added softly.

Harriet looked up at him in silence for a moment, her eyelashes damp. 'This is so hard to believe sometimes, James. You and me, I mean.'

'It is for me now and then,' he admitted, 'but only when we're apart. When we're together it feels so right I wonder how I existed without you all these years.'

Harriet buried her face against his shoulder, soaking his shirt with tears she couldn't keep back. 'Sorry,' she said thickly. 'Lord knows why I'm crying.'

'Then stop it at once,' he said huskily. 'I can't handle it.'

She sniffed inelegantly. 'Give me some tissues, please, and then I'll make tea.'

James mopped her up, and ordered her to sit down on one of the crescent sofas. 'You look tired. Switch on the television we never got round to watching last night and *I'll* make tea.'

The weekend was all the more wonderful to Harriet because James hadn't made it back from Scotland for the previous one. And, just as Tim had predicted, his brother was not at all averse to spending a great deal of this weekend in bed.

'Not just to make love to you,' he informed Harriet as he set up the new television in his bedroom. 'We both need the rest.'

'I thought that television was for my snug,' she reminded him as she watched the operation.

James scrolled through the various channels until he was satisfied, then smiled at her smugly. 'I'll borrow it until you move in. Or maybe even buy another one for the spare room,' he added as two English batsmen came out for the last session of the day.

'Ah, cricket!' Harriet laughed. 'No wonder you were so keen to lug it back here yourself today!'

'They couldn't deliver before Monday, and the test match may be over by then,' James said absently, his eyes on the wicket.

'You could have watched it on the mega screen out there,' she pointed out.

He grinned. 'I'll enjoy it a lot more in bed with you.'

'A good thing I like cricket, then.'

'I was the one who taught you how to hold a bat, remember.' James took her in his arms. 'Cricket is only one of the many things you and I have in common, my darling. We were made for each other.'

Because James was going away for the week to check on the transformation of a Gothic mansion into a super luxury hotel, Harriet stayed over for the first time on the Sunday night and let James drop her off at work next morning on his way to pick up Nick Mayhew for the drive to the north of England.

Giles Kemble eyed her holdall with interest. 'Good weekend, Harriet?'

She smiled at him radiantly. 'Perfect!'

The week that followed was anything but. As it wore on it became an endurance test for Harriet. The phone calls from James each night were the only high spots of days that seemed endless as she struggled with fatigue, which increased as she worked late most evenings to keep on top of her workload. Tim came round one evening to announce that he was off to see Francesca over the weekend, but he left early when Harriet couldn't control her yawns.

'You look as though you could do with a good night's sleep, my girl. Surely you got *some* over the weekend?'

'Of course I did,' she said, flushing.

'When are you actually moving in with Jed?'

'Soon.' She told him about the new furniture for the spare room.

'Good God! He *must* be crazy about you,' said Tim, impressed. 'He thinks the place is perfect the way it is.' He frowned. 'And where am I supposed to sleep when I stay over, may I ask?'

'Where you always sleep. Your bed's still there.' She smiled. 'I sleep with James, remember.'

'I still can't get my head round that.' He gave her a hug. 'Goodnight, angel.'

During his nightly phone call James told Harriet to go straight to his apartment the following evening and wait for him. 'Don't worry about dinner. We'll order in.'

The wait for James that Friday night seemed endless. Harriet stood at one of the big arched windows, gazing down blindly at the river, feeling hot and cold by turns. Excitement and delight gradually gave way to dread, which seeped icily along her nerves until she was on the point of bolting by the time James finally arrived. He strode in, his smile fading as, instead of hurling herself into his arms as usual, she stayed rooted to the spot.

He seized her by the shoulders to kiss her, and straightened slowly, frowning at her lack of response. 'Darling, what's the matter? You look shattered. Have you been fainting again?' he demanded.

'Just once,' said Harriet.

'Have you seen a doctor?' he said urgently.

'Yes, this afternoon.' She stepped back, her dark-ringed eyes fastened on his. 'I thought I had some virus, but apparently I'm having a baby.'

James stared at her in shocked silence that grew to unbearable proportions before he found his voice, and asked the question she'd been dreading.

'Is it mine, Harriet?'

CHAPTER TEN

A WAVE of such anguish engulfed her at his words Harriet felt physically sick. 'No, it's not.' She took fierce satisfaction in watching the blood drain from James Devereux's haggard face. 'It's mine.'

She took her phone from her bag and rang for a taxi, then tossed his door key on the counter, but before she could make it to the door he barred her way.

'Where the hell do you think you're going?' he demanded furiously. 'You can't throw something like that at me and just take off.'

She gave him a flaying look. 'Just watch me!'

'I'm entitled to an explanation, Harriet. Now,' he snapped.

'What is there to explain?'

'How this happened.'

'In the usual way, of course,' she said wearily.

James took a deep breath, fighting to get his emotions under control. 'You told me you took the pill.'

'I do.'

'Did you miss a day?'

'No. Nor did I take antibiotics, have a stomach upset, or do anything else to stop them working. But the single-hormone pill fails in one or two cases out of a hundred. I didn't realise I was one of the unlucky statistics.' Her mouth twisted. 'I was strongly advised to give you the glad news, but I wish to God I'd kept it to myself now.'

'Who advised you?' he demanded, looking so grim she wanted to run. 'Who else knows about this?'

'No one except the doctor I saw today. She said that a

father always has a right to know. True, of course. But you obviously doubt that you are the father, so get out of my way, please, I want to go home.'

'Home?' said James scathingly, ignoring the rest of her tirade. 'That one-room glory-hole in Clerkenwell?'

'After your gut reaction to the news, James,' she said bitterly, 'your opinion of where I live is irrelevant. Let me pass, please.'

'Like hell I will.' He took her by the shoulders, his eyes narrowing dangerously when she cringed from him. 'For God's sake stop that, Harriet. You've got to let me help you.'

'Whether you're the father or not?' she threw at him, then swallowed convulsively, her eyes widening in panic as her stomach heaved. Beads of perspiration broke out on her upper lip, and she threw James an agonised look as she fled to the kitchen sink. She gesticulated wildly for him to go away, but he kept an arm round her and put a cool, supporting hand on her forehead while she threw up.

Coughing and gasping in utter misery, Harriet scrubbed at her eyes and wiped her nose on kitchen paper, then sipped the glass of mineral water James gave her.

'Where are your things?' he asked, when he returned from paying off her taxi.

'I didn't bring any.'

'You can have something of mine. I'll fetch your clothes tomorrow,' he said, and picked her up.

Harriet struggled wildly, but he held her fast.

'I'm putting you to bed whether you like it or not,' he said roughly, his face grim with determination as he strode off with her.

'I'm going to be sick again!' she gasped, and James raced to his bathroom and held her head again while she retched until her ribs ached.

Wishing she could just die and get it over with, Harriet

straightened eventually, shuddering as she saw her ashen face in the mirror. She turned her back on it in disgust, and pushed James away as he bent to pick her up.

'Don't *do* that. It makes me dizzy.'

Apparently convinced she would collapse without some kind of support, James put an arm round her waist again and took her into the other room. He sat her down on the bed, and crossed the room to slide back the section of wall that hid his wardrobe. He took out T-shirt and boxers, and put them down beside her. 'Shall I help you undress?'

'No, thank you, I'll manage.' If it killed her, she added silently as he left the room, which was showing a disquieting tendency to revolve. Illusion due to the curved walls, she assured herself. But when she stood up the floor undulated beneath her feet like the deck of a ship, and she sat down again sharply.

James knocked on the door. 'Are you in bed yet?'

'No.'

'May I come in?' he called.

'It's your bedroom.'

James put his head round the door. 'What's wrong?'

Was he serious? 'I feel sick, giddy and utterly miserable—and I'm pregnant,' she added bitterly. 'Otherwise I'm just dandy.'

For once in his life James Devereux looked at a complete loss. 'What do you want me to do?'

Kiss me better, she thought despairingly. 'I'm afraid you'll have to help me undress, after all.'

James crossed to the bed and knelt to take off her shoes. 'Heels like these are a bad idea in the circumstances,' he said tightly.

'I didn't know about the ''circumstances'' until I saw the doctor. This afternoon,' she added, in case he'd missed the point.

James hadn't. His mouth twisted as he got up. 'It must have been a hell of a shock, Harriet.'

'It was. I thought I had some kind of flu.' She began to unbutton her black linen suit jacket. 'This bit I can do. It was the standing up part that beat me.'

James took the jacket from her and with infinite care, as if she were attached to a stick of gelignite, swung her feet up and laid her back against the stacked pillows. 'Undo your shirt.'

Harriet did so clumsily, all fingers and thumbs under the tense eyes watching every movement. 'Hold your arms up,' he instructed when she'd finished, and she obeyed, face burning as he tossed her once crisp pink shirt aside.

James shifted her enough to unfasten her bra and remove it so he could slip his T-shirt over her head. By the time he put her back against the pillows his hands were shaking and he looked as hot and bothered as Harriet.

'Now for the skirt,' he said, clearing his throat.

She unhooked it and slid the zip down and James drew the skirt away, his jaw suddenly clenched at the sight of lace-topped stockings. As he slowly peeled them off Harriet found her voice.

'Not the knickers,' she said gruffly.

'Right.' He drew the quilt up over her legs, his face rigidly blank. 'What else can I do for you?'

'Just go away, please,' she said wearily, and turned her face into the pillows.

Harriet woke later to find it was nearly two hours since she'd sprung her bombshell on James. She sat up with care, and crawled gingerly out of bed. Her head still felt like a balloon about to float away, but at least her legs seemed willing to hold her up. She lingered in the bathroom for a while in case there was any throwing up to be done, decided there wasn't, washed her pallid face, dragged a comb through her hair and went back into the bedroom.

James was waiting for her, still dressed in formal shirt and suit trousers. 'I heard you moving about,' he said stiffly. 'I thought you might need me.'

'No, I don't.' She gave him an icy look as she got back into bed. 'Now or in the future.'

His eyes glittered ominously. 'You're never going to forgive me?'

Harriet shrugged. 'You know that some of my friends are men, and as a wild card there's even Tim to bring into it if you're keeping score, so I suppose you can be forgiven for questioning rightful paternity. But not by me,' she added flatly.

'Harriet, will you just listen?' said James with sudden violence. 'You've got it wrong. It's not long since we became lovers, so when you said you were pregnant I was bloody terrified that the child *was*n't mine, not that it was!'

Harriet desperately wanted to believe him, but his initial doubt had cut so deep she couldn't. She raised a sardonic eyebrow. 'Or maybe were you ''bloody terrified'' that I'd played the oldest trick in the book to get you to marry me.'

'It never crossed my mind,' he retorted, so emphatically Harriet gave him a mocking smile.

'Methinks the gentleman doth protest too much.' She shrugged. 'Don't worry, James. I didn't come here to propose.'

His eyes hardened. 'That's usually a male prerogative.'

'You would know. Did you go on bended knee to Madeleine?'

'No. I'm not going on bended knee to you, either, Harriet.' He sat on the edge of the bed and took her hand. 'But I am asking you to marry me.'

'How kind.' Harriet detached her hand. 'Thank you, James. But the answer's no.'

'You haven't thought this through,' he said with sudden passion, a pulse throbbing beside his mouth. 'This isn't just about you, Harriet. There's a child involved. Our child—'

'You're sure about that?'

'Of course I'm sure,' he said scornfully. 'Otherwise why would you have told me?'

'I could be palming another man's child off on you.'

James eyed her with distaste. 'This isn't a joke, Harriet.'

'Dead right it's not,' she agreed. 'But I'm in the mood to lash out at someone.'

'And I'm the nearest.' To Harriet's surprise he smiled a little. 'But not dearest right now.'

She looked away. 'I'm not lashing out at you because of the baby—'

'Our baby,' he said very deliberately. 'Now lie still for a while. I'm going to have a quick shower and make some supper.' He got up to take some clothes from the wardrobe. 'While I'm doing that you can mull over the idea of lawful wedlock.'

Once she heard the water running Harriet sat up cautiously, wondering where he'd put her clothes. But when she put her feet to the floor it was obvious that making a run for it wasn't an option. She subsided against the pillows again, defeated. She would have to stay put and go home tomorrow. But that was the hell of it. James was right. The Clerkenwell flat wasn't home. Neither was the one in Bayswater, and in any case Dido's sister was moving in there shortly. The plus in her life was the money for End House, which was no fortune, but at least she wouldn't be penniless when she had to give up her job. The minus factor was a total lack of relatives and nowhere to call home.

James emerged from the bathroom in jeans and the twin to the T-shirt Harriet was wearing. 'How do you feel?'

'Depressed,' she said morosely.

'You need food.'

'No way,' she said in a panic. 'I need a bath, not food.'

'Right. I'll find you another shirt.'

James helped Harriet out of bed, waited until he was sure she could stand unaided then let her get to the bathroom in her own time while he turned on the shower to the correct temperature.

'Make do with a shower tonight,' he ordered. 'Do you need help?'

'No.'

'Leave the door ajar. Shout if you want me,' said James, and left her to it.

Harriet used James' shampoo on her hair, and lathered herself with his shower gel and then stood for a long time under the jet of water, one hand smoothing her stomach as she came to terms with the fact that there was a life in there.

'Time to come out, Harriet,' said James.

She switched off the water and took the towelling robe he held out, amused when he kept his face averted. 'It's all right, James. You've seen me naked before.'

'I know damn well I've seen you naked before.' His eyes burned into hers as he handed her a towel to rub her hair. 'This evening has been more of a strain for me than for you in some ways.'

'And just how do you work that out?' she demanded.

'You felt ill while I was undressing you. I, unfortunately, was in my usual rude health. Must I draw pictures?'

'Even though you'd just seen me throwing up?' she said astonished.

'Yes,' he said, the glint in his eyes bringing colour to her face. 'The stockings were the last straw. Now do you want to go back to bed?'

'I feel better in bed,' she admitted, 'but...' She trailed into silence and looked away.

'I can sleep in the spare room if that's your problem.'

'Thank you. I'd prefer that.'

'I was sure you would,' he said tersely, and made for the door. 'I didn't do anything about food earlier in case the smell penetrated in here and made you ill again. Could you cope now if I made myself an omelette?'

'Yes, as long as you don't make one for me.'

'Are you sure there's nothing you want, Harriet?'

She thought for a moment. 'After you've had supper would you make me some tea?'

'I'll make it now,' he said promptly.

'No. I'll enjoy it much more after I've brushed my teeth and dried my hair and so on. But at my current energy level this could take some time.'

'Have you eaten anything today?'

'Not since breakfast. My visit to the doctor early this afternoon put me right off lunch.'

His jaw clenched. 'And of course you worked for the rest of the afternoon?'

'With mind-numbing industry,' she agreed acidly.

Heat flared in the tawny eyes for an instant before James turned on his heel and made for the door. 'I won't be long. Shout if you want me.'

It was amazing what feeling clean could do, thought Harriet as she finally made it into the bed James had re-arranged for her. Unfortunately she was also pregnant, which meant some serious thinking now James had asked her to marry him. This was by no means unexpected. James Devereux had always shouldered his responsibilities. But there was no way she could accept a man who not only harboured doubts about this particular responsibility, but hated the thought of marrying again.

Harriet told James this when he brought her tea accompanied by some toast she found to her surprise that she quite fancied.

He placed the tray on the steel and glass table beside the

bed, handed her a plate of toast, then poured tea into a tall white mug as he heard her out.

'My turn now, Harriet,' he said, when she'd finished. He sat on the edge of the bed and looked at her with disquieting intensity. 'When I found you in the tower room that night my brain shut down at the sight of you in my bed. I forgot the protection I always carry with me, forgot that you belonged to Tim. I forgot everything other than the desperate desire to make love to you. So the responsibility is mine. Eat your toast,' he added.

Harriet nibbled warily, trying to hide how deeply his words affected her. 'Odd that the pills didn't work, either,' she said at last.

'Presumably they have done in the past?' asked James casually.

'They haven't been put to the test much. The one time I really fancied myself in love my hero objected to my closeness to Tim, and dumped me a few months into the relationship—if you could call it that. I was so humiliated I jumped at the chance to salvage my pride when Tim suggested the fake engagement.'

'And saved you for me in the process.' James smiled triumphantly. 'You didn't stand a chance, Harriet. Fate obviously meant you to marry me.'

'You hate the thought of marriage,' she reminded him.

'With you—and you alone—I can cope with matrimony.'

She shook her head. 'No, James.'

'Yes, Harriet. Living together isn't enough.' He took the mug from her and placed it with precision on the tray, then took her hand in a firm grasp. 'A child alters everything. Antiquated though it may be I want my child—and his mother—to have my name. So for the second time of asking will you marry me?'

She looked at him in sombre silence. 'If cohabiting isn't

enough for you I may have to swallow my pride and say yes. You know my situation only too well, James.'

He shrugged. 'There is another option. If you really can't face the thought of marrying me I can still buy you the house with a garden.'

Her eyes narrowed. 'And you would live here and I would live there, wherever "there" might be?'

'As I said, it's an option.' He released her hand. 'It's not what I want, but it's something for you to think about.'

Harriet thought about it so much she couldn't get to sleep. The night before she'd been so happy at the thought of seeing James again, and for a while she'd been even happier today at the thought of having his baby. Then the doubts had crept in as she waited to give him the news. And her doubts had been justified. His reaction had turned her life upside down. Not your fault, she whispered, patting her stomach. In the normal way of things she would have been euphoric about having James' baby. But not like this—forcing him to marry her. She didn't care for his other suggestion, either. The thought of living alone and pregnant in some house in the suburbs was even less appealing than in her studio flat.

At three in the morning Harriet gave up trying to sleep. She switched on the bedside lamp and got out of bed, opened the door quietly and peered out into the living room, which looked even bigger by night, with only the city lights outside to light her way. She stole barefoot across the cool, uncarpeted floor to the kitchen area, wondering if she could manage to butter some bread without putting lights on to disturb James. But before she reached her goal the door to the spare room slid back and he hurried towards her, shrugging on a dressing gown.

'Harriet, do you feel ill?' he demanded, and switched on the lights over the central island.

'No, I'm hungry, not ill—sorry I woke you up.'

His dark-ringed eyes captured hers. 'Do you imagine I was asleep?'

She looked away. 'For obvious reasons I couldn't sleep, either. Do you mind if I make myself something to eat?'

'For God's sake, Harriet,' he snapped, 'do you have to ask?'

'Yes,' she said simply. 'I do.'

James breathed in deeply, very obviously trying not to lose his temper. 'Go back to bed. What would you like? More toast?'

She inclined her head graciously. 'Lovely. That's very kind of you.'

'Kind?' he said through his teeth. 'Go.'

Harriet went. When she got back to James' room she remade the bed and settled back against the pillows, hoping he'd make her a lot of toast.

When James arrived, after a longer interval than promised, he had himself well in hand and the toast he brought was piled with glossy, perfectly scrambled eggs. 'No nonsense,' he said sternly. 'You need to eat.'

'Yes, James,' said Harriet meekly, and the moment he was through the door fell ravenously on the food, and only by superhuman effort managed to leave one square of egg-crowned toast uneaten by the time he came back.

'Eat it all, please,' he ordered as he set a mug of tea beside her.

She gave a martyred sigh and, with James standing over her, slowly finished the last piece as though she were conferring a favour. 'There,' she said, handing him the plate. 'Thank you. Perfect scrambled eggs,' she added with justice.

'When Tim was ten, and unhappy, sometimes it was all he'd eat, and sometimes I was the only one around to cook it, so it's my signature dish,' said James. 'These days Tim's tastes are more sophisticated.'

'He's gone to Florence this weekend,' said Harriet, sipping her tea.

'I know.' He shot her a look. 'It's not long to his wedding. Are you going to let me pay for your air fare?'

'No, thank you, James. I can manage that myself.'

'I don't know why I bothered to ask,' he said savagely. 'Is there anything else you need tonight?'

'Nothing at all.'

'In that case we'll leave further discussion until tomorrow. Hopefully, you'll feel better disposed by then to the sensible solution to our situation.'

She gave him a mocking smile. 'If you're alluding to marriage do try for a more attractive way to describe it, James. First it's the cure for love, now it's a sensible solution.'

His eyes took on a dangerous gleam. 'For you and me, and our child, it's the *only* solution, Harriet. By the way,' he added as he took clothes from his wardrobe. 'I'm going out early in the morning. We need food. I'll try not to wake you, but if I do, stay in bed until I get back. Now try to sleep. Goodnight.'

Harriet slept eventually, but woke early to listen for James. It seemed like hours before she heard him leave the spare room. She lay with eyes closed in case he looked in, and at long last heard the outer door close behind him. She slid carefully out of bed, relieved when the room held still and her legs held firm. She took her phone from her handbag and rang for a taxi, and soon afterwards, with only teeth brushed and hair combed by way of grooming, she was in a cab on her way to Clerkenwell. When she got to the flat she changed her clothes and collected the weekend bag she'd packed the day before, in that other lifetime before she'd seen a doctor. And only then left a message for James on his phone at the flat.

'I need some time to myself. I'm not in Clerkenwell or

with Dido, so don't try to look for me, and please don't worry. I feel much better today, and I'm perfectly safe. I'll ring you tomorrow.'

She knew perfectly well that James would worry. But right now she didn't care. She needed time to herself to put her life in order before she saw him again. It was cruel, maybe, but she just couldn't forget those three little words that had cut her to the heart. Nor did she believe for one minute the explanation he'd made for them. Harriet's eyes hardened. For a split second James had doubted that her child was his.

After several hours of such hard thinking her brain threatened to shut down, Harriet curled up on a sofa later that afternoon to watch an old Hollywood musical on television. In a break in the music she heard footsteps in the hall and shot to her feet, heart pounding, looking round wildly for something to use as a weapon.

But the man who strode into the untidy room was no burglar. James Devereux glared at her furiously, dangling a key in front of her eyes. 'I've got one of these, too. Tim's only just told me that the other two are on holiday, so I never thought of his house. I hope you're pleased with yourself, lady. I rang Dido before Tim, so you've sent three people off their heads with worry.'

'*You* worried the others. I rang you to say I was safe,' she said, and took her phone from her bag to reassure her friend, who was in such a state it took Harriet some time to calm her down. 'I'm fine, Dido, honestly,' she said at last. 'Come to my place for supper on Monday evening.'

James came in from the hall, snapping his own phone shut as she finished. 'I've just let Tim know he can enjoy the rest of his weekend in peace.'

'You can do the same, now,' said Harriet, and sat down on the sofa again, only to be hauled summarily to her feet.

'You're coming with me,' James informed her grimly. 'Now,' he added in a tone that dared her to disobey.

She might as well, she decided as she repacked her bag in Tim's chaotic bedroom. She'd done her thinking and made up her mind, which had been her main object in coming here. She would put James in the picture once they got back to the apartment.

When she went downstairs James took her bag from her, made sure the house was secure, and then drove her home in silence, his face set in such angry lines Harriet couldn't imagine telling him anything for a while. He helped her out in the basement car park and marched her over to the lift. When they got to his floor he unlocked his door, dumped her bag down and seized her wrist to lead her to the spare bedroom.

Harriet felt a sharp stab of compunction when she saw that the room had been rearranged to make space for the new chestnut leather sofa and chair. 'It arrived, then.'

'Delivered this morning, as I ordered,' James informed her. 'I went out early to make sure I was on hand when it came. I wasn't long, but you were too quick for me. I suppose you took off the moment I left.'

'Yes. I needed time to myself to think.'

'Is that the truth, Harriet?'

She frowned, taken aback by his air of desperation. 'Of course it is, James.'

His eyes bored into hers. 'You didn't go somewhere else on the way to Tim's, by any chance?'

'I went to a couple of places. I collected my things from the flat, and then I took my suit to the cleaners and bought some food.'

'No visits to clinics?' he demanded.

'Clinics?' she repeated blankly, then stared at him, incensed, as the penny dropped. 'Oh, I see! Well, you're wrong. A termination was one possibility I never even considered. I'm hardly likely to get rid of the only blood relative I might ever possess!'

He exhaled slowly, and rubbed a hand over his eyes. 'I had to ask, Harriet. My imagination went into overdrive when I couldn't find you.'

'I just needed breathing space, James,' she said, calming down. 'I knew Tim's place would be empty so I went there to think things over.'

He looked at her in silence for a moment, then crossed to the kitchen counter and leaned against it as though he needed support. 'And have you come to any conclusion?'

'Yes. Do you still want to marry me?'

'Yes, Harriet,' he said with weary emphasis, 'I still want to marry you. But something tells me you're about to make conditions.'

She nodded. 'You have to do something first.'

His eyes narrowed. 'What, exactly?'

'Take a DNA test. We'll have one, too,' She patted her midriff. 'That way you'll never have to ask again if the child is yours. You'll know. One way or the other.'

'To hell with that,' said James, appalled. 'I know I hurt you, Harriet, and I regret it bitterly. But this is pure retaliation.' He seized her hands. 'Look me in the eye, Harriet, and tell me there's even a remote possibility that I'm not the father.' He nodded in triumph as her eyes fell. 'You know you can't.'

'I still want you to have the test,' she said stubbornly, pulling away. 'Otherwise no wedding. I'd rather bring my child up on my own.'

'Over my dead body!'

Harriet shrugged and picked up her bag. 'I'm going back to the flat. You need time to think it over. Call me when you've decided.'

'I've already done that, so I'd rather you stayed here so I can look after you.' He took the bag from her, looking every year of his age for once. 'When I made a promise to your grandmother to look out for you I didn't know what I was letting myself in for. Nor that I would fall so hopelessly in love with you that I'd do any damn thing you wanted.' He shrugged wearily. 'You win, Harriet. I'll take the test.'

'This isn't a contest, James, it's not a case of winning,' she said, her voice purposely acid to disguise threatening tears.

'No. In my case it's losing.' He put the bag down and took hold of her by the shoulders. 'But remember this. You're the one insisting on the test, not me.'

'You're afraid of the result?'

'God grant me patience,' he said bitterly, his eyes locked with hers. 'I *know* the result. And so do you. But if that's what it takes to get you to marry me, I'll do it.'

'Thank you. Thank you for the furniture, too,' she added belatedly.

'Not at all,' said James with formality, and took her bag into the newly furnished spare room. 'There. It's all yours, Harriet. Put your feet up, read, watch television, or anything you like, then later perhaps you'll join me out here for dinner.'

She nodded, feeling suddenly forlorn. 'Do you want me to cook?'

'No. I'll send out for something. You need to rest. On Monday,' he said on his way to the door, 'you can serve notice that you're vacating the flat, ready to move in here next weekend.'

'James,' she said urgently.

He turned. 'Yes?'

'I'm sorry I worried you.'

His eyes softened a little. 'Next time you go walkabout leave a note, please.'

Once James closed the door behind him Harriet sat down

in her new, supremely comfortable chair. She looked at the furniture grouped so carefully with the television, the pile of new books on the bedside table. She had her own private sitting room, just as she'd asked for, but James obviously meant her to sleep in it as well. And after the dance she'd led him on, she could hardly complain.

The rest of the evening passed in a polite truce, with no physical contact between them other than James' kiss on Harriet's cheek before she retired to bed in her newly furnished room. After more of the same during Sunday, by early evening she was more than ready to go back to Clerkenwell.

'I'm London-based this week,' James informed her when they arrived at her flat.

She eyed him warily as she switched on lights. 'Will I see you before next weekend?'

'Do you want to?'

'If I don't want to, there's not much point in moving in with you,' she said tartly.

'Do you want to see me?' he repeated very deliberately.

'Not if it means a repeat of this weekend.'

'In that case maybe we should give each other some breathing space this week. But I'll be here first thing on Saturday morning. Until then take great care of yourself, please.' James took her in his arms and, for the first time since her life-altering announcement, kissed her very thoroughly before he let her go. 'Goodnight, Harriet. Sleep well.'

CHAPTER ELEVEN

DIDO PARKER, for all her candyfloss exterior, was the one person in the world Harriet knew she could trust with her momentous news. Not Tim this time, she thought with regret. This was one piece of news he'd have to learn from James.

'So that's why you fainted,' said Dido, once she'd recovered from the shock. 'I thought people only did that in films.'

'Me, too.'

'How do you feel about it? The baby, I mean.'

'Astonished, mainly.'

'Morning sickness yet?'

'The one time I've been sick was when I gave James the glad tidings.'

'How did he take it?'

'He asked if the baby was his, then held my head when I threw up in his kitchen sink.'

Dido shuddered. 'How *hideous*! Is that why you ran off to hide in Tim's house?'

Harriet nodded wryly. 'I was so hurt and angry I wanted him to suffer for that one split second of doubt.'

'James suffered all right! He was in a terrible state when he rang me. So was I,' added Dido with feeling.

'Sorry about that. I needed time on my own to think over James' proposal.'

'So he wants you to marry him then. Are you going to?'

'Of course I am.' Harriet smiled wistfully. 'He's the love

of my life, Dido—has been since I was thirteen years old, if we're counting. Otherwise I wouldn't dream of marrying him, baby or no baby.'

At the weekend James drove round to Clerkenwell to collect Harriet's belongings. He'd offered to hire a van for the purpose, but she'd assured him it was unnecessary.

'I can see why,' he said, surprised, when she let him in. 'Is this really everything?'

'I had to be ruthless when I moved in here. You see before you the sum total of my worldly possessions, other than the things you're storing for me.' Harriet smiled. 'Radio, books and CDs in the boxes, clothes in the cases, and the plant pot you gave me. That's it.'

When they got to the apartment James took her suitcases straight to his bedroom. 'I've cleared a space for you,' he said, sliding back one of his wardrobe doors. 'Your books can go downstairs in the office.'

After a week of little conversation with James other than a brief nightly phone call to inquire about her health, Harriet was relieved that the question of where to put her belongings had been answered before she'd asked it. 'I'm meeting Dido for lunch, by the way,' she said as she unpacked her clothes. 'We're going shopping for wedding gear. Tim's wedding,' she added awkwardly.

James leaned in the doorway. 'You'll need something for ours, too.'

'The same one will do for both, surely?' She turned to smile at him. 'It's pointless to buy things that won't fit me for long.'

'You only get married once—'

'Not always, James.'

The tawny eyes locked with hers. 'I intend to make very sure it's only once for you, Harriet.' He took out his wallet. 'You'll need some money.'

She shook her head. 'I'll pay for my own dress, James. Save your money for later. Babies cost a lot.'

'Have you told Tim about ours yet?'

'No, only Dido. Tim gave me such a telling off for worrying you—and him—last week, I left you to break the news.'

'In that case we'd better break it right away! I'll ask him round this evening. Or are you spending that with Dido, too?'

'No, I'm not.' She looked at him uncertainly. 'I'd assumed I'd spend it here with you.'

His eyes softened. 'So had I. Tim can share the meal I had ready for our lunch.'

'Sorry about that, James.' Harriet zipped up the last empty case and turned to face him. 'Your phone calls were so brief I never managed to tell you I was meeting Dido today.'

'It doesn't matter. I arranged about the test, by the way,' he added casually.

'Oh, right. Thank you,' she said, flushing.

'So now that's out of the way we can discuss the wedding.'

'Hold on,' said Harriet. 'We need test results before thinking about a wedding.'

He shook his head decisively. 'No, we don't, Harriet. All I need is a straight answer. Do you love me?'

'Yes,' she said simply.

He took her in his arms and kissed her victoriously. 'Then nothing else matters, test results least of all. Let's get married next Saturday. I'll make the arrangements while you're out.'

'As soon as that!' She stared at him in astonishment. 'James, are you serious?'

'Never more so. What point is there in waiting? You're

already here in my home and my life—and my heart,' he added, in a tone that finally settled the matter for Harriet.

'In that case, why not?' She smiled at him radiantly. 'Saturday it is.'

When Harriet got back from the shopping expedition James looked so worried she felt deeply contrite as he relieved her of a large hatbox and numerous smart carrier bags.

'Thank God,' he said fervently. 'I've been pacing the floor for the past half-hour. Why did you stay out so long? You look exhausted.'

'I am.' She kicked off her shoes with a groan and limped to a sofa. 'I may never go shopping again—at least, not with Dido. I didn't mean to worry you, James. I just lost track of the time.'

His eyes softened. 'What would you like to drink?'

'Water, please. Dido Parker, she I used to call friend, dragged me through every floor of Harvey Nichols on what must surely be the hottest day of the year!' She accepted a tall glass of mineral water and gulped it down thirstily.

James joined her on the sofa. 'Did you find what you wanted?'

'Yes.' She pushed her hair back from her damp forehead, and smiled at him. 'I found the perfect dress for the wedding, but I'm definitely wearing it to Tim's, too. And before you start lecturing, I ran out of energy, not money.'

'I suppose I'm not allowed to see this perfect dress until the day itself?'

'You bet. It's not a real wedding dress, by the way. You needn't wear a morning suit.'

'I'm going to just the same.' He smiled smugly. 'I look rather good in mine.'

She grinned. 'I bet you do. Talking of weddings, did you manage to get everything sorted for next week?'

'All arranged. The ceremony is at four next Saturday at

the church in Upcote, with a reception afterwards at Edenhurst,' he announced, his lips twitching as she stared at him, astounded. 'The only thing left to do is the licence.'

'Upcote?' she said faintly.

He shrugged. 'It seemed the obvious choice, for both of us. Your grandmother would certainly approve. I took it for granted you would, too, Harriet.'

'I do, I do. It's a lovely surprise, James,' she assured him. 'I'd assumed we'd just make for the nearest register office here in London.'

'I did that last time with well-known results.' James took her hand in his. 'Because I was the innocent party in the divorce the vicar's agreed to perform the ceremony. So I can make my vows to you, Harriet, in the sight of God as well as man.'

Deeply moved, she curled her fingers round his. 'James.'

He moved closer. 'What is it?'

'Now that we're actually getting married on Saturday— something I can't quite take in yet—can we go back to the way things were?'

He met her eyes squarely. 'Am I forgiven, then?'

'Yes,' she said soberly. 'Otherwise I wouldn't have gone shopping for a wedding dress. I hope you like the one I chose. It's a bit different from the normal things I buy. It wasn't on sale, for one thing. It's a size bigger than usual, too.'

James gave her a leisurely top to toe scrutiny. 'I can't see any difference.'

'I've put on an inch or so already round here,' she said, tapping her chest.

He grinned. 'You can hardly expect me to look on that as a disadvantage!'

Harriet chuckled, and James nodded in approval. 'That's better. I haven't heard you laugh much lately.'

'Sorry.' She patted her stomach. 'She's to blame.'

'It could be a he.'

'True. Would you prefer a boy, James?'

His grasp tightened for a moment as he helped her to her feet. 'All I ask is a healthy baby, Harriet, who gives its mother as little trouble as possible when it arrives.'

'Amen to that,' she said with feeling. 'I'd better hang my wedding finery away in my little retreat. And no peeking,' she added, smiling up at him.

'I wouldn't dream of it. I shall wait to be dazzled on the day. I'll carry the bags, and then leave you to it. Tim's coming at eight, so collect whatever you're wearing tonight, and then lie in the bath for a while, or better still, have a nap.'

'I think I will, but I'll be out in time to help with the meal,' she said, yawning widely as she trailed behind with her hatbox.

'There's nothing for you to do,' James assured her as he laid the bags down. 'It's just a selection of cold cuts and salads from my favourite food hall.' He grinned suddenly. 'If it isn't filling enough for Tim he can buy some fish and chips on his way home.'

When Harriet emerged from the spare room later in the terracotta dress, she was touched to see James had gone to some trouble to make the table look festive with champagne flutes and candles.

'How lovely,' she commented as he came out of the main bedroom.

'So are you,' said James. 'I like that dress.'

'Which is why I wore it,' she told him.

The tawny eyes lit with a heat she knew of old, but as James started towards her the bell rang and he smiled wryly, and went off to let his brother in.

'Sorry I'm late, folks,' said Tim, and gave Harriet a hug and kiss before standing back to look at her. 'Are you feeling better? No more faints? What have I said?' he added as she looked daggers at him.

'Faints in the plural?' demanded James.

'Oh, God,' groaned Tim. 'You didn't know?'

'About the one I witnessed, yes. Have there been more, Harriet, apart from the one when I went away?'

She nodded apologetically. 'When I had supper with Tim and Dido.'

'Scared the hell out of us,' said Tim, and raised his eyebrows as he saw the table. 'Hey, it's a special occasion! I should have worn my party dress.'

'Keep it for the wedding,' said his brother casually.

'No fear. I've got a really great suit for that,' said Tim with satisfaction. 'Francesca chose it.'

'Our wedding, not yours,' said James, removing the cork from a bottle of champagne.

Tim looked from his brother's face to Harriet's, then gave a whoop of triumph as he hugged the breath out of her then clapped James on the back. 'That's fantastic news! But you told me you were just moving in together, Harry.'

'We decided to tie the knot more permanently,' said James.

'Congratulations. When are you tying it?'

'Next Saturday,' Harriet informed him.

'*What?*' Tim sat down with a thump on one of the chairs at the table. 'This is all a bit sudden. You said you didn't want to get married last time the subject came up, Harry.'

'I changed my mind.'

'I changed it for her,' said James. 'We're having a baby.'

Tim stared at him, stunned, as he took a glass of champagne.

'Aren't you going to congratulate us, Uncle?' said Harriet, laughing.

'Lord, yes, it's marvellous news.' He raised his glass. 'Your very good health, both of you. Especially yours,

Harry. No wonder you fainted. I almost did myself just then. I can't wait to tell Francesca.'

'Tell her now,' said James, to his brother's delight. 'Ask her over for the wedding. You can both stay here with Harriet, if she's happy with that. I'll be in Upcote all week until the big day.' He smiled at a totally bemused Tim. 'I shall then take my bride to La Fattoria, and stay there until your own wedding, so if you want to show Francesca more of London you can use this place as a base.'

Tim leapt to his feet and hugged his brother, his eyes suspiciously damp. 'Thanks, James. I really appreciate that.'

'Go into the other room to ring Francesca,' said Harriet. 'Only don't fall over the furniture.'

Tim dashed off, exclaiming loudly over the new arrangement before sliding the spare room door closed behind him.

James handed a glass to Harriet. 'That obviously went well. He called me James for the first time.' He smiled wryly. 'I hope you don't mind sharing this place with Francesca for a night or two.'

'Of course not. Though I didn't realise I wouldn't see you for the entire week before the wedding.' She sighed. 'I'll miss you.'

He kissed her swiftly. 'I'll miss you a damn sight more. Let's drink a toast.'

She eyed the champagne warily. 'Should I be drinking this?'

'Just a sip or two for a toast.' James smiled into her eyes as he touched his glass to hers. 'To the three of us.'

'To the three of us,' echoed Harriet, her answering smile so blindingly happy James caught her in an embrace that lasted until Tim had to cough theatrically to interrupt them.

'Break it up, you two. I'm starving!'

At four o'clock to the minute the following Saturday, Harriet gave Dido a kiss in the doorway of St Mary's

Church, linked her arm through Tim's and, to the triumphant strains of Mendelssohn on the newly restored organ, walked down the aisle towards James, who looked so spectacularly handsome in his formal wedding clothes that after no sight of him for a week Harriet wanted to throw herself into his arms there and then. Instead she handed her posy of white roses to Dido and returned James' smile radiantly as he took her hand in his. Her dress, in double layers of pale pink chiffon printed with trailing white roses, coupled with a huge white straw hat, were both of them so foreign to her usual taste she'd been worried all week that she'd made a big mistake. But the look in James' eyes made it clear he thought she looked ravishing and she relaxed as Reverend Faraday, the vicar who'd known her since she was thirteen, began the words of the marriage service. When James received the ring from Nick Mayhew he looked down into Harriet's eyes as he put it on her finger, the conviction in his voice audible to everyone in the church as he made the vows that accompanied it. But when she slid a matching ring on his hand as she made the corresponding vows only Harriet heard his sharp intake of breath.

In the vestry, later, amongst all the kissing and congratulations James said in an undertone, 'The ring was a surprise. Thank you, Mrs Devereux.'

'I took a chance that you'd like it, Mr Devereux,' she whispered.

'I do. Enormously. I've never had one before.'

'I know. I did some research.'

When she took James' arm to walk down the aisle through a surprisingly crowded church Harriet smiled warmly on the familiar faces who'd come to wish her well, and laughed in delight when a silver horseshoe was thrust at her by a small person held aloft in his father's arms near the door.

'Robert!' exclaimed Harriet. 'Thank you.' She blew the little boy a kiss, and a smartly dressed Stacy grinned happily at her as she restored a rather chewed cuddly lion to her son.

Outside in the sunshine the bride and groom endured the usual photo shoot before escaping in a cloud of confetti to the car waiting to take them on the short journey to Edenhurst, where they received congratulations from the assembled staff before James finally managed to get his bride to himself for a moment before the guests arrived.

'You look so beautiful. I'm almost afraid to spoil your perfection,' he said softly, taking her in his arms. 'I love you, Harriet.'

'I love you, too.' She raised her face for a kiss that was all too brief before the others began to arrive in the flower-filled dining room reserved for the purpose on this special day.

Tim rushed in first, swept Harriet into his arms, and hugged the life out of her before apologising to them both in an anguished undertone. 'Sorry! I forgot.'

'Baby and I don't mind hugging,' she whispered, and slid a look at James as Tim wrung his hand. 'In fact we like it.'

Her new husband grinned at her as Francesca kissed them both and wished them great happiness. 'You are a lucky man this time, James.'

He nodded in heartfelt agreement. 'The luckiest man in the world, Francesca.'

'I'm jolly glad this waterproof mascara's living up to its promises,' sniffed Dido as she kissed Harriet. 'You look utterly glorious today, sort of glowing.'

'It's a bride thing,' said Harriet as she hugged her friend. Then she held out her hand to Giles Kemble, accepted his kiss, introduced him to James, and passed him on to Dido, whose tears dried like magic when Giles acquired two glasses of champagne from a passing waiter and led her across the room.

'Brilliant idea to invite your boss,' murmured James, watching.

'In more ways than one,' Harriet said with satisfaction, and then turned with a smile as the Mayhews arrived to bestow congratulations, plus an invitation to the Cotswolds for a family weekend in the country when the newlyweds returned from honeymoon.

Because both bride and groom were short of relatives, the guest list was composed of colleagues and friends accompanied by partners of various kinds, and it was a congenial little crowd who enjoyed the excellent meal and the entertaining speeches. It was late in the evening by the time the tables were cleared and a trio began to play the kind of standards it was possible to dance to cheek to cheek. Amid cheers James led his now hatless bride onto the limited floor space.

'I asked for this type of music,' he murmured, 'so I could hold you in my arms at the earliest possible moment after the wedding.'

'How clever of you,' she said, impressed. 'You dance well, too.'

'So do you. Rather surprising for one of your tender years.'

Harriet chuckled as the music changed tempo and other couples joined them on the floor. 'A woman must always be able to surprise her man. I read it in a magazine.'

She was allowed only the first dance with her husband. After that Harriet danced with Tim, then one man after another until James led her to her seat at last, gave her a glass of water and told her she looked tired.

'At the risk of being misunderstood,' he said in her ear, 'I think I should get you to bed soon. You look tired.'

The moment James said it Harriet realised she was very tired indeed.

'I am,' she said apologetically. 'But I don't want this lovely day to end.'

He smiled with tenderness that turned her heart over. 'Nevertheless, bride, I'm going to carry you off. No one will be surprised that I want to.'

James stood up, signalled to the leader of the trio, and then tapped on his glass when the music stopped. 'My wife and I,' he began, and grinned at the catcalls and applause, 'thank you all for coming to share in our happy day. Please stay as long as you like to enjoy the party, but we have a journey to make tomorrow and my bride is beginning to show signs of fatigue, so—'

'Come off it, Jed,' hooted someone. 'You just want to take her off to bed.'

'You're absolutely right, I do,' said James, unruffled, and held out his hand to Harriet.

She smiled on the assembled company as she got up. 'Goodnight, everyone. Enjoy the rest of the party.'

After kisses from Tim, Francesca and Dido, James took Harriet's arm and led her from the room to the strains of the Wagner Wedding March from the trio, but once in the hall he said goodnight to the porter, and took his yawning bride out into the starry night instead of up the main staircase as she'd expected.

'Where are we going?' she asked, surprised.

'Home to my place.'

It seemed a very long way across the cobbled courtyard to the stable flat. By the time they reached it Harriet was too tired to do more than give a cursory glance at her surroundings. But as James swung her feet up on a very comfortable sofa she smiled as she spotted her grandmother's cabinet and lacquer screen.

'Just like home,' she said drowsily.

'Want some tea?' he asked, undoing his tie.

'More than anything in the world at this moment,' she assured him.

But when James Devereux got back with the tray Stacy had put ready for them, his bride was fast asleep. Smiling wryly, he picked Harriet up and carried her into the bedroom. With infinite care he undid the fragile dress and slid it off, decided she could sleep in what little she had on underneath, and pulled the covers over her, then kissed her cheek before going into the other room to drink tea. He grinned as he filled the delicate cup Stacy had considered appropriate to the occasion. This wasn't exactly standard procedure for a wedding night. But now Harriet was safely married to him he was a happy man just the same.

It was late on the following day, under a sky too bright with stars to be totally dark, when James drove through the archway into the courtyard of La Fattoria, where welcoming lights shone from the windows, but otherwise all was quiet.

'After spending time with Francesca and Tim, plus Dido the night before the wedding, I thought you might fancy a little peace and quiet,' he said as he helped Harriet out of the car. 'I told the Capellinis they could wait a day or two before they met my bride.'

'Thank you for that, James. Peace and quiet sounds very appealing. I like Francesca very much, but I had to keep reassuring her that I was happy about her marriage to Tim,' Harriet told him ruefully. 'It got a bit wearing.'

'I'm more interested in whether you're happy about your marriage to me,' said James, and picked her up. 'Time-honoured custom,' he reminded her as he carried her over the threshold.

Harriet smiled with pleasure as he put her down in the cool, familiar kitchen. 'I love this place, James.'

'So do I.' He went out to fetch their luggage, refusing her offers of help. 'You had an exhausting day yesterday,' he reminded her when he came back.

'But a happy, lovely day. I like your friends, the Mayhews. Did I tell you Lydia asked us for a weekend in the Cotswolds when we get back?'

'Good, but don't think about going back right now.' James took her hands. 'Let's enjoy our time here first.'

'Since this is the only honeymoon I'll ever have I'm in full agreement.'

'You do look on it as a honeymoon, then?'

Harriet looked up at his tense face in surprise. 'Of course I do. After such a beautiful wedding day yesterday, what else could it be?'

'Just a holiday, maybe?' He looked at her very directly. 'I rushed you to the altar so fast you might well need breathing space. To get used to being my wife,' he added.

Harriet looked at him in silence for a moment. They hadn't shared a bed since James had learned about the baby. After her shopping expedition with Dido their reconciliation had been sweet, but it had been followed by the celebration dinner with Tim, after which she'd been so tired that James had insisted on sleeping in the spare room before he left next day for Upcote to make the wedding arrangements. And when she woke this morning, surprised to find she was in her grandmother's brass bed, Harriet had found to her dismay that her wedding night had come and gone, and her smiling husband stood fully dressed at her bedside, bearing a breakfast tray.

'I can see why you might think that way,' she said at last.

'What do you mean?'

'I've been a pretty unsatisfactory bride so far!'

'Not to me,' he assured her.

Deciding that it was time to make things clear Harriet chose her words with care. 'You made our wedding day as perfect for me as any woman could wish for, James. And today we've flown here first class—which *was* a first for me—and then we had a delicious meal in that little trattoria tonight on the way to this beautiful, peaceful house.' She reached up and kissed him lightly. 'If this isn't a honeymoon, James Edward Devereux, what is?'

She could hardly make it plainer than that, Harriet thought as she followed James up the winding stairs to the tower room, where a vase of pink and white roses stood on the chest, filling the air with their perfume.

'I've left the rest of the luggage downstairs,' he said, putting her overnight bag on the settle. 'Let's leave the unpacking until tomorrow.'

'Amen to that,' she said with a sigh, and with loving care laid her wedding hat on the top shelf of the armoire.

'By the way, I've got something for you, Harriet,' said James, taking an envelope from his jacket pocket. 'Stacy handed it to me first thing before you got up.'

She felt a little thrill when she saw the envelope was addressed to Mr & Mrs Devereux, and took out a card embellished with hearts and horseshoes, and a photograph of a beaming toddler.

'Congratulations and best wishes from Stacy and Greg, and a big kiss from Robert.'

'How lovely,' said Harriet, delighted. 'We must put it with the others. Thank Stacy for me when you go down to Upcote.'

'Come with me and thank her yourself,' he suggested.

'I may well do that, now I've seen your flat. I love it, James.'

'I once asked you to dinner there,' he reminded her, 'but you turned me down.'

She felt her colour rise. 'I was afraid.'

His eyebrows shot together. 'Of *me*?'

'Not exactly. But I was still pretending to be Tim's bride-to-be at the time, remember. The fiction was a bit difficult to keep up when one touch of your hand was enough to turn me to jelly. It still is,' she added, looking him in the eye.

James let out a deep sigh and took her in his arms, leaning his forehead against hers. 'Thank God for that.' He kissed her fleetingly and let her go. 'I'd better leave you to your bath. Shall I make you some tea?'

'No, thanks. I'm off tea, big time. I'd like a big bottle of mineral water, please.'

'Now?'

Harriet gave him a look designed to make her expectations crystal clear. 'Bring it when you come to bed.'

She spent such a short time in the bath it seemed ages before James came back. She smiled at him from her perch on the settle by the window, hoping he approved of the brief apricot silk nightgown she'd chosen alone one day in her lunch hour.

'You were a long time, James.'

He smiled as his eyes travelled over her with apprecia-tion. 'You normally like to wallow in the bath so I had a shower while I was waiting,' he said, and put a tray with glasses and bottles down beside the roses. He joined her on the settle and took her hand in his. 'You looked utterly beautiful as you came down the aisle to me yesterday, Harriet.'

'Brides are required to,' she informed him. 'It goes with the job description. Thank you for my bouquet, the roses were perfect. Did you choose white as a safe bet?'

'Not at all. I consulted Dido.'

'Did you arrange for these, too?'

He nodded. 'But I think they should go somewhere else tonight. The scent is overpowering. I'll put them in the other room.'

While James was gone Harriet drank some water, and sat gazing out into the starlit darkness as she thought over her glorious wedding day. She was glad James had liked her choice of bridal finery. If she'd looked beautiful for him it had been worth every penny of the outrageous price she'd paid for it all.

When he returned she got up, knowing that before she could get on with being married to James Devereux she had to give him the information that was the only cloud on her horizon.

'I've got a confession to make, James,' she said baldly.

He eyed her in alarm. 'There's nothing wrong with the baby?'

'No. We're both fine. It's just that, well, I didn't have a DNA test,' she finished in a rush. 'I was going to tell you not to have one, either, but you were too quick for me. You'd already had one.'

James let out a deep breath. 'Is that your big confession?'

She nodded dumbly.

'I've got an even bigger one.' He met her eyes squarely. 'I didn't have the test, either. I just said I did to make sure you turned up yesterday.'

'You *lied*?'

'With the best of intentions,' he said, unrepentant, and tipped her face up to his. 'You're mine, both of you, and if I had to lie to make sure you married me I don't care a damn.' He kissed her fiercely, and she kissed him back.

'There's something else I haven't told you,' she informed him, smiling at him radiantly.

'It can't be bad if you're smiling,' he said warily.

'Our baby's birthday will be nine months from the night you first made love to me in that bed over there.'

'I was sure of that already.' James picked her up and carried her over to the bed. 'I want to make love to you in it again right now,' he informed her.

'I should think so,' said Harriet, kissing his throat. 'After all, this is our honeymoon, Mr Devereux.'

'Thank God for that, too,' he said as he set her on her feet. 'At one point I had serious doubts that I'd get you to marry me, darling, baby or not.'

'I married you because I love you, James, it's as simple as that.' She reached up to kiss him. 'Besides, I've always known you were the father of my baby.'

'So have I. But I was afraid, in that first, blood-curdling moment, that you were going to tell me someone else was the father, so I asked the question that could have ruined our lives. My life, anyway.'

'Mine, too.' She lifted her face to receive his kiss, and James touched a hand to the silk covering her breasts, and made a relishing sound as he traced the new fullness with a not quite steady hand.

'I've been too long without you. Come to bed,' he urged, shrugging off his dressing gown. 'This thing you're wearing is very pretty, my darling. Take it off.'

Harriet obliged, laughing, and flowed into his arms, relishing the feel of skin against skin as James began kissing her.

'You said this is the only honeymoon you'll ever have,' he whispered. 'So we'll savour it together, my darling.' He drew her down with him to kiss her with slow, erotic kisses that were an end in themselves instead of merely the overture to what would come next. Harriet gave herself up to the joy of his skilled, lingering mouth, shivering in delight as his hands slid over her skin to shape her breasts and hips, and move tenderly over the gentle swell between them.

'I love you, Mrs Devereux,' he whispered.

'I love you, too, Mr Devereux.'

He kissed her with sudden urgency. 'Show me how much.'

Harriet slid a caressing hand over his shoulders and down his back, glorying in the tightening of his muscles under her questing fingers. She kissed him, open-mouthed, caressing his tongue with hers, and then slid her mouth down his taut throat and caught his flat nipples between her teasing teeth before moving her lips down his flat stomach and James breathed in sharply and pulled her beneath him, kissing her with a ravening demand that thrilled Harriet to the core. She writhed in hot, delectable anguish as his seeking fingers found the proof of how much she wanted him, and pleaded with him in such husky desperation James lifted her hips and fused his body to hers. At first, in deference to the baby, he made love to her with all the care and restraint at his command, but soon his bride demonstrated a fiery urgency he was powerless to resist, and they surged together in such harmony they reached the final pinnacle of sensation in unison.

They lay locked in each other's arms afterwards, unwilling to separate. It was a long time before James raised his head to look into Harriet's eyes.

'You know what, Mrs Devereux? I've just discovered an incontrovertible truth. Marriage is not the cure for love, after all.'

Harriet smiled lovingly, and stroked the damp hair back from her husband's forehead. 'We haven't been married long enough to know, surely!'

'You're missing the point.' James kissed her stroking hand. 'I meant that the love I feel for you is with me for life. There is no cure.'

'You mean you're stuck with it.'

He laughed. 'Yes, my unromantic darling, I'm stuck with it.'

'So am I.' She met his eyes with a look so blazingly happy it took his breath away. 'For as long as we both shall live.'

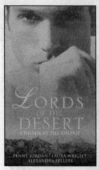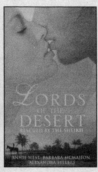

millsandboon.co.uk Community

Join Us!

The Community is the perfect place to meet and chat to kindred spirits who love books and reading as much as you do, but it's also the place to:

- **Get the inside scoop from authors about their latest books**
- **Learn how to write a romance book with advice from our editors**
- **Help us to continue publishing the best in women's fiction**
- **Share your thoughts on the books we publish**
- **Befriend other users**

Forums: Interact with each other as well as authors, editors and a whole host of other users worldwide.

Blogs: Every registered community member has their own blog to tell the world what they're up to and what's on their mind.

Book Challenge: We're aiming to read 5,000 books and have joined forces with The Reading Agency in our inaugural Book Challenge.

Profile Page: Showcase yourself and keep a record of your recent community activity.

Social Networking: We've added buttons at the end of every post to share via digg, Facebook, Google, Yahoo, technorati and de.licio.us.

www.millsandboon.co.uk